PRAISE FOR *THE INVISIBLE COLLEGE*

"Jeff Wheeler weaves a deep and unique world filled with magic, danger, and hope. Readers will fall in love with the characters and root for their triumphs. (And I may have a crush on Robinson now.)"

—*Wall Street Journal* bestselling author Charlie N. Holmberg

"What a ride! Jeff Wheeler really brings out the big guns—literally, there are cannons—with this amazing introduction into the world of *The Invisible College*. From the prologue, I was absolutely hooked! With a world of inventive magic, a doomsday war on the horizon, and a romance you can't help but want to cheer for, this story showcases some of Jeff Wheeler's best work. Old and new fans of his masterful storytelling are going to gobble this right up and come back begging for more."

—Allison Anderson, author of the Cartographer's War series

"Jeff has written an engaging story full of ancient magic, secret handshakes, devious antagonists, and a charming hero just discovering his power."

—Luanne G. Smith, author of *The Vine Witch*

THE ALCHEMY OF FATE

ALSO BY JEFF WHEELER

Your First Million Words

Tales from Kingfountain, Muirwood, and Beyond: The Worlds of Jeff Wheeler

The Invisible College

The Invisible College

The Violence of Sound

The Alchemy of Fate

The Dresden Codex

Doomsday Match

Jaguar Prophecies

Final Strike

The Dawning of Muirwood Series

The Druid

The Hunted

The Betrayed

The First Argentines Series

Knight's Ransom

Warrior's Ransom

Lady's Ransom

Fate's Ransom

The Grave Kingdom Series

The Killing Fog

The Buried World

The Immortal Words

The Harbinger Series

Storm Glass

Mirror Gate

Iron Garland

Prism Cloud

Broken Veil

The Kingfountain Series

The Queen's Poisoner

The Thief's Daughter

The King's Traitor

The Hollow Crown

The Silent Shield

The Forsaken Throne

The Poisoner of Kingfountain Series

The Poisoner's Enemy

The Widow's Fate

The Maid's War

The Duke's Treason

The Poisoner's Revenge

The Covenant of Muirwood Trilogy

The Banished of Muirwood

The Ciphers of Muirwood

The Void of Muirwood

Whispers from Mirrowen Trilogy

Fireblood

Dryad-Born

Poisonwell

The Legends of Muirwood Trilogy

The Wretched of Muirwood

The Blight of Muirwood

The Scourge of Muirwood

Landmoor Series

Landmoor

Silverkin

THE ALCHEMY OF FATE

JEFF WHEELER

47NORTH

This is a work of fiction. Names, characters, organizations, places, events, and incidents are either products of the author's imagination or are used fictitiously. Otherwise, any resemblance to actual persons, living or dead, is purely coincidental.

Published by 47North, Seattle

www.apub.com

EU product safety contact:
Amazon Media EU S. à r.l.
38, avenue John F. Kennedy, L-1855 Luxembourg
amazonpublishing-gpsr@amazon.com

ISBN-13: 9781662528613 (hardcover)
ISBN-13: 9781662521904 (paperback)
ISBN-13: 9781662521911 (digital)

Cover design and illustration by David Curtis

Printed in the United States of America

First edition

To Jeff & Aurora

Iskandir
Halt
Daylen
Andover
Tanireh
Summer
Palace
Winterthur
Nirshoye
Krier
Telimar
Tanhauser
Yverdon
Bishopsgate
Torin
Greenholh
Covesea
Auvinen
Rexanne
Ashmull
Tyburn
Siaconset

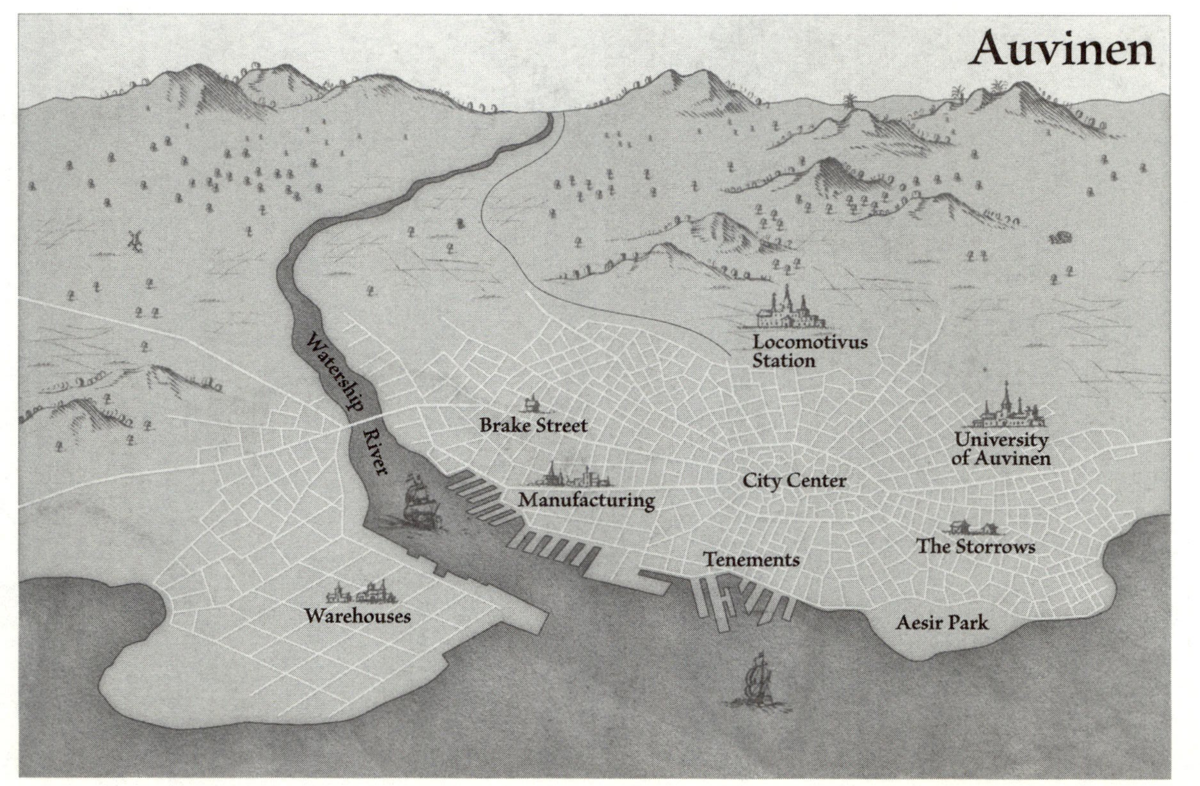
Auvinen
Locomotivus
Station
University
of Auvinen
Watership
River
Brake Street
City Center
Manufacturing
The Storrows
Tenements
Warehouses
Aesir Park

My niece insists, after all these years of living with me, that I must leave a record of my earlier life and doings. That every sorcerer of the Invisible College is compelled by duty to do so. So like her to leverage my own words against me. I was born in the town of Flamsteed, and my father, whom I am named after, died three months before my birth. My mother remarried when I was three. I detested my stepfather and as a young child was sent to be raised by my maternal grandmother, who educated me in the rights and privileges of my station and birth and provided me as well with an unimaginable variety of books. She was a patient woman, one uniquely endowed with a curious mind and a willingness to indulge in my precocious and varied interests even when I was very young.

I was born too early, my mother said, and came out of the womb craving knowledge, which she neither understood nor admired. She wanted me to become a country gentleman and manage my inheritance and lands, but I wanted none of it. My schoolmaster persuaded her, after I'd threatened to burn the family farm down, to send me to the prestigious University of Nirshoye. He was fascinated by my creation of sundials in the schoolyard and believed I had many gifts of the Mind worth exploring. Mother relented eventually and, at nineteen years of age, I went to Nirshoye. I made infrequent return visits to my grandmother's estate, but the university was my true home. And that, dear reader, is all you need know about my childhood.

—Isaac Berrow, Master of the Royal Secret,
the Invisible College

Isaac Berrow

PROLOGUE

A Measured Life

Fifteen years before the founding of the Invisible College

Isaac used the littlest measuring spoon to scoop a heap of wood ash into the mortar. Then, with vigorous strokes of the pestle, he began to mix it into the combination of chymicals he'd already pulverized. The creak of the door sounded behind him.

"I'm busy," he said, not looking back.

"I'm leaving," said his roommate Blake Sherburn from the doorway.

"Can you fetch me some more saltpetr while you're out?"

"I'm not going *out*, Isaac. I'm going home. Back to Telimar."

Isaac stopped working the mortar and pestle and turned his neck, looking at Blake with confusion. His roommate wasn't wearing his scholar robes but a traveling cloak and riding boots. "Why are you going to Telimar?"

Blake heaved a dramatic sigh. "I told you weeks ago. My younger sister is getting married. I'm going to be gone a fortnight."

"A fortnight!"

"You act like this is new information, Isaac. I've told you all of this before. I'll be gone a fortnight, maybe more. It's not easy to travel in winter."

"But how long does it take someone to get married?" Isaac asked, feeling a surge of restlessness in his chest. He'd come to rely on the help Blake offered for his various experiments. His roommate had more friends and social obligations, but he was interested in Isaac's work and keen to learn from him. They'd gotten along well together since joining the university. "The boat ride to Telimar is several hours, then the carriage ride to your family's home can't be more than two days. The ceremony is maybe . . . twenty minutes . . . and then the return. Six days at the most."

Blake sighed. "Just because you despise your family, doesn't mean everyone does. I miss them, and my sister and I are close. It may be longer than a fortnight. At least my snoring won't keep you up at night."

"It doesn't keep me up. I just make it a point to tell you when you *do* snore is all."

"That is so helpful," Blake said with another prolonged sigh.

"If you think so."

"I was being sarcastic."

Isaac paused, mouth open, and then he shut it. "I still need some saltpetr. Can you get some before you go?"

"I'm afraid you will be running the errand yourself this time. You need to get outdoors more anyway."

"I don't like . . . people," Isaac said, wrinkling his nose.

"That may not be entirely their fault," Blake said with an arch look that Isaac interpreted as a subtle rebuke.

"Off with you, then," Isaac said. "You're right. I can get my own things, thank you very much."

"Good. Because I need to leave for the ship. You seriously haven't noticed me packing and talking about the harbor schedule?"

Isaac thought on the question a moment and then shook his head and turned back to the work in his alchemy. He loved the little closet he'd turned into his private sanctuary, a place that smelled of burnt metal and fragrant chymicals.

"Have a safe journey? Give my regards to your family? Hope all goes well? Hope you encounter a young lady you'd like to get to know better?" Blake's intonation made it sound like he was asking questions at every pause, but that was absurd since Isaac wasn't the one leaving.

"You're the one going," Isaac said gruffly. "Fare you well."

Another sigh. The door shut, but Isaac had already gone back to grinding his powder after tipping in another small dose of ash. Several hours must have passed because the closet was getting darker and darker, and he found himself squinting before realizing with a jolt that he hadn't procured the saltpetr.

He was about to call out for Blake, to see if he'd get some, but remembered abruptly that his roommate had already departed.

"Bother and nonsense," Isaac grumbled and scooted his chair back. He extinguished the candle on the table with a pinch—waste not—and hurriedly fetched his long jacket and a cloak. Winter had already settled on other parts of the realm, discernable by the snow line in the mountains, a distinguishable feature manifesting the temperature difference at certain altitudes. He added a wool scarf around his neck, counted the coins in his purse, and then left his tiny abode, locking the door securely behind him. There was too much riffraff in the town, including more than its fair share of burglars. Some students were robbed the week tuition was due, so elaborate means had been constructed to safeguard the transfer of coin from student to bursar.

The breeze was bitingly cold, so Isaac walked briskly, keeping aware of his surroundings. The streets were mostly empty, as folk preferred to keep indoors in such cold, and the lateness of the hour and the hastening dusk meant shops were already closing. He should have left sooner, but he'd been distracted by his work, which he did in addition to the studies required by the masters of the university during the term. Thankfully, he could focus on his own work at the moment, as the term had ended. The lunar fortnight break between terms allowed students the opportunity to visit family, which Isaac was loath to do.

Two merchants were bickering about the price of an old loaf of meat bread, and Isaac hastily dodged to the other side of the street. He was careful to watch his steps, lest he put his foot in a pile of human refuse tossed out from an upper window onto the street.

As he passed a tavern, he heard some lively—meaning drunkenly—manifestations of pleasure happening inside and quickened his pace. Several students owed Isaac money for their regular urges to drink ale and spirits. He didn't feel it immoral to profit off their proclivity to spend money on things that required frequent urination. He always expected interest on capital lent.

His ears and the tip of his nose were tingling with the cold, but it wasn't an unpleasant sensation. Once he had passed two other taverns, the street became quiet again. No one else was about, and that would make him a target of the cutpurses and criminals inhabiting the notorious island and its famous university. The dichotomy of life in such a remote location was an endless source of provoking thoughts. Why did this part of society wish to uplift a student's thoughts through deep learning and reason but permit them to be surrounded by an atmosphere of temptation?

"I don't care if you have to roam the streets all night, you scabby little wench! You find a customer this time, you bring me cuppers, or you'll freeze to death tonight."

Isaac heard a frail cough and a desperate voice. A woman's voice. "I can't. I can't."

"What's it to me?" tossed back the angry man. "Another girl will have the bed. Cuppers or cold. Your choice. Now git!" Isaac heard the smack just as he reached the gap between two buildings. He glanced down the alley, seeing a brawny man towering over a woman who wore too little clothes for such an evening. Isaac's stomach shriveled with pity and repulsion, and he strode by, but not before the man had caught a glimpse of him.

"There's a student," he hissed at the woman. "Now's your chance!"

As soon as Isaac left their line of sight, he bolted down the street and ducked into another alley, his heart racing. He hated men like that who compelled women to prey on the financially insecure students—and some of the faculty. It was an old, unhealthy dynamic that had festered around universities for ages and led to squalid and unseemly living conditions for all concerned, but there was nothing he could do about it. He was just grateful he'd passed by before she'd tried to entice him. The poor woman must have encountered horrible circumstances to have been forced to such wretched means of earning her room and keep.

Isaac arrived at the shop that sold chymicals and reagents and found, to his dismay, it was indeed closed. He stamped his foot in frustration and let out some harsh epithets about the owner's apparent laziness for wanting to close shop so early. He knocked soundly on the door, hoping the promise of a transaction might lure the proprietor back down from the living quarters above. But to no avail. Fuming at the inconvenience of having to return the next day, Isaac set out for his dingy but comfortable dwelling, choosing a circuitous route to get there so he wouldn't need to pass that alley and the poor soul assigned to haunt it. It was worth going well out of his way to avoid that encounter!

Yet, to his utter astonishment, there she was. He recognized the shabby and all-too-revealing chemise. She appeared to be shivering with cold, waiting on the next corner. Watching him with a look he found disconcerting. What an impossible situation. He averted his gaze and felt the misery of his gut-stabbing dilemma.

"I've been looking for you," she said. "I've been looking for so long this time."

"I'm sorry, um, miss," he stammered. Her voice sounded . . . familiar. Impossible. "I'm not interested."

"I know. You aren't the kind who would be." He'd passed her, but she'd already fallen in beside him and was keeping pace with him. That was dreadful.

"Please . . . go away," he said as delicately as he could.

"You don't understand what I want."

"I think I do." He fumbled in his pocket for his purse and hurriedly spilled some coins into his hand. "Just take them and go. Don't follow me."

He scattered the coins on the ground and was amazed by the loud, sharp noise they made. He'd been foolish dropping the coins in the street, but he didn't want to even risk touching her. Afraid she might grab him and try to persuade him with more than words. This encounter had not been of his choosing, but he still felt ashamed of himself for treating another person with such dismissive cruelty.

Risking a backward glance, he saw her kneeling in the street, watching him leave in a hurry. One by one, she picked up the coins as he dashed away, his heart pounding. He'd go to the shop early the next morning. Criminals liked to sleep in, didn't they? In all likelihood, there would be a lower risk of a repeat encounter.

Finally, having set a hurried pace, he made it back to his dwelling and unlocked the door. He looked back, seeing the street empty. He had a preternatural feeling he was being watched, even though he couldn't see anyone. After going inside, he locked the door again, then rubbed the tension from his mouth, grateful to be home. Grateful for the solace of being by himself again. At his family manor in Flamsteed, he would have had servants to answer the door. To fetch the things he needed. But this isolation, and the immersion it allowed, was worth trivial inconveniences and the occasional criminal ones. The few cuppers he'd tossed in the street were easily replaceable.

After relighting the candle, he pulled off his cloak and folded it nicely before tucking it back into the chest he'd gotten it from. Next, he unwound the scarf and folded it up as well before putting it away. A little gurgle in his stomach reminded him that it was time for supper, so he went to the small pantry where he had his stores of food. He picked his food and produce on the same day every week to minimize the amount of time spent haggling for it and bought things in greater quantities to get a lower cost and avoid the necessity of repeat shopping trips.

He economized the allowance he'd given himself from his inheritance, determined to prove to his mother that he was a rational and—

A knock sounded on the door, interrupting his thoughts. He set down the half a cabbage he'd just picked up, stunned at the intrusion. No one ever visited him for a social call. Blake had friends, but he did not bring them over. That was an ironclad agreement between them.

With his heart galloping, he walked to the door soundlessly, careful to avoid the squeaky floorboards. Another knock sounded, followed immediately by a quick series of raps.

He was about to part the curtain to see who'd intruded on his peace when he heard an incantation, a song that was unfamiliar and exotic. The lock turned before his astonished eyes. The thrill of magic made gooseflesh prickle down his forearms.

The woman he'd left kneeling in the street came in and shut the door behind her.

Robinson Foster Hawksley

CHAPTER ONE

The Ashes on Brake Street

Present day

Parts of the rubble and cinders were still steaming. The fire in the Fosters' home on Brake Street had burned until the entire dwelling was consumed, except for the skeletal bones of two chimneys and a corner of the house's brick facade, which were intact but terribly scorched. Even the glass had melted.

Robinson Hawksley squatted in the middle of the mess as the morning light exposed the horrible scene. The night before, he'd been lauded and celebrated for achieving a higher rank within the Invisible College, but he and the Fosters had left the celebration early only to find his in-laws' home engulfed in violent, magical flames.

There was a tightness in his chest that refused to loosen as he stared at some rubble encased in a resolidified puddle of glass. Mr. Foster stood in another part of the ruins, nudging through the debris with his shoe, but Mrs. Foster had taken their youngest child, Trudie, to a hotel, hoping to calm her. Trudie had been home when the fire had started, and she believed her sister—Robinson's wife, McKenna—had perished.

Another throb of anguish pulsed in the young sorcerer's heart. This feeling was . . . familiar. He'd lost his brothers to Aesir-inflicted diseases. He'd knelt by their graves before coming to Auvinen to start a new life. A life that had been transformed by his pupil, McKenna Foster. Marrying her was the best thing he'd ever done, and despite all evidence to the contrary, he clung tenaciously to the hope that she'd gotten out of the building. This was not a natural flame. It was a sorcerer's fire, caused by a chymical combustible in air, and the temperature would have incinerated anyone caught inside. He squeezed the bridge of his nose and shut his eyes, trying not to let grief and anxiety overwhelm him.

The sound of footsteps crunching through the ruins roused him. He looked up and saw Wickins and Clara approaching him. They'd arrived at the same time he had and had borne silent witness to the destruction of the Fosters' fancy house. Not even the greenhouse had been spared. All of its many panes of glass had melted into soot-covered lumps amid the ash and stones.

"Have you found anything, old chap?" Wickins asked gently. "Any sign that could tell us what happened?"

Investigators from the Marshalcy were already working through the rubble, trying to gather clues and evidence. They'd had officers guarding the house when the fire started, but the blaze had engulfed the home swiftly. Some of the neighboring homes had caught fire too, but thankfully the fire crews had managed to prevent further major loss.

"Nothing," Robinson said in a dead voice, rising from his crouch. It seemed the fire had started in the basement. That was all they'd really learned so far.

He'd tried summoning the doglike intelligence—the spark left behind by the dog he'd befriended in Covesea before its untimely death. The creature had not answered his call. Had another sorcerer captured it? Was something preventing it from lending assistance? It had been so willing to help him in the past. He'd used it to track the owner of a lost coin and find his stolen parts from the exhibition display.

That thought unleashed a surge of wrath in his heart.

He suspected that the military was behind this attack. Particularly one General Colsterworth. Was the fire his way of eliminating another Semblance that he perceived as a threat to the empire? Yet, if one of the general's henchmen wearing a kappelin had tried to approach the house, the bulbs would have revealed his presence.

If Colsterworth had killed McKenna . . .

The thought threatened to overwhelm him in a surging tide of grief.

No, Robinson had to stop his dark thoughts from going even darker. Anger was better. It was understandable. It was actionable. Grief . . . loss . . . those feelings might destroy him if he allowed them to take over. He felt that truth deep inside.

Clara put her hand on Robinson's shoulder. "What are you thinking? The look on your face is terrifying."

He clenched his jaw muscles. "I'd rather not say," he told her. "This is all my fault. I should never have left her at home alone."

"Dickemore," Wickins said with a sigh, "she was protected by the Marshalcy! What could you have done that they did not?"

What if the *strannik*, Gregor Skoye, had been involved? He'd been relentless in his pursuit of McKenna, believing her to be a Semblance of the Erlking's forsaken daughter. And at least part of that was true, for she truly was possessed by a Semblance. It had happened when she'd nearly drowned in the sea by her aunt's home on the isle of Siaconset. Afterward, she'd started having nightmares and had become sensitive to heat. Everyone knew that the Aesir could only endure in the cold, which was why they only waged war in winter. But while the military believed that once an Aesir inhabited a mortal host and became a Semblance, death was the only release, Robinson refused to accept that. Surely there was another way to save his wife.

If she wasn't lost to him already.

He felt sobs threaten to choke him, but he squeezed his hands into fists and willed them to subside.

"If I had been here, she wouldn't have faced whatever she faced alone," he said, wrestling with his emotions. Images of General

Colsterworth flashed in his mind. The general was willing to be ruthless when it came to stamping out any possible Semblances. He'd once sent a man to kill Robinson, wrongly believing *him* to be one, before shifting his attention to McKenna.

Clara looked at him so piteously, her own eyes wet with tears, that he nearly lost all composure. Wickins put his arm around Robinson's shoulders, his face expressing the depth of his own turmoil.

"You need to leave this place," Wickins suggested. "Get some sleep."

Robinson looked down the street and saw a small crowd had gathered with the dawn, held back by Marshalcy officers. Neighbors, well-wishers, gawkers.

"Sleep," Robinson chuffed. "I don't think I can sleep until I know what happened here. She was my *wife*."

Was. Past tense. Did he truly believe she was gone? He wanted to scream. To bellow his rage and promises of revenge. Anything to relieve the pain in his despoiled heart. No military officers had come in response to the fire. No decorated colonel offering pat condolences. Were they afraid of what he'd do?

No, he couldn't think like this. Maybe she was alive still and had been clandestinely spirited away. If so, he would find her.

Fresh rage rolled over him as he considered what the military might have done with her. Was there no end to their malfeasance? First, they'd tried to kill him, and then they'd stolen his invention, claiming his design for an Aesir-detecting lightbulb had been patented by another sorcerer first—one Elizabeth Cowing, the famous inventor. He'd met her in Bishopsgate. She was part of the legal turmoil that was, as of yet, unconcluded, although he suspected she was in the dark about the military's duplicity. Hadn't the founder of the Invisible College, Isaac Berrow, warned that great power could lead to deceit and underhandedness? He had tried to guard his own organization against it. One did not rise in the ranks of the college through subterfuge and deceit. It was skill and knowledge and integrity that provided the opportunity to advance. Anyone who had a sound mind, persistence, and a strong moral compass could enter the order of sorcerers and receive their divulged secrets. But in the centuries since its founder's demise, the Invisible College had become moribund. As did all things created by the hand of mortals. Only the Aesir created things that could last.

Robinson noticed Mr. Foster approaching with an officer from the Marshalcy. Both men had grim expressions, and the coil in Robinson's chest tightened further. More bad news? He didn't know if he could bear it.

Wickins gripped Robinson by the elbow, and even though his injury had not fully healed, he was more of a crutch to Robinson than the other way around. Clara stood at Rob's other side.

"What did you find?" she asked the two approaching men.

Mr. Foster looked careworn, troubled, and older than he had just a day before. No doubt Robinson looked the same. McKenna's father cleared his throat. "This is Detective Lieutenant—"

"I don't care about proper introductions," Robinson said. He looked at the detective. "What did you find?"

"That's the problem, sir," said the bluff-faced man. Judging by the lack of emotion in his voice or care in his countenance, he dealt in death and arson on a regular basis. "I've interviewed all the neighbors. We searched for signs of passage. Footsteps in the snow. That sort of thing. There's no evidence anyone left this house other than those who are accounted for. It is my professional belief that your wife perished in the blaze."

Clara let out a little gasp but said nothing. Wickins squeezed Robinson's arm to bolster him.

"Your 'professional belief'?" Robinson said in dismay. He'd been clinging to the hope that evidence to the contrary would manifest itself in the rubble. "Can you tell who started the fire?"

"No, sir. There are no witnesses. And no footprints in the snow."

"And don't you find that odd?" Robinson asked, realizing he was sounding skeptical and possibly even disdainful of the man. Someone burned down the house from the *inside.* How had that happened without anyone noticing it?

If the detective was offended, he didn't show it. "I'll be sending my report straightaway to Master Drusselmehr and Mr. Guiteau, head of the Marshalcy. They've asked for this case to be given particular attention."

Master Drusselmehr. The highest-ranking person in the Invisible College—the Master of the Royal Secret. An ally, or so Robinson had believed. But Master Drusselmehr could not be totally trusted either, as he had exhibited a willingness to achieve his goals at any cost. He'd invented a toy cannon that could eavesdrop on private conversations and alert the Marshalcy to those sympathetic to the *strannik* and his goals of surrendering to the Aesir.

"Have you already told someone in the military?" Robinson asked, his nostrils flaring with contempt.

"Colonel Harrup," said the detective. "He is my liaison officer with the garrison here in the city. I must now ask you all to abandon the premises while we continue to go through the ashes for clues."

"You think if there is something to find, *I* won't find it?" Robinson demanded. "It will be my sole focus."

Mr. Foster put his hand on the detective's arm, made a curt nod for him to depart, and the detective, without so much as a flinch, acquiesced and turned away. Mr. Foster approached Robinson and gave him a look full of compassion yet firmness. "Mr. Thompson Hughes arrived with the carriage a little while ago. I think you should go to the hotel where your parents are staying. Try to rest."

"I can't rest until I find her," Robinson said thickly.

"I know, my boy. I know. This is painful for us all. Maybe a little food. Something to drink."

"I'll take him," Wickins offered. "Come on, old chap. We can come back later. I promise."

"I could come too," Clara offered.

Mr. Foster frowned. "We should go see your mother and Trudie. Tell them what we know."

Clara looked to be on the verge of protesting, but she, too, relented. She touched Wickins on the arm and then leaned up and kissed his cheek. The two were not officially engaged yet, but everyone in the family knew it was only a matter of time. Clara kissed Robinson as well before offering a parting hug.

Wickins led him away from the smoke, ash, and debris toward the family carriage—the one they'd taken from his advancement ceremony at the Storrows back to the house. The driver sat on the pilot bench, gazing at the destruction with a mournful countenance.

"Take us to the hotel the Hawksleys are staying at," Wickins said to the driver, rousing the man from his reverie.

He nodded briskly and adjusted himself on the bench. Wickins opened the door and helped Robinson inside. The battle between rage, loss, and hope was making him dizzy. Why was this blend of feelings so familiar? What was it about this situation that made it feel as if it had happened to him before? He'd thought it was because he'd also lost his brothers tragically, but that didn't seem quite right . . .

He climbed into the cab and lowered himself onto the bench. His knee collided with a violin case. *His* violin case. He stared at it, having forgotten that he'd taken it to the Storrows. He had been asked to demonstrate his magic through his musical abilities, which was part of every such ceremony.

McKenna had arranged for the violin as a gift for him. So he could play songs for her family. Their favorite was the aria of the Erlking's daughter from the Shopenhauer opera. He'd finally seen the opera in Tanhauser with McKenna at his side. Had heard the brilliant soprano sing the part amidst the swell of the orchestra. McKenna had beamed at him, sharing in his joy even if the experience was, naturally, different for her.

The pain was so intense he thought he might black out.

As the music echoed in his thoughts, he buried his face in his hands and began to cry with great, trembling sobs.

MaKenna Aurora
Hawksley

CHAPTER TWO

STRANNIK

The early rays of dawn pierced the clouds scudding against the snow-patched mountainside. McKenna had thought it would never come. If her wrists hadn't been bound with an Aesir-made chain and fastened to a metal hook on the floor, she would have risked jumping out of the wagon to escape her captors. Through the interminable night, the sway of the carriage had continually lulled her to sleep only to be reawoken with every jolt. The carriage had taken the north road out of Auvinen around midnight. Why hadn't Rob found her yet?

But she knew the answer to that already. The *strannik*, who had abducted her from the house on Brake Street, had used a magical glamour that could fool everyone's senses except hers. She saw him for who he really was—a half-crazed wanderer with an unkempt beard and piercing, uncanny eyes that made her fearful. He claimed to be her friend, not her enemy, but she couldn't trust such a man.

In her room the previous evening, the first sign of danger had been smoke curling in from under her door. She'd hurried to open it only to encounter the *strannik* at the top of the stairs, his dark brown peasant jacket looking more suited to the hinterlands than her family's fancy house. She'd slammed the door in his face, but he'd kicked it open and then warned that she was in grave danger. General Colsterworth had been ordered by Master Drusselmehr to execute her while her family was gone because she was a Semblance, a being with two souls inhabiting the same body, a feat of ancient Aesir magic. They wanted her dead because of who her *real* father was.

The Erlking. The dark ruler of the Aesir, the founder of the plagues that had tormented mortalkind for thousands of years.

Come with me. Or you perish tonight!

She'd read his lips. It had been worded as an entreaty, but truthfully, she'd had little choice. He'd hunted her for weeks, his minions dogging her steps from Tanhauser to Bishopsgate to Covesea to the emperor's own palace in Andover! The man was relentless, which wasn't to say she doubted his message. She did believe the general capable of ordering her murder and Master Drusselmehr of duplicity. It appeared to her that he'd formed a friendship with Rob with the intention of luring him away from her.

She'd chosen to go with the *strannik*, but she felt confident that she could find a way to send a message to Rob. Their invisible friend, the doglike intelligence, might be able to help. All along the journey, she had kept looking at the black night behind her, watching for the wisp of summoned light any young sorcerer could conjure. But there was nothing. She'd even submitted to wearing the chains, believing that her rescuers would be in pursuit immediately.

The *strannik* had another Aesir device, a cuff of gold and gems, which had sheathed them in a thick plume of winter frost as they went down the steps and left the house. She'd begged him to save her sister Trudie, but the *strannik* claimed he'd seen her outside the house with the Marshalcy officers. She didn't know whether he was lying, so she was still worried about her sister. About what her parents would think. About how frantic Rob would be trying to find her. But he *would* find her. She didn't doubt it for a moment.

The wagon began to veer down another road, slowing some but not enough to make the bed lurch. They left the main road and proceeded into a wooded area. She and her family normally took the locomotivus to leave Auvinen, so she had no idea where she was or how far they'd traveled. They'd left the city hours earlier, and the scenery, muted in darkness, robbed her of any information about her whereabouts.

The carriage trundled through the woods until it reached a decrepit mansion deep within them. It was overgrown with wisteria vines, and both the door and some of the upper windows were broken. Weeds choked the seams of the flagstones, which caused the conveyance to tremble as they approached a circular driveway. The scuffed front door opened, and a pudgy older man wearing a scowl ambled out with a pronounced limp, joined moments later by a graying woman. They both wore outfits that were decades older than the current fashions. They even had square brass buckles on their shoes. It had been ages since she'd seen anyone wearing those.

The carriage stopped, and the *strannik* jumped down from the pilot box. He rushed up to the man and vigorously shook his hand. The scowl immediately disappeared, and the man gestured toward the ramshackle mansion. They were too far away for her to read lips, so she was ignorant of any communication. The driver got down and began attending to the horses, giving McKenna a better view of his face than she'd previously had. She recognized him as the accomplice who'd attacked Rob alongside the *strannik* at the grave site in Covesea. The man had also been part of the *strannik*'s attempt to kidnap her after the opera in Tanhauser. Her stomach shriveled with fear, but she clenched her hands into fists as she felt the urge to box him in the nose.

The conversation at the front of the mansion ended, and the *strannik* strode back to the carriage. He said something to his accomplice, but he'd arranged his body—deliberately or not—so that she couldn't see his mouth. The fellow nodded and went back to caring for the horses.

The *strannik*, Gregor Skoye, walked to the wagon tailgate, unhooked the pins, and lowered it. "You will be staying here for a while. A day or two, no more. Then we'll go to another location. If the military believes you are dead, you will be safe. But if not, we must elude them."

"Where are you taking me?"

A triumphant smile beamed across his bearded mouth. "You will see. There is some food waiting inside. A change of clothing."

She felt very uncomfortable being in her nightgown, but what kind of garb could this impoverished couple provide her with? The *strannik* fished a key from his pocket and unlocked the cuff around her wrist. Then he gave her a stern look.

"Don't try to escape. We are leagues away from the nearest city. I came here during my journeys. This couple sheltered me. They are loyal to me." He paused, letting his warning sink in. "Come." Then he seized her wrist and pulled her out of the wagon with too much force. She nearly sprawled on the ground, her legs unaccustomed to walking after the long ride, but he placed her near his side and escorted her to the mansion. The driver glanced at her as she passed and then looked away. There was an expression of awe in his eyes. She understood why—they thought she was the daughter of the Erlking.

Once inside, she smelled fresh sausages cooking, and her stomach twisted with hunger. Instead of taking her to a kitchen or dining room, the *strannik* took her to the cramped servants' hall. There were cobwebs everywhere. He picked a small room without any windows and summoned a flare of light by singing the command for Hoxta-Namorem.

The room was dusty, the mattress smelled of mildew, and there was an ugly chamber pot peeking out from under the mattress. The *strannik* turned and looked back, and McKenna followed his gaze. The older woman she'd seen earlier was hurrying down the hall after them, clutching two garments in her flabby arms.

The *strannik* pushed McKenna into the little room with the light and then examined both articles of clothing, which appeared to be moth-eaten peasant dresses from a century earlier.

"These will do nicely!" the *strannik* gushed, his eyes widening with delight. McKenna thought he was absurd to say so, but then she wondered if the woman was under the influence of a glamour spell. Her perception of reality could have been upended. For all McKenna knew, the woman and her husband might believe they were living in the lap of luxury. And the mysterious *strannik* was their gracious benefactor. She probably thought she'd brought two of the finest gowns in the mansion as an offering to the Erlking's lost daughter.

Gregor Skoye handed the garments to McKenna as if they were truly regal gifts and then motioned for the woman to leave. The woman had been trying to get a better look at McKenna but obeyed the dismissal.

The *strannik* turned again. "I'm locking the door with a spell. Pick whichever you want to wear. Or keep the nightgown if it suits you. Knock on the door when you are ready to eat, and I will come."

McKenna nodded and was grateful when he left, the door shutting behind him. The will-o'-the-wisp of magical light he'd conjured revealed there wasn't much else in the room except the bed, a little nightstand and washing bowl, and the chamber pot. Of the two rustic dresses, she picked a dingy white kirtle with an overdress that buttoned in the front. She quickly stripped off her nightgown and changed into it, leaving the extra garment hanging off the bed.

After her harrowing trip to this secret location, it wasn't as easy to believe Rob would show up imminently. If he suspected General Colsterworth was behind the attack, wouldn't he wait before setting off to find her so that he didn't inadvertently lead her would-be murderers to her again? And how would he even know where to look?

Feeling claustrophobic in the tiny room, she knocked on the door, and the *strannik* opened it and brought her into the little servants' kitchen. The couple was nowhere in sight, but a generous meal had been provided—eggs from the henhouse she could see outside the window, several thick sausages that had been burned, and a little pot of paste-textured oats with treacle and butter. She ate ravenously, and so did the *strannik*, helping himself to a second and third link of sausage and licking the grease from his fingers with the manners of a lowborn peasant.

"What will happen to me?" She finally summoned the courage to ask.

"We're going north, to the ice chasms," he said. "I promised to bring you to your father."

"But what about . . . me?" McKenna said worriedly. "I'm McKenna. Part of me is. What will happen to me?"

He gave her a confused look.

"I know I'm a Semblance," she said. "But will I die when I'm separated from her? Or will I still be myself?"

He was chewing rather vigorously as she spoke. "Your body—your *true* body is still amidst the ice. What will happen to you? I don't know. It depends on the Erlking. Only he has the power to revoke a Semblance. You might die. You might not." He shrugged with unconcern.

McKenna didn't feel at all comforted by his statement. Quite the opposite. Considering the history of animosity between the races, McKenna found it unlikely that the Erlking would remove his daughter's spirit from her body and leave her intact. Besides, she could sense, as she had before, that the entity inside her didn't *want* to go back to her father.

"How did you know that General Colsterworth was going to try and kill me last night? From my understanding, they normally send someone with an elfshot pistol to attack a suspected Semblance."

The *strannik* gestured to her mostly uneaten bowl of pasty gruel, but she wrinkled her nose and shook her head. He picked it up and shoveled the contents into his mouth. He had a relentless appetite, which was strange considering he was so thin. Then he smacked his lips and proceeded to lick the edge of the bowl before setting it down.

"Your father gave me an Aesir device that allows me to read the thoughts of others," he said. "I was imprisoned by them, you know. The military. They tried to murder me, but I tricked them. That is how I knew they were coming for you. Why you are only safe with me protecting you."

I think you are an imbecile and a buffoon, she thought, gazing into his eyes. "Can you read my thoughts, Mr. Skoye?" she asked with an innocent air.

He shook his head. "Yours, I cannot. But your husband . . . aha! I can read his. He wants to keep you to himself. He deceives you. I learned this for myself in Covesea."

"What did you learn?" She prodded.

He shook his head. "I must go and do my work," he said. "I must destroy the Invisible College. Then I will return you to your father. Kovya will keep watch over you. If anyone comes looking for you, he will disguise you as a servant!" He grinned at that. "You, the Erlking's daughter, a servant! Ha!" Then he fixed his finger at her. "Do not try to escape. I tell you, the military will *kill* you. And then all is lost. Our only hope for peace . . . lost!" His teeth showed the ravages of time and ill use. "If I do these things—destroy the Invisible College and bring you to your father—he promised to end the war and bring us to a new world we can live in. Far away. No more emperors. No more rifles. No more clickety-clackety machines." He waved his hand dismissively. "A new world for us." He beamed. "He cannot lie. The Erlking cannot lie. These promises will come to pass. Or else . . ." He frowned darkly and folded his arms, shaking his head, as if the other outcome were unutterable.

"When the time comes, I will go with you willingly," McKenna said, using every art she possessed to keep her look sincere. "If we can stop this war, I will even lay down my life."

The *strannik* beamed at her. "We have much to talk about, you and I. But later. I must go do the work. It is great work! Mighty work! I was chosen by the Erlking to save our people from war, and you will help me. You will help me!" He grinned in triumph and rose from the table.

McKenna kept her eyes downcast. He seemed to believe her, which was good. She needed to find a way to get back to her husband, her family, her life.

And that would be easier if the *strannik* and his friends didn't know her true intentions. The Erlking might not be able to lie.

But McKenna could.

Robinson Foster Hawksley

CHAPTER THREE

Seeking the General

Four days of searching. Four days wasted. Even Robinson's parents believed that all that could be done to find McKenna had been—if she were even alive. The Fosters had left for their home in Bishopsgate along with their servants. The family could not afford to rebuild the house on Brake Street at present, but at least they had another home—a smaller one—in that other city. They had implored Robinson to come to them.

Not sure what to do, he'd contacted Master Drusselmehr through his special ring and demanded to know if the military had been involved in the fire. He'd received a message from the head of the Invisible College professing his own ignorance on that score and promising to investigate the matter fully. Robinson had reached out again, several times, requesting information, but had received no further messages. The Marshalcy investigation into the cause of the fire had also been inconclusive. The flames had been caused by a pyrophoric substance, but no further clues had emerged as to where the rare and hazardous substance had been acquired. A limited number of suppliers even had it, and it was mostly sold for military contracts—which added to Robinson's suspicion that General Colsterworth was behind the destruction.

"I don't know what else you can do, old chap," Wickins said as he watched his friend pace restlessly. They were in Wickins's apartment, which he'd rented after he was discharged from the military due to his injuries. He was still recuperating from his wounds, but thanks to assistance from Rob's device—the little pocket watch–style invention no one knew the origins of—he had regained his ability to walk. His limp was mild considering the damage that had been done to his leg. "Maybe you should go to Bishopsgate for a while. I could go with you. I feel well enough to travel now."

Robinson scratched his scalp, feeling restless and guilt-ridden. "I'm afraid to leave," he said. "I'm worried about staying. I don't know the right thing to do. I suppose I could tell Master Drusselmehr where I'll be in case he learns new information."

"There you go. The Fosters are in Bishopsgate. Why don't we take the morning locomotivus? Your parents went home, so they won't miss you, and we could be there in time for dinner."

The decision felt neither right nor wrong. The faithful dog intelligence was still nowhere to be found, so he'd tried summoning other dog intelligences to help find McKenna, but the flames had scorched away any scent of her. The intelligences had roamed about, become disinterested, and then left, which had only stoked his feelings of desperation. Time was running out. He needed to find her *immediately*, before that madman managed to spirit her even farther away from him. And yet, every step forward seemed to lead to another step back. He'd interviewed neighbors himself, hoping to uncover a clue that had eluded the Marshalcy, but they'd been thorough and diligent. No obvious stones were left to be turned.

"Yes? I suppose?" he answered Wickins. "Why not. If General Colsterworth is at Gresham College, maybe I can ask him myself." His anger was still raw. The general would probably refuse to see him. He'd send an underling. Mr. Stoker, perhaps? Very well. Maybe Mr. Stoker would be more forthcoming.

Wickins slapped him on the back. "Let me pack some things, and we can go at once. I think it would be good for you to be with friendly faces again. Better than going off to Siaconset by yourself."

"I think I left some clothes in Bishopsgate," Robinson said. "I can always get more. Grab your things and let's be on our way."

"It's a steady thing to do, Dickemore. I'll be ready in a trice."

Robinson smiled at the familiar nickname. His friend had assigned it to him after their first meeting, because Robinson's mother's family were Dickemores, and Wickins had a connection with someone of that name, a cousin maybe. It had stuck.

While Wickins prepared to leave, Robinson pulled his device from his pocket and flipped open the lid. While it resembled a timepiece, it was much more complicated, with a series of dials surrounding a marbled brown stone in the center. There were some Aesir runes set into the face, a numbered sequence that no one understood. It had changed after Rob's wedding to McKenna, progressing one digit. But they didn't know the cause of the change or what the buttons at the top did. Rob had figured out that the dials were a sort of tumbler combination that released a hidden ring—a sorcerer's ring with the symbol of the Invisible College on it. He'd found a similar ring during their honeymoon in Covesea, which he'd given to Wickins so they could communicate both ways while his friend was stationed at the front.

Robinson entered the combination, which was based on a geometric calculation of a circle, and released the inner ring. He slid it onto his thumb and experienced the jolt of pain in his temple that always accompanied using it, which was why he didn't wear the ring continuously. He squinted, suppressing the painful throbs as best he could.

He sent a thought to Mr. Foster to alert him that he and Wickins were coming to Bishopsgate and would arrive that evening.

After the communications, he twisted off the ring and reinserted it into the device, adjusted the dials, snapped it shut again, and stuffed it into his vest pocket. Action helped temper his swinging moods. At least a little.

Soon he and Wickins were taking an iron-horse tram to the locomotivus station. They procured two tickets and had to wait an hour before the next one was ready to depart. Thankfully, there were extra seats in first class, so they had a pleasant enough trip, although everything reminded Robinson of McKenna, even the plume of fog expelled from the main engine compartment. She'd liked to bathe herself in the cold when she was feeling too warm. Evidence, of course, that she was a Semblance.

The ache didn't dissipate until they were well into the countryside. He gazed out the window, watching the little hamlets and villages as the locomotivus whizzed past, hovering above the iron rails as they were conveyed by the magic of the Aesir. Wickins fell asleep during the journey, and Robinson just gazed out the window. He wanted to be positive when he saw the Fosters. But he worried that they might be giving up hope. Anger and despair began to choke his mind. Was McKenna even alive? Was he deluding himself?

Once more he thought on the loyal doglike intelligence that had followed him from Covesea. It had warned him, multiple times, when he'd been in danger. It had followed him to Auvinen, to Bishopsgate, to Siaconset, and back again. Why had it left him at the most inopportune time? Perhaps it had been reborn into another animal and was a little pup somewhere in Auvinen? He didn't understand how all of that worked. No one did. All that was known was that the intelligence of deceased creatures could be harnessed with magic and used to print books, make clothes, light quicksilver bulbs, and so much more. The cooperation between intelligences and sorcerers had been in effect for centuries. But it wasn't until the time of Isaac Berrow that the study of magic had been formalized and the Invisible College had been created.

What would it have been like to be alive in those days? When magic was raw and new and discoveries were being made every day.

The locomotivus arrived in the evening, and Robinson and Wickins disembarked at the crowded station. There were many military people waiting to get on the southbound trip, and there was an overt sense of worry and distress among their ranks. Robinson overheard some of their remarks as they passed.

"What will we do this winter?"

"We'll be slaughtered. We can't win now."

"Do you really think it was an accident?"

There were more comments, all of them bleak, and Robinson realized something important must have happened. Wickins was scanning the crowd, seemingly oblivious, and then he broke into a grin and pointed.

It was Clara. The two met amidst the throng, and she gave him a quick hug and then a more consoling one to Robinson. "Mr. Thompson Hughes is here with the carriage," she said. "Follow me."

"Has something happened?" Robinson asked her as they began to wind their way through the dense crowd. "I overheard some soldiers worrying about the future of the war."

"You haven't heard?" she said. "It will be all over the presses in Auvinen tomorrow. We just learned of it earlier today."

"What's happened?" Wickins asked, his brow furrowing.

Clara gave him a guarded look. "General Colsterworth is dead."

That made Robinson stop mid-stride. "What?"

"Come. I'll tell you in the carriage. It's too noisy here."

Robinson was rigid with shock. He'd been so certain the general was behind the fire, and perhaps he had been, but the timing was suspicious. No wonder the soldiers were worried. Even though he'd despised the general, the man had been in charge of the war effort. Losing him at such a critical time, right before winter set in and the war resumed, was indeed a terrible blow.

They reached the carriage and the driver tipped his hat to them in recognition. The three hastened inside, but it took several minutes before they were able to get moving because of the crowd.

"Was he murdered?" Wickins asked, his face slack from the shock.

"All we know is he was having a lunch meeting with Master Drusselmehr at his favorite restaurant here. He stopped breathing and died."

"He choked on his food?" Wickins asked in disbelief.

Clara shook her head. "From what we heard, he had hives all over his body. He stopped breathing because of something he *ate*."

"Anaphylaxis," Robinson said with certainty. "Some people cannot tolerate certain foods. Poison would not have caused hives."

"Yes, that's what the news is saying," Clara said. "I didn't know that word. But in a way, he *was* poisoned. The restaurant knew that he could not abide certain seafood."

"It could be an accident," Wickins suggested. "A careless server brought the wrong dish?"

Robinson wrinkled his brow. "I think the general would have noticed it. He was meeting with Master Drusselmehr, you say?"

"Yes. He's the one who called in the Marshalcy to investigate."

"When did this happen?"

"Two days ago. It was kept secret until the cause of death was revealed." The carriage lurched and jolted to avoid hitting another vehicle.

"I don't think it was an accident," Robinson said, shaking his head. He'd sent a message to Master Drusselmehr, who had promised to investigate the matter. No further messages had been returned. What had Drusselmehr learned about the general's involvement in the fire on Brake Street?

It seemed entirely probable that General Colsterworth had been murdered.

CHAPTER FOUR

Master of the Royal Secret

The driver brought them to the front door of the Fosters' home, and even before Robinson and Wickins had disembarked, the front door was flung open and Trudie came rushing out to give them earnest hugs. She hadn't smiled since the terrible night of the fire, and the smudges under her eyes showed she was still suffering from the family trials.

"Did you find her? Is there anything?" she pleaded, gripping Robinson's arms tightly.

He felt a lump in his throat as he shook his head no. She wasn't crestfallen, though. She'd expected this answer.

"I thought so," she sighed. "You would have told us if you had. Hello, Wickins. Clara."

Wickins gave the younger girl an embrace and then helped Clara out of the carriage. Mrs. Foster stood at the doorway, watching the scene, and then came out to greet them. Robinson greeted her with a kiss, and they all started toward the house as Mr. Thompson Hughes took the carriage away. Robinson noticed an elegantly dressed woman standing farther down the street.

It was Elizabeth Cowing. The last time they'd met in person had been at this very house in Bishopsgate. She offered no communication, nor did she approach. It was odd seeing her there, especially with the rivalry between their competing patents. Could it really be coincidence that had brought her to the Fosters' home at the moment of his arrival?

Robinson gave her another glance and then followed the family inside. Mr. Foster appeared from his study and welcomed them warmly.

"I'm so glad you decided to come," he said. "I've a meeting with Master Drusselmehr this evening, and I'd like you to come with me."

That was startling news, especially after what he'd learned about the general. "This evening? Yes. I should like to join you."

"Perhaps we could speak in my study?"

"Dearest," said Mrs. Foster. "They just arrived. They're probably hungry."

Robinson's appetite had dwindled since the fire, but he had been looking forward to Mrs. Foster's dinner. So they retreated to the small kitchen, instead of the dining room, and Mrs. Foster procured some food for them—a tasty split-pea soup and bread. Robinson noticed all the furniture had been uncovered and much had been returned from storage, giving the home a more lively feeling. Mrs. Foster said that he and Wickins would share McKenna's room upstairs and Trudie would move next door to Clara's room. That would all be proper. Robinson wiped his mouth on a napkin and thanked her.

"Could you play a song for us?" Trudie asked when he was finished. "You brought your violin, did you not?"

He hesitated, but he could not let McKenna's sister down, so he told her he'd play anything she wanted. Thankfully, she didn't ask for the aria of the Erlking's daughter, which he was far from sure he could bring himself to play at the moment. She picked a livelier piece from another famous opera about two enemies who became friends, and he played it for them in the parlor.

After that, Mr. Foster got his wish, and they were able to speak more privately. Wickins and Clara joined them, and Mrs. Foster said she'd return if Trudie fell asleep. Judging by her tone, that had been a problem of late.

"Before we speak of Master Drusselmehr," Robinson said, "can you shed any light on the general's death? Clara informed us of it at the station."

"I spoke to a Marshalcy officer whom I went to school with," Mr. Foster said. "The cause of death was asphyxiation. The general's throat closed, and he couldn't breathe. The hives are indicative of a reaction to shellfish. But why would he knowingly eat something he couldn't tolerate? That's the riddle."

Robinson glanced at Clara and Wickins, then shifted his gaze back to Mr. Foster. "Do you think he was murdered?"

"For what reason? He was indispensable for the war effort."

"What if he was killed by Gregor Skoye, the *strannik*? He's already proven himself adept at glamour spells, which he may have learned from the Aesir, and he wants to help the Erlking. That's the reason he kept trying to abduct McKenna. From what Master Drusselmehr told me, the *strannik* and the general are enemies."

Mr. Foster brooded on this for a moment, stroking his beard, and then adjusted his pince-nez glasses. "I hadn't thought of that, Son. Murdering the top general of the military might indeed weaken the men's resolve to keep fighting."

"Who is next in the chain of command?" Robinson asked.

"General Ambrose," Wickins said confidently. "But it's the emperor who decides." He grunted. "You can imagine the politics happening in Andover at the moment."

Robinson had some idea. He and Wickins had been awarded one of the highest civilian honors the Invisible College could bestow for the role they'd played in repelling an Aesir attack using Robinson's device. A ceremony had been arranged to take place at the summer palace, but it had since been canceled due to the threat of the *strannik*. The honor had been bestowed from afar. which was for the best as far as Robinson was concerned. He wouldn't have left the area at this time anyway. This was where McKenna would look for him if she were able to get away.

Mr. Foster nodded. "The emperor is decisive. I think he'll choose General Ambrose. We need experienced men leading the war. Now, for the matter at hand. The meeting with Drusselmehr."

"What did he want to meet you about?" Robinson asked.

"The patent suit."

Robinson sighed and felt like walking out of the room, but he wouldn't be rude to his father-in-law. "I think I saw Miss Cowing outside as we came in."

Mr. Foster looked confused. "Here?"

"She was standing down the street watching."

"That's peculiar behavior. Her barrister is fighting like a hound over a bone for her rights to your invention. Even though you had actually produced glass tubes, whereas she had not, she had a design for a comparable device, down to the wiring at the ends. It is too similar to be coincidence. Miss Cowing's barrister has given the date for which the idea of the invention came to her. Her application happened immediately after. Do you recall the date you invented it?"

"The invention didn't happen on a specific date, Mr. Foster. I'd been working on the idea for months."

"Didn't you keep records? Notes?"

Wickins snapped his fingers. "He did. He always does. And McKenna organized them. Remember?"

Robinson nodded. "When we were courting. Before our official engagement. She used to come over and help out in my alchemy."

Mr. Foster's eyes twinkled with delight. "And those notes were transferred to your alchemy at Mowbray House in Siaconset?"

"Yes," Robinson said. "I think they are still in storage, though. I could contact Mr. Swope and ask him to find them and bring them here."

"Those notes are evidence we need for the case," Mr. Foster said. "If we can prove that your work predates that of Miss Cowing, then we shall win the lawsuit and the patent rights. By all means, summon Mr. Swope!"

Robinson did not care about the lawsuit, not when McKenna was missing. But he understood Mr. Foster's feelings. His home on Brake Street had become cinders. It would cost a lot of money to rebuild, money that he no longer had in abundance. Unless they won the lawsuit against Miss Cowing and the military. He'd explained earlier that the military was liable for treble the damages if they'd knowingly and willfully violated Robinson's patent by stealing his invention and replicating it for their own use without payment or permission. That would be a fortune indeed and would help the family during such a difficult financial setback. If the patent were instead given to Miss Cowing and she sided with the military, it would bankrupt the Fosters.

He had never met Miss Cowing before that day at the exhibition when he'd caught her handling one of his tubes. They were *his* invention, not hers. He didn't know how she could have learned about his idea from so far away, but the similarities between her concept and his invention were probably too great for it to have been a coincidence. Her invention also used quicksilver gas as the illumination ingredient, and like his, it was triggered by sound inaudible to human ears. He did not know whether or not hers used Aesir gold as the conductor. She hadn't struck him as a very dishonest person, however. There might be another explanation he hadn't fully considered yet.

They continued the conversation a while longer, discussing the latest news. Sarah Fuller Fiske had offered them use of her apartment whenever they needed to come back to Auvinen. That was kind of her, and Robinson realized that her future—and the Mrs. Fiske's School for the Deaf she ran—also hung in the balance. Mr. Foster had founded it and was the chief investor. If one was ruined, so too was the other. Things could not be more fraught. He used his ring once again to contact Mr. Swope at Mowbray House and ask him to bring the documents McKenna had organized, along with the materials related to the ring—like the cuttlefish mold—to Bishopsgate. He also communicated her disappearance in case word had not yet reached Siaconset, telling Mr. Swope that the Marshalcy was still investigating the ruins at Auvinen, but no sign of her had been found.

At last it was time to depart for the meeting, and Robinson and Mr. Foster left Clara and Wickins in the study. Night had fallen over the town, though it was well illuminated, and the carriage rocked as it trundled down the street. Robinson noticed, out the window, a mechanical contraption that looked like a turtle was brushing the curb. Was it removing debris? He hadn't seen its like before but was impressed by the invention.

"Where is the meeting?" Robinson asked.

"Master Drusselmehr's home." Mr. Foster pulled out his pocket watch, checked the time, and nodded in satisfaction. He was a punctual man. If anything, they would arrive early.

Drusselmehr's home was an ivy-strewn mansion in the wealthy inner district of Bishopsgate. Tall fences with spear-tip points fronted the house. Uniformed servants opened the gate, allowing the carriage inside. There were four triangular peaks on the front facade and two separate wings jutting out to either side. The interior was lit with quicksilver lamps, but not all the windows glowed with light. A flagpole and a listless pennant protruded from an inner circle set into a lawn, beyond which was ample space to park the carriage.

They were greeted by a servant with a billowy wig. "Mr. Foster, welcome to Overreding. Master Drusselmehr is expecting you. Who is your companion?"

"This is Professor Hawksley. He just arrived from Auvinen on the last locomotivus. I invited him to join us."

"Welcome, Professor. Your reputation precedes you. Come this way!"

As they walked up the gravel path to the door, Robinson noticed symbols from the Invisible College decorating the brickwork. They were subtle references, but anyone who was part of a quorum would recognize that this home was different, which was not to say they would be able to interpret everything they saw. Master Drusselmehr's rank was clothed in secret. No one but he knew "the royal secret." It was the highest rank in the Invisible College, the thirty-second degree, although there was supposedly one degree above it that was honorary. Robinson himself had just been promoted to the fourteenth degree, Sublime Master.

As the servant brought them into the main hall, Robinson heard the hasty clip of boots on the marbled floor and recognized Master Drusselmehr's bodyguard striding toward them with an unfriendly expression. He was in a hurry and clipped Robinson's shoulder as he walked past, not even pausing to offer an apology. Robinson rubbed his shoulder and shook his head as the servant escorted them down the corridor.

There were magical artifacts aplenty on display, and Robinson wanted to pause and admire them, but their pace was too quick to do so. There were also glass cases with a variety of toys inside—different pieces Drusselmehr had undoubtedly invented during his illustrious career as a toy-making sorcerer. He heard a violin playing somewhere inside and wondered if it was Master Drusselmehr.

When the servant reached a set of large doors, he twisted the handles and pulled them open before gesturing for Mr. Foster and Robinson to enter the glowing room beyond.

Where they found Master Drusselmehr slouched back in a huge stuffed chair, his silk shirt stained with blood around his heart and the sulfurous scent of elfshot still lingering in the air.

MaKenna Aurora
Hawksley

CHAPTER FIVE

Escape

The man's name was Kovya. Although she detested him, she *did* appreciate his name. He was the *strannik*'s assistant, the one who'd been with him when he'd come after her before. Unlike the *strannik*, who had a spare frame and greasy, unkempt hair and beard, Kovya had the build of a laborer—tall and broad chested—and an irascible nature. When McKenna tried to engage him in conversation, he sulked and hardly answered her at all. It seemed to her that he was always around and was never far from sight unless she needed to use the privy. And that's what inspired her to make her escape.

The *strannik* had departed to who knew where two days earlier, leaving her with the couple and Kovya. While the older folk provided her with food and the little bed in the servants' quarters, they kept their distance. Kovya was her shadow. He walked the grounds regularly, keeping an eye out for the *strannik*'s return. But once McKenna started to pay attention to his movements, she found that amidst his other chores, he would always check on her, at least once an hour. No conversation. Just to make sure she hadn't left. And at night, he slept on the floor in the corridor outside her door. She'd discovered that when she'd tried to slip away to explore and had awoken him.

Another day passed with little to show for it. Not a single visitor had come by. The old man and woman fed the chickens, tended a small garden behind the ramshackle mansion, and generally went about their ordinary lives. She had fresh milk to drink and plenty of food, but no one to talk to, and that stifled her.

She hated using the chamber pot in her room, so the privy outside was where she met her needs. It was a little shack housing a wooden bench with a hole in it. The walls were made of planks nailed to posts and some of the nails were loose. So loose, in fact, that she'd started pulling them out one by one, using a fork she'd swiped from the kitchen for that purpose. Kovya never stood guard at the privy door—thankfully—but he'd wander outside and sometimes help in the garden, always keeping an eye on the shack.

By the fourth day, in the morning, she'd removed enough nails to be able to dislodge part of the back wall of the privy stall and squeeze through the opening. The wood was so splintered that she needed to be careful or she'd snag her peasant's dress on it and rip it, which she had no doubt Kovya would notice. "Caution" was her watchword. She propped the wood back in place without affixing it and felt it would pass all but the closest inspection.

Her escape plan was simple. She'd been hiding food from her meals in her dress and then in her room. Food she would take on her journey so she wouldn't starve to death. She wasn't concerned in the least about being cold. Kovya would have every advantage in hunting her, since she couldn't hear the noise she made. So she'd decided to sneak away after dusk, thus depriving him of one of his senses—sight. There were gaps in the wooden slats of the privy, giving her a fair enough view of the dilapidated manor and Kovya's wandering. She'd wait until he left to make his rounds, sneak out of the privy, and hide in the tree line. Once he started looking for her, she'd sneak back to the house, grab her food, which she'd wrapped up in her nightgown for easier carrying, and wait there in the darkness in another room. She didn't think he was clever enough to look for her in the house and would spend most of the night searching for her in the woods while she slept comfortably indoors. Before dawn, she would slip away from the house and walk up the road they'd come down. The road, in her view, was her best opportunity not to get lost and to find civilization.

All in all, she thought it a rather clever plan, and her anticipation heightened as the day progressed. It had been four days since the fire. Since Rob hadn't found her yet, even with his magic, she felt it wasn't prudent to wait to be rescued.

As the afternoon progressed, she found it increasingly difficult to maintain her poise. She was fidgeting more than normal and wondered if Kovya had noticed her shift in mood.

At dinner, she was so nervous she didn't want to eat, but she did anyway and tried to disguise her lack of hunger by showing additional appreciation for the food. Kovya gave her a wary look, which was unnerving, but she continued to act as if nothing was wrong while the sun sank lower in the sky.

Dinner was nearly over when she noticed the older couple lifting their heads and looking out the kitchen window. Kovya jumped up from his chair, eyes blazing with concern, and rushed to the window. They'd clearly heard something she hadn't. McKenna pushed away from the table and walked to the window as well, trying to appear unworried.

Kovya slapped his hand on the glass and then rushed out of the kitchen. In the dark, she saw a wagon coming up to the house pulled by two horses. The driver was wearing a cloak that concealed his features. The older husband and wife were talking together when McKenna turned her head.

"Is it him? Is it the *strannik*?" the husband asked.

"I can't tell," the woman replied.

McKenna's heart began to race. Moments later, she saw Kovya running up to the wagon. The driver threw back his hood, revealing the *strannik*'s face. He leaped from the driver's box, and the two men embraced.

Disappointment stung her. If she continued with her escape plan, it would fail. The *strannik* had some way of tracking her. Just like Rob could usually do with their dog-intelligence friend. If she tried to hide, he'd use his magic to find her. All her effort—wasted.

The two men returned to the house, and the couple greeted the *strannik* warmly and with great respect. Gregor Skoye looked at her, his piercing eyes jabbing into hers. She gave him a little nod, but inside she was reeling.

"I'm ravenous!" the *strannik* declared as he took a seat at the table and began to help himself to the fare with gusto.

McKenna went back to her chair and sat down, her mind racing. Should she still try to run away? The privy wall was ready to fall down without the nails. Her food was wrapped in the nightgown beneath the bed. But if she made the attempt and was caught, she believed the *strannik* would treat her more harshly. If he and his companions believed her to be compliant, resigned even, then their guard would come down. Her better hope of escape was to lull them into carelessness.

Finally, after indulging in a copious amount of food, the *strannik* leaned back in his chair, offered what she imagined was a noisy belch, and wiped his mouth on his sleeve.

Kovya leaned forward. "Is it done? Is he dead?"

The *strannik* grinned. "Yes, my friend. They both are. I disguised myself as his manservant, his bodyguard. Heh. And now he's dead and our plan can continue."

"Who did you kill?" McKenna asked, shocked at how carelessly they were discussing murder.

The *strannik* tilted his head and eyed her. "Drussel*storph*. The man . . . the preening inventor of toys. As well as the general." He said it dismissively. "The head of the Invisible College and the leader of the war against the Aesir are no more." He lifted his cup and took a drink in celebration.

He turned to Kovya and laughed as he shared how he had tormented the dying general by telling him Drusselmehr was already dead, even though that was a lie. The man was rarely alone, so he hadn't gotten access to him until he managed to get to the inventor's manservant and take his place.

Kovya looked excited, the most emotion he'd displayed since she'd been with him.

McKenna felt her jaw hang open. "Master Drusselmehr is dead?"

"Bah! A pompous, rich, selfish braggart," the *strannik* said. "He wanted me to *hang*, you see. A rope tight around my neck. Swaying this way and that." He made comical gestures as he pantomimed the scene. "They are the murderers. They are the liars. Even your husband. Everyone in the Invisible College uses lies and deceit to chain the minds of our people. They want war with the Aesir." He held up his index finger. "It is better for one man to perish than for a nation, no? When the Aesir come this winter, they will find a people ready to submit to their ways. We have gone astray." He lowered his hand and drummed his fingers on the table. "And you will help us bring peace once again."

McKenna felt nothing but revulsion for this man. Master Drusselmehr was dead. Killed by a man he'd believed he could trust. The *strannik* posed as Mr. Leishman, the manservant that she and Rob had met earlier.

"Will they not replace him?" Kovya said. "There is always another willing person to be Master of the Royal Secret. They will find another if we do not hurry."

"Patience, old friend. Patience. Our numbers swell every day. Their numbers shrink. When the Erlking comes to reclaim his daughter, he will find a willing and submissive people. The fear is spreading now that the general and the toy inventor are dead. It will happen as I said. You will see." He slapped his palms on the table. "Now we must go. Away. Into the wagon."

McKenna's stomach lurched. "Now?"

"Yes, while it is dark. We will ride all night." He looked at her and then his mouth formed words that did not make sense to her. She realized that he was using his sorcery on her. She felt gooseflesh prickle up her arms but nothing happened.

The old man and woman blinked in surprise and stared at McKenna with open mouths.

The *strannik* smirked. "You appear to be eight years old, my dear," he explained to her. "Golden hair in ringlets. So pretty. You will be my granddaughter Mika." His grin broadened. "Kovya is your father. Mika and Kovya. Simple names. Farmers. That is the way life is supposed to be. These big cities will fall into ruin, and all will go back to its natural state again. You will see."

He rose from the table and bowed in appreciation to the old couple.

"Where do you go next, *strannik*?" the man asked. "You travel so much and work so hard."

"We worry about your health," said the woman.

The *strannik* stretched. "We go to a village in the Lake Country to await the Erlking's return. They will not find his daughter there."

And his gaze fell on McKenna with a look of smugness that made her disgusted with herself for not having attempted to escape sooner.

The idea for founding the Invisible College came when I was a young student at the University of Nirshoye. My roommate, the congenial Blake Sherburn, left to attend to a family matter for a fortnight. The solitude and wintery conditions kept me indoors throughout this period. In that condition of perfect quietude and reflection, I conceived the notion of an organization to facilitate the transfer and knowledge of arcane matters. I did not, at this time, establish the hierarchy of ranks, the customs, symbols, and various methods for members of the order to reveal themselves to one another. That would all come later.

No, the seedling of the idea that sprouted and blossomed was the idea that such knowledge should not be limited to the wealthy or the elite. Many students at the University of Nirshoye came from impoverished conditions and struggled to afford shelter, food, and tuition. The town surrounding the esteemed university teemed with prostitutes, pickpockets, and cheats forced to live in squalor due to a lack of opportunity to better themselves when each one *might have been taught the secrets of harnessing intelligences, mixing chymicals, or disciplining the mind with arithmetic, logic, and rhetoric.*

Our shameful Society rides on the backs of pitiful creatures helpless to improve their position because of where, when, and to whom they were born. I myself could have been one of them. These wretches I saw living in the streets with no shelter, food, or hope. So often I passed them thinking, "There but for the grace of the Sovereignty of the Mind, goes Isaac Berrow."

—Isaac Berrow, Master of the Royal Secret,
the Invisible College

Isaac Berrow

CHAPTER SIX

A Semblance Comes

Fifteen years before the founding of the Invisible College

"Do you have any food?" the woman asked, leaning back against the door and looking as if she might faint. "I'm starving to death."

Isaac gaped at her, still shocked by her sudden appearance in his dwelling and her use of magic to get past his locked door. He shut his mouth and hastened to provide her something to eat, and all the while his mind reeled and his insides churned with dread at being all alone with her. In his little pantry was a heel of older bread, the crust requiring some exertion to cut through. He added some butter, sparingly at first, as he did with his own slices, then silently rebuking himself for being stingy with a guest—albeit an unwelcome one—he slathered it on. His hand trembled as he ladled a cup of water from his water barrel. He had some cheese too—the soft-rinded kind he liked—and took out a little knife to cut it in half.

When he turned to proffer these to his guest, he found her rearranging a shawl over her bare shoulder, which was smudged with soot and bruises. She was walking around the living space, observing his table and the mortar and pestle. Then she reached out and touched her finger to the lip of the stone bowl.

"H-Here you are," he said, his voice cracking with nerves. He had a little wooden tray for the bread and cheese and the cup. The only cup he owned. He was still astonished to think that she, of all people, knew sorcery.

The woman hastily put her wrist to her mouth to stifle a raucous cough. When she lowered her hand, he saw flecks of blood on her skin from where she'd touched her lips. He swallowed with increasing nervousness. She was sick and starving. Her hair was loose, but it hadn't been brushed in a while. A bit of fake jewelry, a clasp, held part of it up. Her clothing was threadbare and distressed.

She took the piece of bread and began to devour it, even though the crust was as tough as leather. He set the tray and cup on the edge of the worktable, his mind working fiercely. Should he fetch someone from the university to drive her away?

He felt sorry for her. But truly, her situation was not his fault, nor was he in a position to remedy it. He'd given her money, and she'd hunted him down. Only . . . *how* had she hunted him down? That was a mystery. His stomach was so constricted it made him nauseous.

"Thank you," she murmured after eating the little wedge of cheese he'd cut for her. Then she gulped down the water, draining the cup.

"I'm sorry for your plight, truly I am," he said. "But you need to go. I don't . . . r-require . . . your services."

She shook her head. "I don't have much time to explain things. I'm dying."

"That's dreadful," he said. "I'm sorry, but we're strangers to each other, and I'm not sure what you feel the need to explain."

"I'm not a streetwalker. Well . . . this body is one. But she died of hunger and cold and misery."

Isaac stared at her, perplexed. "I'm sorry, but that r-rather confused me. 'Her' body? Your body?"

"I'm a Semblance," she said.

"A what?"

"A Semblance. My intelligence is inhabiting her body. We share it. It happened when she died. That is when the magic can take place. It allows us to take control without resistance."

He began to gape again, realized his mouth was open, and closed it.

"As I said, I don't have much time to explain things to you. This poor thing was already sick before I took over, too sick for her body to last very long. I don't begin to remember things until death is near." She began to approach him, and he retreated toward the door.

"I'm not going to hurt you," she said.

"I think you should go."

She shook her head. "That won't do. Let me explain what I can with the little time I have left. This throat tickles so much, I can hardly talk." She began to cough again, choosing to cough into her shawl. He saw the blood again and flinched from it.

She wasn't a physical threat to him. Her weakness was obvious. But still, her intrusion into his dwelling was unwanted and unwelcome. And what she was saying was utterly nonsensical. He'd never heard of Semblances before, and while he knew the word, the way she said it implied a different meaning.

"What's your name?" she asked him once she'd recovered.

"Isaac Berrow."

"I am the Erlking's daughter."

Isaac's eyes widened as he stared at her. His first impulse was to question the revelation, but she'd used magic to get inside his home, and he could see an ancient intelligence in her eyes. Curiosity and wonder poured into him. The way she'd opened that locked door was remarkable—far beyond the magical capacity of anyone he knew or had heard of. Only a handful of spells had been handed down over the centuries, and those typically impacted light and sound. Most magical knowledge was about chymicals and mixtures. He didn't disbelieve her. He wasn't sure why, but he knew she was telling the truth. He felt it down to his muscles and bones.

The Erlking was the fabled ruler of the Aesir. The conflict between mortals and Aesir had been going on for thousands of years if not longer, and no living mortal knew how the conflict had started.

"You're one of the Aesir?" he asked cautiously. His stomach had started tingling, but the feeling wasn't quiet dread anymore.

"Yes."

"The door was locked. How did you open it with magic?"

"I harnessed an intelligence to control the lock. I communicated with it and empowered it to move the right parts. All without touching it. Magic can do so much more than mortals remember."

"Show me," he said, testing her.

She stared at him a moment, then began to hum, her voice soft and coaxing. He gaped at the kettle on the stove as it began to rattle and hiss.

"I chose exile to help the mortal world against my father," she told him. "I've taught generations of sorcerers. And now I must teach *you*. I will die in a few days. Maybe a week. That's all the time we have, Isaac."

"Wait . . . you want to teach me? Why me?"

"Because I chose you," she answered as if that made perfect sense. And it did not.

He tried to find words, but they failed him. "I'm just a student here. There are others who would be far more suitable."

She shook her head. "I chose *you*, Isaac Berrow." She approached him, looking up and down. "You must believe me. I want to help the mortal world before my father destroys it. And if he's allowed to do so, he will, Isaac. He will."

"But why? Why do the Aesir fight against us? What did we ever do to them?"

"You can't remember—none of you can—but you violated your oaths and covenants. You betrayed the Aesir and the knowledge that was given to you. My father believes in the immutable principle of justice. You did wrong, and so you must continue to pay. But *I* believe you deserve mercy. You cannot remember those oaths because nothing you teach endures the ages. This island was once an Aesir stronghold. You were permitted to live here among our people, to care for the land while we were under the Skrýmir."

"The . . . what?"

"That is when we sleep. The Skrýmir lasts for years and years. You were stewards, so to speak. Stewards and caretakers. Your ancestors agreed to this. Willingly. But when the Awakening happened, so many generations had passed that your people had forgotten and believed those things and places and magic were yours alone. When we returned to reclaim what was rightfully ours, you fought us. Not duplicitously. You no longer remembered who'd given you so much."

Isaac listened with fascination and growing interest. What little he knew of the Aesir he had learned in books. They were immortal beings who lived in the coldest of climates. Their creations didn't age or wither, and neither did their bodies. They could only interact with mortals during seasons of frost and snow because they were vulnerable to heat, the fierce rays of the summer sun, and certain metals forged in the hottest of fires. They were immortal, but they could be killed. A blue-skinned people with smudges of darker blue or violet beneath their eyes. This woman, this Semblance, looked nothing like the proud effigies he'd seen at the university.

"So we are attacked, randomly it seems, because of an ancient agreement we don't remember?"

"It isn't random, Isaac. The cycles of the Skrýmir are not happenstance."

"You mean there is a pattern?"

"There is always a pattern. You are a scholar. You know arithmetical concepts. We taught them to your kind. Triangles, squares, circles. The ratios of such."

"And you are saying that there is a pattern in all the numbers?"

"Yes. The whole universe moves in harmony with it."

"The universe . . . as in this world and everything that revolves around it?"

She shook her head. "No, Isaac. I always have to keep explaining this part. The universe is infinitely more vast than this particular world and its particular sun. There are billions of other stars and worlds in the universe. The world we came from was dying. The energies that powered our solar sphere were failing."

"Failing? Like a fire running out of fuel?"

"Not exactly like that. All the stars you see in the night sky are other suns, just farther away. When a sun loses its heat, it implodes and destroys everything near it. Our world became colder and colder. We adapted to it. But we knew through calculations what would happen once it eventually extinguished. We came to this world because of how cold it was."

"Were we . . . already here?" Isaac asked. "Mortals?"

"Yes. Mortals have . . . always . . . tenaciously . . . clung to life." She tried to speak through an avalanche of coughs that had begun again and did not stop until she was sitting on the floor, shoulders heaving. He struggled with feelings of sympathy, watching her pant and try to regain control of her breathing again. He refilled the cup with water and crouched near her, offering it. She drank from it slowly, trying not to choke.

"Is there any medicine I can get for you?" he asked softly.

She shook her head. "It's too late for that. This disease I'm suffering from . . . it was unleashed by my people."

"They can create illness?"

"Illness already abounds in the mortal world." She was wheezing still but at least able to communicate. "Our magic can alter it. Tailor it to the purpose of exterminating your kind. It was part of the covenant. That if you betrayed us, we would unleash these horrors on you. Your rulers, long ago, agreed to the pact."

"Why would they?"

"Do you know how many times I've had to repeat this story, Isaac? How many times I must keep retelling it? Memory shouts at first. Then it speaks. Then it whispers. Then it falls silent. You've forgotten who you are."

"*I've* forgotten? Or mortals in general? My father died before I was born. That fact alone precludes me from ever truly knowing him."

"You have *all* forgotten the promises made. But I came to help you remember. To remind you of what once was." Her eyes were feverish in their intensity. "We don't have much time, Isaac Berrow. Sit and listen to my story."

Robinson Foster Hawksley

CHAPTER SEVEN

Transmutation of Thought

Present day

"Thank you for coming," Mr. Foster said after the inspector general had seated himself in the parlor.

Abram Howard Guiteau was in charge of the Marshalcy and had come once again to update them on the investigation of Master Drusselmehr's murder. Robinson was unable to sit and continued to pace with agitation. The murders of the two highest-ranking members of the Invisible College had filled him, and every sorcerer he'd come upon for two days, with great anxiety. Worse, he'd seen the victim. He could still see in his mind the image of the wound, the crimson stain on Master Drusselmehr's shirt, the final groans he'd uttered before succumbing to death.

"It's the least I can do, Mr. Foster," said Guiteau in a steady voice. He was a plain-looking man with a thick, brushed mustache and hair parted in the middle and slicked with pomade. He was likely in his early forties and wore the uniform of the Marshalcy officer except he had a star symbol sewn onto each shoulder.

Robinson had met him for the first time the night of the murder. He'd rushed to Master Drusselmehr with his device, hoping the magic would prevent the death of the senior official, but the wound was too serious and he'd died before their eyes. The Marshalcy had come at once to begin their investigation. Robinson had slept little since then, haunted by what had happened.

It was his opinion that Drusselmehr had been killed by Gregor Skoye wearing a glamour to look like Mr. Leishman, the aged sorcerer's bodyguard. He'd collided with Robinson on his way out of the building, and it seared Robinson's gut to think of how close he'd been to the man who might have abducted McKenna.

He realized his raging thoughts had blocked the inspector general's words and that he'd missed some of the update. ". . . and we discovered the body in his room, pushed under the bed."

"Unfathomable," Mr. Foster said. "How long had Mr. Leishman been dead?"

"The coroner estimated it happened two days prior to Drusselmehr's murder. The elfshot pistol used in the crime and left at the scene was indeed Mr. Leishman's. It seems Professor Hawksley's intuition matches the evidence precisely." He looked at Robinson and gave him a nod of respect.

Robinson cared less than ever about accolades. "And so he disappeared like a . . . a ghost," he said with frustration. "He fled the estate, became someone else, and walked away."

"That is correct," answered Guiteau. "My officers interviewed every person. We are still following up on leads, but it seems you are correct. I wonder, Professor, if you might want a job in the Marshalcy. You'd be a great help to us." He'd asked with a half-serious tone.

Robinson shook his head curtly. "What happens now?"

"We find him. I have people searching for him—"

"No, I mean what happens to the Invisible College," Robinson interrupted.

Mr. Foster took off his pince-nez glasses and began cleaning them with a handkerchief. "The order was created to withstand such a calamity."

"Oh? I've never heard of the recourse for such an event," Robinson said.

"That knowledge is restricted to higher orders, naturally," said Guiteau. "But there are precedents for it, beginning with the death of Isaac Berrow himself. When the position of Master of the Royal Secret is vacated, there are three individuals who are chosen, in advance, by the Master of the Royal Secret to assist in the ascension of a new master. Each of these individuals gives a key, or token, to someone else within the order to safeguard."

"What are these keys or tokens?" Robinson asked.

"They unlock certain boxes. Small boxes, like the kind jewels are stored in. I've not seen them, so I cannot tell you what they look like, nor can I tell you where the boxes are. That knowledge is kept tightly guarded."

Mr. Foster finished cleaning his glasses and put them back on. "Master Drusselmehr did not know which individuals hold the tokens, so he could not have revealed the information to any enemy. It was designed thus to prevent him being tortured into a confession. Those three individuals will choose the next sorcerer to become Master of the Royal Secret. They'll hand over the keys, and he or she will become the new master after opening the boxes to gain the knowledge of that role. Then the master will entrust the keys to three new sorcerers."

Robinson thought about what he'd been told. It was an interesting way to establish a transfer of power and authority. It was, in a sense, like the combination of a lock.

"Do these three choose from within the hierarchy, then?" Robinson asked.

Guiteau shook his head. "They can pick any sorcerer who has achieved the rank of Sublime Master or higher."

That was astonishing. "You mean *I* could be chosen?"

Guiteau leaned forward, giving him a piercing look. "Above the fourteenth rank, Professor, there are surprisingly few within the Invisible College. So yes, you are a candidate. All who have achieved the fourteenth rank will be summoned to a convocation, where they will be interviewed by the three sorcerers. They will choose someone they feel best espouses the virtues required in the Invisible College. This person must also have the resources to further its aims. Wealth is not a prerequisite, mind you. But as there is no stipend for assuming the role, one must have the means to support oneself and invest in the future."

"Master Drusselmehr was of the eighteenth rank, if I recall, when he was chosen," Mr. Foster said.

"Seventeenth actually," said the inspector general. "I myself am a sorcerer of the thirtieth degree. There are only a few higher than me, but I have no greater claim to it than any other sorcerer of suitable rank. One of the reasons I am explaining this to you, Professor, is so that you understand an invitation will come to you by an authorized messenger of the order. As I understand things, you were already going to be invested with accolades along with your business partner, Mr. Wickins?"

"Yes," Robinson said offhandedly. "That seems of little consequence now."

"It is of significant consequence, sir. You have a reputation that makes your candidacy a real possibility."

Robinson's eyes widened. "Me?" He chuckled.

"Don't dismiss it out of hand, my boy," Mr. Foster said. "When the convocation of sorcerers happens, when all of us are gathered together, your life will be highly scrutinized. Every deed you have done, every act of self-interest or unselfishness will be discussed."

"It is not my decision to make," said Guiteau. "But I expect you stand a greater chance than most. Your contribution to the war effort has already been highly valuable and esteemed."

"Can I refuse?" Robinson asked.

Mr. Foster frowned. "If you are chosen, you are *chosen*. It would be an honor and a privilege. Some aspire to that rank. They feign the virtues you exhibit naturally."

"You mean they only have a semblance of virtue?" he said and then caught himself when he thought of the word's other meaning. His wife was undoubtedly a Semblance. Likely a rather important one. Mr. Foster did not know this, but his wife did. Robinson felt self-conscious and guilty.

"Your modesty is commendable," Guiteau said.

"Oh, it's not modesty," Robinson said, feeling chagrined. "I truly do feel I would not be a good choice. But I'm not going to borrow trouble when I already have so much of it."

"Your wife," Guiteau said, nodding. "I have men continuing to look for her."

"Yes, but they wouldn't recognize her if they found her," Robinson said with a sigh. "She was abducted in the middle of Tanhauser in front of witnesses who did not seem to notice anything amiss. The *strannik* has a stunning ability with glamours. I have to find her, sir. That is my highest priority."

"And my highest is to bring to justice this *strannik* who wants to destroy us all by surrendering to the Aesir," said Guiteau. "Do you have any other suggestions for us to consider? Your ingenuity has saved us time and trouble."

Robinson stopped pacing and scratched the back of his neck. "I've given you my reasoning, and that is all I can do. Master Drusselmehr was with us during my advancement. The *strannik*'s glamours do not work on McKenna. She has always been able to see the *strannik* for who he is, whereas the rest of us cannot." He paused. "Perhaps it is because she is deaf. We may be able to use that to our advantage against him."

Guiteau frowned. "You mean use the deaf to help us? How?" He frowned, and Rob got the sense he didn't like this idea, but at least he hadn't rejected it out of hand.

Mr. Foster adjusted his position. "I'd not considered that."

"Neither had I until just now," Robinson said. "My mind has been a fog of worry since she was taken."

"There is no evidence that she was abducted," Guiteau said slowly, sympathetically. "My men have been very consistent on that point."

"The nature of the flames at the scene would lead to that idea," Robinson said, trying to keep his emotions from rushing away as he spoke. The sleepless nights were taking their toll, his confusion and misery compounding day by day. But still he hoped. It was the hope that kept him going. "They wiped away all traces of her. I'm not trying to cling to false hope, Inspector. The sequence of events leads me to believe that the *strannik* fulfilled his intention to capture her."

"But why would he want *her*? Revenge against you? Or . . ." He paused, his eyebrows lifting. "If he suspects *you* might be chosen as the new Master of the Royal Secret, it would give him compromising leverage against you."

Mr. Foster looked startled by the comment. "Indeed it would."

Indeed, Robinson thought. Had Gregor Skoye killed General Colsterworth to remove someone else who knew McKenna's secret? Was he going to systematically kill everyone in the military or the order who did know about her?

"I think that the Marshalcy would benefit from my suggestion, an idea, of trying to use the deaf to penetrate the *strannik*'s glamour."

"Yes, but my officers do not know manual communication."

Mr. Foster brightened. "There is a school in Auvinen run by a very capable sorcerer, Mrs. Sarah Fuller Fiske. I myself have sponsored it."

"That's right. It is the school that also teaches its children to read lips and talk?"

"And one of the students," Mr. Foster said proudly, "has even begun to use magic."

Guiteau gave a pensive frown. "I'd not heard that. But I do know of Mrs. Fiske. I'll arrange a meeting with her."

Robinson fumbled in his pocket for his device and quickly released the inner ring. He withdrew it and held it up for the inspector general to see.

"An Aesir ring?" asked the other man.

"This is information that Master Drusselmehr was apprised of. And took to his grave. With this ring, I can speak directly to your thoughts. My partner, Mr. Wickins, also has one. At my home in Siaconset, I have a ring mold to make more. I only paused the work after my friend was injured. Then the fire and McKenna's likely abduction kept me from going back. I'm sure you can see the importance of these rings. They'll allow our military to communicate over vast distances without needing Signals Intelligences. That is how I communicated the Aesir threat to Master Drusselmehr in time for him to alert the military. I think this invention would also be advantageous to the Marshalcy."

The look on Guiteau's face was more than interested. It rekindled Robinson's own delight over the discovery. Before he'd met McKenna, his only driving interest had been to find new ways to be of service with magic. "By what principle does it operate?"

"The transmutation of thought," Robinson explained. "The Aesir have always been able to communicate with each other this way. The ring allows mortals to tap into the same tonal frequency that enables them to do so."

"May I see it?" he asked.

Robinson dropped it into his outstretched palm.

He looked at it, studying the design, and then paused when he saw the symbol of the Invisible College on the inner band. A peculiar look came over his face. Robinson couldn't decipher it.

"I've seen a ring like this before," said Guiteau.

"Really? Where?" That was surprising information. Robinson leaned forward.

"Miss Elizabeth Cowing showed me a ring like this," he said, handing it back. "She wanted to know if I had ever seen its like. I had not . . . until now."

CHAPTER EIGHT

Warning Voice

After the inspector general left, Robinson felt himself in a quandary. He wanted to help the war effort. He wanted to help protect people from the upcoming Aesir attacks. But the military had been less than cooperative with him so far. What about the Marshalcy? Was Guiteau trustworthy? Did he take his commitment to the Invisible College seriously? Rob had learned a high rank was not always an indicator of integrity. Or would the inspector general use whatever Robinson said against him? Against McKenna.

Mr. Foster had that twinkle in his eye again—the one that showed his mind was piecing together facts and how to present them in a case. He was a shrewd barrister, and Robinson was indebted to him for his business guidance thus far.

"So Miss Cowing has a ring too, hmmm?" his father-in-law said, his eyebrows lifting slightly.

Robinson wanted to reveal more information to the older man—especially about McKenna—but he knew he should consult with Mrs. Foster first. It had been her advice to keep her husband in the dark about McKenna being a Semblance.

"I found another ring in Covesea," Robinson said. "It stands to reason that there are more out there."

"Do you think she's figured out how to use it?"

Robinson grimaced. "I can't say. But I did notice she was near the house when Wickins and I arrived. I thought it a rather strange coincidence, but now I begin to wonder."

"If she was wearing her ring when you communicated you were coming here, she may have picked up the thought. Is that what you're suggesting?"

"It will take some experimentation to reveal that, but yes . . . it's possible that she heard my message if she was wearing the ring. I can't bear to wear it for very long because of the headaches it gives, but maybe hers doesn't affect her. I don't know."

Mr. Foster nodded sagely. "If she had the ring before you discovered the one embedded in your device, she may have overheard your first transmission. She may have learned about your invention unwittingly and believed the idea was her own."

Robinson hadn't even considered that. "If that happened, then the court case could come down to the timing of our patent applications."

His father-in-law shook his head. "The same argument could be applied both ways. That you derived your invention from *her* thought. I'd like to reach out to her barrister and see if I can learn about this ring she has. This is new information. I'll go to my office and see if I can arrange a meeting."

"That's a good approach. If we can resolve this matter out of court, it would be in all our best interests."

"I couldn't agree more. I believe you are the true inventor. You shared your idea for the quicksilver tube long before you invented it. I know the exact date in fact when we discussed it, as I keep a diary. I'm going to try to persuade Miss Cowing to resolve this amicably. They are still manufacturing her invention just as we are manufacturing yours. Whoever wins this case will have claim to them all."

"I hope you can persuade her, then. Thank you."

Mr. Foster nodded, then grabbed a hat and a walking cane and set off for his offices, leaving Robinson at the house alone with the servants. Mrs. Foster and Trudie had gone out shopping and hadn't returned yet, and Wickins and Clara were at the foundry offices of the glass tube manufacturer they used in Bishopsgate.

He was intensely curious about how Miss Cowing had come to possess the ring. Had it been handed down to her, the way the device had been handed down to him? How strange that both of them should have one.

After he'd spent about half an hour ruminating on the situation, the front door opened and Mrs. Foster and Trudie stepped inside carrying parcels. Robinson sprang to help and greet them. Trudie gave him a hug before setting down her packages, then walked to the kitchen with a forlorn air.

Mrs. Foster watched her go with a sigh and a look of parental concern. Then she glanced at Robinson, who was staring at her intently.

"Her sorrow and guilt are so deep," she said. "I don't know what I can do but listen. My own feelings are of lesser importance to me than hers. I just want her to be happy again."

Robinson nodded and tried to judge whether it was a good time to discuss the interview with the inspector general or whether he should wait.

"And I'm worried about you too," she said, pressing her palm to Robinson's cheek in a motherly manner. "This has been difficult for all of us. I wish the Marshalcy had been able to discover more. And now that Master Drusselmehr has been killed, they'll be too busy to look for McKenna, especially if they believe she's already dead."

"Can we speak confidentially?" he asked her. "I need your advice."

In the house on Brake Street, there were many places they could have had a private conversation, but the Bishopsgate house was much smaller. They went to Mr. Foster's study since he would be gone awhile, and Mrs. Foster shut the door and locked it.

"Hoxta-namorem," she sang, summoning a globe of light to illuminate the room. She sat down on the edge of her husband's chair, but Robinson was too restless to sit and just paced.

He quickly informed her of what they'd learned from the inspector general. They hadn't known he was coming or else she would have remained home to hear the news firsthand. She was already familiar with the rite of succession. She hadn't ascended to the position of Sublime Master yet, so she would not be considered to attend the convocation in her own right, but she could come with family members who were.

"So far I've managed to persuade the Marshalcy to keep looking for McKenna," Robinson continued, "based on the fact that she's been the *strannik*'s target ever since we were married. The inspector general believes she's dead, even though I don't. If Guiteau had reason to suspect she's alive, he would be more inclined to invest resources into finding her."

"You want to know whether you should tell him about what she is . . . and especially *who* may be sharing her body."

Robinson nodded mutely. He scratched his head, feeling at a loss.

"And that would also require telling my husband," she said, looking away.

"He's not the kind of man who likes being kept in the dark. As a barrister, he is bound to uphold the law. And we know from General Colsterworth that the laws don't exactly *apply* to Semblances."

She turned and looked at him, her jaw firm, her eyes blazing with resolution. "Which is exactly why we will tell them nothing. We'll keep looking for her ourselves. When is Mr. Swope due to arrive? He was going to bring evidence for the case, was he not?"

"Yes. I've summoned him, so he should be arriving imminently. Unless the weather was poor at Siaconset and the crossing was delayed. I've had no message from him, but I assume he's on his way. I'd like to go back to Auvinen and keep searching for McKenna myself."

"No," Mrs. Foster said. "You belong with the family. We need to let the experts in the Marshalcy do their jobs. If you can make more of those rings, it can further the search for the *strannik* and McKenna. The ability to communicate across great distances would be an advantage. That is what you can do to help."

"I asked Mr. Swope to bring the cuttlefish mold from Mowbray House." He sighed, feeling conflicted again. He wanted to be the one to find her. To find the *strannik*. Part of him needed it.

"We can't give up hope. McKenna knows we'd come here. If she can escape from this *strannik* fellow, she will."

Robinson blew out his breath and put his hands on his hips, preparing himself to give voice to one of his fears. "But what if she was persuaded to go with Gregor Skoye willingly? If she was persuaded that sacrificing her life would save tens of thousands. Millions even. She promised me she wouldn't make a decision like that without me, but . . ."

Mrs. Foster shook her head. "She wouldn't go against her word. She's being held against her will. I'm sure of it."

"That makes the most sense to me as well," Robinson agreed. "But I've been second-guessing myself."

"That's only natural, Robinson. No, we must think about what is most probable. Skoye set the fire to scare her into coming with him and hide evidence of their flight. His ability with glamour means they could have taken the locomotivus, but I have a feeling he would prefer a subtler route. He may be hiding her in Auvinen or on the outskirts of town. We'll ask Mr. Swope to start his search there." Robinson knew he'd been an officer in the Marshalcy earlier in his career. He didn't know why or when Aunt Margaret had hired him to be her bodyguard. Or manservant. Or whatever title he possessed.

"The Marshalcy already interviewed people across town, and so did I," Robinson said. "No one saw anything. I did mention to Guiteau about using deaf boys and girls to try and help. They may be immune to glamour, the way McKenna is, which could help us spot the *strannik*."

Mrs. Foster beamed. "I'm sure Sarah would help!"

"We already gave him her name. Thank you, Mrs. Foster. I feel slightly better now. We'll keep this a secret for now. Between us."

Mrs. Foster rose from the chair and embraced him. Then she took his hands. "McKenna changed me after I became a mother. I was very selfish and flighty when I was younger, but no longer. I will not let anyone harm her. I will protect her like a lioness."

"I will do anything to protect her," Robinson vowed. The longing for her made his heart swell again.

"You've been good for each other, Rob. Whatever happens, you're part of our family now."

The words were heartening, but nothing would fully comfort him until he found his wife—alive. Sleeping in her room with Wickins was a painful reminder of what had been.

He needed to find her. He needed to help her.

There was nothing else for it.

They concluded their interview and unlocked the door to the study. Mrs. Foster went to consult with the servants and Robinson began to pace yet again. Then he got the idea to join Wickins and Clara at the foundry offices. Anything to distract his mind from the intense dread he was feeling.

On his way out, he found Mr. Foster coming up the street, his expression stern and roiling. That didn't portend good news.

"I take it the meeting didn't go well?" Robinson asked.

Mr. Foster shook his head. "They refuse to meet with us. Her barrister insists you stole the invention from his client and claims he will prove it in court. He said if any of us try to contact her by any means, he will complain to the judge overseeing the case."

"What about the ring?" Robinson said, feeling a sharp edge of anger stab into his chest.

"I asked, and he said he didn't know anything about it. I don't think he was lying to me. At least I hope he wasn't. She may not have told him about it, feeling it had no relevance to the case."

"So he threatened us basically," Robinson said.

"More like an ultimatum. But it has the same effect. We will present our cases in court and see who believes the facts."

But Robinson knew it wouldn't just be a contest of facts. The jury would look at him and at Miss Cowing and decide based on how they *felt* about the facts.

McKenna Aurora
Hawksley

CHAPTER NINE

Follow the Mountains

McKenna peeked around the tree, her palm sticking in some sap where she leaned against the trunk, and gazed at the bobbing lights heading away from her. Her heart was still racing, as was her breathing, although she tried to muffle it. The orbs of light had been summoned by the two men searching the woods for her.

After their initial rush to get away from the area outside Auvinen, they had switched to traveling during the day and bedding down beneath the wagon at night off the main road. She'd made her run for it on the second night they had stopped to rest.

The impulse to flee had risen as they'd gotten closer to the mountain range. At first, the looming peaks had seemed far away in the north. But steady progress in the wagon had brought them closer and closer to the gray mountains with white peaks. The range looked familiar to her, although she couldn't remember traveling that way before. They'd passed no settlements and only the occasional farm, but even those were at a distance. There wasn't much to run to, but she knew, deep in her core, that if they went into those mountains, she would be lost to her family forever.

So she'd pretended she needed to relieve herself behind a tree and had instead fled into the darkness. They had pursued her almost immediately, but the darkness had given her the advantage she'd hoped for and neither man had proven capable of tracking her. Which was odd, since the *strannik* had located her so easily before. After both had summoned magical lights, allowing her to keep track of them, she'd circled back to the camp to steal some food and grab a blanket before fleeing in another direction.

She imagined they were staying within earshot of each other, judging by the nearness of the floating orbs. The zigzagging of the lights showed they were randomly searching for her instead of using a pattern.

McKenna's plan was rudimentary. An appropriate word considering the circumstances. The nearest mountain range she knew of was north of Auvinen and separated that area from the Lake Country and Tanhauser. If she followed the mountain range to the east, she would eventually run into Bishopsgate. There was a city called Torin along the way, and she imagined she was east of it. That meant she could reach Bishopsgate, if she walked hard, in three or four days on foot. It was possible she'd find a farm along the way and could seek help there.

She was worried about the glamour that the *strannik* had disguised her with, but it occurred to her that it might help her situation rather than harm it. People would take more pity on her if they thought she was a young girl. She had enough food for two days and hopefully, with mountains nearby, she'd find some streams in which to get something to drink. Rob had told her that glamour spells were very powerful and only the highest-ranking sorcerers were allowed knowledge of them. Would the glamour wear off after time? She had no idea.

Within the hour, the light from her pursuers had disappeared, so she felt safe walking again. She wouldn't know if she was going east until the sun came up, so it was possible she'd lose her way in the night, but it was important to get as far away from her abductors as possible. She walked until her legs ached, and once the moon rose, she was able to see well enough to avoid the trees. Sometime after midnight, she left the little wilderness of trees and found herself in grassland. That enabled her to pick up the pace. She found a little creek shortly afterward and was able to scrub the sticky sap from her hands before cupping water and drinking it. It was cool and refreshing.

McKenna kept going, wishing she knew more about navigating by the stars. She'd read about it in books, but she didn't know the constellations well enough to get her bearings. After walking for miles and miles, she decided to rest and wait for the coming sunrise to reveal her path. So she huddled in the blanket in the tall meadow grass and dozed. It was cold enough that dozing was all she managed to do.

Eventually, after an interminable wait, the eastern sky began to change color. That was her course. She took a hasty meal from the provisions she'd stolen and then started her march again, using the skyline as her compass and the blanket as a shawl.

Dawn made the splendor of the mountain range visible. It also revealed the woods in the distance behind her, but there was no sign of her pursuers. No cattle grazed the land. She did see an elk herd in the distance and watched it awhile as she walked. Midmorning, she came upon a flowing brook that blocked her way forward but provided a much-needed drink. It was a tributary from the mountains, too small to have been on any map.

She scouted the bank, looking for a place to cross, and then picked her spot where some eddies had slowed the speed of the water. A few tentative steps revealed the water was about to her knees, so she felt safe maneuvering across it, being careful not to stumble and plunge in. Even though she preferred the cold, she imagined it would be dangerous to be soaked to the skin.

A thought wafted through her mind. The idea that if she submerged herself in the river, it would wash away the *strannik*'s enchantment.

McKenna stepped carefully on the stones, the water getting deeper as she approached midstream. Soon it was about to her waist. She felt her jaw quivering with cold, although it didn't feel unpleasant.

The thought came to her again—the idea to immerse herself in the water, letting it cover her head to toe.

Are you trying to talk to me? she thought inside, wondering if the entity trapped in her body could even hear her thoughts.

Just as before, she felt a sickening feeling that communicating with the Erlking's daughter, or whichever entity inhabited her, would be dangerous and harmful. She felt a shiver of fear and decided against further inquiry.

At midstream, the water had reached her navel and soaked through the peasant's dress, causing it to cling to her. In hindsight, she should have removed the dress and carried it under her arm so she'd have something dry to wear on the other side. She frowned at her lapse of perspicacity. She did manage to keep her blanket out of the water as she continued. After a step that brought her plunging down in the middle of the stream, she let out a gasp, for the water level had reached her breasts, but then she was past that part and able to get into shallower waters again.

As she was reaching the far side, she'd mulled the idea of submersion thoroughly and made her decision. She was already mostly soaked, so finishing the job wouldn't cause much additional harm. After stepping from the river with her waterlogged shoes, she set her blanket down on the dry bank. Then she stripped off the dress and wrung it out as hard as she could. In her clinging chemise, she went back into the river and reached the middle point easily. She held her breath and dunked herself. The cold wasn't as shocking this second time, and she quickly stood and wiped her face and eyes. She hadn't bathed in days, so it actually felt pleasant and not too chilly. Glancing around to make sure she was still alone, she saw nothing but a doe and two younglings farther upstream. She didn't know if the dunking had worked, and the deer couldn't tell her, but she hoped it had.

Then she wrapped herself in the blanket and hung the damp dress over it so it could air dry and catch the rays of the sun. Like she was a walking clothesline. It made her laugh. She turned back after walking a ways and still didn't see any sign of her pursuers. She could see for miles, so she felt safe.

She paused to eat again at midday and had to negotiate with her hunger pangs in order to save the rest of her provisions. She scolded her stomach for being voracious and disciplined herself. Always, she kept looking back the way she'd come.

When night came, she put her dress back on, which had dried, and huddled in the blanket again to bed down in the meadow grass. The smells of the wilderness were eerily familiar, even though she'd never spent a night out-of-doors until her abduction. She found herself fast asleep after the long walk and slept soundly until morning.

Cautiously, she lifted her head and gazed in the distance and was relieved to see no one. She had no idea what the *strannik* was doing at this time, how frantic he was, but so far he'd been unable to follow her in his usual way. Perhaps there were fewer intelligences to capture and command in the wilderness.

McKenna took a few nibbles from her dwindling stores and then started marching again. There was a tiny stream to cross, which she chose to do barefoot, and then she tugged on her shoes again and kept going. She'd encountered not a single farm along the way so far, and she began to wonder whether she'd done something incredibly foolish. But those worries were tempered when she saw, in the distance, a parallel set of metal rails heading from southwest to northeast. As soon as she saw the mounds of earth they cut through, she realized with a thrill that she'd found the locomotivus rails heading to Bishopsgate. Following the rails would bring her directly to her destination.

The rails looked miles away, but the discovery had settled her worries and dread. Then, to her astonishment, she saw a northbound locomotivus approaching from the distance. If she reached the rails in time, she could perhaps use her blanket to flag the conductor! McKenna began to run through the grass, trying to close the distance that separated her from the tracks. Running was alien to her, but she kept at it, huffing for breath, trying to get there in time.

But the locomotivus covered vast spans of ground in moments. She wasn't going to make it. McKenna unslung her blanket and waved it over her head, hoping one of the passengers might see her and tell the conductor. She panted, thirst ravaging her, as she waved the makeshift banner.

But the locomotivus rushed on past her. She stopped running, dropping her hands to her knees as she gulped for breath. Her throat was sore, and her joints felt loose. It *was* the northbound locomotivus. She was certain of it.

She scooped up the blanket again and continued toward the tracks, her back straightening as purpose pulsed through her. The locomotivus would be back, headed to Auvinen in the next few hours. It was a minor setback, that was all.

After some time, a preternatural feeling that she was being watched tickled her spine. She looked around, trying to see if anyone was there. But no . . . she was still alone. Panting, McKenna continued to follow the tracks toward Bishopsgate. She would not make it there by nightfall, which would mean another night in the meadow. The breeze cooled down her heat as she trudged forward.

She gazed back once more, wondering if that feeling from earlier was a warning of sorts. No matter. She would forge ahead. After turning around, something peculiar caught her attention. Something else was coming down the tracks. The locomotivus was gone . . . and yet, whatever she was seeing was also mechanized. She squinted, trying to make sense of what she was seeing.

It was heading from north to south. Which was strange because only one locomotivus could use the tracks at a time. Especially if the two were going in opposite directions. Then, with growing anticipation, she realized it was the last compartment of the locomotivus. It must have detached from the longer piece. Two men were standing at the back rail, gazing at her. She waved her arm, feeling an impulsive surge of relief, and started to jog forward.

Someone had seen her! Someone on the locomotivus must have said they'd seen her, and they'd detached the back compartment and sent it back on the rails to investigate. She started to laugh with relief.

Two men.

Her chest lurched with dread. What if it was the *strannik* and his minion? Had they somehow managed to get ahead of her? Surely not.

Doubts swarmed her mind, but if it was them, she was too winded to run away.

The locomotivus compartment drew nearer and nearer. She gazed at the men. One wore a uniform from the line. The other man was in a suit. Relief twined through her. She was impervious to glamour spells, so she knew neither wore a disguise.

The man in the suit waved at her. She waved back, squinting more to get a better look. It wasn't the *strannik* or his companion, but he did look familiar. As the compartment drew close, she gaped in shock and recognition.

"Mr. . . . Mr. Swope!" she exclaimed, recognizing her aunt's manservant, who was in charge of Mowbray House.

The locomotivus stopped, and he jumped off and ran to her, his eyes wide with wonder. She raced into his arms and began to sob with relief.

Robinson Foster Hawksley

CHAPTER TEN

The Hinge Moment

It was the night before Closure, and the Foster family was gathered around the little table in the dining room at the Bishopsgate house. The meal was delicious, as Mrs. Foster always had a flair for such things, but the mood was somber, so it was silent but for the clink of silverware and the occasional murmur of voices.

Mr. Foster had revealed that the fire in Auvinen had damaged other properties, and at least one of the owners was seeking restitution and threatening legal action. Clara and Wickins were sitting by each other, but they were likely at odds because neither had said a word to the other. Trudie hadn't eaten much and was just sitting in her chair, looking occasionally from face to face and seeming very distressed. The overall tension in the room made Robinson's shoulders ache, and his own disquiet made him a surly companion.

"Whatever the Gilderbrandts decide, we will face it," Mrs. Foster said to her husband, reaching across the table and taking his hand. The family was in a difficult financial position, from the fire to the lawsuit against the military and the patent dispute with Miss Cowing.

Mrs. Fiske's school needed money as well—money that was not in abundance.

"The clean-up of the burned-out house is costing more than we anticipated as well," Mr. Foster replied with a heavy sigh. "I may have to secure a loan from a bank while all this sorts out."

Mrs. Foster nodded in agreement. The two maintained holding hands across the table.

"Surely not," Robinson said, shaking his head. "I don't think McKenna would hesitate to offer help. I'm not the legal owner of her property, at present, but surely we can make things work."

Mrs. Foster gave him an appreciative smile. "Thank you for offering, Rob. There are so many things we still don't know. I didn't want to presume."

"It actually may not be possible, though," Mr. Foster said bleakly. "There was an entailment clause in McKenna's inheritance that forbids just such a situation as this. It could take months to sort it out."

That was new information, and it made Robinson feel glum and irritable. An entailment clause? The kind that prevented disreputable men from stealing an heiress's fortune. But his heart softened when he saw Trudie looking at him, and he gave her a smile.

And it was in that moment, when their eyes were locked together, that a jolt of energy shot through him, his senses responding to the doglike intelligence, which had been absent since the fire. It couldn't bark, but it had all the exuberance of doing so—bringing an urgent, excited mood into the solemn dining room. It couldn't communicate in words so much as impressions, but he felt its silent urging for him to come out to the street at once.

Incapable of speaking after such a surprise, he jumped from his chair and bolted for the door.

His sudden departure caused a commotion of activity—chairs squealing against the hardwood floor, exclamations of confusion and dismay, and an avalanche of footfalls chasing after him. He was the first to the front door, startling one of the servants who'd been polishing furniture in the front room. Grabbing the handle, he twisted it and raced outside into the dusk. His invisible friend's excitement was palpable. He glanced around, eager, hoping but not wanting to hope too hard in case his hopes were in vain. There were people walking toward him in the gloom. At first he could only make out the uniforms worn by two officers of the Marshalcy and the peasant's dress of one of the people who accompanied them. But an aching sense of familiarity filled him, and he hurried forward until he was close enough to see their faces. *Her* face.

He took two long strides and stopped, his heart unable to conceive the truth of his eyes. Surely, this was a dream he'd wake up from. But the smells of the city, the hard pavement beneath his shoes all bore witness to reality. That was McKenna's thick glossy hair, gathered in a coil on one side. McKenna's shining eyes. She was alive. His wife was alive!

As soon as he recognized her in the flesh, as soon as he allowed his heart to believe it wasn't a phantasm, he cried out in relief and ran to her. She broke from her companion—Mr. Swope, he realized—and flung herself into his arms as soon as he was close enough, giddy with laughter and tears as they embraced. He lifted her off her feet and spun her around, amazed and confused and relieved. He set her down, taking her face in his hands, watching as the rest of the family came rushing up.

Robinson turned and gaped at Mr. Swope. "How on earth did you . . . ?" He was at a loss for words.

Mr. Swope must have realized that it wasn't the right moment for explanation as the family came crashing together, reunited at last. But it was the relieved groans from Trudie that wrung Rob's heart most as she fell at her sister's feet, hugging her legs, and panted over and over, "You're alive! You're alive!"

Mrs. Foster and Clara were suddenly embracing McKenna too. Mr. Foster was wiping tears from his eyes, unable to maintain his usual taciturn reactions. McKenna disentangled from her mother and middle sister and then knelt down, cupping Trudie's face in her hands. Trudie was sobbing uncontrollably, but McKenna kissed her again and again.

"I'm all right, Trudie. I'm all right. It's not your fault. None of it was your fault!"

Trudie squeezed her eyes shut and just hugged her sister. Tears were stinging Robinson's eyes at the scene. There was so much to say, so much to explain, but at the moment, he just wanted to enjoy the outpouring of feeling.

McKenna, likely confused by all the words coming at her, everyone talking at once, rose and then hugged each of them—Wickins included—before burying her face in her mother's bosom. Robinson had never felt such stirrings before. His heart was filled to the brim. No, it was overflowing with joy.

"How did you find her, Mr. Swope?" Mr. Foster asked in disbelief. "This is truly a miracle."

Robinson sensed the giddiness of the dog intelligence. And he realized the truth before Mr. Swope could offer an explanation.

"I was going to take the ferry to Rexanne and then the locomotivus to Bishopsgate, but I felt an unusual urge to stop by Auvinen first. I can't explain the feelings I had. I went by the Brake Street house and saw the destruction. I have friends in the Marshalcy still and asked for details. Then I took the northbound locomotivus to Bishopsgate. While I was riding on it, I was sitting by a window seat, and it felt like something was nudging me to look out the window. We were in the middle of nowhere. But I saw a young woman in the fields waving a blanket. It looked so much like Miss McKenna."

"It was me," McKenna said, joining the conversation, her voice thick with tears. "I'd escaped and had been walking for so long. But the locomotivus just kept going. I thought I'd be walking all night."

Mr. Swope smiled tenderly at her. "I went to the conductor and told him I'd seen someone flagging us down. Someone who looked like they needed help. He wasn't going to stop the entire locomotivus, but he did grant permission to release the last cart. Since I'd witnessed it, I went with him and we retraced our journey back to where I'd seen her. And there she was, looking like a farmer's daughter."

McKenna squeezed Robinson's waist and leaned her head against his arm. He wrapped his around her shoulder. The dog intelligence had never abandoned them. It had followed McKenna throughout her ordeal. She couldn't sense it, so she hadn't known. But Robinson felt its satisfaction for having arranged the rescue. His heart nearly burst with gratitude.

Well done, he thought to the intelligence. *You brought her home. Thank you! A thousand times, thank you!*

The solemn dinner of earlier had transformed into a much more festive mood with McKenna returned. After they made it back inside, still bewildered by the change in circumstances, the inspector general arrived, having been summoned by his officers at the locomotivus station. McKenna, still wearing the dress she'd been found in, related to the entire family and the Marshalcy officers everything she could about her abduction, where she'd been taken and concealed, and how she'd escaped. Her information also gave them insight into the *strannik*'s whereabouts and his intended destination. It was also abundantly clear from her testimony that the *strannik* was likely responsible for the murders of both General Colsterworth and Master Drusselmehr.

"We have highly trained bloodhounds we use when hunting for fugitives," Guiteau told the family. "Professor Hawksley, if I can get word to my men in the city of Torin, they can begin the hunt immediately. We know we're looking for two men and a wagon. We must assume they're somewhere east of Torin at present. I can have dozens of men sent out from Torin and dispatch others from Bishopsgate. What would be incredibly helpful is if we could borrow one of your rings so that I may communicate with my officers directly instead of trying to have a message delivered by morning."

"You can use mine," Wickins volunteered immediately, reaching into his pocket and producing the ring. "My training is in Signals Intelligences with the military. I can be of help to you."

Guiteau nodded encouragingly. "Helpful indeed. It may be prudent to let General Ambrose know about this." He glanced at Mr. Foster. "He has more men at his command than I do, and they are better trained for this sort of thing. If Skoye hides in the mountains, it will take a lot of people to locate him, and winter is coming." He shifted his gaze back to Robinson as he completed his statement, inviting a response from both men.

Mr. Foster pondered the situation carefully before speaking. "He clearly has loyalty among his followers. That run-down mansion, for example, that McKenna told us about. There will be others like that. I don't know General Ambrose, so I cannot judge how he would handle this."

"I know him personally," Guiteau said. "He's a fine officer, but they're all political. One must be in that profession, I suppose. There is a lot of ground to cover. What do you think, Professor?"

"With his ability to use glamour, he will be very difficult to apprehend," Robinson said. "Let's use every resource we can."

Guiteau nodded sagely. "Very well. Mr. Wickins, if you can educate me on using the ring, I can begin sending orders. The hunt begins."

"The *strannik* is afraid of dogs," Robinson said. "We've seen evidence of that in the past."

"We'll use that knowledge to our advantage." He turned to McKenna next. "I understand that although you are deaf, you are adept at reading lips. Out of all of us, you probably understand our fugitive the best. Is there any reason he gave for abducting you that you have not told us about? Anything that can help in our search? This man must be brought to justice."

Robinson felt a throb of uneasiness at the question, knowing, as he did, that the answer was yes.

McKenna didn't look to him or her mother for reassurance. "I've told you all that I can," she said simply. "He's quite deranged."

"Well, on behalf of the Marshalcy, I must commend you for escaping your captors. You are wise beyond your years. Another young woman, raised in the city, would have been truly helpless in that situation. With your assistance, we hope to catch this man before he can do more damage."

"I hope you do," McKenna said. "I'm very tired. I think I should like a bath before going to bed."

"Of course. I have officers on guard. But you have very capable sorcerers here inside with you. Mr. Wickins, if I might have you come with me to make sure we get the message sent efficiently? Your expertise in this would be appreciated."

"Of course."

"I'll come with you too," Clara said.

Wickins grinned, and the trouble between them seemed to have blown over like clouds.

Robinson felt McKenna's hand snake into his, their fingers intertwining. When he looked over at her, she leaned forward and kissed the corner of his jaw. Then she whispered an invitation to be with her.

Trouble seemed to shadow their steps wherever they went. During their honeymoon in Covesea, she'd helped bathe him after he'd been attacked with the shovel and left to die in a dug grave.

He was more than happy to return the favor. In fact, he felt it would be a struggle to wait another moment without some privacy.

CHAPTER ELEVEN

The Forgotten Past

The smell of soap mingled with the polish one of the servants had used to clean the floorboards of McKenna's room. Robinson shut the door, muffling the noise from downstairs. His wife was toweling her hair over by the window, which was open, letting in a breeze that was a little too cold for him, but which she seemed to enjoy.

After she finished, she set the towel down and turned in the chair to face him. "When he abducted me, I was wearing your favorite nightgown," she said with an apologetic smile. "It's gone now."

"That's easily replaceable." He left the door, approached her, and played with some of the wet strands of her hair. Then he started kissing her again. He couldn't get enough of the sight, sound, and smell of her. Relief made his kissing even more urgent. The play of her lips against his, the little dash of her tongue. It stirred up excited feelings until something she'd said broke through, and he pulled back.

"They took your nightgown?"

"And gave me that peasant's dress to wear after we arrived at that strange run-down mansion. I'd snuck away some food while preparing to escape, but I didn't get the chance before the *strannik* came back. We left immediately, and I had to leave the nightgown behind. It's probably still sitting under the bed where I left it."

That made more sense and alleviated his surge of worry that something untoward had happened to her. He knelt by her chair and lowered his head onto her lap. Her fingers began to stroke through his hair. Closing his eyes, he just enjoyed the moment of silence and being with her.

Then he lifted his head and looked into her eyes. "Your mother and I still haven't told your father or anyone else about why the *strannik* wants you. I know the inspector general must be wondering."

She shook her head. "I can't talk about it, Rob. Even now, it makes me . . . queasy." She rubbed knuckles into her belly. But this had always been so. Something within her restrained her from speaking on the subject. Or, perhaps, some*one* within her.

He wrapped his arms around her and held her close. The smell of her soap was delicious. He wished they were far away from Bishopsgate.

"We should go back home to Mowbray House," she said, tousling his unkempt hair.

He looked up again so she could read his lips. Sometimes he forgot she couldn't hear. Everything they did to communicate had become so natural to him that it was almost spontaneous.

"I want to go too, but there's the court case and the upcoming convocation. All sorcerers at my level and above will be invited to it."

"Where will it be held?"

"We don't know yet."

"And if they won't let me come?" she asked, her expression betraying not only worry but resentment.

"Then *I* won't go," he answered.

She gazed at him seriously. "The *strannik* wants to destroy the Invisible College. There is some bargain he's made with the Erlking. He's been told he'll be given a new world. He wants to return society to a simpler time, of farming and cows and pigs and no more sorcery."

"He'd like to undo the progress we've made in the last few centuries. I don't think anyone wants to go back to those days."

"Some do," McKenna said. "He's also told me that you're lying to me. That you aren't who you claim to be. He talks a lot of nonsense." She cupped his face. "We're meant to be together, Rob. Whatever happens. But I don't think the future he's racing toward would be a good one. We wouldn't be free."

Robinson rose, took her hand, and brought her to their bed. Trudie was staying in Clara's room next door. Wickins had agreed to stay at a nearby hotel.

"I don't think the Erlking's daughter wants that either," Robinson said, still holding her hand. "She's trying to prevent it."

McKenna shuddered, but not with cold. She looked away, her expression showing the usual discomfort. As much as he'd researched this in Auvinen, he felt he still needed more information about the Erlking's daughter. The best source would be McKenna herself, but he likely wouldn't be able to get such information from her. Where else, though? He'd done the best he could with what resources he had available, including Wickins, who was knowledgeable about the Aesir language, but everything of importance had happened so many years earlier. It had been centuries since Isaac Berrow had established the Invisible College. The banishment of the Erlking's daughter had happened centuries before that. It might have even been thousands of years. Clues were all that remained, mostly found in the spoken legends of the people of Iskandir, an island perpetually sheathed in ice. The famous opera about the Erlking's daughter was probably a mere pantomime of what had actually happened. The famous tale of the Aesir woman falling in love with a human warrior who was magicked into forgetting her was a tragedy that had taken new shape over countless years.

He reached his finger and nudged her chin to face him. "We don't have to talk about it."

"I can't describe it, Rob. The feeling is so visceral. That something bad will happen if I commune with . . . her. I can see the wisdom in trying to. It makes logical sense. But my heart knows something my head does not."

He nodded in sympathy. "There must be another way. When we were honeymooning, I wanted to try in order to find a way to separate you both. Now, the stakes are even higher. The winter storms are coming and, with them, the stormbreaker ships. If we had more of these rings, we could communicate over vast distances. Since Mr. Swope brought the mold, we'll be able to start producing them."

"And what of the lawsuit? You clearly invented the tubes first, Rob. I don't know how Miss Cowing can claim she did."

"Ah, there's something I didn't tell you about that. When I showed my ring to Mr. Guiteau, he said he'd seen one just like it. One possessed by Miss Cowing. Your father tried to contact her, but we've been forbidden to by her barrister. She may believe she invented the tube, but it's possible she overheard my thoughts about it while I was wearing the ring."

"I don't like her very much," McKenna said with a hostile look.

"There is so much money at stake. I'm not surprised her barrister counseled her to resist. If we win the patent, then the military will owe us treble the damages. They've since licensed the invention from her, so there is no such punitive measure if she wins it. It's not about the money, although I'm afraid your parents are going through hard times. One of your neighbors has threatened to sue them because of the fire."

"But that wasn't their fault." She frowned with offense.

"Still. The hardships have become pressing."

McKenna firmed her lips. "I'll talk to Father in the morning. I'm wealthy in my own right. We both are. We can help shore things up until this court date happens. How far away is it?"

"It was postponed for a few weeks. I agree with you. Let's use some of your inheritance to help your family and Sarah's school. In fact, I was so certain you'd feel the same way, I offered to help earlier this evening, just before you came home."

She clasped their hands together. "I would like that."

"I think the students at the school could be of great help right now," he said and then explained his theory that she might be immune to the *strannik*'s glamour because she was deaf. How Robinson had counseled the inspector general to ask for the older students' help in seeing past the man's illusions.

"My intelligent husband," she said, before leaning forward and kissing him on the nose. Then she leaned against him, resting her head against the crook of his neck. He wrapped his arm around her and clung to her fingers with his other hand.

"We'll get through this somehow," she said after a prolonged silence. She looked up into his face.

He kissed her damp hair just above her forehead. "We will. I was a wreck when I lost you. Maybe it was just stubborn pride, but I didn't believe you were dead. I couldn't."

"No, you just knew that the *strannik* wasn't going to give up. He's going to come for me again, Rob. There can be no doubt about it. I just hope the Marshalcy finds him first."

"I think Mr. Swope should be enlisted to help protect you. I used the ring to summon him, but I had no notion he'd find you on the way to Bishopsgate. The Unseen Powers are truly amazing. It was not a coincidence."

"You yourself told me that our little dog friend helped make it happen. That he followed me and was by my side the whole time. I believe it, even though I couldn't sense his presence. We should give him a name."

"Do intelligences have names?"

She shrugged and offered a playful smile. "It doesn't have to be a mortal name. How about . . . Loyal?"

Robinson could sense the intelligence in the room with them, hunkered down in the corner. Dogs liked to sleep, but intelligences didn't require rest. It seemed to respond immediately to her thoughts.

Would you like a name? Robinson asked in his mind.

He could sense a tail wag.

"Loyal it is," Robinson said. "I can't think of a better one."

There was a quiet knock on the door.

"Someone knocked," he said to McKenna, and then he rose and answered it. Trudie was standing at the door in her nightdress. She craned her neck to look at her sister sitting on the bed.

"I just wanted to tell her good night."

Robinson stepped out of the way, and Trudie rushed in and hugged McKenna tightly for a long time. There was a scuff on the floorboards, and he turned to see Clara. She had a shawl over her own nightgown, and her hair was braided back. Leaning against the doorjamb, she called gently, "They want more time alone, Trudie." Then she gave Robinson a rather knowing look and a devious smile.

Robinson wondered how much had been heard from the bathroom downstairs and felt his cheeks begin to burn.

Trudie kissed McKenna's cheek. "I'm so glad you're home," she said, squeezing her sister's hands.

"I'm sorry for what you went through," McKenna said. "I was worried about you too."

Trudie hugged her once more, and then she and Clara retired to the other room. Clara gave Robinson another knowing look and grin before he shut the door. And locked it.

There was a haunted look on his wife's face. He approached her, lowering down on one knee by the bed.

"Are you all right?" he asked tenderly.

She swiped a tear from her eye. It took a few moments of slow breathing to compose herself. "I just had this feeling. It'll pass."

"What kind of feeling?"

She bit her bottom lip. "How much it's going to hurt her. Trudie especially. It will hurt all of them." She gazed into his eyes. "When I'm gone."

A feeling of foreboding smote him in the chest, causing a strangely familiar ache. "Don't say that. I won't lose you again. We're going to grow old together."

McKenna looked anguished. "I know this sounds strange, but it feels like this has happened to me before. The pain of losing my family. Of losing *you*." She closed her eyes and began to shudder. "Hold me, Rob. I feel like I'm slipping away right now. Hold me. Don't let me go."

They lay down on the small mattress, huddled close together, his arms wrapped around her. She began to cry softly, and the sound broke his heart. Then she started kissing him, kisses of sorrow and desperation, and he tasted the salt of her tears.

Of all the words in Cawdrey's book of words, I think the most important may be "remember." Scholars of the Invisible College are required to recall certain facts, arithmetical equations, poems, and lines from famous speeches. Not only for the betterment of the individual, but to sharpen the dull sense of memory. What we do not repeat in our minds is no longer important to us and will fade. A wise farmer will record efforts prior to harvest as well as the results thereof in order to improve the yield. Should not sorcerers, the farmers of the Mind, do the same?

The most important things to remember are the promises we have made. When one commits to repay a fellow for loaning him cuppers, why should the lender be left with the inconvenience of providing to ensure the requirements are enforced? The proof is often buried within the conscience, which reminds us relentlessly what is owed and what is due. Until we smother it with excuses, choke it with self-deception, or squander it with broken pledges. If I, as a young student at a prestigious university, could feel so wronged when a fellow reneged on his pledge, how much more severe would it be if a matter of infinitely more weight and consequence were forgotten. "Our greatest need," writes Professor Kimball, "is to remember."

—Isaac Berrow, Master of the Royal Secret,
the Invisible College

Isaac Berrow

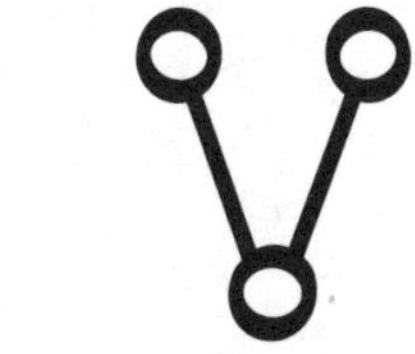

CHAPTER TWELVE

That Which was Lost

Fifteen years before the founding of the Invisible College

The faint rays of dawn were beginning to creep in through the edges of the closed curtains. Isaac was exhausted physically, but his mind was still reeling from all he'd learned during his prolonged interview with the Semblance who was the Erlking's daughter. What he'd learned had kindled excitement and interest within him that went far beyond anything he'd learned in his formal education.

"Would you allow me to repeat back a summary of what you've told me?" he asked her while she sipped from a mug of tea and honey he'd made for her. The tea had helped subdue her cough, which kept sucking away her energy until he'd feared she'd die in front of him. He'd kept the teapot on the small stove in the corner of the room so he could continually warm her drink. The two bedrooms in the tiny lodging were adjacent to each other, but neither had a door. They opened up to the shared living space, which contained a few chests, a single bureau, and the equipment for Isaac's alchemy crowded near the chimney and flue. The only chairs in the lodging were the two uncomfortable wooden ones at the little rectangular table by the front window. Offering her the use of his bed had been the only decent thing to do.

"You don't believe my words?" she asked after setting the mug on the floor next to his bed.

"I just want to make sure I have the facts ordered properly in my mind."

"I was jesting, Isaac. I know that was your intent."

"Oh." He struggled at times to understand humor or sarcasm. "Very well. I shall try to be succinct since there is so much I wish to learn from you still."

She gave him a wan smile. At least, that's how he interpreted it. He was still amazed that this poor shabby creature who'd been dying of illness and starving was actually one of the most powerful beings in the universe. He was incredibly humbled to be in her presence, let alone to be the recipient of her tutelage.

Isaac swallowed and tried to organize the story in his mind. "The Aesir's world was dying. This one provided a suitable habitat, but its climate was different when your people first came. This place we're in now was all under a great volume of snow and ice. Glaciers, as you called them. But those glaciers began to recede?"

"Yes. It happens very slowly. Imperceptibly to mortal eyes. Over your lifespan, you may notice it. But for us, the change is quite dramatic."

"Admittedly so. Therefore, as the glaciers retreated north, the land in this area became inhabitable by mortal tribes, who came from warmer climates closer to the planet's equator. These tribes fought each other for territory and resources until the Aesir began to teach them patterns of civilization. One might call those early interactions . . . benevolent?"

"The patterns we taught created longer life spans, greater health, more stability. So yes, I think that word is fitting."

Isaac nodded with interest. "These interactions were primarily led by your mother, the Erlqueen, who personified the Aesir virtue of mercy. Mortals ceased to be nomadic and began to found cities of great renown based on the patterns of the Aesir. But these "conglomerations," for lack of a better word, inspired feelings of resentment, ambition, and lust."

"Coveting."

"Yes, and that was when the high king, who'd usurped power from the other kingdoms, betrayed and murdered your mother with a silver-tipped arrow. That is what started the war between mortals and Aesir. Have I left anything pertinent out?"

"No, Isaac. You have remembered well so far."

"Thank you. The war lasted for centuries, broken intermittently by the Aesir resting state called the Skrýmir. But at each Awakening, it would commence again."

"Yes. Both sides were determined to subjugate the other."

Isaac began to feel giddy. "Yes, until a nobleman from Auvinen came looking for his brother. The brother had survived a costly battle and had been chosen by the Aesir to serve in the Erlking's realm. Only the most perfect of mortals were given this opportunity."

"It is still considered a great honor," she said.

"Yes, but the younger brother did not realize this and believed his brother had been carried away, captive. Fraternal love prompted him to hazard his life to seek his brother's return. And you met this devoted brother and fell in love with him. Even though it was forbidden by custom and quite prohibited."

"I wanted to experience a mortal life," she said. "To understand the creatures who had betrayed and murdered my mother. I saw the good in you. There was much to be admired."

Isaac nodded eagerly.

She continued. "My father was opposed to the match, believing mortals incapable of constancy to anything or anyone. A truce was made and terms were set. The young nobleman fulfilled his end of the bargain, and it created a period of peace between mortals and Aesir. We were permitted to marry, but I could only do so as a Semblance. Otherwise, I could not have survived the climate outside of winter. One season per year I would return to the Aesir to share what I'd learned, so long as the mortals upheld their end of the truce. Every facet of the agreement had to be met precisely."

"And what were those terms? You were vague on that point."

She shook her head. "What's important is the terms were originally broken with the murder of my mother. My marriage was intended to heal that breach. To make another attempt at peace between our races. Because by then it was clear mortals would never remember their side of the covenants."

"Because they were not written down?"

"No, they were written down, Isaac. How long does paper last? Then they were written in stone. But the wind and rain destroyed it. They were written in metal. That lasted even longer, but still it was not enough. They needed to be written in a metal that was impervious to entropy."

"Aesir gold," Isaac said. "A specific alloy of gold, platinum, palladium, and cobalt."

"But the more we taught you, the more knowledge your kind coveted. And the knowledge we'd already shared was turned against us. You discovered new ways to kill our kind."

"Which I apologize for, Your Highness," Isaac said meekly. "None of what you've told me has survived to this era. Only the enmity between our peoples has endured. If we honored our end, would the Aesir be forced to honor theirs? Is that correct?"

"Yes, because the Aesir . . . *ahem* . . . prize justice above all." Her voice gave out at that point, and the cough began to rattle and shake her. Isaac hurriedly fetched another rag to replace the bloodied one from earlier. He pitied her for the weakened state she was in. He'd learned that part of her self-exile from the Aesir courts was that she was doomed to repeat mortal life after mortal life, her intelligence being transferred from one recently dead victim to another. Sometimes she was reborn as an infant. Sometimes a crone. Her latest incarnation, a desperate prostitute from the slums of Nirshoye, hadn't been her choice either.

Her father selected the mortal vessels she was transferred to. And she only was able to recover her memories, the memories of the Erlking's daughter, when the body she was in was near death and the magic binding her to the mortal body began to fail. Each time she tried to coax mortals into remembering the forgotten covenant, but nothing she'd done had endured.

When the hacking cough finally subsided, he steadied her shoulder with one hand and lifted the mug of lukewarm tea with the other, coaxing her to drink. She was so weak, she could hardly do more than swallow.

"Thank you," she whispered hoarsely. "For your kindness."

"Are you hungry again? I could go to the market when it opens and get some fresh food."

Before she could reply, the door flew open and a burly man barreled inside, bringing in a whorl of snowflakes. The sudden intrusion sent a jolt of fear through Isaac's chest as the man stomped in, slamming the door behind him. The door he'd absolutely forgotten to lock.

He *never* forgot to lock the door . . .

"You've 'ad her all night, lad, and you'll pay plenty of cuppers for it!"

Isaac blinked, confused, then realized this was the man he'd seen with her in the alley. The man who'd been so cruel to her. Isaac rose to his feet.

"This is my dwelling. Leave at once, or I'll—"

The man lunged across the room and backhanded him across the face. In the explosion of pain and distress, he found himself shoved against a wall while the man's greedy hand searched his pockets. He kept Isaac pinned to the wall with his other arm—easily holding him captive with his superior size and strength.

"Where'd you keep all your cuppers, boy? I'll take all of them, or I'll skewer you like a rat! You've had your fun. Now it's my turn!"

Isaac tried to shove the man away, but to no avail. His cheek stung from the blow, and the swelling urge to do violence against this fellow began to blaze in his chest. But he hadn't the physical prowess to back up the feeling, and before he knew it, the man had him on the floor, face down, his arm twisted behind his back.

"Call for help, and I'll cut out your tongue! Look at me, and your eyes go. Understand, you little brat? Where do you keep your cuppers? I want all of them. Get them for me. Now!" He released Isaac and backed away, blocking the exit with his bulk. He jabbed a finger at the woman on the bed visible through the open archway. His eyes radiated a smoldering fury that was truly frightening.

"Get back to my place," he spat at her. "I'll deal with you later."

Isaac rubbed his shoulder as he got shakily to his feet. *"A-Apoxtos sigorum!"* he said, pointing at the man. But he'd slurred the word and only precision would invoke the Unseen Powers.

The man's eyes flared with hatred. He drew a knife from his belt, the blade mottled with rust. Or was it dried blood?

Isaac felt terror freeze him in place.

He needed a shield. What was the shield spell? He was just a novice still. But his mentor, a professor at the university, had taught him some basic defensive spells.

He heard a low melodic sound and then felt the tingling of magic, a force that made the hair on his arms stand up. A shield spell enveloped him, but he hadn't summoned it. He'd been too panicked.

It was the Erlking's daughter. And then she sang a command that cracked like a whip. The huge man clapped his hands over his ears, his face contorting with pain as blood leaked through his fingers. He swooned with pain and started for the door, leaving the fallen knife on the floor.

The Erlking's daughter lifted her hand and sang another word. Isaac couldn't hear what she said, but her words struck the man in the back as he wrenched the door open. More snow came bursting in as the fellow lunged into the street.

The shield spell shrank from Isaac, who rushed to the door and hastily bolted it. A lot of snow had blown in during the brief time it had been open. Tugging apart the curtains, he saw the man staggering down the street, hands still on his ears. He careened as he fled, the blizzard swirling around him.

Isaac let the curtain fall back in place and turned and looked at the woman in awe. "What did you . . . what did you do to him?"

"I burst his eardrums," she said. "Then I ruptured his appendix. He won't be coming back."

"And you injured him by singing? I thought sorcery was only good for tricks or summoning light, other than its use in preparing elixirs, but you've been harnessing intelligences to do so much more. Can sorcery truly affect the organs of a mortal body?"

"Isaac, it is so much more than that. It can also damage or heal the impurities in a body and restore youth. Let me teach you all it can do."

Robinson Foster Hawksley

CHAPTER THIRTEEN

Wulfram College

Present day

"Look at this one," Wickins said eagerly, drawing Robinson's attention away from the book he was perusing. He, Wickins, and Clara were in a private study room at Wulfram College in Bishopsgate, in the quorum of the Invisible College that was popular among the members of the Marshalcy officers in the city. Its library also had the oldest books, and Robinson was fiercely determined to find every reference he could to the Erlking's daughter. He hadn't revealed his reasoning to Wickins or Clara, of course, but they were helping, nonetheless. They'd spent hours each day at Wulfram in the weeks since McKenna's return to Bishopsgate. Since McKenna could not work magic and was thus not allowed inside—nor would she have been able to bring herself to do the research even if those weren't obstacles—she was remaining under the protection of Mr. Swope and in easy contact. Robinson and McKenna had rented their own apartment in Bishopsgate so it would not be common knowledge where they were staying. Her inheritance had helped the family with their crisis, and she still had more than enough funds to rent the apartment.

"What did you find?" Robinson asked, keeping his thumb in his own book. Clara was still fixed on the book she was reading, a translation of some sort.

"This is interesting, very interesting," Wickins said. "I haven't read this record before, Dickemore. Let's see . . . it's *The Saga of the Mysing*, an epic poem of Iskandir. Look here. It's a translation, not the original."

"Good, because I can't read Iskandir," Robinson said, bemused. "Tell me."

"The translation is abominable, but it speaks of a witch-wife. Well, that's the translation."

"Witch-wife?" Clara said, looking up from her book. "What's the Aesir word for that?"

"I've no idea. I'll have to find the original version. But here's the interesting part. It talks about a queen from the mortal world sitting in her bower, whatever that is, and she's approached by a being called a witch-wife who asks her to change Semblances together."

Robinson put his book on the table and leaned forward earnestly. "It uses the word 'Semblance.'"

Wickins pointed to the line and handed over the book. The tale, a very short one, was about an Aesir who'd exchanged bodies with a mortal queen named Sigridur. It did not talk about how the magic was done, but the two had exchanged bodies willingly and for a limited time.

"This is amazing," Robinson said, his heart beginning to beat faster as he read the tale. His mind was on fire with new information.

"Isn't it? I thought Semblances could only inhabit the recently dead. This proves it's not the only way."

"'By her wiles she brought it about that they changed Semblances,'" Robinson quoted, running his finger under the words as he read them. "'And now the witch-wife sits in Sigridur's place according to her rede'—I'm not sure what that means."

Wickins snapped his fingers a few times with thinking. "Oh, I remember! It's from the Aesir word *'raed,'* which means, um . . . *a tale or prophecy*. A figure of speech. Whoever wrote this is repeating a tale they'd heard. Go on!"

Robinson read the next line. "Oh, the witch-wife wanted to sleep with the mortal king! 'And he knows not that he has other than Sigridur beside him.'"

"That's rather sordid," Clara said. "The Aesir are too cold to have conjugal relations, but they crave them anyway?"

"We don't know," Wickins said, giving her a smile. "Meanwhile, Sigridur, in another body, goes and seduces someone else . . . Sigridur's brother."

"That's disgusting!" Clara objected.

"I didn't create the story. It's the founding of a dynasty. Anyway, read the next part."

"'Thereafter, she fared home, and she found the witch-wife and bade her—'" Robinson stopped reading, his eyes caught by the next words, shock abruptly silencing him, but he recovered and said in a whisper, "'. . . and bade her change Semblances again, and she did so.'"

"That's the part," Wickins said, his eyes bright. "This reveals that a Semblance can swap bodies again and return the former person. The military had said it was impossible!"

A buzz of hope filled Robinson's chest. What if the term "witch-wife" was a reference to the Erlking's daughter? What if it were possible for McKenna to be released from her hold?

"Wickins," Robinson said, shaking his head. "We've spent weeks digging up scraps of information from the past, but this record . . . Do you think you can find the original? Maybe this translation is wrong?"

"I can try," Wickins said. "My Iskandir grammar is pretty shabby, but I know Aesir, and there's a chance this came from that language originally."

"Well done," Clara said, stroking Wickins's arm.

The bulb in the small quicksilver lamp sitting in front of them started to glow, snapping Robinson's attention to it. He'd asked the foundry they were partnering with to prepare a travel-sized lamp for him so he could be alerted to the presence of any Aesir magic, and he'd taken to leaving it out wherever he went.

"It's glowing," he said, then ducked his hand into his pocket to put on his thumb ring. A crease of pain unfolded along the side of his head, the usual repercussion of transmitting thoughts.

A knock sounded at the door. Clara was closest to it, and when she opened it, she blanched, finding Mr. Stoker, the new head of the military department in charge of hunting Semblances, standing there in a kappelin cloak, the invisibility charm disabled. Robinson felt a frisson of concern, but as long as his device was on his person, he felt he would be protected if the man had ill intentions.

Robinson sent a thought to Mr. Swope. *Get McKenna to Straethen's. Mr. Stoker just arrived.*

"Pardon the intrusion," Mr. Stoker said, sidling past Clara, who wasn't retreating from him. She folded her arms and glared at him, and little wonder. The last time they'd interacted, at the Great Exhibition, he'd ended up arresting her and Robinson.

"What do you want?" Robinson asked distrustfully.

He sensed Mr. Swope's mental reply. *On our way. We'll meet you there. Do you need me to summon help?*

I can do that myself. Thank you.

Robinson hadn't just spent his time researching. He'd been making copies of the rings he'd found. The inspector general and his top commanders each had one. Wickins and Clara had them. So did Mr. Foster and Mr. Swope. There were great advantages in being able to communicate from a distance.

General Ambrose had demanded access to the rings for the war effort, and more were being created daily at a foundry in Bishopsgate. Robinson wanted to do his part to help stop the Aesir from slaughtering people.

Mr. Stoker gave Robinson a measured look. "I wanted to come in person and tell you that we've called off the hunt for the *strannik* and his accomplice in the wilderness. Too much time has passed since your wife escaped, and with no trail to follow, we're wasting our time looking out there."

"It's only been a few weeks," Robinson said as he removed the ring so he could concentrate on the conversation at hand.

"It started snowing last night in those mountains. Any trail they may have left will be impossible to follow, and the dogs have been useless. With winter nearly here, the general needs my men at the front and at the upcoming convocation. If he shows up in one of the cities again, we'll be watching, and the Marshalcy will be continuing their investigation elsewhere of course."

"So you're quitting?" Clara asked, arms still folded.

Mr. Stoker gave her a sidelong look. "We're being realistic, Miss Foster. I was the one who originally arrested him and have come to the realization that he *wanted* to be found so he could infiltrate the military. But his interest has been focused, all along, on your wife, Professor Hawksley."

Robinson's stomach clenched with dread. "He's a fanatic."

"I think it would be for the best if she were under the military's protection," Mr. Stoker said in an attempt to be compelling. "The Marshalcy failed to protect her at the family house in Auvinen. I urge you to consider this. I urge it most strongly considering where the pyrophoric came from that burned down the house."

"What do you mean? We weren't told they'd found the source," Robinson demanded in a confrontational tone.

"It came from someone in the Marshalcy. So Guiteau didn't tell you?" The smug look on his face was provoking.

"He did not."

"There aren't just sympathizers in the military, Professor. The *strannik*'s followers are everywhere. One of the Marshalcy guards assigned to protect your wife was one of them. One of *my* men discovered his treachery only recently. I know you and your wife are hiding in Bishopsgate. That's prudent. But it would be wiser still if you let *us* protect her."

Robinson saw Clara's nostrils flare with contempt. Wickins had looked away but was slowly shaking his head. They mirrored his own feelings.

"I appreciate the offer, Mr. Stoker. I'll give it due consideration once this lawsuit over my patent is over."

Mr. Stoker sighed. "That was General Colsterworth's mad scheme, and he's dead. What you are doing is going to cost the empire millions in damages."

"It's hardly my fault it's come to this," Robinson replied evenly. "Are we done, Mr. Stoker? Is there anything further you wish to discuss?"

Mr. Stoker looked disappointed he hadn't made headway. He shook his head and walked back to the door. After he left, the glow of the lamp dimmed and then winked out.

"I despise that man," Clara said, closing the door.

"Men like him exist in every hierarchy," Robinson mused.

Wickins gave him a sympathetic look. "Do you think he was telling the truth about Guiteau? It makes the most sense now that I think on it. The *strannik* only needed one of those officers to be corrupt to help him get inside the house with the chymical."

"Here's the thing about truth," Robinson said. "There's Stoker's version of events. There is Guiteau's version of events. And then there's what actually happened. I'm disappointed, but I'll withhold judgment until after I've heard Guiteau's side."

"That's fair enough," Wickins said.

Robinson pushed away from the table. "I'm going to meet up with Mr. Swope and McKenna. We can come back tomorrow to continue our work."

"Tomorrow is the first day of court," Wickins said. "You haven't forgotten about it?"

Robinson had forgotten. He massaged his temples, feeling vexed. The last thing in the universe he wanted to do at the moment was sit in a courtroom and listen to witnesses and barristers and a judge. The man presiding over the patent dispute was Judge Mark Riddoch Bache—a magistrate judge in Bishopsgate. According to Mr. Foster, he was fair-minded but incredibly stern and was perhaps the most seasoned judge in the city.

"I wish it were over already." Robinson sighed, then pushed back his chair and stood.

"We can clean up here," Clara said.

Robinson thanked her and Wickins and then hurried out of Wulfram College. After alerting Mr. Swope that all was well and he was coming, Robinson summoned the dog intelligence, Loyal, and requested that he linger and observe whether anyone was following Robinson. He took the main street first, in order to lose himself in the early-evening crowd, and then he began to crisscross side streets to shake off any followers. Mr. Swope had given him a hasty education in the methods of deterring people trying to follow him. After about twenty minutes of proactive efforts to lose a possible tail, he continued on his way to Straethen's, a little teahouse near the apartment they were renting.

There was no sign of a pursuer, thankfully, and he reached his wife and Mr. Swope about thirty minutes after leaving Wulfram. They were seated inside Straethen's at a little round table with three seats. McKenna had her elbows on the table and looked uneasy, but she brightened when she noticed him coming up the street.

"I wasn't followed," Robinson said, taking the empty chair and then squeezing his wife's hand.

"Caution is always the best policy," Mr. Swope said. "What did Mr. Stoker want?"

"My absolute and complete trust," Robinson said acerbically. "He suggested someone in the Marshalcy was behind the fire and that Guiteau has been hiding the truth from us."

Mr. Swope blew out a breath and shook his head.

"Why wouldn't he tell us?" McKenna asked with concern. "I'm tired of all this underhandedness. I thought sorcerers from the Invisible College were supposed to be paragons of integrity."

"He also said it has begun to snow in the mountains and they've called off the search. No sign of the *strannik*."

McKenna's shoulders drooped. They'd all been hopeful that her information about the *strannik* would lead to his arrest. But as each day passed, that outcome seemed less and less likely.

The *strannik* had been very adept at hunting down McKenna thus far. Robinson had the sick feeling that neither the military nor the Marshalcy would be much help in stopping him from taking her again.

"This will cheer you up," McKenna said, pushing a little plate toward him.

"What is it?"

"It's a tart. Apples, almond paste, and a shortbread crust. It's delicious. I know you'll love it."

He hadn't even noticed being hungry after working all day at the foundry and then spending several hours at Wulfram College. He wanted to keep reading, to keep learning, but it was time to shut off that part of his mind and be present with McKenna.

"Shall we go for a walk afterward?" he suggested, lifting up the corner piece of the tart. Dusk was settling quickly, which was an ideal time for taking a stroll incognito.

"I'd like that," she said. "I'd like to hear what you learned today."

He was about to put the tart in his mouth but paused just before biting. He couldn't help wondering how the being inside her would react if he called her a witch-wife.

McKenna Aurora
Hawksley

CHAPTER FOURTEEN

The Magistrate

Being in the courthouse reminded McKenna of the time, years ago, when she had gone with her father and Miss Trewitt to a hearing about . . . well . . . *hearing*. Being so young and unacquainted with the world, she had found the experience rather bewildering. This time, instead of having capable Miss Trewitt at her side, she was sitting by Mr. Swope. Rob was next to Father at one of the front tables. Her husband looked restless and agitated. During breakfast that morning, he'd revealed the stress he was feeling by barely touching his food and lamenting that he had to spend all day in a courtroom instead of at the foundry or Wulfram College. He twisted in his chair, looking back at her, and offered a resigned smile. She gave him an encouraging one in return.

Others in attendance began craning their necks, so McKenna joined in and watched as Miss Cowing arrived with her barrister. McKenna was well aware of Miss Cowing's reputation as a fine dresser, a brilliant inventor, and a charming woman, and indeed, she was beautiful and poised. People were talking to each other with great interest about the new arrival, but the woman herself said nothing and simply went to the table adjacent to Rob's with her barrister, seating herself in a most elegant manner. McKenna felt her lip wrinkle involuntarily but tried to appear unmoved.

Mr. Swope touched her shoulder and surreptitiously pointed to the front of the court. An officer of the Marshalcy was standing to deliver an announcement. McKenna only caught the final words, which were instructions to rise for the entrance of the magistrate judge.

Judge Bache was an older gentleman, probably in his sixties, with wavy gray hair that was slick with pomade and a notable tuft of a beard on his chin and lower lip, the latter curled into a surly frown. His eyes were piercing in their intensity. He wore his robes of office, and his only accessories were a pin designating him as a member of the Invisible College and a cravat, which was not stylish, just a plain black cloth. McKenna could feel the quiet of the room in her chest. Judge Bache sat down and eyed both tables before speaking. The gallery was full—every seat taken—and officers from the Marshalcy guarded all the doors.

"This session will come to order," he declared, and everyone sat down. McKenna smoothed her skirts, feeling apprehensive yet interested. She wished that she'd chosen a seat where she could get a better view, but at least she could observe the witness stand and read the lips of the speakers who were there. She wouldn't be able to follow the barrister's questions very well, but she should be able to surmise them from the answers.

She missed several words of the judge's speech but was able to piece the meaning together quickly and seamlessly, the result of years of long practice and her innate ability for lipreading. "I handle approximately four to five hundred divorce cases every year, custody cases, paternity cases. Patent cases are rarer because the parties typically resolve their differences out of court and reach an agreement. I will hear both sides fairly and impartially. I must stress that I wish to hear facts and not opinions. I respect evidence. At the end of this case, I will render a decision in favor of one party or the other or none at all if the situation warrants it. I understand a great sum of money is involved." He shook his head. "That carries no weight at all with me. We will take the needed time to hear the details, arguments, and rebuttals. This may take several weeks. We will adjourn for Closure each week and allow our minds to refresh. Let us proceed." He gestured to McKenna's father. "Mr. Foster. You will go first."

⁕

After a long and mostly tedious day in court, the Fosters gathered at their home to share a meal. Wickins had spent the day in the foundry—he wouldn't be asked to testify until later in the week so he wasn't allowed in the courtroom until then. Father had already told McKenna that he was not planning to invite her to testify, to shield her from any prejudice that might be directed toward her for being deaf. That disturbed her, but she trusted his judgment and knew he would want what was best for both her and the case. Rob had fidgeted often in his seat during the proceedings, sometimes taking notes, sometimes gazing out the window.

Dinner was a delicious roast lamb with broiled purple potatoes. The meat was succulent and the potatoes crispy, but Rob poked at his food. She rubbed his back and shoulder, giving him an encouraging nod to eat more. When she'd gotten back from her ordeal with the *strannik*, she'd found that her husband had lost weight again.

Questions were asked and answered about the events of the day—so many that it was difficult for her to keep up with the conversation, even though they all sat at a circular table. Wickins, in particular, wanted to know all the details in between bites of food. His appetite was truly prodigious. But it made it difficult to understand him.

"So the issue raised today was the ownership of the patent," Wickins said. "The military clearly used Dickemore's invention unlawfully, but that will not be decided in this dispute?"

Father shook his head. "Correct—it is the ownership of the patents that will be decided in this case. Once ownership is established, then the consequence of the military using Robinson's invention will be brought into consideration."

"But why not resolve both matters here? I don't understand that. They stole the idea straight out. I was at the front last winter, and those tubes saved our lives on many occasions, but they acquired them illegally, and they know it!"

Father wrinkled his nose and sat back in his chair. "I understand your fury, Mr. Wickins, but if Miss Cowing is granted the patent, then they did not use them illegally, since she has now granted them permission. In fact, we will be held liable for violating it."

"So it sounds like all day was spent setting the stage," Wickins said after demolishing more potatoes. "What a waste of time."

"Cases must be presented logically and persuasively," Father said. "Every word spoken is part of the record. What happens here will impact other patent cases in the future. Admittedly, the process does feel tedious, but I'm confident it will produce the results we require. When we win this case, it will change our family's fortunes forever. And your fortunes too, Mr. Wickins," he added wryly.

Rob turned and looked at McKenna. "I can't sit here any longer. Are you finished eating? I need some fresh air."

McKenna wasn't quite done, but she nodded, recognizing his restlessness. Mr. Swope wiped his mouth on a napkin and rose from his seat.

"You're leaving already?" Trudie asked with a pout. "I wanted you to play some music. Can't you play some music for us?"

"Maybe another evening, Trudie," Rob said as he rose.

"It's been a long day," McKenna concurred, standing as well. They bid their farewells and then slipped out the back door leading to the alley behind the row of homes. They walked with their arms hooked together, and one backward glance revealed Mr. Swope in the shadows, trailing after them. The alley was too dark for lipreading, so they didn't converse until they reached the main street, which was well lit by lamps. Rob gazed at her face as they walked. "Thank you for leaving early. The last thing I wanted to do was endure the miserable day all over again."

"I thought it rather interesting," she said.

"I don't think this is what Isaac Berrow had in mind when he created the Invisible College."

"Yes, but it's a legal matter, Rob. The court should decide it."

"But what if we'd resolved this matter with Elizabeth out of court? It would probably have taken no more than an hour to discuss where our ideas came from and when. If she truly were first, I would have given way without any fuss." He chuffed and shook his head. "Now it's all about money and defending interests."

"Can you blame them?" McKenna said. "With such large sums at stake, there needs to be a way to handle the matter dispassionately."

"We're two intelligent people. If we'd simply sat down together and observed the facts, we could have reached a civil conclusion about who was in the right and who in the wrong. It is how members of the Invisible College would have handled this in the past."

"Perhaps you are too idealistic about the past," McKenna said. "I read a book about Mr. Berrow once that said he was an incredibly stubborn man and could hold resentments for years."

Rob smirked and shrugged. "Maybe I can't help being idealistic. Or maybe I resent the idea of being forced to spend so much time sitting in a chair in a courthouse to finish this case when I could be inventing a device to bring down an Aesir stormbreaker."

"Does your mind ever stop working, Husband?" she said teasingly.

He smiled at that, but then he glanced back sharply and looked at her.

"What's wrong?" she asked.

"Someone is following us. Mr. Swope just warned me."

McKenna felt her mouth go dry at the words. Who was it this time? She dreaded another attempt at an abduction. Squeezing Rob's arm, she matched his increasing pace. Rob reached into his vest pocket, and she realized he was putting on his own ring.

"Is someone behind us, then?" McKenna asked. She itched to turn around and look, but there were many people roaming the streets of Bishopsgate that night, and it would be hard to tell who might be trailing them.

"We'll turn up ahead. Mr. Swope has already alerted the Marshalcy. They're on their way."

McKenna bit her lip, her pulse racing. That sickening feeling of worry was worming its way through her stomach.

"This way," Rob said, tugging her into a dark alley they'd almost passed.

Without the streetlamps, it was dark indeed. They stopped, and Rob pushed her gently against the alley wall, made of brick, shielding her body with his own as he gazed back toward the street they'd just left.

A few moments later, a burly man appeared in the gap. He wore a cap and seemed to be in a hurry. Because the light was behind him, she couldn't make out his face or discern whether he was saying anything.

And then Mr. Swope came up behind the fellow and jabbed a pistol into his back. In the space of a moment, he had him shoved up against the wall, the pistol held against his spine. The dim light didn't reveal much, but she could tell the man was yelling. Then, from the darkness of the alley, two officers of the Marshalcy rushed in to help Mr. Swope subdue the man.

After a quick search, they found the man had a knife in his pocket. McKenna saw the light glint off the metal, and it made her shiver. Not with fear but a feeling of excitement. The situation and the predilection for violence of the being inside her was tangible to her. It was the opposite of reassuring.

Rob summoned his ghost light and faced her. "They want you to look at the man and see if you recognize him."

She nodded, and as they approached, she got a better look at the man with the close-cropped beard. His cap had been knocked off during the melee, and she saw that he was mostly bald with some stubble across his scalp. She'd never seen him before in her life.

"I don't," she said flatly.

They had reached the fellow, who was protesting against the men keeping him subdued.

"I just need some cuppers is all," the man said angrily in the struggle. "I wasn't gonna hurt anyone. You can't hold me for that! I didn't do nothin' wrong!"

Mr. Swope motioned for them to follow him back into the street. "I suspect he was just a desperate man in a desperate hour," he said to them. "The Marshalcy will take it from here."

McKenna put a hand on his arm. "Thank you, Mr. Swope. Thank you for everything."

He gave her a determined smile. "I won't let anyone take you again, Mrs. Hawksley. You have my word on that."

Hopefully, it would be enough.

CHAPTER FIFTEEN

Testimony

McKenna and Rob were sitting together on the bed, cross-legged, when she noticed the change in color of the sky through the open skylight window.

"It's nearly morning?" she asked, startled by the realization that they'd sat up talking all night. After the mishap in the alley, they'd ensconced themselves in their room on the highest floor and prepared to go to bed, but they had ended up having a series of deep conversations, the room lit by one of Rob's ghost lights.

He looked up at the skylight just as a little bird flew past it. "I've been hearing the birds for an hour at least," he said. "I guess I hadn't noticed. It was too enjoyable talking to you." He grazed her knuckles with his thumb.

It had been enjoyable. The privacy, the seclusion, just being together after all the tumultuous events of their young marriage. Even stranger, it had felt *familiar*. They'd often stayed up late talking, but never all night. And yet . . . there was a visceral feeling, one that knocked on the door of her memories. A door she didn't dare open.

"What's that look?" he asked, tilting his head.

She shook her head and gazed down at her lap, where their hands were intertwined.

He reached up with his other hand and tilted her chin back up, giving her a questioning look.

"It's silly."

"I don't mind silly, McKenna."

She sighed. "Well, I just had this strange feeling that we'd done this before. Stayed up all night talking, I mean."

"I don't think we ever have," he said, then shrugged. "We've endured so much uncertainty recently that we needed some uninterrupted time together." He shifted his hand and began massaging her neck.

"We should probably try to get some sleep before going to court this morning. We only have a few hours left."

"Might as well sleep in court," Rob said flippantly. "Nothing exciting is going to happen anyway."

"Boring is usually a good sign, Husband," she said. "You heard my father. Cases must be laid out logically, one point building on another."

"Don't get me started," he said with a chuckle. "Having to endure the tedium once is difficult enough. I wonder if Guiteau is going to contact me today about the fire. I don't think Mr. Stoker was lying about it. After all the help we've tried to provide to the Marshalcy, you'd think he'd at least inform us of a matter that concerns us so closely."

"I agree," McKenna said. "But no one likes to admit they're in the wrong. There's a certain stubbornness inherent in all of us." She gave him a wry smile. "Some have more of it than others."

"Are you accusing me of being too stubborn, Mrs. Hawksley?"

"For your many virtues, you're entitled to one fault," she said teasingly. Then she leaned over and kissed him on the mouth. "My husband requires sleep before we go. I insist."

"And I'd better not be stubborn about it?" he asked. The glowing orb of light that had illuminated the room during the whole of the night faded and vanished.

"Lie down," she said, pushing against his chest, and he complied. She could think of several ways that might enable them both to fall asleep quickly, but before she could entertain the delightful notions in her mind, another echo of memory resounded through her. She slipped off the bed, padded to the door, and locked it.

There was no rational reason to fear someone bursting into their room, not with Mr. Swope on guard below and the lamps Rob had magicked to warn them of intruders. But the memory of someone crashing in on them after they'd spent all night talking flickered in the back of her mind. And that memory brought with it an emotion she didn't understand the source of either.

Sadness. A deep, penetrating sadness.

"State your name and address for the court if you please," said Mr. Jeppson Savage, hands clasped behind his back. He was partly facing the court, partly facing his client. The barrister who represented Miss Cowing was a handsome man with a well-maintained physique and no facial hair at all, just smooth cheeks that made him look younger than his likely age.

"Elizabeth Cowing of Marchtown Street, Bishopsgate," she replied confidently. She wore another highly fashionable dress, along with a feathered hat that matched it perfectly. She was the epitome of poise and grace.

"How long have you been an inventor, Miss Cowing?"

"Since I was a student at the University of Nirshoye. I made several inventions there."

Mr. Savage adjusted his position, so McKenna couldn't discern the next question he asked.

"I don't work for free, Mr. Savage," Miss Cowing answered.

McKenna noticed Rob had shifted to look at the assembled court and realized that Miss Cowing's words must have gotten a reaction. She turned and saw a few recovering from laughter.

By the time she turned back, she'd missed the barrister's next inquiry.

"Yes, I worked for several firms after my years at university. I worked at Cuddelston Blakley's for two years. Then at the Harper Shaw foundry for one year. After that, I decided to go into partnership for three years before dissolving it."

Another question was asked, and McKenna felt another stab of annoyance at not being able to see it.

"I was cheated on a contract by my barrister, who was also my business partner," she answered. "I learned firsthand that some men cannot be trusted."

McKenna's father raised his hand and interposed an objection. "This has no bearing on the current case."

Judge Bache turned to Mr. Savage with uplifted eyebrows and then gave his attention to Miss Cowing. "I'll remind the witness to constrain remarks to the facts and not to wrongdoings wholly unrelated to the present case."

McKenna wondered if Miss Cowing's words had been intended for the public who had assembled to listen to the case rather than the judge. Was she trying to turn public opinion against McKenna's husband and make it seem like he was just another untrustworthy man who had taken advantage of a partner or colleague? It made her bristle with outrage because Rob had more integrity than anyone she'd ever met.

The barrister turned in a way that allowed her to see his face again. "Your Honor, I feel it pertinent to the case to establish that not all sorcerers from the Invisible College uphold the ideals of the institution."

"I am a magistrate judge, Mr. Savage. I know this already. Proceed with your line of questioning."

"Miss Cowing, after your business partner betrayed you, was there any other man or woman you trusted as a partner?"

Miss Cowing offered a pretty smile. "One cannot succeed in this world without partners, Mr. Savage. I lacked the capital to produce my own inventions. But I never had partners in the actual inventions."

He turned again, infuriating McKenna.

"Twelve. When I lacked specific knowledge, I would find those I could learn from, but I did not reveal what I was trying to invent. I didn't want my ideas to be stolen."

Mr. Savage said something else before shifting enough that his face was once again within view. "Tell us about the patent under dispute. When did you come up with the idea for it?"

"Many of my inventions have military applications," she answered. Her expression and demeanor had not changed in the slightest since she had taken the witness stand. She portrayed herself as a professional, cool-tempered genius with a flair for fashion. "They are highly profitable as well as useful to Society. I have many friends who are officers in the military, and with the coming of the Awakening, they lamented that there was no way of knowing where the Aesir would attack next."

"Can you be specific on the timing, Miss Cowing? We all know when the Awakening occurred. The Aesir attacks impacted all of us. When, specifically, did the idea about using quicksilver lamps come to you?"

"I remember it distinctly, Mr. Savage. I wrote an entry in my diary."

He turned suddenly, gesturing in a questioning way.

"I do, Mr. Savage."

Another question must have been asked because it caused an instant reaction from Miss Cowing. The inventor straightened her spine and produced a small leatherbound book. She flipped to a marked page and began to read.

"It's dated in the upper right corner," she said and mentioned the date aloud. "I will read the entry verbatim. Word for word. 'Theory—Aesir artifacts modulate on subacoustic pitches. Decode such and amplify to discernible degree.'" She closed and set down the diary.

"Can you translate that for us, Miss Cowing?" Judge Bache asked.

"All Aesir magic operates according to sound—although many of the sounds they can hear and replicate would be unheard by mortals. That is why spells need to be sung. Since our hearing can only distinguish sounds within a certain spectrum, my theory was that we could train intelligences capable of superior hearing to notice the frequencies of Aesir magic and trigger a reaction."

McKenna noticed Rob leaning over to whisper something in Father's ear.

"Your Honor," Mr. Savage then said while facing the judge, "the diary is evidence that Miss Cowing invented the idea first. While it is true that Professor Hawksley was the first to bring such an invention to market, the origin and timing of the idea is the pivotal matter in this case. Unless the professor can prove that his occurred chronologically before my client's, then she should be given the patent rights for this invention. My client has a proven record of inventions. Mr. Hawksley does not. He is an elocutionist by training. A speech teacher."

The disdainful look on the barrister's face made McKenna's blood quicken with heat and offense. Her husband was more than just a teacher. She'd sat in the parlor of the house on Brake Street and observed the in-depth conversations he'd had with her father. She'd worked alongside him in his alchemy. She knew the depth of his brilliance and innovation. And Miss Cowing's attorney was trying to present him as a thief. She glanced at Rob and found him slouching in his chair. Fear surged inside her that he'd dozed off. But that concern was alleviated when she saw him rub his eyes and sit up.

"Your witness, Mr. Foster," said Mr. Savage with a gleam in his eye.

McKenna's father waited until the other barrister had seated himself before he stood. She didn't want to miss any of it. As she had known he would, her father took pains to face the audience so his questions would be understood by her.

Father stood silently a moment. Then he repeated her early words. "'Theory—Aesir artifacts modulate on subacoustic pitches.' Translation: *We can't hear Aesir magic. Mortals have a limited bandwidth for hearing.*

'Decode such and amplify to discernible degree.' Translation: *Make the sound louder.* Your diary said nothing about harnessing intelligences to do this. It said nothing about which alloy might be required or the composition of Aesir gold. In other words, Miss Cowing, it was just an idea that popped into your head with no practical way to apply it. Is that true?"

Miss Cowing seemed unaffected. "All ideas begin that way. Inventors are explorers. Discoverers."

"Indeed they are. A suitable description. Miss Cowing, do you possess a ring made of Aesir gold with a symbol on the inner band of the Invisible College?"

McKenna saw Mr. Savage's hand shoot up. "Your Honor, Miss Cowing's possessions are completely irrelevant to this case!"

"Your Honor, my client also possesses such a ring, which enables the transmutation of thought. The ring is very old, although untarnished, as you'd expect from an Aesir artifact. The inspector general of the Marshalcy told us that he observed such a ring in Miss Cowing's possession. I merely seek to establish that fact."

Mr. Savage waved his hand. "It has no bearing on this case! Strike the question."

Judge Bache looked at the rival barrister coldly. "I would like to hear a little more about this ring if you please."

Robinson Foster Hawksley

CHAPTER SIXTEEN

Heirlooms and Invitations

The fatigue Robinson had felt up to this moment in the trial melted away as he fixed his gaze on Elizabeth Cowing and awaited her answer. So far, her barrister had done exactly as Mr. Foster had predicted—he'd sought to diminish Robinson's credibility as an inventor while establishing her reputation as the preeminent one. It was time to turn the tables. The truth, he believed, was on his side.

"I do have such a ring," Miss Cowing said in a neutral tone. "I asked Mr. Guiteau about it, to see if he understood its origins. He did not."

Mr. Foster took a step closer to her. "Professor Hawksley also possesses such a ring and has discovered one of its unique properties is the ability to transmit thoughts from one person to another. One ring he was given as an heirloom by his father, Mr. Joseph Hawksley, who is in attendance in this very courtroom should this information need to be verified. Professor Hawksley found a similar ring in Covesea, detected the alloy used to make it, and produced functioning replicas of it. Where did you acquire your ring, and have you uncovered the properties I described?"

Robinson was keen to hear her answer.

"The ring was sold to me by a man from Andover," she said, her brow furrowing in an enigmatic way. "A pawnbroker who'd bought it for cuppers from the estate sale of a bankrupt nobleman. He'd hoped it would possess some intrinsic magical powers. I was able to determine the use of the other items, but not this one. I bought it from him for thirty cuppers because I was intrigued."

Mr. Foster nodded as she concluded her words. "You suspected it might be more valuable than he knew?"

"I suspected, yes, but it did not respond to any of the magical commands I tried with it. The pawnbroker made a profit on it. If the ring did nothing, I risked being the losing party of the deal."

"But you have connections. You know sorcerers in the upper echelons of the Invisible College."

"I do, Mr. Foster. And none of them had seen such a thing before either."

"When you put it on, did you experience discomfort? A sudden headache?"

"Yes."

Mr. Foster turned and looked at Robinson, who couldn't help but smile. They'd just confirmed the similarity of her ring to the one that was nested in the device his father had given him.

"Were you wearing the ring on the day you wrote in your diary?"

"Your Honor, this is preposterous!" Mr. Savage protested. "The line of questioning is absurd. We're talking about magic rings that cause headaches now? Please! How desperate this seems!"

Judge Bache was unmoved. "Be silent, Mr. Savage. Miss Cowing, you will answer the question."

"Yes, I was," she said. "I have often endured the headaches as I've tried to unravel its mysteries. To no avail."

"Your Honor, my client informed me during Miss Cowing's testimony that the date of her diary entry coincides with an experience he had with his own ring at his alchemy in Auvinen. The ring can connect individuals regardless of distance. If they were both wearing their rings, simultaneously, it is possible that thoughts were unintentionally exchanged between them. For myself, I discussed such a concept with Professor Hawksley one evening after dinner on Closure in my parlor. We discussed his ideas regarding the transmutation of thought at length. This was well before the date of her journal entry."

"Your Honor," said Mr. Savage, chuckling derisively.

The judge cleared his throat. "Before we can continue, we will need an unbiased third party to test both of the rings and confirm they possess the properties that have been described. Opposing counsels will work together to identify such a third party, agreeable to both, who can inspect and use these rings to determine the veracity of the claim. The court will be adjourned until that has happened."

"Your Honor!" Mr. Savage burst out.

The judge shook his head. "We will adjourn, Mr. Savage."

Because court was adjourned early that day, the family met at a restaurant to discuss the events of the trial. In attendance were Robinson's parents, Mr. and Mrs. Foster, Trudie, Mr. Swope, and of course, McKenna. Wickins and Clara were still working with the foundry and were not able to join them. The restaurant was called the Civitas, and they were pleased that it had a private room available for them.

Lack of sleep was making Robinson's head loll, but he was grateful for the respite from another dreary day in the courtroom. McKenna nudged him encouragingly to eat more food. He was more tired than hungry, but he obliged and took another bite from the saffron and chicken dish.

"I know a sorcerer here who might be able to do the test," Robinson's father said eagerly. "Splendid fellow by the name of Leonardson. He is a twenty-fifth degree if I recall. Teaches at the military college."

"I would prefer a sorcerer unaffiliated with the military," Mr. Foster replied, then took off his pince-nez glasses and cleaned them with a table napkin before putting them back on.

"Oh, I see. They stand to lose a great deal of money in this case," Joseph Hawksley said. His wife, Robinson's mother, was neglecting her food in order to follow the conversation at the table by reading lips.

"We will need to come up with at least a dozen potential names," Mr. Foster said. "Hopefully, there will be some shared names in our lists, but in case there are not, we will have to investigate the names one by one before determining suitability."

"Which will drag the case on even longer," Robinson muttered.

"Inconveniently. I would have preferred to settle this out of court. We might have managed it if Mr. Savage had allowed us to speak to his client."

"I could speak to her right now," Robinson said, thinking of the ring in his pocket. "Without his consent."

"That would be unwise," Mrs. Foster said, giving her husband a sidelong look.

"They're right, my boy," Mr. Hawksley said. "Listen to your barrister. Follow his counsel."

"I have been, Father," Robinson said. "And he's steered us right so far. I'm sorry, I just didn't sleep well last night. Feeling a little out of sorts." McKenna stroked his arm, and he smiled at her.

A waiter entered their room. "The inspector general just arrived."

Shortly following the introduction, Mr. Guiteau entered and shut the door behind the waiter as he left. He greeted the family pleasantly, shaking hands with each member, even Trudie, who looked very bored.

"Do you have news?" Mr. Foster asked. They'd been hoping to hear from him for days, but his arrival during the meal was wholly unexpected.

"Yes. I do have news that will hopefully be welcome." He fished a hand into his vest pocket, pulled out an envelope with a broken seal, and wagged it at them. "This is from the emperor himself. It arrived this morning."

"The emperor?" Mrs. Foster said in a startled voice.

"First, some facts," Mr. Guiteau said. "I learned recently that one of the officers of the Marshalcy on duty the night of the fire was a secret disciple of the *strannik*. He purchased the chymical that caused the destruction and turned a blind eye to the *strannik* when he came. He did not believe anyone would be injured, but he's confessed his wrongdoing and is under arrest and awaiting trial."

This was news Robinson already knew, but he was grateful it had been shared at last. Some of the fatigue melted away. "Thank you for telling us," he said sincerely, feeling a greater trust for Mr. Guiteau than previously.

"His involvement in the affair has put some culpability on the Marshalcy. I didn't want to share the news of this until I had proposed and secured a remedy. I proposed to the emperor that the Marshalcy reimburse your family for the loss of your home on Brake Street. He refused." That shocked everyone into silence. But only for a moment. "Instead, he insisted on paying for the rebuilding of the home himself from the royal coffers." He grinned at them as he finished the sentence, knowing it would be welcome news.

Robinson's chest flooded with a surge of relief and pleasure, and McKenna took his hand as a grin spread across his mouth and he shook his head in disbelief.

"That is very generous," Mrs. Foster said, her throat catching.

"The emperor will also reimburse the damages caused to the neighboring homes," Mr. Guiteau said. "And, as I understand, there was also a little greenhouse on your property. The empress herself asked that it be rebuilt. She has a fondness for flowers and sunroom plants. The construction will begin immediately as long as you agree not to hold the Marshalcy liable for any further damages."

"Even in winter?" Mrs. Foster asked.

Mr. Guiteau nodded. "Those are the commands. The construction will begin immediately. General Ambrose agreed wholeheartedly with the arrangement and offered his condolences to your family."

McKenna squeezed Robinson's hand even harder, and when he looked at her, he saw the tears in her eyes. One danced off her lashes, and she quickly grabbed her napkin to blot it away from her cheek.

"May I read the emperor's letter?" Mr. Foster asked, holding out his hand.

Mr. Guiteau handed it over with a flourish and watched as it was examined.

Mr. Foster showed no expression other than a twinkle in his eye as he glanced up at Robinson upon finishing. "Seems you made a strong impression on him when you visited his family. Everything is as described. I will not refuse such a generous offer. It is"—his voice began to break, but he mastered himself—"appreciated."

Mr. Guiteau nodded with satisfaction. "Also, I have other news to relate. The convocation of sorcerers will be held at the University of Nirshoye. This is not public knowledge at present, but let me indulge in my authority by giving you the information early. All who are qualified will receive an invitation to attend. The university dormitories will be used to house all the guests."

Robinson felt a premonition of concern. He leaned forward. "I will not attend if my wife is—"

"Your wife will be permitted to come," Mr. Guiteau interrupted. "She cannot participate in the ceremony, of course, but she will be near you at all times, except for your interview. Even then, she will be outside the door with family and friends and"—he paused to glance at Mr. Swope—"guardians. This is a convocation of sorcerers, Professor, meeting at the place where the Invisible College was founded. I assure you that all precautions are already underway. The individuals with the three boxes containing the transition artifacts have been identified and are being safeguarded separately."

The pressure in Robinson's chest began to ease.

"Has the date been established?" Mr. Foster asked.

"Yes, but it is secret at the moment and I cannot share it. Those who receive a formal invitation will learn of it then. I'm sure we'll all have more information soon, but for now, I must be on my way."

Robinson rose from his chair and shook Mr. Guiteau's hand. Everyone else joined in thanking him before he took his leave.

"Might I have a quick word, Professor?" Guiteau asked at the doorway. Robinson stepped into the corridor with him, cocking his head slightly. They were alone.

"Yes?"

"Two quick things. First, I would like to try and test your theory about deaf children being immune to glamour spells. Or at least the kind of illusions employed by the *strannik*. I have some contacts in Auvinen who may be helpful in that regard. Second, your wife may be of some help in catching this enemy."

"How so?" Robinson asked, feeling concern bubble inside.

"We might be able to entice him to make his next move if he thinks he knows where he can find her. I would prefer doing this in Auvinen, of course, because of the resources available to us there."

Robinson frowned. "You want to use her as bait."

"Wasps attack where there is honey, Professor. He's eluded us thus far. If I could persuade you to bring her to Auvinen, I assure you, we would take the utmost precautions."

"Yet the ashes on Brake Street persuade me otherwise." He shook his head firmly. "I don't think so, Mr. Guiteau. Sorry to disappoint you."

The Marshalcy leader nodded, but whether his response boded acceptance or delay, Robinson wasn't sure.

When he returned, the mood in the room had altered. Trudie was grinning from ear to ear, and Mrs. Foster was dabbing tears from her eyes. Robinson's parents extolled the generosity of the emperor and expressed hope that they might get a chance to meet him in person someday.

"What a welcome relief," Mr. Foster said, gazing bemusedly at his wife.

When Robinson glanced at McKenna again to judge her reaction, he saw her look of pleasure had faded and she had a cynical expression. It made him quirk his eyebrows.

"What are you thinking?" he asked her.

She seemed reluctant to answer at first, but he coaxed a response from her.

"I'm pleased with how it turned out, Rob. Relieved. But I can't help but wonder at the timing of the news and the convocation. I think Mr. Guiteau hopes this public display of kindness will secure his place as Master Drusselmehr's successor. The general can't have it because he's military. Was this all a show, or was he sincere? I can't tell."

He thought of the favor Mr. Guiteau had requested out in the hall but after thinking about it longer, he decided he was right not to mention it. He could not take the chance that his wife might feel obligated to help in any way she could. And how could he support bringing additional danger to her after all they'd been through?

"I'll take whatever good luck we're due. Master Drusselmehr was a political man. Ambitious. That didn't disqualify him from the position. I think Mr. Guiteau shares similar qualities, but he might be good as the new Master of the Royal Secret."

"So would you," McKenna said with confidence.

Robinson felt a flush begin to creep over his cheeks at his wife's praise.

CHAPTER SEVENTEEN

Dangerous Mixtures

The secret entrance to Wulfram College was an annex filled with snorting horses, part of a series of paddocks used in rotation to meet the military's needs of hauling equipment and munitions to and from the locomotivus stations. The smell of dung and the annoying buzz of flies were part of the ambience. Robinson gave the hand gesture to a laborer leaning over a muck rake. The fellow nodded, allowing him to pass, and Robinson went to the farthest stall, emptied of animals, and lifted the trapdoor to climb down.

"Hoxta-namorem," he sang, conjuring the whorl of light, and he followed it to the underground entrance of the quorum of the Invisible College.

With the delay in the trial, he'd had more time to spend at Wulfram to try to discover everything he could about the Erlking's daughter. He'd spent the entire morning there actually. There had been no further breakthroughs, but he was determined. His wife's future might depend on what they learned.

At the end of the musty corridor was an iron-bound cellar door. He gave the appropriate knock, answered the password question, demonstrated a handshake, and was allowed inside.

He went to the private room that he and Clara and Wickins had been using for research, and when he opened the door, surprised the two of them in an amorous embrace. Clara sat on Wickins's lap in a business dress, her hat on the table and her hair disheveled. Robinson's arrival had clearly startled them, and Clara blushed fiercely and nearly leaped to her feet. Wickins looked suitably chagrined.

Robinson gave them both a patient but rebuking side-eye and chose not to comment on the inappropriateness of the situation.

"Well, old chap," Wickins said, still flustered, "H-How did your interview with the barrister go?"

"Tedious and obligatory," Robinson answered. Clara had picked up her hat and seemed to be deciding whether or not to try to fix it on her head. She put it down again, trying to suppress a mortified smile. "My father vouched for giving me the device. He'd never figured out how to unlock it, so his story corroborated mine."

"She stole the idea from you, Dickemore," Wickins said. "I know she did. The timing says it all."

"She did it unwittingly perhaps," Robinson said. "I'm willing to concede that. But her attorney knows that a fortune is at stake, and he's not going to give ground willingly."

"Not all barristers are as honorable as my father," Clara said, trying out her voice. There were still smudges of pink in her cheeks, but her embarrassment seemed to be fading.

"Or as shrewd," Wickins added. "I'm just glad he's on our side."

"I'm sorry I'm late," Robinson said, changing the subject. "The interview took longer than expected. Did you discover anything new?"

"I've been reading a new translation of that Iskandir saga I told you about. Clara has been spending her time studying Isaac Berrow."

Robinson nodded. "And?"

"This other translation calls Semblances by another name. Skin-changers. And . . . interestingly . . . it talks about gold rings being part of it."

"Oh? Show me."

Wickins retrieved the book he'd been reading and quickly turned to one of the pages that had a bookmark. He traced his finger down the row of text. "Ah, right here. 'They find a certain house and two men with great gold rings are asleep inside of it. Now, these twain were spellbound skin-changers.'"

He showed the passage to Robinson, who sat down in a nearby chair. He read a little more, but nothing stood out to him. The cryptic wording didn't help.

"What do you make of it?" he asked his friend.

"It's hard to say. This saga was written thousands of years ago. They used different words for things from the ones we use now. A 'may' is a young unmarried woman. They would also fight the Aesir alongside the men. They were called 'shield-may.' These old stories are full of strange happenings. There are magical drinks that could make a hero forget his wife or that he was even married. You know, the legend of the Erlking's daughter features that. It's all a giant riddle."

Robinson rubbed his eyes and set the book down. Scholars and elocutionists had studied the speeches and poetry of the island kingdom that had the first recorded interaction between mortals and Aesir. Maybe he would have to travel to Iskandir to find the knowledge he sought. Unfortunately, that wouldn't be possible in the winter. The island was farther north, and some years, the seas froze around it, making it impossible to get there.

"Other texts I've looked at are full of stories of kings and queens, of treachery and poisoned drinking horns. Fascinating, but there's so little about the Aesir or their magic."

"Thank you for trying," Robinson said, feeling a prickle of disappointment. But he was grateful for their help in searching for answers. He glanced at Clara. "And what did you learn about Isaac Berrow?"

She was still standing, and she leaned against the table close to where he was seated.

"He was a very strange sort of man. He loved the color red. Well, a specific shade of red. We know he invented certain kinds of arithmetical equations and ways to calculate large numbers. In his older years, he was in charge of the imperial mint. Did you know that?"

Robinson frowned and shrugged. "I think I'd heard that somewhere."

"His niece came and lived with him. She's the reason we know anything about him at all, for he was very secretive. I've been trying to learn more about his time at the University of Nirshoye, since we're going there for the convocation. Not only did he graduate from there, but he also taught there for most of his career."

"That makes sense since it's where he founded the Invisible College."

"I read that he was required to give lectures to get his salary, but it was not required that anyone *attend* them. His lectures were so advanced and baffling that he often delivered them to an empty room."

"What?" Robinson asked, chuckling.

"Are you joking?" Wickins asked with a startled laugh.

"I'm not. If a student happened to wander into one, he'd just pretend they weren't there and keep on talking. He didn't really care for university students. He relished time in his alchemy the most. He never married and was buried with little fanfare."

"I can see why he never married, then," Wickins observed. "He was rather aloof, I should say."

"That describes him perfectly. Even people who knew him when he was a student say he was miserly and socially inept. More interested in the immutable laws of nature than in caring for the feelings of others."

"He founded the Invisible College as a professor, though," Robinson said. "As a way of educating new generations of sorcerers. So he must have cared about the students to some extent."

"That is true," Clara confirmed. "But they say most of his greatest thinking happened during an Awakening."

Wickins snapped his fingers. "I'd forgotten that part! It was while he was a student. Another Aesir disease had begun to spread. The septicemic plague. I think it killed a quarter of the population of the empire."

Robinson shuddered. "And everyone knows what happened next. The university was canceled and everyone fled. Berrow returned to his childhood estate and proceeded to have the most prolific creative period imaginable."

"There's something about being bored," Clara mused.

"I don't think he ever got bored," Robinson said. "I recall an old philosopher said that if you do the same thing over and over again, you not only create boredom, but you are also allowing yourself to be controlled by what you do, rather than having control. When I'm working on a problem or an invention, I'm trying to find a new way to accomplish something. It's endlessly invigorating. That's why I don't want to spend time at the foundry. *That* is boring."

"I find the foundry fascinating," Clara said, tossing her head. "And so does John." She looked at Wickins for confirmation and looked pleased when he nodded.

"I do like reading ancient literature, though," Wickins said sheepishly. "I don't get tired of it. I'd give a lecture to an empty room if I could do it."

"Stop," Clara said, shaking her head. "Do you really want to be a professor of ancient languages?"

Robinson could tell that she didn't respect the idea, and he watched as Wickins shrank a little inside himself and gave a half shrug.

"Frankly, I would rather be at my alchemy in Mowbray House with McKenna, trying to solve problems," Robinson said to ease the tension. "If only we could end this awful trial."

"You won't think it awful when you win, Dickemore," Wickins said.

"Having to fight over my invention has soured me on the whole process. Sorcerers used to share ideas in Isaac Berrow's time. To impress each other with their inventions. They'd help each other improve on them."

"That doesn't exactly explain why Professor Berrow lectured to an empty room," Wickins pointed out.

"Do you think those students even knew who they had in their midst back then?" Clara said, shaking her head. "He was probably the smartest man who ever lived, and they skipped his class because they didn't understand it. I wish I'd lived back then."

"And risk catching the septicemic plague? No thank you!" Wickins disagreed.

"We have our own plagues," Clara said. "The Aesir keep inventing new ways to destroy us."

The door opened and another sorcerer poked her head in, her face anxious. "You're Professor Hawksley, aren't you?" she asked.

Robinson pushed the nearby book away. "Yes. What is it?"

"A message arrived from Auvinen. A courier was looking for you." She backed out and made a motioning gesture. "He's in here, sir."

"What's this nonsense about?" Wickins muttered.

Robinson shrugged and waited. A smartly dressed man with a pencil-thin mustache arrived, wearing round glasses and a bowler hat. His suit was certainly professional. "Professor Hawksley?"

Robinson stood and the two shook hands. "Who are you?"

"I'm Mr. Featherkile from the law firm of Brocklehurst, Minchin, and Creakle. We received a message from a partner firm in Siaconset claiming that your wife, Mr. Foster's daughter, is actually still alive. Is that true?"

"Yes. She's here in Bishopsgate."

The man's brow wrinkled. "I'm afraid I must impose on you both to return promptly to Auvinen. Her aunt's will has strict stipulations regarding inheritance and the rights of transfer, so she must prove she's alive by swearing an affidavit in front of a magistrate. I'm terribly sorry to impose this on you on such short notice, but we did not want the Siaconset estate to become entailed to another relative."

"Can we not swear the affidavit here in Bishopsgate? Mr. Foster can vouch—"

"I've already spoken to Mr. Foster, and I'm afraid the will makes this stipulation. My apologies. It must be done in person. I'm just the messenger, Professor Hawksley. There were protections built into the will in case the inheritor, your wife, died prematurely. I sought your wife at the family home and was directed here to Wulfram, because you would know where she is and can contact her."

Robinson scratched his neck. "We'll take the locomotivus to Auvinen as soon as we can."

"Thank you. My charge is finished, and I'll be returning to my office should you have any further inquiries. Brocklehurst, Minchin, and Creakle—the office is downtown in Auvinen on Selby Street. Thank you." He bowed stiffly and left them.

"He was as friendly as a sore throat," Clara said, wrinkling her nose. "Aunt Margaret had an entailment clause? That's odd."

Wickins looked confused but gave Robinson an encouraging nod. "You could go this evening and take the southbound locomotivus to arrive when the law office opens. You could be back as soon as tomorrow night."

Robinson had been feeling confined to Bishopsgate, and the same was true for McKenna. Leaving town for a brief trip might be a refreshing change of pace for both of them. He reached into his pocket and pulled out the device, quickly turning the combination to release the ring.

"We'll leave after dinner," Robinson said before slipping the ring on his thumb.

McKenna Aurora
Hawksley

CHAPTER EIGHTEEN

The Saltpetr Factory

The locomotivus yard in Auvinen was full of frenzied activity. McKenna had to grip Rob's arm tightly as they were jostled by the teeming crowd. They were followed by the agile Mr. Swope, who was never farther than an arm's length from her. She hadn't been in such a crowded station since the Aesir had attacked Bishopsgate.

Once they were free from the masses trying to cram onto the northbound locomotivus, the crowd was sparser, although the mood in her home city had altered. Everywhere she looked, people were reading the news, and the street trams were all packed. Her gaze fell on a young man standing near the Marshalcy officer talking to Rob. He wore ordinary clothing, the typical shirt and suspenders that were expected of a youth, but she noticed a pin at his collar with the symbol of the Marshalcy. His gaze was darting from person to person.

"What's your name?" she asked the young man, curious. He didn't respond to her question, his eyes still searching the crowd. Then she realized he was deaf.

She positioned herself more directly in front of him and repeated the question, this time using manual communication as well.

"Sorry, miss. My name is Albert, but I can't talk right now. I have a job to do." He both said the words and signed them with his hands.

"Are you from Mrs. Fiske's school?" McKenna asked, getting his attention again.

"Yes, miss."

She felt a tap on her shoulder and turned, looking into Rob's face.

"The Marshalcy have asked Sarah's older students to help them find the *strannik*. They're posted at every station and road out of the city. The inspector general took our advice after verifying that a glamour spell does not work on them. Sarah has been very helpful in this effort. The Marshalcy is going to make a sizable investment in her school."

That made McKenna smile. "That's wonderful news. Should we take the tram to Selby Street?"

"It would probably be faster to walk." He was looking around as he spoke, giving his surroundings a closer degree of attention than usual. That was not surprising with the *strannik* on the loose.

"That suits me," McKenna said. "Any objection, Mr. Swope?"

The manservant shook his head, and the three of them departed. They had each packed a change of clothes before their hasty leave-taking to the station. But after seeing how crowded the station was, McKenna realized it might be difficult for them to get out of Auvinen as quickly as they'd planned. Then again, money and privilege facilitated most conflicts, and she didn't doubt they could book passage back to Bishopsgate when they desired—for the right price.

As they walked, she smelled the burnt-sugar smell of the peanuts they favored, but she wasn't in the mood for a treat. Like Rob, she was eager to get the legal matter concluded. Rob had also expressed a desire to see how Mrs. Farmer's family was doing if time permitted.

The office of Brocklehurst, Minchin, and Creakle proved easy enough to find. The barristers in the office made them wait while they arranged for the affidavit to be recorded and sent to a magistrate. They did provide some refreshments to the visitors while they were seated in the waiting room, but Robinson tapped his fingers on his knee with an air of impatience. She took his hand in hers and squeezed it.

It took a few hours to accomplish the task, but finally the affidavit was signed and they were permitted to leave. When they started back on Selby Street, Rob asked if she wanted to stay longer or if they should send Mr. Swope to arrange for tickets for the next locomotivus.

"Are you sure you want to leave already?" McKenna asked him as they walked, gazing at his face. "The station was quite crowded earlier. I thought it might be easier for us to stay the night."

"I just . . . feel—" Then he stopped abruptly.

She'd felt it too. Tremors under the soles of her feet. Vibrations rippling through her chest and throbbing against her eardrums. Robinson was gazing around with a wild look in his eyes. She turned and saw that Mr. Swope's expression mirrored her husband's.

"What was that?" McKenna asked, feeling her voice tremble. Something had shaken the city.

Robinson gripped her hand and they started walking. People were rushing out of the buildings and onto the street. The smell of saltpetr stung McKenna's nose. Gray roiled through the sky above the buildings, but it was not a thundercloud. It was smoke.

By the time they reached the next main intersection, all the trams had stopped. People with worried expressions were thronging the streets. Some pointed to the cloud of smoke coming from the south.

Robinson stopped a passerby and asked a question McKenna couldn't make out. The impossibility of following the conversation only made McKenna feel more disoriented and frightened.

It took some time before an explanation was found. One of the saltpetr factories near the tenements had exploded.

⁂

The tenements in Auvinen were vast, so it was unlikely—improbable even—that the Farmer family had been impacted personally by the blast. But the uncertainty was agitating, and Rob and McKenna wanted to find out in person and render assistance if they could.

"We should find shelter ourselves before there isn't any left," Mr. Swope advised. "There's no sense trying to search the rubble for the family you know. It could be impossible to find them."

"It won't be," Rob said sternly. He looked at McKenna. "Loyal can find them. I've already sent him to look. I have to make sure they're all right. Go with Mr. Swope and find shelter. I'll rejoin you later."

"No," McKenna said firmly. "We'll help you."

"Ma'am, in this chaos, you are vulnerable," Mr. Swope said. "We should all get to the locomotivus station at once and get out while we can."

Robinson shook his head. McKenna saw the anguish in his eyes and felt a fiery determination in her own heart. She turned to Mr. Swope. "I'll not be separated from him so easily. I'll be safest if I'm with Rob, and we need to find the widow's family and make sure they're safe first. We can find them. I promise."

"Isn't it possible that the *strannik* set this up just to find you?" he retorted.

Rob frowned. "He might have. But she can see through his glamour, and you have a pistol." He looked at McKenna directly, his gaze imploring. "I want you to be safe. I want that above all else."

"And I don't want to be parted from you. The quicker we stop debating this, the quicker we'll get to safety."

Rob considered this for a moment and then nodded resolutely. They walked several blocks to the edge of the city center. Pieces of rubble had punctured the streets, blown a great distance by the force of the blast. None of the trams were functioning, as most had been abandoned by the drivers. People were fleeing the destruction zone, covered in dust, some holding bloodied rags against injuries. McKenna had been down these streets before and knew the way to the widow's lodgings, and the closer they got, the more fearful she became.

When they arrived, the area was covered with rubble that was being carted off, and there was a haze of stone dust in the air so potent she could smell it and feel the grit of it in her teeth. It seemed every available cart and horse team had been summoned to help haul away the mess. And she saw, to her horror, that they were carrying away the remains of people as well that had been torn asunder. Several of the passenger trams operated by metal horses had also been conscripted to help with the cleanup.

A feeling of heaviness came over her as they moved through the chaos. People were sitting on the sidewalk, heads in their hands, stunned by the evidence of destruction all around them. A few blocks in, McKenna's jaw dropped. Entire rows of buildings had been pulverized, and with each step, the sulfurous smell in the air grew more pronounced.

"Oh dear," she murmured. "Oh dear, oh dear."

Glancing at Robinson's face, she saw a mixture of emotions on display. The damage was appalling. The suffering abundant. She also sensed a building fury inside her husband, a determination to aid these people. He'd done this before, going to Mrs. Fiske's school after the students had been afflicted with an Aesir plague. While others offered sympathy and gifts, he'd exposed himself to the illness in order to help.

They tried to go deeper into the tenements, but the main roads were all blocked, requiring them to backtrack and try alternate routes. People using push brooms alongside magical contrivances were sweeping ash and dust from the streets. They stared in shock and wandered for longer than they imagined through the horror of the destruction. And then the day was waning and McKenna imagined it would be difficult if not impossible to fall asleep. And with such wreckage, most of the hotels would likely be filled to the brim with those who had lost their dwellings. Thankfully, there were friends they could call on.

Rob guided them through the streets until they were able to find an opening to get into the tenements. And then he halted, dumbfounded by what he saw. McKenna stared in disbelief. The buildings had fallen down there too. *All of them.* The explosion from the factory had clearly blasted straight into the tenements. People were combing through the rubble, some of them with their bare hands. Although she could not hear the sound of the women shrieking, she *knew*. Small shawls and blankets had been draped over stacks of bodies. The suffering of these people was horrifying and unimaginable.

"W-Was this the street?" she asked, her voice breaking with sorrow.

Robinson looked at her, grief-stricken. "It doesn't look the same, but this is it. Loyal led me here. He's searching for her family now."

"I am so sorry," she said, gripping his arm.

He looked more determined than sorrowful. He wasn't giving up hope. A film of dust had settled on their clothes, infiltrated their hair. They wandered the ruined street, passing the many diggers and mourners. Some held lamps, others candles, as they clawed through the mess. There were no sorcerers there. No, the sorcerers were probably combing through the factories, not the dwellings of laborers.

Rob suddenly grasped her hand and pulled her with him as he marched down the street with purpose. In the middle of the densest avenue of destruction, they found the widow, weeping in misery, as she knelt in the debris and tried to remove it piece by piece. McKenna gaped in horror when she recognized the woman, a trickle of dried blood on her chalky face. Their invisible friend had brought them directly to her, but she was a mother of three, and there were no children with her. None. McKenna feared the worst had happened.

Robinson let go of McKenna's hand and climbed onto the rubble where the woman was digging. She didn't recognize him at first, but when she finally did, her face contorted with grief. She spoke so fast, so miserably that McKenna couldn't read her lips. The expression on her face spoke of a mother's devastation. Robinson knelt next to her in the rubble, hand on her shoulder, looking into her face and listening to her horrific tale.

"What's she saying, Mr. Swope?" McKenna asked thickly. "It's getting darker and I-I can't understand her." She gazed up at Mr. Swope, who was battling his own emotions.

"From what I can make out, she was shopping for food when the explosion happened. The children were here. There haven't been any survivors found in this part of the rubble so far."

McKenna covered her mouth, tears stinging her eyes. Robinson listened and then began climbing into the hill of rubble.

"It's too dangerous," Mr. Swope said. "He could be killed."

"Rob! Rob!" McKenna called out to him. He didn't respond but a will-o'-the-wisp of light appeared and then another and another. The whirling orbs began to move slowly amidst the ruins, extending away from Rob like tentacles.

McKenna admired him and feared for him simultaneously. She began to march forward to help, but Mr. Swope caught her by the arm and shook his head.

McKenna was about to order him to release her, but he nodded to indicate someone was approaching. Turning her head, she saw Mrs. Farmer clambering toward her.

"Oh, my lady," the widow sobbed, grabbing McKenna by the arms. "I didn't know ye were coming. I didn't know, but bless you! Bless you by a hundred! If my little ones are still alive, the professor will find them. I know he will! But if not, even if not, bless you for coming! Bless you!"

McKenna hugged the widow, feeling tears streak down her own cheeks. It was an awful scene, one that tugged and twisted at her heart. Who could have survived the collapse of a building? It just wasn't possible. But McKenna had always steadfastly believed in the impossible.

No mother should have to endure a trial like this. It was beyond imagining.

As the darkness fell, Rob continued to search the debris, his little ghost-lights wandering up and over and down through the pile. He paused twice amidst rubble and shouted something down to them.

"What is it?" McKenna asked Mr. Swope. "What did he say?"

"He found two corpses. Adults. Not children. He's still looking."

A quarter hour later he found someone who had survived the blast, an old man living in the tenements who had lost his shirt or had not been wearing it at the time of the explosion. Rob extricated him, and others climbed the mound to help the dazed older man scrabble down to safety.

Rob rose and kept looking. She could tell he was being guided by their dear Loyal.

While she comforted the widow as best she could, Mr. Swope stood guard. She'd asked him why he wasn't helping Rob search, and he'd replied that his paramount duty was to safeguard her. If the explosion had been rigged by the *strannik*, his minions might still be in the area. In fact, he grew more and more uneasy about remaining on the street at dusk.

Rob must have called out to them because Mr. Swope pointed to the top of the mound. Her husband was waving them up. McKenna's heart wasn't sure it could bear the news if the children had died, but she joined Mr. Swope and the widow as they carefully mounted the pile.

"They're under here," Rob said once they'd arrived. "We need to remove the pieces carefully, one by one."

"Are they alive?" Mr. Swope demanded with a look of incredulity.

"I think so," Rob answered, nodding his head. "But they won't be for long if they remain trapped. Help me clear away the fragments." He hummed some bursts of magic, which began to levitate some of the heavier pieces off the stack, and he sent them down to be taken elsewhere.

Mr. Swope straightened and made a command for help, and soon others had joined in the rescue. McKenna felt her dress rip as she swiveled back and forth, but she didn't care a whit about that. People climbed up on the mound, and she handed chunks of stone, wood, and plaster down. She cut her hand on a bit of broken glass and hissed in pain but continued to do her part.

More arrived to help, and a hole began to open in the midst of the ruins.

Then the widow sat up rigidly, covering her mouth with her hands. When she lowered them, she was gazing at McKenna with wonder in her eyes.

"I hear her! I hear my little girl singing! She's trying to make light!"

CHAPTER NINETEEN

The Injustice of Determination

All McKenna could think of was rescuing the children from the rubble, but it took hours, even after they were joined by random strangers who had responded to their calls for help. She sobbed with relief when the youngest children were found, crammed beneath a broken table, which had sheltered them from the worst of the collapse. But the oldest, the boy, was pinned beneath other sediment. The widow gathered her little ones around her, brushing the chalky plaster from their dirty faces as she kissed them again and again.

Efforts were redoubled to save the son, who went in and out of consciousness. Will-o'-the-wisps of light had gathered around the area, providing illumination for the workers. That the youngest children had been discovered alive was nothing less than a miracle. And everyone was rallying to extend that same miracle to the eldest boy, Jake, the lad that Rob had encouraged to grow in education so that he might someday become a sorcerer of the Invisible College. And then, finally, they reached the timber that had crushed his arm and kept him pinned in place, and they carefully removed it. McKenna recoiled at the injury and wondered instinctively if the boy would even survive, but he was immediately carried by Rob to an awaiting carriage to be rushed to a hospital.

Those who had gathered to help out clapped their hands in a cheer she felt in her chest. Rob's hair was gray with dust, giving her the impression that he'd aged into an old man during the ordeal. He motioned for her to join him at the carriage, and Mr. Swope followed.

He gazed into McKenna's eyes. "We need to go with him. I put the device in his pocket so it can try to heal him. If I don't stay near him, it will come back to me."

That had happened before. The device with the ring was magically connected to Rob.

She understood and agreed wholeheartedly. "What about Mrs. Farmer?"

"Let me see if Sarah can help her," Rob suggested. Using the ring, he contacted her mentally, and McKenna watched his brow furrow as he awaited a response. She didn't know when Sarah had gotten a ring or from whom, but it was clear her husband knew she had one. Then a relieved smile appeared on his face. The driver of the carriage wanted to get going and complained about the delay, but Rob insisted it would only be a few more minutes. He gave the widow the address to Sarah's home in the Storrows and then deposited some coins in her hand to pay for a conveyance to bring them there. The widow kissed Rob's cheek in gratitude, and he promised to inform her immediately, by messenger, when they arrived at the hospital.

The carriage lurched and they were underway. When they arrived at the hospital, which was overcrowded with injured people from the explosion, the lad was carried to a bed and a doctor was summoned to examine his injuries. The doctor had a thick mustache and perspiring bald head, but what McKenna noticed was the spattering of blood on his apron. Even though he'd probably been working nonstop since the explosion, he seemed determined to help the boy.

"He'll likely lose the arm," the doctor said to them. He pulled up the lad's eyelid to examine his eye, and Jake hardly responded. "Head injury too. And his leg might also be broken. Nothing we can do but wait for now. I'll make a decision about the arm in the morning." Then he hurried away to see another desperate patient.

Every chair in the massive hall was taken, so Rob and McKenna sat on the floor by the bed. Mr. Swope offered to find some food but insisted they should contact him immediately if trouble arose.

As she and Rob leaned against the bedframe, McKenna felt her exhaustion and relief quickly overpower her.

Rob's fingers slid through her dusty hair and she looked over at him.

"You were very brave," he said.

"I'm proud of you," she replied, then nestled against his shoulder and promptly fell asleep.

Rob jostled her awake, and as her bleary eyes opened, she was blinded by the sunlight coming in through the diaphanous curtains, which jarred her from the dream of walking through a snowstorm amidst dead horses and dead soldiers in rustic, ancient armor. Confused by the surreal scene, she needed a moment to remember where she was. And *who* she was. Rob helped her stand and she recognized the arrival of Mrs. Fiske along with the widow. Mr. Swope was nowhere to be seen at first, but after a quick search, she noticed him patrolling the hall.

The widow hurried to the bedside of the little boy, and McKenna watched as Robinson explained the doctor's grim assessment of the situation.

"If he loses his arm, he can't become a sorcerer," the widow said with a mournful expression. "Can he?"

Mrs. Fiske shook her head. "Society would reject him," she said, her expression showing a look of disgust and tempered anger.

"If his voice isn't damaged, he should be able to summon intelligences regardless," Rob said.

Sarah shook her head. "His abilities would be irrelevant. Coming from the tenements already imposes on his future. He wouldn't be able to give the sorcerer's handshake—"

"He could with his left hand," Rob interrupted, displaying annoyance.

"Professor, I would like to agree with you, but I myself have been subject to the discrimination of Society," Mrs. Fiske said, anger sparking in her eyes. "When I didn't fully recover from my illness, I lost my position at the quorum. I was demoted in rank."

Robinson gaped at her. "I didn't know."

She smoothed her dress and then faced the widow. "I wish it were otherwise, but your son may not be able to become a sorcerer if he loses his arm."

"Even though more sorcerers are needed for the war effort?" McKenna objected.

Mrs. Fiske shrugged. "Even so. Society still controls who is acceptable and who isn't. I know this firsthand, I'm sorry to say. One of my deaf students has been able to sing a spell, but I was told in no uncertain terms not to encourage her further."

"That is absolutely ridiculous," Robinson said with hot anger in his eyes.

McKenna felt as if she'd been punched. She'd wanted desperately to learn magic. She'd heard about Mrs. Fiske's successful student, Sandra Clegg Pond. According to reports, the deaf girl had learned three spells already. The injustice of denying her the chance to join the Invisible College made McKenna furious.

If Rob became the head of the Invisible College, perhaps he could persuade the system to change. Would he have the authority to mandate it? She hoped so.

The widow looked crestfallen by the news, but she sat down beside the bed and stroked her boy's cheek. His lashes fluttered and he awakened for the first time.

"M-Mama?" He gazed around in bewilderment.

"Rest, Son. Just rest."

"Where are the others?" the boy asked. McKenna positioned herself so she could see both of their mouths better.

"They're at Mrs. Fiske's grand house. Eating cakes and resting. You need to rest too." She smoothed his hair, giving him such a tender look it made McKenna's heart throb.

The boy noticed Robinson standing by the headboard. "S-Sir!" he gasped.

"You'll be all right," Rob told him. "You're going to be fine."

The frazzled doctor returned and asked the others to back away so he could examine the boy again. McKenna held her husband's hand and watched the doctor's face keenly as he studied the wounds.

"The swelling has gone down considerably," the doctor said with confusion. The device had been working slowly but surely, and the wounds and scratches on his face from the night before were gone. But would it be enough? "Can you lift your arm, lad?"

The boy complied and lifted it. He winced with pain, but it seemed more like soreness than anything deeper.

"I'm bedeviled," the doctor said, turning to face the adults. "I must be confusing this young man with another patient I saw last night. The arm was so badly mangled it seemed inevitable amputation was the only option."

"You can save his arm?" the widow asked with excited eyes.

"It wasn't in any real danger," the doctor said. "He's clearly in some pain, but the injury was far less severe than I thought. If he can walk on his own power, you can take him home. I need the bed for more injured patients."

McKenna felt Rob squeeze her hand. She gazed at his face, grinning, beyond grateful for him and for the device that had helped the boy.

"We need some rest and a change of clothes," Robinson told her. "I'll have Mr. Swope find a hotel."

"Nonsense," Sarah said. "I've plenty of room at my home. I insist that you all stay with me."

McKenna felt an unusual wariness. She knew and trusted Mrs. Fiske, but their friendship with the older woman was common knowledge. The *strannik* and his minions might be keeping an eye on Sarah's home. The widow and her children would be safe there, but they might not be.

She caught Rob's gaze as he was about to reply and gave a subtle shake of her head.

"That's generous of you, Sarah, but we'll find a hotel. It would be better if no one else knew where we were staying, and we should get back to Bishopsgate as soon as possible. I would like to meet your young student, though. Can we come by the school later and see Miss Pond?"

McKenna felt a little pinch of envy inside herself, but she rebuked the emotion as being too petty. After all, the girl wouldn't have been allowed to join the Invisible College anyway since deafness was prohibitive. "I'd like to meet her as well."

"You know you are always welcome at the school," Sarah replied. "I'm relieved about the boy's improvement. There may be hope for him becoming a sorcerer after all."

"I'm going to be one," the boy said with a look of total commitment.

Mrs. Fiske gave the child a look that was difficult to interpret. Like she was proud of him for wanting to achieve greatness but pitied him because it wasn't going to be easy.

"You can do anything you want to," the widow said, cupping her son's chin. "I know you can. Don't give up."

McKenna felt a twinge of unease as she witnessed the exchange. She'd believed that herself. But the world had been made in such a way that dreams were often dashed before they could ever be fulfilled.

A sorcerer once said that you can easily judge the character of a person by how they treat those who can do nothing for them. I found this platitude dull until I experienced the truth of it for myself. Friendly smiles and courteous offers will, more often than not, transform into the barking of dogs when a favor is asked or denied.

Kindness is often a deception. It is often a ploy that is self-serving and dissembling. This is true even of my own behavior. My willingness, as a well-to-do student, to lend money concealed an inner craving to be accepted by the fellowship of students. We both masqueraded our true intentions. It is not virtue if it is feigned. It is but a semblance of it.

—Isaac Berrow, Master of the Royal Secret,
the Invisible College

Isaac Berrow

CHAPTER TWENTY

That Which Tempers Justice

Fifteen years before the founding of the Invisible College

"I could buy you some new clothes, you know?" Isaac suggested after summoning the courage to pose the question. He and the Erlking's daughter had spent three days together while the snow silently fell outside. Days spent in deep discussion. Days in which he'd learned more magical knowledge than in all his time at the university. He was chagrined it had taken him so long to offer her new garments to replace the threadbare ones she'd been wearing. The thought of shopping for women's clothing was unappealing, to say the least, but once he'd put the offer out there, he could not in good conscience rescind it.

"I'm going to die in a few days, Isaac," she answered softly. The coughs had become worse. She was fighting feverish chills as well. "What I'm wearing then will make little difference when they lay my body in a pauper's grave."

"Isn't there anything I can do to help you?" he asked, feeling anguished at the thought of losing her so soon. "To slow the illness . . . to reverse it? Do not the Aesir have healing magic?"

"Some do," she said. "If they lay hands on you, recovery is possible. But the Aesir are still asleep, and there's no time for us to try another way. It takes a long while to make a philosopher's stone."

She was sitting on his roommate's bed, and he was sitting on a chair beside it. Close enough that he could see the dimples of gooseflesh on her arms as she shivered.

"How long does it take to make one?" he asked.

"Ten years. It's a meticulous spell. I'll show you the ingredients after I rest."

"You'd share that with me?" he asked in surprise.

She nodded, offering a kindly smile. "Knowledge should be shared, Isaac. Not hoarded. But not every person is willing to accept its burdens. You are."

He smiled sheepishly. "I'm pleased you think so. Isn't there anything I can do to help you? Anything at all? You've given me so much."

She looked down at her hands. There was something. He wasn't adept at reading expressions, but for some reason, he could tell.

"Tell me," he pleaded.

She started to cough again in great heaving spasms. Isaac hurriedly rose and fetched her some water. The coughing fits usually left her too weak to talk, sometimes for hours, and he dreaded that each episode might be her last. He had no idea how he was going to explain the bewildering events of the last few days to Blake when he returned from his family obligation. Actually, it would probably be better if he *didn't* say anything about it at all.

Isaac had learned secrets of magic that few other sorcerers knew. Almost anyone could summon a whorl of light by singing the right notes, but he could do so much more. The possibilities of magic went well beyond what the sorcerers of the day had derived from memoirs left by cryptic men ensconced in their alchemies. He'd learned the intricacies of harnessing intelligences, how those intelligences were persuaded most to obey sorcerers with sterling characters and integrity. He'd learned the arithmetical equations of how the universe worked, how planets and light and sound traveled astonishingly great distances. During her times of unconsciousness, he'd written copious notes in a cipher he'd invented to keep the knowledge she'd given him secret.

She accepted some water, but the convulsions had exhausted her, so she lay down on the bed and promptly fell into an exhausted sleep. He quietly removed the cup from her grip and set it down nearby. Hair had covered part of her face, and he had the urge to brush it aside. But that would mean touching her, and he'd never really touched a girl in such a way. Other than his mother and grandmother, of course, but that was different. She was closer in age to him, had given him knowledge and secrets that buzzed in his mind like the bees in the apple orchard near his family manor at Flamsteed. He wished he could bring her there, instead of keeping her cooped up in these humble lodgings. He would have loved to walk the grounds with her. In his mind, he envisioned them holding hands as they did so, and he felt a trembling rush of deep emotion that nearly overpowered his senses. He'd never been able to imagine himself falling in love. In the past, he hadn't been sure his heart was even capable of it.

Isaac took up his notebook and sat in his chair, but he hesitated writing down the latest batch of information she'd shared. His fancy of them in the orchard together kept distracting him. He couldn't dislodge the thought of seeing the apple blossoms and crooked branches with her, feeling the lush grass under their shoes. But it was winter, and spring was quite far away. He cleared his throat, trying to suppress the confusing swarm of feelings. Feelings were dangerous. Feelings were reckless. Feelings were illogical.

Yet there they were. Hinting. Hoping. Exciting. He gazed at her sleeping expression, feeling protective and worried and all sorts of things.

A knock sounded at the door, startling him. Her eyes flickered open.

Isaac left the small bedroom through the opening in the wall and hurried to the door. He gazed out the window first. Dusk was approaching again. How quickly the afternoon had passed. There was a fellow student outside, Alvin Thuernagle. He had borrowed money from Isaac at the beginning of the term, having pulled him aside to ask after one of their shared classes.

Isaac saw Alvin glance at the window with a look of desperation on his face as he pounded on the door again.

Isaac unlocked it but only opened it a few inches.

"Thank the Mind you're here," Alvin said. "I heard Blake was gone and was afraid you'd left as well."

"W-What can I do for you?" Isaac asked, keeping his foot against the door. If Alvin discovered a young woman in the rooms, asleep or not, it would cause a scandal.

"Can I come in?" Alvin pleaded.

"Just tell me what you want." The cold coming in from the door stung Isaac's nose.

"I'm out of funds," Alvin said. "I spent my last cuppers two days ago. I know I haven't paid you back from the previous loan. I thought I could make it stretch farther. I don't know who else I can turn to. I haven't squandered it. But . . . it's been so cold, and I was shivering and needed fuel for the stove. And then the landlord made an unjust demand."

Isaac felt annoyed by the disruption and also the request for more coins when the first batch hadn't been repaid, let alone with interest. Adding to the debt wouldn't be prudent for either of them.

"Please," Alvin said miserably. "I haven't eaten all day."

There was a part of Isaac Berrow that was made of flint, and that part of him wanted to shut the door in Thuernagle's face. There was no moral obligation to loan someone money who was a risky prospect. The other student was only in this position because of his own poor choices.

But Isaac knew he *could* help him. He had the means. Other students had repaid their debts on time, with interest, so he had enough to spare. And he realized, belatedly, that his first impression of the Erlking's daughter had been a profound misjudgment on his part. She had given him knowledge worth a king's ransom. How could he not be generous in return? If Isaac had been robbed days before, it would have been a different situation.

"I will repay you," Alvin insisted, his eyes looking frantic. "On my honor, I will."

"Just a moment," Isaac said. "Wait outside." He shut and locked the door. Then he walked to his room, where he kept his purse, and opened it. He reached in and felt the coins and then counted them into his hand one by one. And then added several more. And then another. He squeezed his fist around the money and walked back to the door and unlocked it.

Alvin looked on the verge of crying. He was shivering with the cold but also from his pent-up fear. It was a sign of his desperation that he'd come at all.

Isaac held out his fist, knuckles up. Alvin opened his palm beneath it, and Isaac poured the pile of coins inside. The other boy's eyes widened with shock.

"That's too much," he said, shaking his head. "I only need a little to tide me over."

"It's a gift," Isaac said. "You don't need to pay it back. Just . . . just help someone else when you can. Don't tell anyone I did this. It's just between you and me. Will you keep it a secret?"

Alvin's mouth hung open a moment, and then he grinned and nodded. And he reached through the door and hugged Isaac so hard he nearly swept him off his feet. Then, closing his hand around the coins, he offered a makeshift gesture of thanks before hurrying off into the snow, saying something about finding some dinner.

Isaac felt a warmth fill his chest. He shut and locked the door again, a smile, of all things, on his mouth. He felt almost giddy. It was a feeling he hadn't experienced very often, especially in his childhood being raised by his intellectual grandmother.

Turning his head, he saw the Erlking's daughter standing at the door to the room. She had a look of respect and even admiration on her face. That made the giddy feelings start to bubble up.

She closed the distance between them and wrapped her arms around him, burying her head against his chest. It was a second unexpected hug.

"I'm proud of you, Isaac. So proud."

He was abashed by her praise and attention, and confusing feelings continued to leap about inside his chest and his stomach. There was a little jig happening inside him at the moment, and it baffled him.

She looked up into his eyes.

He felt like laughing but didn't. "After all you'd given me, so freely, it felt . . . well, it felt *wrong* to turn him away. I know he can't repay me. But strangely, I don't care."

She nodded as if she understood him perfectly. "Justice is implacable. It is harder than ice a mile thick. It is the principle that my people hold in the highest esteem. Only one thing can temper it. Mercy. My mother taught me this. And there is too little of it in the world today. But you just brought about a little more." She reached up and caressed the side of his face.

Unbidden, he caught her hand as she tried to lower it. The feelings inside him had grown too strong. They surged like primordial lava venting from a cracked mountainside.

"There is something I can do for you, isn't there? Tell me what it is. If it is within my power, I will do it."

A sadness came over her face. "I don't think you will."

"If it is within my power, I will. I don't say this lightly."

"I know you don't, Isaac."

"Then why won't you tell me?"

"Because what I must say will frighten you. And I don't want to frighten you."

"Tell me what I can do for you. Do not fear me. Just *tell* me."

She lowered her head and pressed her forehead against his chest. "You must marry me before I die."

MaKenna Aurora Hawksley

CHAPTER TWENTY-ONE

The Deaf Girl's Song

Present day

McKenna felt a surge of nerves as the street tram made the stop near Brake Street. The magical mechanical conveyance wasn't as crowded as when they'd first boarded it, and she grabbed the rail to stand and stepped off into the street. As was her practice, she looked around to make sure nothing was coming, but Rob grabbed her hand and squeezed it, and she felt comforted by that small gesture. Glancing back at Mr. Swope, who had also climbed off the tram, she nodded at him and they started up the street together.

No words could have prepared her for the sight awaiting her up the street. Clenching her other hand into a fist, she pressed it into her stomach to try to quell the anxious feelings worming inside her.

The house was entirely gone.

"Oh, Rob," she breathed in devastation.

Brake Street was altered. A missing tooth was the first thought that came to mind, seeing the gap in the row of houses. Every childhood memory rushed to the surface. It was a home of love and tenderness, where Mother had discovered her own selfless nature and ability to nurture. Where her father had come home from his legal practice to sit in the parlor and listen to his daughters talk about their day. It was a place where Mary Trewitt had become a teacher, a confidante, a friend.

Much of the rubble had been carted off. The adjacent buildings, which had been scorched, still showed evidence of the damage caused by their proximity to the flames. It had been cleaned enough that it was not quite the horrifying scene that had been described to her, but that made no difference to McKenna Foster.

She thought of herself by her childhood name in that instant.

As they approached the ruins, she gazed at the pocked ground. Amidst the memories swirling inside her were recollections from the previous day when they'd clambered through the debris caused by the explosion of the saltpetr factory.

This was the *strannik*'s legacy. Destruction. He wanted to break down the cities, to bring life back to a simpler time. Of docile obedience and toiling over the land. If he had his will, her beloved Auvinen would be reduced to rubble.

A feeling of rebellion surged in her heart. She gazed up at her husband's sorrowful face. "We can't let Gregor Skoye win. We have to stop him."

He nodded, still gazing at the scene, lost in his own dark thoughts.

"Even the greenhouse is gone," McKenna said with another pang. "Memories of *us* were in that little shack. I wanted to show our children that place." She stamped her foot, shaking her head and fighting the hurt in her heart.

He caught her gaze. "Your home wasn't the wall and paint and nails. Everything it was, you still carry inside you. It's those intangible things that made it a home."

He was right. The most important things were the people who had lived there and made memories together. The dinners at Closure, the discussions in the parlor, the amorous kisses in the greenhouse. Those were memories that the *strannik* could never take away from her.

She sidled closer to him and squeezed his arm. "He tried to convince me that you weren't who you claim to be, but I never, for a second, believed him. Glamour doesn't work on me, so I see you for who you really are, Robinson Hawksley. And I love you for it."

She saw his cheeks burn a little with embarrassment and perhaps a little gratification. What man didn't want to be doted on by his spouse?

Seeing the ruins on Brake Street had been painful and difficult. But it had firmed her resolve to defy Gregor Skoye and his machinations with the Erlking. Part of her hoped he came to seize her again. She wanted Mr. Swope to put a bullet in him.

Where was the horrid man, anyway? He was probably skulking like the coward he was.

"I've seen enough," she said. "It will be rebuilt. And hopefully we can make it the same as it was before, even down to the delicious draft that makes the attic so cold. I think I'm ready to go to Mrs. Fiske's school. I want to meet this little girl who learned magic."

McKenna hadn't visited Mrs. Fiske's school very often and felt a little nervous doing so—mostly because she was older than the students and felt out of place—but she was set at ease as soon as she walked through the doors. There were posters with the Hawksley method on the walls in the classrooms they passed, familiar to her with its various symbols representing configurations of the mouth, teeth, and tongue. It brought back pleasant memories of her teacher, before he was her husband, and she squeezed his hand. She was also delighted to see how fond the children were of him. Several ran up to hug him, remembering the role he'd played in comforting and helping them during the plague that had hit the school. Sarah herself had been stricken by the grievous illness, which had made her lose her voice for a while. And, they'd come to find out, her standing in the Invisible College.

Mary Trewitt was their guide—she had taken a permanent position at the school—and McKenna and her old governess were able to catch up for a little while outside Sarah's office since she was in a meeting.

After a while, the door opened and an officer of the Marshalcy stepped out in his dark uniform. He nodded to them in greeting as he passed, and then Sarah appeared in the door to welcome them.

Before McKenna stepped inside, Mary pulled her into a quick embrace and promised they would see each other soon. McKenna had missed the opening of the conversation between Rob and Sarah, but she was able to catch up quickly. They were discussing the Marshalcy.

"We have officers coming every day now asking for help and assistance," Sarah explained while ushering them inside her office. "I'm worried because of the explosion. I don't want to put my children at risk, but they've been quite useful. And will be useful in the future. I've been asked to send as many children as I can to the University of Nirshoye for the upcoming convocation. You can imagine how excited and nervous they are to be of service."

"They would be. I don't think many have left Auvinen before, have they?"

"We have children from different countries actually. But most are from Auvinen. At least Society is beginning to acknowledge how special these children can be." She looked very pleased to be able to say that.

"I don't know why Society feels it must shun others," McKenna said, feeling a strong alignment of feeling with Sarah.

"Such as yourself?" Sarah said, her mouth curling with disapproval. "What you endured with all those wealthy families who had invited you over to hear about your husband's invention still rankles me."

"Now is our time to prove them wrong," McKenna said. "We came to see Miss Pond. To learn how she was able to start casting spells."

Sarah was suitably proud of the accomplishment and it showed. They were escorted to one of the classrooms where the little girl was working with her tutor, a young man with round-rimmed glasses and a gap in his front teeth.

"Mr. Fludd, I'd like to introduce you to—"

"Professor Hawksley!" the young man interrupted eagerly, coming forward and pumping Rob's hand. "It's an honor, sir, truly!"

"And this is Sandra," said Sarah, introducing them to the smiling ten-year-old with flax-colored hair and keen eyes.

"Hello," Sandra said and bobbed a little curtsy, which made her hair bounce.

Robinson immediately lowered himself to the little girl's eye level and extended his hand. She smiled and shook it.

"Will you cast a spell for me, please?" he asked her.

"Which one?"

"She can cast six now," Mr. Fludd said with a proud expression.

"Six? I'm impressed. Would you summon some light?"

Sandra nodded and softly sang, *"Hoxta-namorem."*

McKenna recognized the incantation—she'd tried to sing it herself a thousand times—but nothing had ever happened in response to her efforts, and a will-o'-the-wisp of light had already begun floating above the little girl's head.

A stab of envy shot through McKenna's chest, but she subdued it. This was the first deaf person who had managed to conjure a simple spell. That opened the door of possibility for all who might follow, McKenna included, and she wouldn't ruin it by being piqued or jealous.

"Very impressive," Rob said. He looked up at Mr. Fludd. "How did you teach her to sing the notes so perfectly?"

Mr. Fludd adjusted his glasses and then escorted them over to a table with two chairs where McKenna noticed a large mirror had been set up. Mr. Fludd held the chair for little Miss Pond, who sat down and scooted in. Mr. Fludd sat down next to her so that their reflections were very close. McKenna was able to read his lips through the mirror. It wasn't difficult at all for her.

"I was a private tutor of music before I became an elocutionist," said Mr. Fludd. "To be honest, I was in desperate need of a situation when I found out Mrs. Fiske and her school were seeking teachers, so I applied at once."

Rob and McKenna stood nearby. Mrs. Fiske was beaming with satisfaction.

"When I saw how well the Hawksley method worked, I was naturally curious to try teaching one of my deaf students to sing. Sandra used to work at a candymaker shop, and her mother always hummed and sang to her. She lost her hearing to the redoubtable fever when she was six. I noticed that she would sometimes hum some sea shanties she'd picked up as a child. That got me thinking."

He paused and then turned to the little girl. "Are you ready?"

"Yes," Sandra said with a bright smile.

They began to demonstrate. He put his hand on Sandra's throat, and she put her hand on his throat. McKenna watched him open his mouth and tilt his head up and down and Sandra did the same, following his motions. She realized the little girl wasn't speaking, she was singing.

Rob squatted by the edge of the table and watched the two of them do a series of what she imagined were singing exercises.

Once they'd run through several of them, the little girl grinned.

"The mirror helps her see what you are doing," Rob said. "And the connecting touches allows her to feel the vibrations."

"Precisely," said Mr. Fludd. "I had a particular student who had no sense of sound at all . . . truly, he couldn't carry a tune in a wheelbarrow. I thought of using the mirror method to help him see what music looked like on his face. How he opened his mouth, where it sat in his chest."

"It must have helped that Miss Pond had memories of music," Rob said.

Mr. Fludd nodded vigorously. "Absolutely critical. It's been several years, but she hadn't forgotten the shanties. Sometimes I use a little drum to help her understand beats." McKenna noticed one on the table.

McKenna was proud of the little girl, but she also felt defeated. She had no memory of music from her childhood. She'd never heard a sea shanty before, although she knew they were songs that sailors liked to sing and that they had interesting rhyming patterns. But she didn't recall ever having heard any. She didn't even have memories of her mother playing the Broadwood grand.

And she dreaded, instinctively, that such an absence in her life would forever bar her from achieving her goal.

Still, it was worth a try.

Robinson Foster Hawksley

CHAPTER TWENTY-TWO

Music and Memory

After seeing the demonstration of the mirror method, Robinson was keenly intrigued. He'd tried teaching McKenna magic a dozen different ways, including with a flame he'd magicked to respond to certain pitches, but the mirror seemed more straightforward. Judging by McKenna's expression, she was also intrigued. He caught her eye, seeking silent permission to ask for a more detailed demonstration. She gave a subtle nod.

"Would you mind demonstrating the technique again?" Robinson asked Mr. Fludd. "I wonder if it would work for my wife?"

"I would be happy to," replied the teacher with enthusiasm.

"I will bring Sandra to her next class," Sarah said. "Take your time. When are you planning to return to Bishopsgate?"

"We haven't decided yet," McKenna answered. "We'll say goodbye before we go."

"Thank you. The convocation is coming up. Do you know when you'll be traveling to the University of Nirshoye?"

"I haven't received my invitation yet," Robinson said.

"Ah. I'm sure they will start delivering those soon. McKenna, I'll be attending as well, though I won't be invited to be considered for the position. We can visit while Robinson is at the convocation."

"I've been given special permission to stay near him," McKenna said. "The inspector general has arranged it."

That triggered a surprised response from Sarah. "Oh. I didn't know. I can see why, after what happened after the Storrows. I'm glad you're allowed to be there."

Robinson discerned a tone of resentment in Sarah's words, which he attributed to her loss of rank due to the prejudices of Society after her throat had been damaged during the latest Aesir plague. He could hardly blame her, especially given all she'd done to help the Invisible College. Her leadership during the Awakening and the Aesir war had been admirable.

"Thank you for everything," he said, reaching out and taking her hand.

Sarah squeezed his hand in response. "Things will change after the convocation. For the better. I feel confident about that."

Was she implying that she believed *he* had a more than average chance of being elevated to the highest rank? It was gratifying, surely, but he was still very young and imagined someone like Mr. Guiteau was a more likely choice. Still, the possibility was . . . interesting. What if he could make some improvements to the order? He didn't want to let the eagerness of his thoughts get ahead of him, though.

After they had commended Sandra for her impressive accomplishments and wished her well, Sarah took her out of the room.

"Now, Mrs. Hawksley," Mr. Fludd said, making sure he was noticed by her, "if you'll take the seat right here. With your permission, of course, I'll need to touch your throat, and you mine?"

"Of course, Mr. Fludd." McKenna seated herself facing the mirror. Robinson caught her gaze in the reflection and gave her an encouraging wink. He intended to observe the details minutely so he could replicate the techniques himself at home.

"Ah, very well. I've trained many vocalists over the years. Singing happens from the diaphragm," the teacher said, demonstrating the position in his chest with one hand.

"I'm aware of the principles, Mr. Fludd," McKenna said nervously. "I just can't do it."

"Well, we shall try. Put your hand on my throat. I will sing a note. A middle-range note."

McKenna lifted her hand and touched Mr. Fludd's throat. He proceeded to sing a C without any assistance from a musical instrument.

"You have perfect pitch, don't you?" Robinson asked, impressed.

"Thank you, I do. Let's try again. *Daaaaaw*," he sang.

McKenna was watching him through the mirror, her brow wrinkling. "'Daw'?"

"It's not a word. Just a representation of the sound at that pitch. You try it."

McKenna screwed up her face and said the word but not in a singing voice.

"Feel the vibration in my throat," the teacher coaxed. "Watch my lips. In the Hawksley method, the tongue is on the palate just for a whisker." He repeated it several times, letting her feel the vibration in his throat. "Now you try it again." He put his hand on her throat. Robinson wondered if that was a principle of resonance.

McKenna tried again but did not produce a note anywhere near the C. Mr. Fludd was encouraging and kept repeating the same note, taking more time to talk about the mouth, the lips, the tongue, but Robinson could tell she was becoming increasingly frustrated.

"I can't do it," she finally said, lowering her hand. No doubt having watched little Sandra perform some spells had made her feel worse about her own inability to do so.

"Mrs. Hawksley, I implore you to keep trying. Sandra was singing before she lost her hearing. She has memories of music. You do not, but that does not mean you cannot learn."

"This isn't the first time I've tried, Mr. Fludd. I just feel this . . . resistance inside me. And, honestly, being observed by you and my husband makes me feel more self-conscious."

"That's perfectly understandable, but look at all you've accomplished. I've been teaching at this school for many months and have worked with children who lost their hearing at varying ages. Your diction, your pronunciation is exquisite. How you follow conversations without missing a word. I'm frankly astonished."

"I do miss words, Mr. Fludd. I just . . . I don't know . . . I can make up for them. Decipher them from context."

"That is hardly commonplace, Mrs. Hawksley. Most children struggle to do what you take for granted. Singing differs from speaking. It activates different parts of your body."

McKenna frowned, but Robinson could see she wasn't ready to give up. Her determination was strong. She nodded and lifted her hand to the teacher's throat. They tried again and again without results.

She looked desperate and sad, but Robinson gave her an encouraging nod.

"Let's try it another way," Mr. Fludd said. He didn't seem the least bit frustrated or annoyed by McKenna's lack of progress. His personality in general was so patient and enthusiastic it made him an excellent teacher. "I want you to try yawning. Think of something very dreary and boring. Counting backward from one thousand. How tedious would that be?" He made an exaggerated yawn, all the while keeping her fingers pressed to his throat. "You try."

McKenna gave an impressive yawn.

"That's it!" Mr. Fludd said. "Did you feel the difference in the vibration? Not the same as talking. Try it again!"

McKenna did so, and Mr. Fludd copied the tone of her yawn. Then he shifted his, yawning a perfect C.

And McKenna repeated it.

"That was it!" Robinson said, feeling a thrill shoot through him.

McKenna looked surprised. "I sang a note?"

"You sang a C," Mr. Fludd said. "Well done, Mrs. Hawksley! Let's try another note. A simple spell usually has three or four different note variations. It's just as important to convey a feeling to summon intelligences as it is to hit precise notes. But singing is very much like yawning!"

They practiced again, and this time McKenna was fully engaged, her eyes bright, a triumphant smile on her mouth. Robinson was so happy for her that he was bursting with pride. He didn't care that he hadn't been the one to teach her. No, it was more important that she was finally having a breakthrough.

"Second note. *Maaaay.* Feel the difference?"

"I can," McKenna said.

It took several tries, but she hit the note. Robinson clenched a fist and felt like leaping in the air. McKenna met his gaze in the reflection, trying to suppress a smile.

"Well done again, Mrs. Hawksley. Those are the first two notes that we'll use to make up the word '*Hoxta.*' *Maay-Daaw! Hox-ta!* In this variation, there are only three notes to learn for the phrase. You've learned two of them. Well done!"

"H-Hox-ta," McKenna sang. It wasn't exactly in tune, but it was close.

"Almost," Robinson said.

She bit her lip. "What's the third note? Is it higher or lower?"

"It's lower than the other two. It's on a lower scale. But not too low for you. More contralto than soprano. I'm sorry for using musical terms. Professor Hawksley understands. This note is 'sow' but an octave lower than what you've been singing. Let's try it on the upper register first." He took her hand and put it on his throat. *"Daaw . . . Maay . . . Soow."*

McKenna tried copying it and got it after her fifth attempt. Robinson couldn't stop grinning. His wife was on the verge of casting her first spell—finally, after all the work she'd put in.

"Excellent. On a musical scale, the notes repeat both higher and lower. Seven total notes, not including sharps and flats. We'll get to that concept another time. This version of Hoxta-Namorem comprises three notes. The sound for 'sow' is what you'll use for 'na' but an octave lower. Feel the difference. *Sooow . . . sooooooow.*" The second one was sung in G but an octave lower.

McKenna wrinkled her brow. "May I?" she asked, bringing her other hand over and putting it on Mr. Fludd's chest.

He repeated the different tones. "The second one vibrates lower in the chest. I'll leave it to your husband to practice that range with you. But you can feel the sound comes from lower than your throat, can you not?"

"Yes," McKenna said, her brow still perturbed.

"Now you try it."

"I don't think . . . I should," she said.

"It's just a different register, Mrs. Hawksley. It's not too low for a female. Try it. *Hoxta-namorem.* We go back to the pattern of the other two notes for 'morem.' *Hox-ta-na-mor-em.*"

McKenna stared at herself in the mirror, as if transfixed by his words, by the moment. Robinson studied her face, hoping she would make the breakthrough and step through the window leading into a new world. He knew how much she wanted it. And, he had to confess to himself, he wanted it *for* her.

She gazed at herself and then sang the lowest tone perfectly. It was a powerful contralto voice, one that sent chills down his spine. He felt the tingle of magic, the awakening of something inside her. He sensed Loyal in the room as if the dog intelligence were perking up its ears and paying attention to that sound.

McKenna's mouth twitched with a triumphant smile, but then her expression melted into a look of absolute terror.

She stood up suddenly and rushed to the door. It happened so quickly that both Robinson and Mr. Fludd were stunned by her flight.

"P-Professor?" Mr. Fludd asked in confusion. "Did I offend?"

Robinson gave the man a squeeze on his shoulder and rushed out of the room, the sound of McKenna's running footsteps telling him where she'd gone. He raced after her and saw her taking the staircase down as she hurried to the front door. He called after her, momentarily forgetting she was deaf, and then ran as fast as he could.

He didn't catch up with her until she was almost to the street corner at a busy intersection filled with pedestrians and street trams. He grabbed her elbow to halt her flight and she spun, eyes feverish and wet with tears.

"I can't, I can't," she sobbed, trying to hug him and wrench away from him at the same time.

"What happened?" he asked in dismay.

She was too agitated to speak. Several onlookers were gazing at them worriedly. There was a bench made of wrought iron and wood nearby, and he guided her to it and helped her sit down. She clung to him, weeping against his shoulder.

"I can't do it, Rob. I can't!"

"But you were so close," he said, stroking her head. Mr. Swope approached with a look of concern, his pistol in his hand, but Robinson dismissed him with a shake of the head. Mr. Swope backed away, concealing the weapon, looking around for the sign of a threat.

McKenna had a wild look in her eyes, the kind she got when she was having one of her nightmares. Her fingers on his jacket dug in painfully.

"If I do it, I will die. Don't you understand? I know it. I don't want to lose you again. Not again. Not so soon."

Robinson realized, with a sense beyond comprehension, that he wasn't talking to McKenna anymore. This frantic, desperate creature was the Erlking's daughter in possession of McKenna's body. A Semblance. He didn't want it to be so public. Couldn't bear the thought of one of the military men showing up and putting a bullet into her skull.

"I'll protect you," he said, face to face, his voice low, whisper-like.

"I will *die*," she insisted passionately. "Believe me, Isaac. Believe me!"

Robinson felt a jolt of fear and curiosity. She'd called him by another name. Isaac. Had the Erlking's daughter known Isaac Berrow?

There was no record of it, not in any of the old sorcerer's written works. He wanted to ask questions, wanted to learn what he could from her, but she was terrified, and he also needed to console her.

"Please," she said, shaking her head and pressing against him, weeping. "Not again. Not so soon." And she wept as if grieving something . . . someone . . . she'd lost long ago.

CHAPTER TWENTY-THREE

The Growing Toil

Robinson saw the gentle rise and fall of McKenna's bosom and knew she'd fallen asleep. The way she lay on the mattress, one hand tucked under her cheek, tugged at his heart. They were back at the hotel, later that same afternoon, and she'd fallen asleep so quickly. After rousing from her panic, she'd begged to return to the hotel to rest. He hadn't hesitated to agree.

Although he was also exhausted, he was too rattled to sleep, so he carefully slipped off the bed and went to the door. He twisted the handle, letting himself into the communal area in the middle of the suite. There was Mr. Swope, pacing, an angry scowl on his face.

"She's going to sleep for a few hours. If you'd like some time to yourself, you're welcome to it," Robinson offered.

Mr. Swope put his hands on his hips. "Is she all right? Truly?"

There were some truths too fraught to be spoken. "She will be, I think."

Mr. Swope sighed. "She's had these little . . . fits . . . since the day she nearly drowned," Mr. Swope said. "I still remember when she came back to Mowbray House, dripping seawater from head to toe. She'd gotten dragged out to sea by a rogue wave. I still feel guilty about it."

"Guilty? It was my fault she was distracted that day," Robinson said, shaking his head. "And I know what you mean. I felt dreadful when I found out. Still do."

"I remember watching her leave that day. A passing thought came that I should accompany her, just to be sure. But my employer had assured me she was safe near the sea. And I had other business at hand." He sighed again. "Things changed that day. Then, as if nearly drowning weren't devastating enough, she was abducted by zealots. In my earlier career, I used to investigate the kidnapping of children."

"I didn't know that," Robinson said. They were both standing in the room, neither making a move for the sofa or a chair.

"I don't like talking about that time. Some neighborhoods were especially prone to such evils. We rarely found the children, but on occasion we did. Some, after we'd rescued them, pleaded to be taken back to their abductor. Being taken away, forcibly, had changed them somehow. I can't help but wonder what else she suffered after Skoye took her." There was a dangerous look in his eye. A look that said he wanted vengeance and was determined to have it.

"We've spoken at length about it," Robinson said. "She was desperate to escape him."

"Why did they take her, though? Were they hoping for a ransom?"

Again, the secret loomed between them. "No. He is as determined as he is wrong-headed."

"If he's so wrong-headed, why have so many joined his movement? A friend of mine keeps me informed of such things. Before he was murdered, Master Drusselmehr made an invention to try to discover who was part of the faction. A toy that would report any talk supporting the *strannik*."

Robinson nodded. "He admitted as much to me. What has your friend learned?"

"Those toys have been shipped to every city. They were working and then . . . they stopped working. The magic responds to people talking in the language of this zealot. Certain words or phrases trigger the intelligence controlling the magic, which will then send out a signal. But there have been no more signals. Not a single one."

That was new information. "He found out. And he's warned his followers."

"But how could he disseminate the information so thoroughly and quickly? It should have taken much longer. I think we need someone to infiltrate the order. Find out where and when they meet. Who the other ringleaders are. I'd like to get my hands on some of them."

Robinson could only imagine the interrogation techniques he'd use to wring information out of them. "The *strannik* is a dangerous foe. Stopping him should continue to be our highest priority."

"I agree, sir. If you don't mind, I'll go take a walk. I feel restless. I'll keep the ring on my thumb and stay nearby. Do let me know if anything happens while I'm gone."

"I will." He paused, grateful for Mr. Swope and his protection. "I appreciate all you've done for us. McKenna does too."

"Glad to be of service," he said, tipping his hat, and then he left the room. Robinson locked the door after he was gone and sat down on the couch. He ruminated, wondering where the *strannik* was hiding himself. Was he in Auvinen, or had he sent his minions to trigger the explosion? It would take months to repair such extensive damage. Not to mention what it would cost the military to lose the factory before the war effort kicked off again. Surely the generals had stockpiled enough saltpetr, but there would be an impact. There could be no doubt about it.

Then his thoughts drifted back to what the Erlking's daughter had said to him while they were on the bench. The deep sadness she'd felt. The loss of someone she'd loved. And she'd mentioned the name Isaac . . .

Isaac Berrow had never married. He'd devoted his life to his research at the University of Nirshoye, one of the oldest universities in the empire. Although Robinson had attended one of his father's lectures there, he didn't remember the place well. Rather, he remembered certain details. Nirshoye had been built on an outcropping of rock connected to the mainland by a natural land bridge, and the ocean crashed beneath its cliffs. There were many little islands in the area, all dating back before the sea had hammered away at the cliffs and begun to break them apart. The streets were narrow and dark, the cobblestones filled with ruts from wagons. It was like stepping into a chasm of time.

He thought about the upcoming convocation, which would take place at Nirshoye, and the process of choosing the new Master of the Royal Secret. What was this secret? The empire had been founded long before Isaac Berrow's time. It was a common belief that the "royal" secret had to do with some information handed down to the royal family. But what if that wasn't true? Or the royal line in question was the Erlking's?

Robinson was not ambitious by nature, but he did wish to know the secret. He pinched his nose and sighed. Best not to get his hopes up.

A thought came to his mind, cutting through the noise of his musings. It had the force and strength of Mr. Foster.

Put on your ring. I have news to communicate.

Robinson ducked his hand into his pocket and quickly freed his own sorcerer's ring. He slid it on his thumb. *I hear you. What is it?*

Miss Cowing's barrister has offered a settlement deal. They want fifty percent ownership of the patent. He believes there will be enough money to make both parties wealthier than anyone can imagine. They're prepared to contest the military's role in this mess and side with us.

There was silence in Robinson's mind for a moment. *What do you think, Mr. Foster?*

I think they believe they're in a bad position. They risk losing all profits and contracts. Better to win half than lose all. That is my assessment. I'm inclined to reject the offer.

Robinson had to agree, and yet . . . *If we don't settle this now, it could drag on for months. I don't really care about the money.*

I know you don't. I would advise not giving away half to this ploy of theirs. They have more to lose than we do.

Robinson snorted under his breath. *We've lost almost everything so far. Well, the house will be rebuilt. That's good news at least.*

It is not the time to let emotions rule. Do I have your support to reject the settlement offer?

I wish to speak to McKenna about it first. I'll go with whatever she decides. My shares belong to her. She should decide what to do with them.

A brief moment of silence. *Understood. Will you talk to her now?*

She's resting. We're both exhausted. We'll talk later, and I'll let you know her decision.

Very well. Thank you.

The connection ended, and Robinson took off the ring and massaged his aching temples. He didn't want to wake her. Not for this. But he did wish to talk to someone about what had passed between them earlier. The only other person who knew it all was Mrs. Foster.

After another quick rub of his temples, he put the ring back on.

Dinner was at a small local restaurant later that evening. It was on a secluded street, nestled between a couple of shops selling scarves of all things. McKenna was more subdued that evening and Robinson was still nursing a blistering headache from using the sorcerer's ring so much. The meal was a pleasant-tasting clambake with some savory herbs and fresh baked bread. There were only three other couples in the restaurant, and the noise from the kitchen was louder than the sounds the guests were making.

"What do you think of your father's advice?" he asked during a lull in the meal after explaining about the settlement offer from Miss Cowing.

McKenna answered immediately. "We should reject it."

"Tell me your thoughts on it. You made up your mind so quickly."

"I used to discuss Father's cases with him when he'd come home for dinner. This kind of ploy is typical among unscrupulous barristers. That man's serving his own interests as much if not more than his client's. If he thought they were going to win, he'd have not made the offer."

Robinson would have been interested in eavesdropping on those conversations in the parlor. It didn't surprise him that McKenna's father had been interested in her insights, even at such an age.

"I don't really care about the money," Robinson said. "I'd rather end the dispute. But this isn't just about the financial impact."

"No." She looked him in the eye. "General Colsterworth's schemes are behind this, and his actions were reprehensible. I don't believe Miss Cowing invented your bulb. She may not have stolen it from you, but you had the idea first. Settling out of court is now her best option. It's not ours."

"If my patent proves to be the legitimate one, then we'd next have to pursue a case against the military."

"If they're smart, they'll try to reach a settlement with you. General Colsterworth is dead. There is no punishment we can contrive that can possibly injure him. I would accept a settlement if they offered a fair one."

Robinson nodded. "I agree, and I'm glad you feel the same way. All of this has been a distraction." He reached across the table. "I'd rather be back at Mowbray House with you, inventing new things."

"Rob, that may not be our future."

"Why do you say that?"

"I think you were destined for greater things. We'll always own that home, but you might end up needing to travel a great deal."

He furrowed his brow and shook his head. "What you're implying would be a great burden."

"Some men are born for greatness," she said with a charming smile and squeezed his hand.

He felt his cheeks begin to get warm. "I don't have any delusions that I'll be able to overturn the sentiments of Society, although I vehemently disagree with them. The posturing is especially galling to me."

"And I love you for you. Perhaps in this case your *stubbornness* will prove the deciding factor."

"Stubbornness isn't a virtue, Mrs. Hawksley."

"What Society needs most is someone who doesn't give a dropped plum about their ways or sentiments. Besides, Society won't choose the next leader of the Invisible College. Your peers will."

Her words had made his stomach start to act strangely. It was more than just raw excitement. Strangely, he felt as if the decision had already been made. He was about to ask her a question when he noticed she was staring at something.

"Someone stopped in the street," she said softly, eyes still fixed elsewhere. "He's watching us. He's so close, I can see his features clearly. I don't recognize him."

Though his skull was still throbbing from the last time he'd used the ring, Robinson reached into his pocket and slid it on.

Mr. Swope. Are you near the restaurant?

The reply came immediately: *I'll be right there.*

"I've summoned Mr. Swope," he told McKenna in an undertone, then began to hum a shield spell to protect the two of them. Would it be enough?

"Is he still there?" he asked McKenna quietly, his stomach beginning to twist with dread.

"He's looking around. I don't like how furtive he's being."

He's standing outside at the window, Robinson told Mr. Swope. *I'm going to take McKenna out the back through the kitchen.*

I'm almost there, Mr. Swope responded.

And then McKenna started when Mr. Swope appeared at the window. Robinson watched as their protector grabbed the man by the arm and proceeded to push him against the window casing, startling the other diners.

Squeezing McKenna's hand, Rob waited until he had her attention, then said, "Be ready."

Mr. Swope was talking to the man, whose back was to them. What was being said? Did either of them have a weapon out? It wasn't obvious from their vantage point.

Then, to Robinson's surprise, Mr. Swope disappeared with the stranger—only for the door to open twenty seconds later, admitting both of them to the restaurant.

Mr. Swope promptly brought the young man to their table. "My name is Jacob Beckley Jones," he stammered, looking unnerved. "I've come from Wulfram College in Bishopsgate as that is your new quorum. Had to hunt you down, Professor. I have your invitation to the convocation in my pocket."

CHAPTER TWENTY-FOUR

Summons to Court

They spent one additional day in Auvinen before another summons came—the court order had been fulfilled, and Judge Bache was ready to reconvene the trial. They'd stayed to help make arrangements for Mrs. Farmer, who required new lodgings and help paying for her injured son's medical bills. The boy was recovering well, which Robinson was relieved to see. While the Marshalcy was still investigating what had caused the blast, there was little doubt in Robinson's mind that the *strannik* was responsible. His devious mind was capable of any atrocity. He had to wonder if Mr. Guiteau was involved, directly or indirectly. At the house in Bishopsgate, the older man had suggested using McKenna as bait to draw the *strannik* out. It made him want to confront the man, but his focus had to be on getting McKenna out and to safety.

Mr. Swope arranged for tickets on the evening locomotivus, and they spent the day saying their farewells. First to the widow and her family. She kissed their hands and thanked them over and over for coming to help. Her son, Jake, gave Robinson a determined handshake and promised he'd become a sorcerer someday. Afterward, they went to Sarah's school and visited with her and Miss Trewitt awhile. McKenna mentioned feeling uneasy being there, however, remembering what had happened after her attempt at magic. She told him she had no desire to bid farewell to Mr. Fludd, and they beat a hasty retreat.

There was time to stroll the promenade near downtown and enjoy a bag of sugared peanuts. McKenna became uneasy amidst the crowd and told him so, worried that one of the *strannik*'s minions was watching them. She gripped Rob's arm and sighed with relief when it was time to take the street tram to the station.

There were still unusual crowds trying to leave town, but they managed to board the locomotivus and find their private car. Mr. Swope had arranged for a lesser fare for himself, his seat close enough that he could keep watch on the door heading to their compartment.

Alone at last, McKenna snuggled against him, and he felt a little thrill at the sense of acceleration as the locomotivus left for Bishopsgate.

"Can I see the invitation again?" she asked, peering up at his face.

Robinson quickly pulled it out of his coat pocket. It was a rectangular piece on heavy cardstock, about the size of a postcard. One side had a painting of the tied island of Nirshoye with its land bridge and surf crashing against the rocks. They'd seen another postcard with a different image of the famous university on it, a picture from the street view with its famous gate and scalloped rooflines. She examined the card and then flipped it over so they could both read it again.

Invitation to: Robinson Foster Hawksley

A convocation of sorcerers

to be held at the University of Nirshoye,

founding place of the Invisible College

by Isaac Berrow, Master of the Royal Secret.

Present card for admittance on 12 Equinox.

Admittance includes: McKenna Hawksley, Arthur Swope.

“The script is elegant,” she said. “And I’m glad they included my name and Mr. Swope’s.” Although it looked handwritten, Robinson knew the technique used and told her that devices harnessing the intelligences of squids had been used to overlay the card with color and ink. Each invitation was unique, not a replica stamped by a machine.

Because of the lateness of the hour, she began dozing off during the conversation. “I’m sorry,” she apologized after catching herself the third time.

Robinson offered his lap as a pillow. She lay down on it, and he started to stroke her hair and her arm. He wished they could be at their own place, Mowbray House, which was thankfully theirs once again, without all the cares and troubles of court cases, rival inventions, and a sinister man trying to upend things.

When they arrived at Bishopsgate just after dawn, Mr. Foster was waiting for them with the carriage, along with the driver, Mr. Hughes. McKenna hugged her father and greeted Mr. Hughes before they all climbed inside the carriage and went to the house.

“Do you have any information from court?” Robinson asked.

Mr. Foster shook his head. “Judge Bache has the final report. He will be announcing the results when court reconvenes the day after tomorrow. He knows about the settlement offer and our response. Neither side has withdrawn their claims thus far.”

McKenna’s look was curious. “Does that mean Miss Cowing is unlikely to withdraw?”

Mr. Foster pulled off his pince-nez glasses and cleaned them with a handkerchief. “Unlikely, yes. If she withdraws her claim on the patent at this point, she’ll get nothing. Their hope is likely that the judge will grant her a portion if the results are muddled. We have a strong case. Robinson kept thorough notes, and we have reliable witnesses who have been interviewed under oath. I believe it will end in our favor."

"But how long can they drag this on?" Robinson asked.

McKenna looked at him worriedly.

"There is an appeals process. The losing side can take that path, and if they do, the trial will continue into next year."

Robinson shook his head in disgust. She patted his leg. "Be patient. I believe we will win."

"It shouldn't have to take this long," he said.

Mr. Foster nodded in sympathy. "Unfortunately, that's how the law works. The cogs of justice might turn slowly, but this is a better system than what was used in the past, when such matters were dependent on the whims of rulers. Or favors they wished to bestow. Certain privileges were awarded because of marriage alliances."

"You have a point," Robinson admitted.

"Has there been any word about the upcoming convocation?" McKenna asked. "Rob received his invitation."

"Twelve Equinox is coming soon," Mr. Foster said. "There may be another delay in court because of it. I hope not. We'll take the locomotivus to Telimar and then a ship to Nirshoye. Some will have to travel quite early to get there in time. We are fortunate to be so close to the coast."

"Rob's been to Nirshoye before. But I don't think I have."

As she said the words, her expression began to alter. She put her hand on her breast, as if in pain—and a wave of intuition hit Rob hard. The memory she was having in that moment wasn't her own.

⁂

Judge Bache had a stern look on his face as he glanced down at the sheaf of papers displayed on an elevated stand on the desk in front of him. Robinson sat solemnly by Mr. Foster, in turmoil over what might happen. The opposing counsel and Miss Cowing were at the other table. The counsel looked surly, not elated. Was that a positive sign? Miss Cowing's expression was void of emotion. She guarded her feelings.

"Come to order," said the judge. He gazed at the occupants of one table and then at the other. "I have received the report on the findings. The circumstances surrounding the acquisition of the rings, and the rings' properties, have been established by creditable sorcerers. Their properties have been too. It is also my understanding from the inspector general of the Marshalcy that they are being used to apprehend criminals. But that is not the purview of this court. This court's purpose is to determine who owns the patent rights to the tubes that glow in the presence of Aesir magic." He paused and looked at the two parties again.

Robinson clenched his fingers. Tension hung in the air. The judge seemed disturbed by something.

"I understand that a settlement offer was presented and rejected. Is that so?"

Mr. Savage lifted his hand. "I would like the record to show that we tried to resolve this out of court."

"Mr. Savage, you are contemptible," Judge Bache snapped. "You have persuaded your client to pursue this matter, even in the face of credible evidence undermining your case."

The exclamation startled Robinson, who sat up straighter in his chair.

"Your Honor," Mr. Savage said, his face turning beet red.

"I'm not finished, Mr. Savage. It is clear to anyone with eyes or a partially functioning brain that Professor Hawksley came up with the idea first. His workbooks lay out the facts. What was unclear to me, until this report, was whether there was any cooperation between the two inventors. There was clearly none. Not wittingly anyway. Because the rings enable transmutation of thought, I find it probable and likely that Miss Cowing was inspired by Professor Hawksley's imagination, and her discovery, as it were, happened after his. He also had the sagacity to implement his idea, whereas your client didn't get that far. Given as such, the timing in the patent office is almost irrelevant to me, but it does matter." He paused again and looked at Mr. Foster. "Do you have any objections, sir?"

"None whatsoever," Mr. Foster said without any change of expression. Robinson found himself holding his breath in anticipation. Was it really ending this way?

"Do you, Mr. Savage?"

"This is highly irregular, Your Honor!" protested Mr. Savage.

"An interesting turn of phrase, Mr. Savage. What is irregular is that this case has proceeded so far given how little merit it has." He looked quite stern. "Were you or your client aware, Mr. Savage, that Professor Hawksley's invention was undermined at the Great Exhibition? That its display location was deliberately altered, the devices themselves tampered with, and the judges—of whom Miss Cowing was one—were directed to avoid the display entirely? Does this not seem unusual to you, Mr. Savage? Or . . . 'irregular' as you called it?"

Mr. Savage's eyes widened with surprise.

"This is not evidence that Mr. Foster presented, nor would I expect a man of his integrity to even suggest such a thing. He has laid out the facts of the patent case. The timing, the dates. As I understand, his daughter, Professor Hawksley's wife, was the person who made and saved records of the timeline." The judge inclined his head to McKenna as he said the words, offering her a nod of acknowledgment. "What is clear to me is that there has been a conspiracy from the start to steal the professor's invention from him and prevent him from being properly compensated for it."

"Your Honor," Mr. Savage said, raising his voice. "My client's only intention has ever been to help improve sorcerous inventions."

The judge's gaze shifted in Mr. Savage's direction. Moments later, the judge said, "Sir, we are at war with an alien race who is intent on our utter destruction. Some among us are convinced that their sense of propriety and justice is superior to our own. That we would do well to lay aside the magic they taught us and submit ourselves to their authority for our survival. I cannot disagree in stronger terms. Justice will be done in my courtroom. I rule that the patent for this invention has been rightly earned and deserved by Professor Robinson Hawksley. I also rule that all contracts, agreements, and inventory made and in the process of being made are the rightful property of Mr. Hawksley—and he can lease, sell, or dispose of such property as he and his business partners see fit."

Robinson, thrilled to his core, shook his head in disbelief at the turn of events. Mr. Foster was sitting back in his chair, observing the time on his pocket watch. He risked a glance at the opposing table and saw Mr. Savage with his head in his hands. Miss Cowing's cheeks looked flushed.

"Now," said Judge Bache, "I am well aware that you are entitled to appeal my decision. It is your prerogative, Miss Cowing. But I implore you, for the sake of decency, to do the right thing and decline such a measure, which would only prolong the inevitable. I was approached by a new witness who told me about the exhibition and the deceit and subterfuge that happened there. I don't believe you were party to it, Miss Cowing. If I believed you were, I would direct the Marshalcy to investigate you, as I have directed them to investigate the others. Your barrister has led you astray. If I were you, I would fire him at once and find better counsel."

"Thank you, Your Honor," Miss Cowing said, her cheeks still pink. She turned to her barrister. "I no longer require your incompetence or your advice."

Robinson turned around to look at his wife. McKenna beamed at him.

"Mr. Foster, I will notify General Ambrose of my decision. You can expect a representative from the military to acquaint you of their . . . *ahem* . . . assets, which you gentlemen are now the owners of. This session is adjourned."

McKenna Aurora Hawksley

CHAPTER TWENTY-FIVE

An Offering

It was Closure and McKenna's family had gathered at the Bishopsgate house for a special dinner. Not only did it commemorate the end of the trial, but Wickins had proposed marriage to Clara that very day and she'd accepted. McKenna was overjoyed by the back-to-back developments, and having the family together under the same roof made it all the sweeter.

Neither Clara nor Wickins were interested in a winter wedding, so the nuptials had been planned for spring. They sat together on one of the settees in the cozy parlor after dinner, their hands interlaced. Clara's coming-of-age party had been postponed due to McKenna and Rob's travels to pitch his invention last summer, and Clara had wanted them there, but it had been long enough, so it was scheduled to follow the convocation.

"I want to have it in Auvinen," Clara said to Mother. "All our friends are there. And some of the officers Wickins is friendly with. We can afford to rent a ballroom, I should think."

"Of course we can have it in Auvinen," Mother agreed. "If Sarah offers her home to host it, we should at least consider it."

Clara's brow wrinkled with stubbornness. "I'm earning my own wages now. I don't want to make it seem like we need charity. Don't you agree, John?" The way she squeezed his hand was enough of a prompting.

"Whatever you think, my love," Wickins said amicably. "Not that Mrs. Fiske's home isn't splendid, mind you. But this should be your celebration, Clara. You deserve it."

McKenna glanced at Rob to see which conversation he was paying attention to, but he had a brooding, distant look as he sat next to her, rubbing his mouth. She wondered if he was thinking about some of the letters that had arrived following Judge Bache's decision. Many of their investors were anxious to know whether an accord could be reached with Miss Cowing to prevent her from appealing the decision. The first hurdle had been passed, but folks were always uptight about money matters, and they wanted to know whether their investment would yield the returns they craved. She hoped she and Rob would be able to go off to Siaconset soon, before the late-winter storms made sea travel more precarious. If they could travel there in secret, they might be safe from the *strannik* or others who wished them ill.

All she wanted was for them to be by themselves. Illogical or not, she felt that was the only way they'd be protected.

Father had a stack of mail and was reading it in his comfortable chair. The next envelope he picked up had the emblem of the military on it. After he unfolded the letter within, he sat up straighter and said, "Listen here." The other conversations lulled as everyone gave him their attention. Trudie was reading a book, but she folded it closed and gazed at Father.

McKenna nudged Rob, who looked at her, and she nodded to her father.

"General Ambrose has asked to pay us a visit," Father said. "In two days. His adjutant wishes to know if it would be agreeable."

"He's coming to our home?" Mother said. "I would think him far too busy for that."

Clara smirked. "They likely owe us a great sum of money. A little sniveling is in order."

Wickins smiled at her, nodding in agreement.

General Colsterworth had sent Wickins to the front for the previous winter campaign as revenge after he'd refused a military promotion. Wickins had begun working for the manufacturer of the tubes triggered by Aesir magic after his injuries took him from service, and his time was spent overseeing production and giving demonstrations. There was a lot of demand for the invention around the empire, including from the wealthy, who all wished for them to be installed at their mansions.

"I don't see any reason to refuse the request," Father said. "I will contact the adjutant tomorrow morning."

McKenna watched Clara sidle closer to Wickins and read her lips when she whispered to her fiancé, "At least you're getting your officer pension. We don't want to ruin that. Not that we need it."

McKenna wondered if Clara's preoccupation with money had much to do with the harsh financial circumstances the family had found itself under. Things had been difficult for quite a while, even before the house had been immolated by conniving interlopers and some unfeeling neighbors had chosen to press claims. McKenna's inheritance from Aunt Margaret had given her and Rob a feeling of security and the ability to help the family. Father's investment in Rob's invention would likely bring great wealth to the family. And surely there was more to come.

"Do you think we should all be here when the general comes?" Mother asked. She was facing Father as she spoke, but her eyes were fixed on McKenna and Rob. It seemed a silent message that they should *not* be around when the general came.

Mr. Swope stepped into the parlor and stopped by Rob's elbow. When her husband looked up at him, he said, "She's here."

Rob nodded in acknowledgment and then turned to McKenna. "Miss Cowing wanted to speak to me. Would you join us?"

That was startling news, but McKenna agreed, and they both rose and followed Mr. Swope to the front door. Miss Cowing waited for them on the porch, her fashionable silk dress and feathered hat illuminated by the bulbs installed there. They weren't glowing because it was nighttime but because she had Aesir magic.

Miss Cowing looked at the couple.

"Thank you for meeting with me on such short notice," Miss Cowing said. She appeared solemn and cautious.

McKenna had always felt a small twinge of rivalry toward this accomplished and distinguished woman. She was the sorcerer McKenna had always wished to be. But Miss Cowing's change of heart in court had altered McKenna's assessment of her. That must have taken courage. The ordeal was a very public failure for her.

"This is my wife, McKenna," Rob said. "She wasn't here the last time we visited."

Mr. Swope gave them privacy to speak, standing unobtrusively by the curb and waiting for the interview to conclude. There were not many passersby on the street at that hour, but there were some, and the bodyguard was ever vigilant.

"Mrs. Hawksley," Miss Cowing said, "I understand that for a deaf person, you read lips exceptionally well?"

"I understand you perfectly, Miss Cowing," McKenna said, bristling at the mention of her deafness. It made her wonder what others said about her behind her back. "I imagine the last few days haven't been easy for you."

Miss Cowing offered a chagrined smile. "That is true. I fired my barrister, Mr. Savage. Several others have offered their services. They all insist I should appeal the verdict."

Rob said nothing. He stared keenly at her, waiting for her to continue.

"I decided I will not," she said. "I'm done listening to bad advice. I regret we didn't speak when you offered to have a discussion at the beginning of all this . . . nonsense, Professor Hawksley. Despite appearances, I hold you in high esteem. I was persuaded by my counsel, and I see now where his advice has gotten me. And what I stand to lose. I should have renounced his strategy from the start. I wanted to apologize to you in person. To you both."

She noticed Mr. Swope glancing their way, a smug little smile on his otherwise stern expression.

How complex the feelings of mortals are.

The thought was not her own. It made McKenna uneasy that the being inside her was so much more active lately. So much more *awake*.

"Thank you for your apology," Rob said with sincerity in his eyes. "You are a notable inventor, Miss Cowing. I'm sure the loss in revenue from the military contracts will be made up another way in the future."

Miss Cowing looked away for a moment and shook her head. "Oh, that's not what I was referring to, Professor." She met his gaze again, and there was a spark of jealousy in her eyes. "I was thinking instead of the convocation of sorcerers. My reputation has been damaged at a most critical time."

Suddenly, McKenna understood everything. Miss Cowing's demeanor wasn't so much repentance as it was thwarted ambition. Perhaps Mr. Savage had persuaded her that a victory in court would assure her the office of Master of the Royal Secret. It was becoming clear how much she'd coveted it. But she didn't deserve it.

Rob nodded. "Well. It'll probably go to Mr. Guiteau. He's very capable."

Miss Cowing gave a startled chuckle. "You're very modest, Professor Hawksley. And it doesn't seem by design."

"Pardon me?" Rob asked, confused. "I've never adopted manners out of anything less than sincerity."

"That makes you unique among sorcerers, then. At least the cohort I rub shoulders with. Your name has been mentioned more than any other of late," she said. "Some prestigious individuals are firmly convinced that you can save us from the Aesir and the faction who wants us to surrender to them. Are you truly immune to gossip?"

"I find gossip rather tedious," Rob said, and McKenna was proud of him for saying so. "But thank you for your candor. I don't aspire to take Master Drusselmehr's place. Truly."

The arch in Miss Cowing's eyebrows could be interpreted many ways, but "incredulity" was the word that came to McKenna's mind. Oh, she wanted this conversation to be over. Miss Cowing was sulking, and she'd only come because she didn't want to make an enemy of Rob.

"All the more reason you deserve it," Miss Cowing said with a false smile. She dipped her hand into her elegant purse and withdrew the sorcerer's ring. With aplomb, she offered it to Rob. "I think you should have this. I don't want there to be any further misunderstanding between us. I don't think I stole the idea of the invention from you. But as long as I possess this ring, people will doubt whether my future ideas are mine or . . . you understand?"

Rob extended his open palm, and Miss Cowing deposited the ring there.

"I can compensate you for the loss of the ring," he offered, looking a little embarrassed by the whole interaction.

Miss Cowing seemed offended, but she smiled anyway. "That's not necessary. I paid very little for it. Consider it a gift. And if you should require any . . ." She stopped speaking. McKenna surmised she'd wanted to ask for a favor should Rob indeed become the head of the Invisible College but had thought better of it. "Well . . . I bid you both good night." And then she turned and walked away swiftly.

Rob examined the ring in his hand before sticking it in his pocket and giving McKenna a sidelong look. "What do you make of that?" he asked.

"I think she came intending to charm you," McKenna said. "And my presence caught her off guard."

"I concur," he said. "Which is why I thought it best for you to accompany me. I shared my reservations with Mr. Swope when she contacted me during dinner, and he insisted you join us."

She saw Mr. Swope sauntering up the walk, looking rather satisfied with himself.

"Thank you, Mr. Swope. Again." She gave him an approving smile.

He tipped his hat to her.

"I believe Mother has made a special berry cobbler for dessert," McKenna said. "You shall have an extra serving."

"I'm only doing my job," he said. "But I won't refuse dessert."

McKenna felt a vibration in her chest, her knees, and her feet. It took her breath away. Mr. Swope spun around, a confused and wary look on his face, and Robinson gripped McKenna's arm.

"Another explosion," he said when she looked to him for an explanation.

Friendly company is bothersome. I much prefer solitude. It is not that I loathe other people. My confidence has increased through reflection and observation, hard work and self-discipline. I have very high expectations of myself and others. Most do not, or will not, even attempt to achieve the full measure of their potential. I cannot help but experience the emotion of disdain for such, which makes me a poor companion.

I'm often asked why I've chosen not to marry. How typical of unimaginative people that they feel entitled to answers from popular strangers of no consideration or connection to them. My private life is my own. I owe no one an explanation for the choices I have made. If I have not married, is it not possible or reasonable to consider I might not have met my rational equal during my tedious sojourn on this orbiting sphere?

—Isaac Berrow, Master of the Royal Secret,
the Invisible College

Isaac Berrow

CHAPTER TWENTY-SIX

The Erlking's Oath

Fifteen years before the founding of the Invisible College

"You want to marry . . . me?"

Isaac had never imagined such words leaving his lips, but he needed confirmation that was what the Erlking's daughter had indeed meant. Her words had summoned within his breast quite a few flutterings of existential feelings he was hardly capable of defining. Amorous attraction was quite foreign to him, and he wasn't sure whether her mind or her personality appealed to him more.

"I do want it, Isaac. And I *need* it too."

So he had not misunderstood her. His feelings became more tumultuous by the moment. "Ah . . . well . . . you see . . ." Words, proper ones, utterly failed him.

"Please understand, I don't ask this lightly," she said. "I am dying. Nothing can prevent that. I grow weaker by the hour. Let me tell you why I need you to marry me. That might help you decide." She paused for a moment before adding, "It must be willing, Isaac. I cannot use glamour on you to coax a decision against your natural will. That is part of the covenant."

"What covenant exactly?" he asked. They had moved back to his bedroom because she had felt faint, and she was sitting up in bed, her legs covered by the wrinkled blanket. He scooted his chair a little closer to her so she wouldn't have to speak louder to be heard. He listened attentively and with great focus.

"Our peoples have fought for millennia, Isaac. As I've already told you. But there was that young nobleman, long ago, who sought to end the conflict permanently through a marriage alliance with me. He wrested a promise from my father. A promise that would compel my father and the rest of the Aesir to abandon this world. Forever. There would be no coming back. My father knew from his experience with the original covenant that mortals were incapable of being constant. He told me that if I married that nobleman, I would experience betrayal, heartache, and despair. But I still have compassion for your kind. I did not want you all to be annihilated, your bones left moldering into dust. And I loved him. Such emotions were new to me back then. I gave myself as a ransom for your people should they forget the newly forged covenant formed from the shards of the broken one. To fulfill it, I must marry a mortal one thousand times. Then, and only then, will my father fulfill his end of the bargain and abandon this world with the rest of the Aesir."

Isaac stared at her. "A thousand times? How many times has it been?"

She closed her eyes. "Nine hundred and forty-six." She looked and sounded very weary as she said it.

"And you have continued to honor this oath, for . . . for centuries? No, it must have been longer than that. Thousands of years. Ten thousand, perchance! Even though we've forgotten everything, you still honor it?"

"That is part of the test, Isaac. I am only allowed to return to my people if I abandon it or finish it." She looked up at the ceiling, her voice throbbing with emotion. "As we have spoken of before, sometimes I am reborn as an infant. Sometimes as a widow. In every case, I am a Semblance. And my father chooses the guise I will wear."

"Are you required to explain the terms before you marry the mortal?" he asked with genuine curiosity.

She shook her head. "That doesn't matter. I chose to tell you because I thought, with your personality, it would be easier for you to accept me if you knew."

She was right, of course. She'd recognized the quirks of his personality. Her experience over so many lifetimes had taught her the vagaries of mortal temperaments. It humbled him that she had chosen him among every person living at Nirshoye.

"Do you . . . often keep this a secret?" he asked her, his heart quivering with delicate emotions.

"It utterly depends on the circumstances," she replied. Then her throat tickled, and she started to cough again. He instantly went to fetch her a drink. His mind whirled with thoughts. The irony of the moment too. His roommate was gone to a family wedding. And when he got back, he'd find Isaac Berrow a married man. No one would believe it. It was unfathomable.

He brought the cup back, waiting for the fit to subside. She lowered the blood-flecked rag and then slumped against him, her eyes rolling back in her head as she fainted. He prevented her from falling by wrapping his arm around her and just waited, cup in hand, for her to revive.

She did, after several long minutes elapsed. "I don't have much time, Isaac." It seemed an effort to lift her head. "I know you like to consider things. To reason them out."

"Yes," he blurted out.

"I thought it best to tell you the circumstances. This life, in this body, will be one of my shortest. But if you're unwilling, I—"

"No, I meant *yes*, I will marry you. Is there a vow I must make? A formality of—?"

He stopped abruptly when she wrapped her arms around him and hugged him. He patted her shoulder as she heaved broken sobs against his chest.

"Thank you," she whispered. "Thank you."

"You've given me so much already," he said, offering her the cup after she released him. He'd spilled some of the water on his pants.

She accepted the cup with both hands and delicately drank from it. All of it. Then she handed it back to him and he set it down on the floor.

"So . . . is a ceremony required?"

"Yes. Whatever is a requirement of the time period. Some have been rather interesting."

"I should think so! This would be nine hundred and forty-seven, then. Why, there are only fifty-three left. You are almost there!"

"It's not that simple, Isaac. The wars between our peoples have become more conflicted. As the population has grown, it has gotten harder to find . . ." She sighed. "I fear that your people might be destroyed before I can achieve the fulfillment of the oath. My father does not want to lose. He's put me in more vexing situations of late. Like this one. He wants me to forsake my promise."

"Your father sounds similar to my mother," Isaac said with a chuckle. "She wanted me to be a country gentleman. To ride around the farms on my family estate and scold tenants about this or that. It would have been unbearable."

She clutched his arm. "You do understand, then. I have borne misery, contempt, and depredations too horrible to imagine. But I've endured them to stop the war. I fear what he may yet impose on me."

Isaac nodded in sympathy. "I didn't know . . . my father. He died before I was even born. Maybe I would have wanted to become a country gentleman if I'd seen his example. I don't know. I don't know what I would have become."

She gazed into his eyes. "You were destined to become a great sorcerer, Isaac Berrow. Your mind is no ordinary one."

He felt a little blush creep onto his cheeks. "You've opened my eyes to possibilities." He reached down and touched her hand. Hesitantly. Nervously.

Her thumb caressed his bony knuckles. "Thank you, Isaac."

"I don't even know your name," he confessed. "Not the prostitute's, but . . . well . . . yours." He gave her a hopeful look.

"I'll pronounce it for you in the Aesir speech. It is Eiríka."

The way she said it made a tingle go down his spine. There was magic in that word.

"What does it mean?"

"It means *ever ruler*. You know my true name. You have power over me now."

Isaac frowned. "I'm not sure what that means."

"Names are powerful tokens, Isaac. Very powerful. I cannot speak my father's true name. I don't even know it, else it would give me power over him. He gave his name to that nobleman from Auvinen. My . . . first husband. It was part of the covenant. So he could force my father into exile should the terms of the covenant be fulfilled."

Isaac thought on that and then nodded. "But he died before that oath was fulfilled. Does that mean he wrote the name down? Could it have survived all these years?"

"It was written on Aesir gold," she said. "So that it would not fade."

"Ah, so someone has it. All these years later. And they don't know what they have."

She touched his cheek. "Indeed, they do not."

Her touch made him shiver with pleasure. "There must be a more efficient way to achieve your goal. To marry more rapidly. A way to hasten the process. Finding a sorcerer today is difficult. I imagine that's an attribute you look for? Someone who knows magic or wants to learn? They don't wear the symbol around their necks, you know."

"They don't," she agreed. "There was once an order of knights who knew my secret. That order lasted for one hundred and ninety-three years before it was destroyed by a covetous king." There was a wistful look in her eye. "Those were exciting days."

She was still touching his hand, and he felt confident enough to rest his other hand atop hers. "Well, Eiríka, the current marriage custom requires a magistrate judge. It's a simple ceremony actually. And ends with the phrase 'till death us depart.' I think there are five or six such magistrate judges here in Nirshoye. Lots of crime, you see. I need to make an appointment is all. Pay a small fee, I think? It's not very difficult. Then he writes our names in his book and on a marriage license, and it's over."

She thought on it. "Will you go find one, then? I don't know if I have the strength to walk very far."

"Nirshoye isn't very big," he said. Then paused. "I should get you a dress. The judge would be suspicious if you came as you are. Let me get you something better to wear."

"There's no need to waste your money on me," she said. "While I'm not allowed to use glamour on you to persuade you to marry me, I can glamour the judge. I can make it so he won't even remember performing the ceremony."

Isaac thought about it and nodded. "I would like to get you a dress. It's bitterly cold outside, and those rags won't do. Will you agree?"

"I will," she said, taking his hand. "But our marriage must not be known publicly."

"It would be a secret between us, then. A secret I will keep."

Robinson Foster Hawksley

CHAPTER TWENTY-SEVEN

Alliance of Necessity

Present day

The explosion in Bishopsgate, as it turned out, was an accident. It had happened in the upper room of an apartment, where it appeared one of the *strannik*'s minions had been attempting to create a bomb. Unfortunately for the creator, it had exploded on him instead. Nothing had been left behind to identify him. But the landlord's information had helped the Marshalcy do so, and they'd also informed them that visitors had been coming by at odd hours dressed in peasant clothes. Inspector General Guiteau had revealed as much to Robinson and the Fosters through the medium of the sorcerer's rings. The explosion had caused a panic all over Bishopsgate, but in the two days that had followed, things had calmed down. The military were doing house-to-house inspections, searching for more makeshift devices, while the Marshalcy investigated who had rented the apartment and others who might have been involved. It was the topic of conversation throughout the city. The second explosion in Bishopsgate hinted at a larger plot—one designed to sow fear.

Robinson had pressed Mr. Guiteau on whether the legal matter that had brought the couple to Auvinen had been exploited by the Marshalcy to lure the *strannik* into the open. Mr. Guiteau had assured him in no uncertain terms that it had not, that he had honored Robinson's request.

Robinson, McKenna, and Mr. Swope went to the Fosters' home in preparation for the visit from General Ambrose. Travel preparations were also underway for the journey to Nirshoye for the convocation. The Fosters had arranged passage for the entire family.

"Are your parents going to Nirshoye as well?" Mrs. Foster asked Robinson brightly.

He nodded. "My father is a candidate himself for the office, but he believes I stand a better than average chance of getting it." His feelings squirmed with anticipation. What if he did get it after all? He didn't want to admit he'd been fancying the idea. "I received a telegram from him that they will be arriving at the university in four days."

"We depart in three days," Mr. Foster said. "Are they traveling by sea?"

"No, by locomotivus and carriage."

"Rob, has your father been to the University of Nirshoye before?" Mrs. Foster asked.

"Many times. He gave lectures there when I was a boy."

"They must be very proud of you," she added with an indulgent smile.

Robinson shrugged, but he knew that they were, especially his father. A feeling of significance hung in the air. It felt as if his life was about to dramatically change. He had no pretentions about becoming the Master of the Royal Secret. He didn't covet the rank or title. But if it could enable him to do more good, he was willing to accept it.

If it was offered to him. And what better way was there for him to protect his wife?

The defensive bulbs flickered on, indicating the presence of Aesir magic approaching the home. McKenna squeezed his hand. Seeing the nervous look in her eyes, he gave her a reassuring nod. He didn't believe the general or his officers had asked for this meeting with the intention of harming her. Mr. Swope left for the door.

"I guess it's about time," Mrs. Foster said, rising and wringing her hands.

Mr. Foster rose as well, and soon the others followed suit. Wickins and Clara were also there, holding hands. Trudie had been sitting by the enchanted heater. Everyone had wanted to be present for the meeting.

Robinson patted his pocket, reassuring himself that the device was still there. As he was wont to do on occasion when he was nervous, he pulled it out and flipped open the circular lid. There was much he'd discovered about it, although the mystery remained as to the Aesir numbering on it. When he'd gotten it from his father, it had displayed the numbers nine, nine, eight. And then suddenly it had changed to nine, nine, nine after his marriage to McKenna. He hadn't noticed it until they were traveling to their honeymoon destination. No change to the numbering had happened since.

Voices could be heard at the door, and then Mr. Swope returned, introducing General Ambrose, Colonel Harrup, and Mr. Stoker.

Colonel Harrup was an acquaintance of the Fosters from Auvinen. Stoker, of course, was part of the outfit that hunted Semblances. He'd broken into Robinson and McKenna's apartment in Auvinen, so he was entirely distrusted.

General Colsterworth had been a spare man with closely shorn hair, probing eyes, and a distinctive bushy mustache. General Ambrose was stockier in build, balding on the top of his head, and had a thick mustache that attached to bearded cheeks. His chin, however, was bare, which gave him the appearance of having tusks.

"A pleasure to meet you all in person," the general said with a husky voice, coming forward and greeting everyone with a handshake. "Mr. and Mrs. Foster. You must be the Hawksleys. Well met! And this is Lieutenant Wickins. I knew your father quite well when he was in command at the ice trenches. Your bravery and quick thinking spared us an unfortunate disaster with the Aesir last year. Well done, young man! And who is this beautiful young woman next to you?"

"Clara Aurora Foster," Clara said, introducing herself as she shook the general's hand.

"My fiancé," Wickins added proudly.

"Well, congratulations are in order!" He paused when he saw Trudie and bent himself lower to more match her height. "And what is your name, my dear?"

"I'm Gertrude Aurora Foster," Trudie said, taking his hand.

"Are you a sorcerer too?" he asked. "Is everyone in the family a sorcerer?"

"I'm too young," Trudie said.

"Well, it is my pleasure to meet you, Gertrude Aurora Foster. You are delightful." He straightened and turned. "May we sit? Where would you like us, Mrs. Foster?"

Robinson was impressed with the general's warm greeting. However, it was very likely his friendliness was politically motivated. His predecessor had left him with quite a mess on his hands.

Mrs. Foster made sure everyone was seated, except Mr. Swope, who stepped out of the room but remained where his shadow could be seen.

"The Fosters are missed in Society in Auvinen," Colonel Harrup said. "It's my understanding that your wonderful house on Brake Street will be rebuilt very soon. Is that true? When will construction begin? I'm anxious to see it restored."

"We hope to commence construction quite soon," Mrs. Foster said. "It will take some time, but yes." She glanced at her husband. "We do hope to return to Auvinen."

Robinson kept his eye on Mr. Stoker, who was perusing the room and, occasionally and surreptitiously, glancing at McKenna. Robinson felt a surge of protective feelings, but McKenna seemed calm. She was trying to keep up with the conversation, shifting her focus to whoever started speaking. Her concentration was exceptional.

Mrs. Foster had seated everyone in a circle to provide McKenna with an uninhibited view of all participants.

"It is certainly a pleasure to visit with your family this afternoon," General Ambrose said. "But, as you are undoubtedly aware, there are some urgent matters that need to be discussed."

"There are indeed," Mr. Foster said. He and Rob had discussed, at length, next steps in dealing with the patent suit. Once the courts had established Robinson's ownership of the patent, the military had known it was in violation of it. And, since the slight had been made deliberately, Robinson was owed just compensation, including damages.

"I'm glad you see it that way, Mr. Foster," the general said. His friendly tone and demeanor grew sterner. "We've been dealing with that fanatic, Gregor Skoye. He and his minions have infiltrated all strata of the empire. He is a skilled glamourist, to be sure, thus giving him his own impunity with the law. His goal of surrendering to the Aesir is unthinkable."

Mr. Foster frowned. "The *strannik* is a problem, indeed, but I don't see what bearing he has on this discussion."

Robinson agreed until he saw Stoker was looking at McKenna with fixed eyes and a little smile.

"Mr. Foster, it does concern your family," the general said. "Your daughter seems to be an object of fixation for this renegade miscreant. He has made multiple attempts to seize her. First, during her honeymoon in Tanhauser. Second, during her stay in Covesea. Third, the very night of the professor's elevation in rank in the Invisible College, which ended with the immolation of your home."

A nauseating feeling of worry bloomed in Robinson's stomach. He snuck a quick look at Mrs. Foster, who seemed to share his concern despite her stern gaze.

General Ambrose leaned forward. "I've asked myself why? Why your daughter? Why the professor's wife?"

Robinson felt his wife trembling. He glanced at her and found her cheeks were pale. She looked desperate and afraid, just as she had before she'd run from the music lessons. He grasped her hand and squeezed it hard.

"Who can explain the motivations of a fanatic?" Mr. Foster said.

"I think I can," replied the general. "My adjutant, Mr. Stoker, has an explanation. I believe, Mr. and Mrs. Foster, that your daughter McKenna is a Semblance. And I have to wonder if you do not already know this."

Mr. Foster pulled off his pince-nez glasses and began to clean them. "That is preposterous."

"Well, Mr. Foster, as any self-respecting barrister would, should we not consider the evidence first? Mr. Stoker, if you would present the case?"

"Yes, sir. Gladly, sir." He leaned forward, his eyes fixed on McKenna, who was watching him with undisguised fear. Robinson noticed Mr. Swope had emerged from the shadows. His eyes were fixed on the newcomers with animosity. "Semblances can only invade a mortal host who is on the brink of death. They often inflict that death themselves in order to transfer bodies. Miss Foster, as she was known at the time, nearly drowned in Siaconset during the war. Near her aunt's residence."

Mr. Foster looked outraged. "That is a private family matter. How did you learn of it?"

"Second," Mr. Stoker said, ignoring the question. "Semblances are more attuned to the cold. She has been observed standing in plumes of locomotivus fog and was ill during the heat wave in Bishopsgate at the time of the Great Exhibition."

"Many people took ill from the heat," Mrs. Foster said in a warning voice. "It was excessively hot that week."

"Third, Semblances can exhibit bursts of unnatural behavior. I've interviewed individuals who have accused Mrs. Hawksley of such outbursts of emotion. And others have heard her screaming during the night. This has happened on multiple occasions, not isolated incidents. It is my professional belief, as someone who has pursued Semblances during my career in the military, that there is sufficient evidence."

Robinson's heart was pounding in his chest. He knew that Stoker was right. But he would not let anyone harm her.

"Does this evidence seem unreasonable to you, Mr. Foster?" General Ambrose asked softly. "Judging by the hostile looks from your wife and son-in-law, this is not new information to them. But you seem . . . surprised."

Mr. Foster was sitting back in his chair, fidgeting with his glasses. He did indeed look stunned. Robinson quickly glanced at Wickins and Clara, who had been helping him with his research. If they spoke up about his sudden interest in Aesir lore, they could add to the facts of the case.

"General Ambrose," Robinson said. Mrs. Foster shook her head, so he paused. She didn't want him to speak for fear of incriminating McKenna any more. And yet, they had to make some response.

"You've known for some time, haven't you?" the general said with sympathy. Or was it feigned?

"General, a Semblance who had infiltrated the military tried to murder me," Robinson said. He gave Stoker a scornful look before turning back to the general. "That is when I first learned about Semblances." Pausing, his mind working furiously, he then added, "General Colsterworth explained the laws concerning how they've been dealt with in the past . . ."

"General Colsterworth believed your wife was a Semblance," Stoker said emphatically. "We were ordered to delay taking action."

"An order that I have upheld," General Ambrose said calmly. "It would be within our rights to take Mrs. Hawksley into custody. But I have a proposition to make. An alliance if you will. An alliance of necessity."

CHAPTER TWENTY-EIGHT

A Rare Semblance

Robinson's feelings were at a knife's edge as he waited for the general to continue. Everything was about to change, and it remained to be seen how.

"I think it would be prudent to forgo further discussion," Mr. Foster said, his haunted expression belying his stern tone.

General Ambrose turned to the barrister. "Oh, come now, Foster. Let's be reasonable and discuss the matter at hand. Your daughter *is* a Semblance. But I think she is no ordinary one." He turned his gaze to McKenna next. "A fourth piece of evidence. We recently apprehended one of the *strannik*'s followers, one who was involved in the recent explosion here in Bishopsgate. We learned after some rigorous interrogation methods that the *strannik* and his followers believe you are a Semblance of particular importance to their cause. That you are, in fact, the Semblance of the Erlking's daughter." He swiftly raised his hand to forestall any questions or objections. "It is their purpose to return you to the Erlking. The *strannik* believes this is what will lead to the peace he's been promised, as well as a leadership role for him. All he needs to do is deliver you . . . to them." Here, he paused, inclining his head slightly, studying McKenna's reaction.

Robinson noticed her trembling had ceased. She was staring at the general impassively.

"I want no part in the *strannik*'s plan," McKenna said. "He said as much to me himself when he abducted me this last time. The man is deranged."

"It may have helped us . . . had you mentioned that part," the general said with a cunning smile.

"We've dealt with these adjutants in the military before," Robinson said. He gave Stoker an arch look. "When the Semblance attacked at the exhibition—"

"Yes, yes, I know," General Ambrose said with a sigh. "But Mr. Stoker reports to me and must obey my orders. In most cases we've encountered, a Semblance is under the direct control of the Aesir, although their mortal host can be oblivious to the manipulation. Their purpose is to undermine our efforts to withstand the Aesir. That does not seem to be the case here. Your work, Professor Hawksley, and I assume it is with her assistance, has only contributed to our resistance to their attacks. Is this not so? You've helped defend us."

"That has always been my purpose," Robinson said before his wife could answer. "I'm the one who invented the tubes. I discovered the magical rings and made more of them."

"Yes, but you must also see that, from the outside, it may appear that your work is influenced by your wife. Also, before I forget to make this important point, your wife has shown no predilection for using magic. We've never heard of this before. Most Semblances are quite capable of using Aesir magic, but she hasn't shown that ability. Is that true?"

Robinson looked over at McKenna again, deciding it best to let her answer the question.

She nodded in agreement.

"Well then, let me make the proposal I came here to make. It has nothing to do with the recent lawsuit regarding your patent. We would seek a settlement. Our focus must be on finding and eliminating the *strannik*. You, Mrs. Hawksley, appear to be the person of interest who is the crux of all his plans. As I understand it from Guiteau, you and the deaf children are the only ones who can see through his glamours. I propose aligning our efforts to capture and bring Gregor Skoye to justice. With the help of your manservant, you've been exceptionally adept at evading the *strannik*'s minions." He shook his head. "And yet . . . we must stop evading him if we are to catch him. After the convocation, we would like to try and trap him, using you, Mrs. Hawksley, as bait."

Robinson almost came out of his chair with indignation. "You're asking us to trust you?"

Stoker grimaced and shook his head.

"I'm asking for your help," General Ambrose said. "We only ask for the opportunity to question her, to see what we can learn from her about the Aesir. About the Erlking himself and his weaknesses. This is something we have never been able to do before. In return, I'm willing to let your wife remain in your custody. If what we learn shows she is not a threat to us, then we can propose new terms of accommodation."

"Such as?" Mr. Foster demanded.

"I don't want to get ahead of myself," the general said evasively.

"Have you shared your findings with Mr. Guiteau?" Robinson asked.

The general shook his head. "We oversee different jurisdictions. Unless he becomes the head of the Invisible College. But I'm placing my bets on you, Professor Hawksley. I'm proposing a temporary truce. Let's see how things play out, shall we?"

Robinson felt some relief from the tension hanging in the room. Mr. Stoker looked disappointed, likely because he'd agreed with General Colsterworth's method of handling Semblances—with a quick bullet. The other military leader, Colonel Harrup, was giving them all an imploring look. He didn't seem to want bloodshed either. It was better than he'd hoped for.

"One more fact for you to consider," Robinson said evenly, deciding it would be best to give them something. "My friend, Mr. Wickins, is an expert in translating the Aesir tongue. In our research at the quorum of Wulfram College, we've found historical sources indicating it may be possible for Semblances to be separated from their host bodies. It is said by *some*," Robinson emphasized the word for Mr. Stoker's benefit, "that this is impossible. However, if the military has records of previous such attempts, I should like to have access to them."

General Ambrose studied Wickins a moment, his expression thoughtful, and then turned back. "The military has many records and secrets not divulged to the public at large. If you indeed become the Master of the Royal Secret, you will be privy to all of them, should you desire. Why don't we see what happens?"

After the visitors were gone, Mr. Foster slumped in his chair, wiping his eyes. The tension had been nearly unbearable for all of them, Robinson suspected. Poor Trudie looked confused and worried and near tears. Wickins was utterly flabbergasted and kept shaking his head, looking vacantly at a pot near the window.

Mrs. Foster went to Clara and put her hand on her shoulder. "Would you and Wickins take Trudie somewhere? Maybe for a dessert? Father and I need to talk to McKenna and Rob."

"I'd like to be here for that part," Clara said. "I'd like to know what other secrets you've been keeping from us!"

"Clara," Mrs. Foster said in a pleading tone.

"Don't I have a right to know?" Clara insisted angrily. But seeing the injured looks on her parents' faces, she steadied herself. Then she took Trudie by the hand. Trudie looked at McKenna nervously before following them out.

Mr. Swope's expression was difficult to read. He'd devoted his life to protecting and helping the Foster family, but what was he thinking about all of this?

"Perhaps we could talk privately first," Mr. Foster suggested to his wife.

Mrs. Foster shook her head. "We've kept this from you, Grandin. Deliberately. Now it's time to share. I know you were caught off guard today."

The agitated look in Mr. Foster's eyes showed her words had *definitely* caught him off guard. He appeared furious.

McKenna rose from the couch and knelt in front of him, her hands on his knees. "Papa. It's still *me.* I've kept it a secret for too long. Please. We want to tell you everything."

Mr. Foster's anger melted, and he took her hands in his, his expression withering with sadness. Then he nodded in acceptance.

"Let's talk in our room," Mrs. Foster suggested.

That was the one room in the house Robinson hadn't been inside. It felt like it should be a private space, but he relented and accompanied them there.

McKenna looked back at Mr. Swope with a tender smile before they left him behind and sequestered themselves in the bedroom.

The Fosters had a very large four-post bed that occupied a good deal of the space. The room was meticulously organized, not an article of clothing out of place. Its windows faced the rear alley, which was visible through a gap in the curtains. There was a little couch, a writing desk and chair—a stack of books thereon—and a closet that showed his suits on one side and her dresses on the other.

Robinson cast about for a place to sit down, and Mrs. Foster gestured to the little couch. He settled onto it with McKenna.

Mr. Foster paced the room restlessly before pausing in front of them. "How long have you suspected this?" he asked.

"McKenna confided in me after she leaped onto that locomotivus to escape Gregor Skoye," Mrs. Foster answered. "Only the three of us knew. No one else."

"You should have told me immediately," he insisted.

McKenna rose from the couch and went to him. "It's not that easy, Papa. I can't even talk about it well with Rob. When I try . . . I feel this . . . I feel profoundly agitated. I'm feeling it right now, actually. This . . . isn't easy for any of us. It can make me shriek in the night."

His mouth drooped with compassion, and he took her hands and patted them.

"And I have the strangest dreams. I can hear in them, and it's like . . . I can remember things that have never happened to me. But then I forget them as soon as I wake. Like they're being blocked from me. I do believe what General Ambrose said is true, though. I do believe she's . . . inside me."

Mr. Foster squinted, and then his shoulders began to shake with sobs. He took off his pince-nez glasses, stuffing them in his pocket, and put his hands to his eyes as he wept bitterly. Robinson had never seen him so affected.

McKenna hugged her father, holding him close as tears streaked down her own cheeks. Robinson felt himself tearing up too as he watched his brave, serious father-in-law spill out his emotions. As he wiped his own eyes, Robinson realized that this was why Mrs. Foster had suggested retreating to their bedroom. She'd known Mr. Foster wouldn't want to be witnessed losing his composure.

"Y-You're my daughter," he choked after a storm of emotion. "I was so afraid . . . so afraid what they'd do to you. What they have the *right* to do."

"I know, Papa," McKenna said tearfully. "We've been living with that risk all this time."

Mrs. Foster touched her husband's shoulder sympathetically. "I did what I did to protect McKenna," she said thickly. "And you. You can claim with justification that you did not know. The decision was mine. Blame me for it."

"There's no need to blame anyone," McKenna said. "I didn't choose for this to happen to me. Rob's been spending every moment he can researching about Semblances. To try and help me."

Mr. Foster nodded, and when he looked at Robinson, it was with an expression of profound appreciation. "Thank you, my boy," he said thickly.

"Mr. Foster, I hold you in the highest regard." Robinson got up and approached them so he could rub McKenna's back in comfort. "McKenna is my wife, and I will protect her with my life. Even if that means we need to flee from the military. I love her too much to let them hurt her."

"We've been given a reprieve," Mrs. Foster said. "I'm relieved, but this is only a temporary truce, not an end to hostilities. If Rob isn't chosen as the head of the Invisible College, they might go back to their original . . . methods."

"I cannot countenance that," Mr. Foster said, reaching up and dabbing a tear from McKenna's chin.

"I love you all so much," McKenna said, squeezing her father and her mother to her simultaneously. Mrs. Foster hooked her arm around Rob and brought him closer too.

It was a poignant moment, one Robinson felt he would always cherish. After some further conversation, McKenna and Rob left the room. Before retiring to their own bedchamber, McKenna thanked Mr. Swope for all he'd done to protect her and said she was grateful he knew the truth at last. He accepted her words and said it didn't change his feelings toward her at all. He'd accompany them to Nirshoye to protect them. And he'd try to find a way to get them out of there in case the convocation didn't go as hoped.

When they were finally back in their room, McKenna shut and locked the door. For a moment she leaned back against it, eyes closed and breathing slowly. Then she opened her eyes and shook her head.

"I could tell you were terrified," he said, coming to stand closer to her.

She reached up and began unbuttoning his shirt. "I wasn't frightened," she murmured.

"You were trembling."

"I was holding her back," McKenna said. "She was going to kill Mr. Stoker first, then General Ambrose. She didn't really consider Colonel Harrup much of a threat."

Robinson gaped at her.

"Well, maybe I'm exaggerating a little. I felt her thoughts, but I wasn't alone in holding her back. She was restraining herself."

"I'm glad," Robinson confessed, chuckling. "That would have made the entire military hunt us."

McKenna shrugged, still feverishly unbuttoning his shirt. "That wasn't what restrained her." She stopped, gazing up at him. "She knew if she came out fully, then I would die. And she didn't want my life to end like that. Not yet."

McKenna Aurora
Hawksley

CHAPTER TWENTY-NINE

Memories of Dying

The ship from Telimar was full of passengers all heading to Nirshoye for the convocation. McKenna had compassion for the poor souls battling seasickness, although she did not experience it herself. The seas were rough and the winds blew voraciously, whipping her hair about her face as she stood on the deck. She gazed at the imposing island of Nirshoye up ahead and felt unbidden memories tease her mind.

She'd been there before—the Erlking's daughter, not McKenna.

The island of Nirshoye was connected to the mainland via a land bridge. There was a town at the bridgehead, which had built stone scaffolding across the isthmus to reconnect the island with the town because parts of the land bridge had collapsed into the sea, but it still looked like a giant arched window ravaged by the waves. There were ports in the town, but most of them were at the base of the rocky island.

The sky was lined with plumes of smoke from the many chimneys over the walled town, and all around them, seagulls kept pace with their ship. The smell of the air reminded her of Siaconset, although the island of Nirshoye was much larger and crowded with old buildings. The university was ancient and had a rich, full history, having been founded in the dark ages.

The late afternoon sun was veiled by clouds as their ship finally reached the crowded dock. Because of the convocation, only those with invitations were allowed to disembark. The crew offered to help the passengers with their luggage, but Father and Mother carried their own valises. So did Robinson. Actually, he had insisted on carrying both his valise and McKenna's, as well as his violin case, tucked under his arm. It made McKenna feel positively empty-handed. Clara and Wickins, just behind them, looked eager to abandon the ship, particularly since Wickins had experienced seasickness. Despite his nausea, the four of them had conversed about her secrets during the journey. It had made her feel more settled, especially since Clara and Wickins had expressed their support. They wanted to save her, just like Rob did. She'd been surprised to learn Rob had enlisted them to help him find all references that they could to Semblances in the hopes of finding a way to separate them without the host perishing.

Turning her head, McKenna noticed Mr. Swope following their group some distance behind, keeping a watchful eye on the other passengers. Ever vigilant. She felt a surge of gratitude for him.

Once it was their turn to head down the railed gangway, they were met by officers of the Marshalcy. They'd been clearing each group of passengers. Each officer was accompanied by an older child.

Father showed his invitation to the officer and then explained that they were all from the same family of sorcerers.

Rob set down his baggage and approached one of the children, using manual communication to greet them as well as words. The young lad brightened and replied in kind. McKenna learned that he was from Auvinen, a student at Sarah's school, and was one of many deaf children positioned at the various entrances to Nirshoye to look for the *strannik*. They were interrupted when the officer motioned for

Rob to approach. He pulled his invitation from his coat pocket and showed it to the man.

"Pleasure to meet you, Professor Hawksley," the officer said. "Mr. Guiteau provided special accommodations for all of you. You'll take the Genowen Flying Chair and go to Heighe Warde Street to the college. He'll meet you there."

"Thank you," Rob said and stooped down to retrieve their luggage again. Mr. Swope followed him. Many of the passengers were climbing the iron stairs, but there were several of the Genowen Flying Chairs, a fabulous and rare invention, and an officer of the Marshalcy directed them to the next available one. They all boarded it together, and McKenna clutched Rob's arm when it jostled to life and began to pull them up.

There was a giant wheel contraption, made of iron, at the base, with toothed gears and pumping wooden pistons. A man stood near the contraption, probably a sorcerer, making it all work.

There was a platform with fencing around it, but she still felt uneasy since she could see through the gaps in the floor as they ascended. The feeling of upward movement tickled her stomach, and the smell of iron was strong. Finally, it locked into place as they reached the appropriate height. The fence gate was opened by another Marshalcy officer, who reviewed their invitations for the second time.

While they waited their turn, she asked Rob if he knew how the mechanism worked, assuming he knew, which of course he did.

"It was invented by a sorcerer named Hammond Darling Watt over a hundred years ago," he explained. "The flywheel down below makes the whole contraption work, and it's powered by the intelligences of bulls, I believe. The flywheel is spinning all the time, even when the platform isn't moving, storing the energy so the compartments can be easily pulled regardless of the weight burden. Quite fascinating. My father explained this to me on a visit when I came here as a child."

After showing their invitations to the officer, they were ushered through a stone gate and entered the city. There were more children posted there, gazing at those who entered. McKenna was proud of the children for helping, and Father had told her they were being paid for their work. They deserved to feel valued and important, and perhaps they would be better appreciated in the future.

She hadn't been able to follow along with any of the directions given to her parents, so she just went along with the rest of the group as they entered the streets of Nirshoye. The streets were narrow, made of stone and brick. The sidewalks were also very narrow, forcing them to walk single file. Carts and carriages lumbered down the street, and she felt a little uneasy at how closely they passed. The town felt like a labyrinth.

A trap.

She gazed at the buildings, mostly dwelling places for students, taking in the gabled windows at the rooflines and turret-like chimneys. Smoke belched from them, filling the air with a chymical smell, suggesting the chimneys were part of the students' alchemies.

When they turned the corner, she could see the university ahead. The sight of it struck her so hard that she nearly stopped walking. An image of the same street, choked with filth and snow, came to mind—the same street and yet different. Rougher. From a different lifetime.

The memory of a cough in her chest made her involuntarily begin a fit.

Rob turned and looked at her, noticing her expression. She gave him a smile and kept going, until they reached an alley. There, a surge of feelings struck her so hard she had to stop. The piercing cold. The desperation of hunger. The horror of the sickness taking hold of her body. The memories were so vivid and powerful, she nearly started crying. It felt like something inside her would rip loose.

She forced herself to keep walking, but someone touched her shoulder gently, and she turned to see Mr. Swope with concern in his eyes.

"Are you all right?" he asked.

The question made her want to cry. Inexplicably. But she felt she could not speak of the sadness inside her. The feeling of loss that made no sense, other than it was a deep shadow caused by an event long ago. To someone else. She nodded to him and kept going.

As they walked past the alley, she tried to focus on keeping her feet moving and not losing herself in the swarm of memories. Then, a few streets farther, she saw it—another dwelling very much like all the others, except a crowd was gathered by the dormitory.

Her father paused and pointed to the crowd. "That was Isaac Berrow's alchemy when he was a student here," he announced. "There is a little sign outside the door. His lodgings, as a professor, are inside the university proper, but this place is very famous. It's where he had many of his early ideas."

As McKenna watched him speak the words, the memories tugged at her again. Sharply. She feared she might faint. Or even worse.

She'd been to that little dwelling. She'd knocked on the door, and Isaac had been on the other side. She'd seen him pass by the alley where she'd been looking for him among the passersby. Where she'd been forced to inhabit the body of a—

McKenna collapsed.

The stench of ammonia roused her and made her gag. She realized she was sitting in the street, surrounded by her family. A stranger crouched in front of her, holding a vial of the foul-smelling stuff that had made her start coughing. The odor was so repulsive she instinctively turned her head away.

Rob was kneeling by her. "You fainted," he explained. He held her hand as he looked at her solicitously.

The memories were still swirling in her mind. Memories of a few days spent in Nirshoye in . . . a prostitute's body while she hunted the streets for someone dear to her and tried to avoid a cruel overseer. Her rapid blinking was caused by the smelling salts as well as the sting of the memories. Her father, the Erlking, had put her into the body of a wretched woman on the verge of death. A streetwalker who was forced to prey on the students of the university. She'd known immediately that her life would be brief, yet she'd still needed to find *him*. To persuade him before the disease stole her last breath.

She felt strong arms hoist her up by the elbows. Her knees were weak, but she managed to stand. As she looked around, she experienced double vision, seeing the present and the past simultaneously. The same street but choked with ash-flecked snow and no modern contrivances whatsoever clashed with the existing landscape. The familiarity of both scenes made her think she had a foot in two different centuries.

"Can you talk?" Rob asked, trying to get her to meet his eyes.

She nodded, but she was afraid to speak. Afraid she'd started screaming in front of everyone.

A carriage had stopped in the street, and she saw her father speaking to the inhabitants. Room was made for her, Rob, and Mr. Swope to go on ahead of the rest of the family. Wickins offered to help with the bags.

McKenna nodded and let herself be led into the carriage, where a well-to-do man and his wife were sitting on the bench. Mr. Swope climbed up to the driver's box to share the bench with him as Rob helped get her settled.

"Thank you for helping us," Rob told the man.

The man's wife said something, giving McKenna a look of sympathy, but in her current state, she couldn't decipher the words at all.

The carriage jostled as it began to move. Being inside helped clamp down some of the memories and feelings. She averted her gaze from the window because everything outside was so startlingly familiar to her. Her stomach roiled with nausea and the fear she'd start coughing up blood. She squeezed her eyes shut at the memory.

They reached a building at the end of a street, one with a wrought-iron fence blocking the way. Officers of the Marshalcy were posted there, and one approached the carriage. McKenna saw Mr. Swope jump down from the box and talk to the officer, who nodded and then waved to another man posted at the gate.

McKenna and Rob shuffled out of the carriage. Rob thanked the husband for his compassion. The wife said she hoped McKenna recovered from her seasickness soon. "Poor dear." McKenna realized she'd missed an entire conversation that had happened between them.

Standing on the street once more, gazing at the entrance to the university, she again felt a strange pulse of familiarity. Of knowing. The huge stained-glass windows. The turrets of stone. The trees behind the gate. They were all familiar. She knew without asking there was a courtyard and a fountain just out of sight.

Then she saw a man walking toward them with a welcoming smile, a scraggly beard, and unkempt hair. He waved in greeting.

It was Gregor Skoye.

Questions abound. Hard as we strive, we cannot answer them all.

Where arises all the order and beauty we see in this world? Is it orderly because we made it so? Is it beautiful because we deem it so?

These are questions that have excited and exhausted my imagination these many decades.

Whence is it that the suns and planets gravitate toward one another? Why is it that Nature does nothing pointlessly? To what end are the comets, and why do planets move in orbs concentric, while comets move all manner of ways in orbs very eccentric? What hinders the fixed stars from falling upon one another?

How came the bodies of animals to be contrived with so much art, and for what ends are their several parts? Was the eye contrived without skill in optics, and the ear without knowledge of sound? How do the motions of the body follow from the will, and whence is the instinct in animals?

Does it not appear from phenomena that there is a being incorporeal, living, and intelligent, to direct these phenomena? I'm convinced the Mind of the Sovereignty established order through laws innate in the universe, and the beauty we behold springs from the manifestation of those laws. Or are my very eyes susceptible to deception?

—Isaac Berrow, Master of the Royal Secret,
the Invisible College

Isaac Berrow

CHAPTER THIRTY

A Glamour

Fifteen years before the founding of the Invisible College

The judge lifted an eyebrow and looked at Isaac askance. That didn't bode well. "And you want to marry this young woman tonight?"

"It is our mutual desire, yes," Isaac said, feeling his throat dry.

"Do your . . . parents know?" the judge pressed. "Or is this an elopement?"

"Have I not filled out the license properly?" Isaac asked, feeling his agitation growing. The Erlking's daughter was standing by his side in front of the magistrate judge's desk. It was near the end of business hours. He was nervous the judge would delay the marriage until the morrow. He wasn't sure she would survive that long.

"Young man, I have been a magistrate judge for many years. It is not altogether uncommon for impetuous decisions to be made at your age. I implore you both, please do not rush into this. In cases like this, it rarely ends well."

"Are you refusing to marry us?" Isaac demanded.

"Of course not. I just think you should consider this more carefully."

"We've made our decision," Isaac said. He reached for and took her hand. "Haven't we?"

She nodded. He wondered if she didn't speak because she was afraid of another coughing fit. After leaving his little apartment, she had used glamour to disguise herself into someone more respectable looking to shop for a new dress she could wear to the judge's office. They found a comfortable and warm wool frock, new stockings, and new shoes. After Isaac paid for it, she changed into the new outfit.

She no longer looked like the wretched creature who had been with him the last few days. Her hair was tidy and pinned, her new dress a conservative yet simple one that made her seem decent in every sense. She still wore the same face as the host body she'd been put into, although illness no longer hollowed her cheeks and eyes. That was the illusion.

He *knew* it was an illusion, but he wished to believe otherwise—that she might yet have many days or weeks left. Maybe even months.

The judge sighed and examined the license again. The fee had been paid. "I've done what I could to save you from making a blunder. Let me see here, do you Isaac Berrow of Flamsteed, agree to espouse yourself to Lydia Brewer of Telimar? To join hands in matrimony, under the provident gaze of the Mind of the Sovereignty. Will you have this woman to be your wedded wife, to love together in this holy state of matrimony? Will you love her, comfort her, honor and keep her, in sickness and in health? And, forsaking all others, keep only to her till death you depart?" He cleared his throat. "If you agree, state 'Till death us depart.'"

"Till death us depart," Isaac said, relieved no other obstructions had prevented it from happening.

"Very well. Do you Lydia Brewer of Telimar agree to take Isaac Berrow of Flamsteed? To join hands in matrimony, under the provident gaze of the Mind of the Sovereignty. Will you have this man to be your wedded husband, to love together in this holy state of matrimony? Will you obey him and serve him, love, honor, and keep him, in sickness and in health? And forsaking all others, keep only to him till death you depart?"

"Till death us depart," she whispered hoarsely, squeezing his hand.

"I require and charge you, as you will answer at the dreadful day of Judgment, when the secrets of all hearts shall be disclosed, that if either of you know of any impediment why you should not be lawfully joined together in matrimony, you confess it now."

He gave Isaac a condemnatory look. He shook his head, and when the judge turned his disapproving gaze to her, she did the same.

The judge gazed down at the license again. "Forasmuch as Isaac and Lydia have consented to join in holy wedlock and thereto given and pledged their troth to each other and joined hands, I pronounce that they be man and wife together. Amen."

Relief and nervousness went through Isaac in that moment. The magistrate judge, whose name Isaac had already forgotten, set the license on the desk and with a feathered quill, signed his name and affixed a stamp to it. Isaac reached out to take the certificate, but the judge shook his head.

"I need to log this in my book of marriages first," he said. "For the official record."

He went to a bookcase near the desk and retrieved a leatherbound volume with ridges on the spine. Carefully he opened it to a ribboned page where several names were already listed.

"Eshi omorfi matia."

Isaac glanced at Eiríka, who had just sung an incantation. She was staring at the judge as he looked at the book and found the next empty space. He reached for the quill and then hesitated. The hand holding the quill trembled.

"Take the license," she told Isaac. "He's already beginning to forget."

Isaac snatched up the license from the desk. The judge's eyes were staring vacantly ahead of him. Still holding hands, Isaac and Eiríka walked out of the judge's office and hurriedly left the building, Isaac stuffing the license into his pocket.

A flurry of snow descended on them as they walked. Down the larger street, he saw the gate leading to the university and its tall spires and intricate stained-glass windows. He paused, gazing at the impressive structure. The cold stung his nose.

"What is it?" she asked, moving to stand closer to him.

"I've learned more from you in a few days than anything I learned over there," he said. He faced her, feeling agitated at the injustice. "Women aren't allowed to learn sorcery. They're treated as inferior. Even in the marriage ceremony. The wording was different for you. It shouldn't be."

"If you had your way, you'd allow women to be taught just as the men?"

"You've explained the equality that exists among the Aesir. Why, from what you've told me, you'd be entitled to rule your people should your father perish. I can't imagine the empire doing that."

"Mortals did things differently in the past," she said. "There were times, long ago, when such equality existed."

"Why did it change?" he asked in confusion.

"Mortals are mutable, Isaac. They change all the time. It is because of entropy."

"There is that concept again," Isaac said with a sigh. "It takes work, effort, and diligence to make lasting change. That means, if I want to change the way things are, it will take a long time to do so."

"But with persistence, you can achieve it."

"Me? I don't think so. Nobody likes me."

She came around and stood in front of him, taking his hands in hers. "It's not about liking or disliking. It is about serving. We love whom we serve. That is the lesson my mother's life taught me. And it's the reason we rebelled against my father." She squeezed his hands and lifted them to her mouth.

"You are my inspiration, Eiríka," he told her. "I think sorcery can do much good for this world. Will you teach me the spell you used on the judge? The glamour?"

"It is a powerful and dangerous spell, Isaac. People believe what they see. But the glamour spell obfuscates the senses. Instead of seeing what is really here, you are seeing what I want you to see. Your eyes become connected to *my* mind. You see my thoughts instead of reality."

It dropped in an instant. She had dried blood on her lips, paired with a grayish cast to her skin. Instantly, he anguished over keeping her outdoors for so long. She'd shown no sign of sickness under the illusion, but without it, he saw the chills making her whole body tremble.

"Let me take you back inside," he said. "You need to warm up. I can get some food."

She shook her head. "No, Isaac. I'm going to die tonight. You've done all that I've asked of you. One step closer. That's all I needed."

He stared at her. "What are you saying?"

"I don't want this life. This body. I'm ready to switch to another. I'm tired, Isaac. I'm very tired."

He shook his head. "I can't bear the thought of you shivering in an alley somewhere."

"Do you know how many times you passed Lydia Brewer in the streets, Isaac? I have access to her memories. She noticed you because you weren't like the other students. The greedy ones looking to waste a few coins. The jealous ones who wanted to control her. The selfish ones who only thought about their own needs, their own pleasure. You were different. She noticed that, and through her memories, I knew it was you. I also knew I only had a short time to find you before I succumbed to this sickness. But you were always so focused on your own life, you rarely ventured outside, and she didn't know where you lived. You've built walls to blind you to the suffering of others. She died a few days ago, frozen and beaten and hungry."

Isaac felt a lump in his throat. Guilt riddled him. "I never noticed her."

"You never chose to see her," she said. "It's like you cast a glamour on yourself." She leaned up and kissed his cheek. "Goodbye."

"No!" he said, trying to grab her by the arms.

"Eshi omorfi matia," she said.

Confusion jumbled his brain. He couldn't remember why he was standing alone in the street. Had he left his comfortable apartment to get some food? There was an errand he needed to run. He turned around, seeing the silhouette of the university against a cloud-strewn sky shadowed by the setting sun. There was an ache in his heart. He didn't understand it.

"What am I doing out here?" he mumbled to himself. The cold seeped into his bones. Sometimes, during his experiments, he lost track of time. But it was unusual for him to experience such confusion while walking through Nirshoye. No, it was totally unlike him. He always went out with a purpose. To get certain chymicals for his experiments. To buy more food.

He shook his head and began to walk quickly back to his tiny apartment in the student quarter. Loneliness hung on him. And sadness. Why was he feeling these emotions? And . . . and guilt?

What had he done wrong to feel guilt for?

A memory niggled at his mind. Had he asked Blake Sherburn to fetch something? No, Blake was away at a wedding.

Wedding.

Another surge of emotions. He felt an instinct to check his pocket for a piece of paper. He reached inside to do so, but there was nothing there except his money purse. Continuing his journey, he passed by an alley. He saw someone had collapsed there. Someone with no cloak. A woman, actually. He could tell by the hair.

Had she been injured? He hurriedly passed the alley. Surely someone would come by and offer help. What could he do? He was just a student at the university. He was no one.

When he got to his place, he unlocked the door. There was a peculiar smell of sickness about the place. He wondered if he was the one who'd been sick. Maybe he'd had a fever and had gone wandering about the streets disoriented?

But a strange feeling continued to nag at him. The woman in the street. He should go help her. It was wrong that he hadn't.

He leaned back against the door, struggling with his feelings, but they refused to abate. He couldn't do much. But maybe he could bring her over and help her warm up a little. That was something he could do. Blake was gone. There would be no awkward questioning.

"You're overthinking this," he muttered to himself. "It's probably nothing. She could have slipped on some ice. She's probably gone already."

The feelings persisted.

"You fool," he griped. He opened the door and went back into the street. Sure enough, when he reached the alley, she was gone. But there was something dark in the snow patch. Had she dropped something?

He approached cautiously. The alley was very dark.

"Hoxta-namorem," he sang, summoning a writhing spindle of light.

He approached the dark smudge in the snow. And the vivid crimson revealed itself to be a bloodstain.

Robinson Foster Hawksley

CHAPTER THIRTY-ONE

Promise Fulfilled

Present day

Robinson waved to Mr. Guiteau, who approached from the gate with several officers of the Marshalcy. He was desperate to get McKenna to their assigned room so she could lie down and rest. Seeing her collapse like that had lit a terror within him.

McKenna suddenly grabbed his arm, her fingers digging painfully into his muscle. "It's him," she gasped in disbelief and shock.

Robinson turned to gaze at her, jolting to awareness when he saw the fear and desperation in her eyes. He looked back at Mr. Guiteau and then at the other advancing officers. Instantly, he realized a glamour spell was in effect, disguising one of them.

"Which one?" Robinson asked, stepping in front of her. He jammed his hand into his pocket to find his sorcerer's ring so he could warn others.

"Guiteau," McKenna whispered.

The next second, Mr. Swope barged in front of them, drawing his elfshot pistol and aiming it at the disguised head of the Marshalcy.

Then everything went to mayhem. Saltpetr flashes and concussions of sound exploded in the alley. Robinson clutched McKenna to him as a hail of bullets swarmed around them. He saw Mr. Swope flinch as he was struck by multiple balls before he could get off a single shot. The bullets whipped past Robinson and McKenna, even though he hadn't summoned a shield. The device in his pocket had already activated and protected them from harm, but Mr. Swope had been too far from them for it to include him in its protection.

The brave Mr. Swope sank to his knees before Robinson could react.

The officers of the Marshalcy were suddenly running toward them, through a haze of saltpeter fog. Another shot rang out, and Mr. Swope collapsed onto the street in front of them.

"No!" McKenna shrieked in anguish, wresting herself away from Robinson and dropping to the ground by Mr. Swope.

Robinson stared in disbelief, seeing the bloodstains on Mr. Swope's coat. He watched him die, his chest stilling.

"It's the *strannik*! He was the *strannik* all along!" one of the officers shouted, aiming his weapon at the comatose body.

"They brought him here," said another one, his gaze shifting to Robinson's face, his eyes full of accusation.

He heard some words of magic sung, but he only recognized one of them in the commotion, "*matia*." The magical word for eyes. And Mr. Swope's body transformed to look exactly like the *strannik*. McKenna was weeping, still holding the body. He seized her beneath her arms and hoisted her away.

"No, no, no!" she sobbed.

"He brought the *strannik* here?" Mr. Guiteau said, his welcoming smile turning devious.

McKenna tried to break loose. Her eyes were full of rage. She looked like she was going to attack the *strannik* herself with her bare hands. Robinson grabbed her around the middle and hoisted her back.

"He's the *strannik*!" Robinson said. "It's a glamour spell. My wife can see through it!"

How had the *strannik* infiltrated the University of Nirshoye? Students from Sarah's school had been positioned at the entry points. How had he slipped past them?

"Take him," Guiteau ordered. "Take them both."

"He's an imposter!" Robinson warned.

McKenna screeched at the *strannik*, her expression full of hate.

Officers of the Marshalcy surrounded Robinson and grabbed him by the arms. One of them yanked his wife away from him. She fought against the man until he covered her mouth with a cloth. Robinson watched in surprise as her eyelids fluttered, and she instantly fell unconscious. He caught the pungent whiff of chlorinated lime and realized they'd used the powerful gas to knock her out. The liquid was dense, colorless, and had a powerful smell and effect.

He struggled against the men holding him, trying to get his hand into his pocket.

"Stop him!" Guiteau barked. Robinson's arm was yanked free of his pocket. The ring jerked loose and landed on the cobblestones with a metallic timbre and then rolled away before settling.

"He's the *strannik*, I can prove it!" Robinson snarled. He was not strong enough to free himself from three men.

One of them chuckled. Robinson looked at the man and saw his knowing smile. He realized these men were all the *strannik*'s followers impersonating Marshalcy officers. A feeling of dread bloomed inside his chest. They were near the university, but in an area devoid of bystanders.

"Take the device from his pocket," Guiteau said. "He's vulnerable without it."

Again Robinson struggled, but one of his captors punched him hard in the stomach. Pain quivered in his midsection, and the air escaped his lungs, making him powerless to stop the hand that dug through his pocket for the sorcerer's device. The man handed it to the *strannik*, who took it and examined it with curiosity for a moment before slipping it into his own pocket.

"I wonder how you stole it back from General Colsterworth," the *strannik* said, eyeing Robinson with a triumphant smile. "He didn't know you'd gotten it back. Interesting."

The man who had drugged McKenna had laid her down on the street. She was breathing softly, hair obscuring her face. The sight of her so vulnerable filled him with rage. He sang a quick command, sending up a sorcerer's warning flare. It popped and exploded like a tincture of magnesia flakes and saltpetr and hung there, glistening in the sky.

The *strannik*, posing as Mr. Guiteau, did not look impressed. "That summons will not help you, fool. It will only help me. Don't you understand? My people are planted throughout the island. I've been expecting you all to come. I will deliver you and your ilk to the Erlking. And I will return his daughter to him too. Thank you for bringing her here. You've been most helpful."

"And what will you get from him? You think he will take pity on you?" Robinson's voice throbbed with fury and frustration.

"Oh, he'll do so much more than that," the man said with an insane grin. "He's giving me another world, Professor. A world in need of a spiritual leader. He will open the portal here after I deliver to him the highest-ranking sorcerers of the Invisible College *and* his daughter. Don't you see? I *let* her go. Why drag her to Nirshoye kicking when I knew you'd bring her here yourself." His grin stretched wider. "You have not learned cunning until you have been taught by the Erlking himself." Turning to the others, he added, "Take them inside."

Dickemore. I see the flare. Are you all right?

He could hear Wickins's thoughts, which meant his friend was wearing one of the rings he'd replicated. But without his own ring, he could not answer back. He clenched his jaw. Oh, he was tempted to burst their eardrums. But he'd tried that spell on the *strannik* and his minions before, and they'd seemed impervious to it. He didn't doubt they'd prepared whatever counterspell the man had used before in advance.

"How did you get past the deaf children?" Robinson asked as they began to haul him toward the gate.

The *strannik* smirked. "They're on my side, Professor. Mrs. Fiske was only too willing to join my cause. Her children will all be saved, and *respected*, in our new world."

The blow stunned him. Sarah Fuller Fiske was working with the *strannik*? Why? Memories chased each other in his mind. She'd lost her position and rank in the Invisible College after her illness. Society openly scorned the children she'd loved and cared for, and when she'd gotten sick, the only person who had come to her aid was Robinson himself.

He understood all too well why she'd turned her back on the Invisible College. They'd given her reason to, and yet she still did wrong. This man was insane, his cause no less so.

Two men lifted up McKenna and began carrying her toward the gate. She looked pale, as if she'd died. He couldn't see her breathing anymore. One of the possible side effects of chlorinated lime was death . . .

"She's not breathing," Robinson shouted, panic-stricken. "Help her!"

Dickemore? Can you hear me? I haven't gotten a reply.

The *strannik* walked over to McKenna's body. He frowned, seeming to notice her still chest. He cupped a hand and put it on her breast, which made Robinson even more furious. To see him touching her. To have to watch while that awful man saw to her care.

He spoke some words, too indistinguishable to hear, and then McKenna's lips parted and she gasped for breath. Her eyes fluttered open. Robinson was relieved, but he noticed the *strannik* had not removed his hand from her bosom.

"Take her to the altar room," the *strannik* said. "We must begin the ceremony of separation. I'll summon the Erlking. The stormbreakers are waiting for the alert that we have fulfilled our part of the oath."

"Get your hand off her," Robinson said threateningly.

The *strannik* lifted his hand and pointed a finger at Robinson. "I want you to see it all fail. I want them to blame *you* for it. All these deaths are on your shoulders, Professor. What began in infamy must now be undone."

Robinson could hear the noise of running footsteps. Surely they were coming in response to the flare. But who was coming? Would it be someone else under the *strannik*'s control? He was baffled by why the *strannik* hated him so much. Or what he believed Rob had done to merit such contempt.

Even if the newcomer wasn't an enemy, the *strannik* was presently disguised as Mr. Guiteau, who was very likely dead. As Guiteau, he would have the authority to control the whole Marshalcy. Worse: The members of the Marshalcy had sorcerer's rings and could communicate instantly with each other.

The seriousness of the situation was at fever pitch.

Without the device, Robinson could be killed. How long would it take before it returned to him? Hours? Days?

The men holding Robinson began taking him in through the gate. Glancing back, he saw the *strannik* gaze down, stoop, and pick up the ring that was lying among the cobblestones. He inserted it into the middle part of the device and twisted it.

"With this, I will live forever," he said.

CHAPTER THIRTY-TWO

Shattered

They locked Robinson in one of the university offices. There was one curtained window, showing only a slim gap of the outside world. His wrists were shackled behind his back with nulling cuffs, the kind used to prevent rogue sorcerers from communing with intelligences. The office had a sturdy polished desk near the window and, along the same wall, a built-in cushioned couch in the corner. There were cabinets beneath the slab-like cushion, and several embroidered pillows lay atop it. The other side of the room had built-in shelves hosting an arrangement of books and sorcerer journals as well as small Aesir statuary and a replica of an ancient Aesir fortress that looked vaguely familiar. Another, smaller desk, likely for an assistant, sat against the opposite wall. There were two stuffed chairs.

Robinson observed these details while he paced, his manacles jingling as he walked the few available steps before swiveling on his heel and going back the other way. He was angry, nervous, and frightened. It defied belief that the *strannik*, the most wanted criminal in the empire, had maneuvered the situation so adroitly. It made it harder to bear that he'd done it in the throbbing heart of the Invisible College, which had served as the birthplace of the order of sorcerers, beginning with Isaac Berrow.

Robinson twisted his arms to try to feel his pocket for the device, but it had not yet reappeared. It was in the *strannik*'s hands, which would likely give him the same protections it had given its true owner. He felt agitation for McKenna, worried about what kind of ceremony was being performed on her. A "ceremony of separation," the *strannik* had said. Would that remove the Erlking daughter's Semblance from McKenna? What would happen to her? Would it leave McKenna's memories and personality intact? Or would the ceremony kill her?

He had to get away. Movement at the window caught his eye, and he tried to slide around the bulky desk to peer outside. He had to use the tip of his nose to part the curtain.

The sky outside was teeming with gray clouds. A few fat snowflakes had begun to fall, which increased his worry. The temperature was dropping.

A key was put into the lock, and he turned around in time to see it opened by one of the *strannik*'s minions, the same man who had helped the *strannik* attack him at Covesea. He knew his name was Kovya. McKenna had learned it during her captivity.

The detestable man was accompanied by Sarah Fuller Fiske, who looked pale and defiant.

Robinson stared at them both.

"We're gathering the children," Sarah said to Robinson. "It's time for us to depart. I know you condemn me for this. I just felt the need to explain myself before we go."

"Sarah," Robinson said, shaking his head in disbelief. He felt her betrayal like a hot poker jabbed into his chest. And yet . . . he knew the injustices she had suffered and seen. He didn't think she had made the right decision, but after what she and her charges had endured, it was understandable.

"Please. If you'll permit me. The Invisible College has been more interested in preserving its power than in helping people. I didn't believe that at first, so I excused their mistreatment of the deaf. Tolerated it, even. Until the Society the Invisible College helped create to uphold itself showed its true colors to me. Many have traveled a great distance to be saved from the destruction that's coming. You see, once the Invisible College falls, nothing will stand in the Aesir's way. We must leave this world. I believe the *strannik*'s cause is a righteous one, but I'm sorry we have to part as enemies."

"We're not enemies, Sarah," Robinson said. "The *strannik* uses glamour to seduce his followers. What you believe isn't necessarily true."

Her expression became more distrustful. "The same can be said of you, Professor. You aren't who you've claimed to be. I've seen proof of that. Everyone thinks that you'll be the next Master of the Royal Secret. But they don't know who you really are."

"Who I really am, Sarah? I am who I've always been. I thought we were friends."

"I can't trust you, Professor. Not knowing what I know about you. I'm taking the children to safety, along with the others who believe. Mrs. Farmer and her family are coming with us." Robinson felt another searing stab of betrayal as she continued to speak, undaunted. "I wanted you to know, so you wouldn't look for them anymore. We're going to a world safe from the Aesir. No more stormbreakers. No more ice trenches. A world of beautiful fountains and waterfalls. This is what we were promised. I wish more had chosen to come with us. But you prevented it by letting this conflict with the Aesir drag on." She sighed. "I'm sorry."

"Sarah, I have never knowingly or deliberately misled you," Robinson said. "I fear for you and for those who are following the *strannik*. He's a murderer."

"Well, I didn't expect we'd see eye to eye. He may have removed a few people who were trying to kill him. But it is nothing compared with the number of lives you've destroyed. I can't tell if you're lying or not.

Maybe you've deceived yourself so thoroughly that you believe it." She was about to turn but stopped. "What you did, marrying the Fosters' daughter, was a truly wicked thing." The look of accusation and sound of hurt in her voice made Robinson quail. Marrying McKenna had been wicked? How could Sarah say such a thing?

"Sarah, it's not too late to stop this," Robinson pleaded. "You have to trust me. I haven't done the things you're accusing me of."

Her look was pitying, but she shook her head and left. Her companion, however, did not.

"You're summoning the Aesir here?" Robinson demanded, feeling nauseous with dread. "What's this ceremony the *strannik* mentioned? What are they doing to my wife?"

"The body of the Erlking's daughter is at the bottom of the lake near the summer palace," he said. "Asleep in the Skrýmir. We're going to loosen her intelligence and trap it in a crystal so the Erlking can restore it to her proper body and awaken her. The ceremony is a severance."

"You mean McKenna will die," Robinson said angrily, his voice breaking.

"She's already dead," Kovya snorted. "She drowned. You've been dallying with . . . with a corpse."

Robinson felt a surge of outrage. "I'm going to stop you. I'm not going to let you kill her."

The man looked smug. "Oh, but you've already helped us so much, Professor. The tubes you invented are everywhere. When the Aesir come, those tubes are going to shriek so loudly that no sorcerer will be able to hear anything, let alone cast a spell."

"My tubes don't do that," Robinson exclaimed.

"They do now. You taught us the violence of which sound is capable. Remember? The soldiers in the ice trenches will be writhing on the ground, helpless in agony, when the Aesir come. Thanks to *you*. Do you know how many Semblances will be unleashed then? They'll make sure no sorcerer is left to protect the mortals. When the next winter comes, no one will be left to stop them."

"And this is what you preach?" Robinson said, outraged.

"We took their world away from them. Is it any wonder they want it back? We've betrayed them at every turn. Should they not desire vengeance? You will be blamed for this. Because *you* are the true deceiver."

"I don't know what you're talking about!" Robinson protested.

Kovya shrugged. "How unfortunate for you."

He left the room, and Robinson heard the key twist and the lock tumble into place.

Robinson didn't know how long he sat on the couch, trying to come up with a solution to the problem. So much of what was said hadn't made any sense, but that was to be expected. A glamour spell, however it was cast, made someone believe a lie to be truth. They were made to doubt their own senses. The glamour spell was a carefully guarded secret only known to the highest levels of the Invisible College. This situation was proof enough that the knowledge was dangerous.

He thought about the manacles on his wrists. They were forged of a certain kind of iron that was anathema to Aesir magic. In fact, using such chains on an Aesir would cause them incredible suffering. He'd read that in a book somewhere, long before. So the chains would prevent him from summoning Aesir magic. He needed to get them off, but iron, as a rule, was a rather sturdy metal.

"Annixe," he sung dejectedly.

The manacles unlocked and dropped to the floor behind him with a thud, startling him. His hands were free. He drew them up and stared at them in disbelief, then touched his pocket. The device was in there. A gleeful feeling leaped in his bosom. Ducking his hand into his pocket, he pulled it out. It was real! It had come back to him.

Robinson quickly opened the lid and twisted the proper combination. When the ring popped out, he swiftly put it on, feeling an instant stab of pain in his skull.

Wickins. It's Dickemore. I've been captured by the strannik. Can you hear me?

His heart raced with excitement. Maybe there was still a chance to stop this catastrophe.

Dickemore! Where are you? They told us you'd been knocked unconscious.

I'm in an office in the university. The strannik is impersonating Guiteau. His minions are the Marshalcy officers. How many, I don't know. Sarah betrayed us.

No! How could she?

We need help. I'm going to find McKenna. Contact General Ambrose and tell him to destroy all—

Robinson paused his thought without finishing it.

Dickemore? Are you all right? Tell Ambrose what?

What if this was part of the *strannik*'s ploy? What if he *wanted* Robinson to have all the tubes destroyed? They'd be the authors of their own demise. And it would, rightfully, be Robinson's fault. A cunning ploy.

Warn Ambrose that the Aesir are going to attack. Tell him Guiteau is an imposter and the strannik and his minions are here. Warn everyone you can, Wickins!

I will. Then I'll try to find you.

Relief surged inside Robinson. *Thank you, dear friend. They're going to kill McKenna. I have to stop them.*

Robinson needed to stay active. He walked to the door and uttered the same command as before. The lock twisted and opened. He grabbed the handle and turned it.

As expected, there was a Marshalcy officer standing just outside, pistol in his hand. He raised the barrel to Robinson's chest.

"Don't move," he ordered.

Robinson walked toward him, and the man pulled the trigger. The magic of the device effortlessly deflected the elfshot.

"Percutis malleo," Robinson sang, causing a rush of magic that shoved the officer into the wall behind him, the impact hard enough to knock the man unconscious.

Little friend, Robinson thought in desperation through the searing pain in his skull. *Loyal. I need you to guide me to McKenna. Are you there?*

He felt the doglike intelligence pad up to him. Another bloom of relief filled him, chased by gratitude. This invisible creature had helped him for so long.

Help me, he thought to it, sending plumes of feeling with it.

The doglike intelligence immediately started down the corridor. Robinson followed, roaming through the familiar halls. He'd come here with his father. There was a door at the end, leading out into a courtyard. When Robinson reached it, he twisted the handle and opened it, and a swell of snow struck him in the face. The snow was coming down in sheets, blanketing the courtyard in white.

He was in the heart of the college—the courtyard surrounded by medieval walls—and he could feel Loyal padding along in front of him, leading the way. Directly across from them were the tall windows looking into the great hall with its impressive dais. A raised fountain took up the middle of the courtyard with a cupola surrounding it. A statue of the Erlking's daughter presided over it, veiled in snow.

As a boy, he used to stare up at it. It was so large it felt like a crypt. He walked briskly toward it, following Loyal, who was in turn following the Unseen Powers.

The interior of the courtyard suddenly flared with light. There were bulbs fixed all around the edges, and they began to glow.

He felt a premonition of dread just before the shadow fell across the university. A stormbreaker was descending through the snow. The bulbs were *his* bulbs, awakened by its magic.

No! Robinson thought in horror.

And then all the tubes began to shriek, an earsplitting sound that made him clamp his hands over his ears and sink into the snow in agony. The noise and pain shattered Robinson's mind.

His last conscious thought was that he should have warned Wickins after all.

McKenna Aurora
Hawksley

CHAPTER THIRTY-THREE

Communion

A horrible smell revived her, acrid fumes stinging her eyes. McKenna felt groggy and irritable and incredibly disoriented. As she looked around the unfamiliar room, she was even more confused. She propped herself up on an elbow, feeling a hard slab of wood beneath her.

Darkness suffused the room, the only light from wisps of sorcerer's fire gathered directly around her, hovering overhead. Where was she?

"Rob?" she called out.

She became aware of pain in her ears—a low, dull throb. It was uncomfortable but not unbearable.

Pushing herself up, she swung her legs off the slab. It was a decorative piece of wood, the interlocking pieces arranged to form the symbol of the Invisible College. The craftsmanship was exquisite. A gold inlay decorated the edges.

Heavy curtains blocked the light from outside, or perhaps it was already after sunset. There was no way of knowing how long she'd been unconscious. She gasped as the memory of the *strannik* surfaced. He'd been waiting at Nirshoye, and someone had covered her mouth with a cloth that had fumes . . .

"Hello?" she called out, looking around for someone.

A figure approached from the shadows, wearing dark robes. She recognized him as the fellow who had abducted her before. Kovya. His arms were folded. His look was confident.

"Where's my husband?" she demanded as he came nearer.

"I can't hear you," he said, wagging his hands. "The noise prevents it." She saw he was wearing a set of Aesir ear cuffs—a form of jewelry popular among the snowborn but not considered fashionable in mortal society.

He also had on a thumb ring and a tidy suit beneath his robes—robes of the Invisible College. She must be within its inner sanctum. The marble floor with its varied striations of color suggested opulence.

She tried to slide off the plinth, but he pushed her chest to keep her on it and shook his head.

A crack of light suddenly beamed from one of the walls, revealing a doorway and daylight streaming in from beyond. In strode Gregor Skoye, clutching three small wooden boxes. He shut the door, plunging the room into darkness again. She couldn't see him, but she felt him as he approached. Fear tickled her stomach. As he got closer, she was able to track his movement and watched as he set the three small boxes on the plinth with her.

She saw Kovya tilt his head and give the *strannik* a questioning look. The crease of a smile came in reply, and she realized the two men must be conversing through the sorcerer's rings they both wore. The *strannik* also wore a set of ear cuffs.

"What is happening?" she demanded again, but neither man looked at her. So she reached out and jerked on the *strannik*'s sleeve. *"What's going on?"* she repeated, mouthing the words in an exaggerated fashion.

The *strannik* arched his eyebrows. "I know you can read lips, my dear. Unfortunately, I lack that skill. Can you sense the sound?"

She nodded, feeling the discomfort in her ears still. She'd experienced this sort of thing before, in the presence of a loud or high-pitched sound.

"It prevents any spells from being cast, thus rendering the Invisible College powerless, but my followers are immune to it. The Aesir have arrived. Your *father* is coming to reclaim you."

A sickening feeling of dread filled her.

"All the sorcerers of the Invisible College here on the island will be dispatched." A wicked grin came over his mouth. "You and your husband have led them all into a trap. At least, that is what people will think. The hierarchy will be destroyed. And without it, no new leadership can be established." He touched the three boxes.

McKenna recalled that three individuals had been given items they would then use to reveal the great secret to the new chosen Master of the Royal Secret. Undoubtedly the *strannik* had hunted those individuals down and claimed the boxes from them.

Her parents were on the island. Her sisters were there. So was Wickins. Mr. Swope had already been shot and killed. The memory sent a wave of anguish through her. These men were going to destroy everyone she loved. Or they'd make it possible for the Aesir to do so.

"What did he promise you?" she asked the *strannik*, feeling rage bubble within her.

"What?" he asked, unable to understand her.

"What . . . did . . . he . . . promise!" she screamed at him.

The *strannik* turned to his companion and then nodded. "What did he promise? A new world! One with no more war. This world belongs to your people. We will forsake it for another. When the Aesir searched for an inhabitable world, they discovered others with mortal life. Worlds that were too warm for them. They chose this one as a suitable alternative for your kind. We cannot keep the bargains we made when you first came here, so we must go somewhere else. Our two peoples will exist separately."

McKenna felt furious. "And everyone who doesn't leave will die?"

The *strannik* looked confused at her words but then seemed to understand. "We've given the warning. Is it my fault mankind is too stubborn to heed it? Those who follow me to this new world will be saved. Those who stay behind will be destroyed. This is justice. It is the law of your people."

McKenna felt helpless and weak. These men had subverted so many to their cause. The Aesir would show no mercy to those who were left behind, including every person she loved. They'd been incapable of mercy since the death of the Erlqueen.

"You are a monster," she said to him.

"I am a savior," he declared triumphantly.

She lunged at him, but his burly henchman grabbed her arms and restrained her.

The two men seemed to have a silent conversation, and then the *strannik* nodded and picked up one of the boxes. Slipping his hand into his pocket, he removed an ordinary key. The boxes themselves appeared plain and unmarked. Each was about the size of a little music box. The *strannik* inserted the key, twisted it, and then opened the box. Inside was a gleaming coin made of Aesir gold. One that would not tarnish.

McKenna struggled to free her arms from the henchman's grip, but he was stronger than her. The henchman frowned at her, then tried to peer at the coin. The *strannik* looked at one side, then the other. When he showed it to his henchman, McKenna discerned a number.

1-6-1-8.

The *strannik*'s eyes widened with surprise. "The divine proportion," he said excitedly.

The henchman wrinkled his brow in confusion.

"The divine proportion!" the *strannik* repeated. He then pulled out another key and inserted it into the lock of the second box. It opened and revealed another coin. "The same," he gasped.

Then the third was opened.

The henchman still looked confused, but he seemed to be listening to something, as if the *strannik* were trying to explain the significance to him mind to mind.

McKenna had a realization. Rob had discovered how to open his sorcerer's device by using the inner rings in a certain combination—something about the ratio of a circle. That had enabled him to access the ring within it.

But what if another combination unlocked something else?

That insight struck her powerfully. Yes, it *would* unlock something. Perhaps even something very important. If Rob had become the head of the Invisible College, he might have gained special access to the Unseen Powers because of the device he carried.

She had to get to him. She had to *help* him.

The *strannik* grinned triumphantly, putting the three coins back into their boxes. He patted his pocket, and then a look of surprise took hold of him. He patted his pocket again and then, in a frenzy of emotion, stuffed his hand into the pocket. Realization struck him.

McKenna understood what was happening. It seemed he'd taken the device from Rob and it had disappeared, just as it had with General Colsterworth.

Kovya released one of his hands from McKenna and grasped the *strannik*'s clothes, shaking his head. They were arguing. Silently. In their minds.

She had to get to Rob. If the violent sound was deafening him, he wouldn't be able to cast any spells to protect himself. But maybe his device would help. Maybe it would shield him from the noise.

The *strannik* looked flustered, but he finally nodded in agreement. The henchman, appearing relieved, suddenly grabbed McKenna and shoved her down against the plinth. Gripping her wrists, he used his body weight to drive her into the unyielding wood.

Beyond him, she saw the *strannik* was opening the buttons of his jacket. From within it, he withdrew a harrosheth blade. A blade that could pierce anything. She knew instantly that he was going to plunge it inside her, severing the connection between her and the intelligence of the Erlking's daughter.

She knew instantly that it would kill her.

Please help me, she cried out in the silence of her thoughts, despite the pain resonating in her eardrums. *Help me save them. You can take over. I won't shut you out. Please help us.*

It was a plea to the Semblance. A willingness to cede control of her mortal body.

As soon as the words crossed her mind, McKenna felt a strange sense of calm wash through her. She felt the urge to relax her muscles, to stop fighting the henchman. Her breathing began to slow. She felt her lips parting for an exhale.

Everything seemed to slow down, to crystalize in her senses.

Kovya pulled McKenna's arms away from her chest, pinning her wrists by her head. She felt each rise and fall of her chest as the *strannik* gazed down at her, holding the harrosheth blade in a sacrificial pose. He gazed at her in awe as she succumbed to the entity inside her.

Knowledge flooded her.

A gush of memories came with it. Along with the realization that she wasn't ceding control at all. There was no exchange to be made. She had always been one soul. McKenna had died as a young child—and that was when Eiríka had joined her as a Semblance.

The realization should have been shattering, but it wasn't. It was suddenly all so clear to her. Surprising, yes. But natural too. She was who she'd always been. Her penchant for words. Her insatiable curiosity. None of that had changed in this body. And she remembered a thousand lifetimes.

"I am ready," McKenna said, although it was not her who said it. She'd yielded herself completely, offering no resistance at all. A willing sacrifice to the *strannik*'s blade.

There was hunger in the *strannik*'s eyes as he gazed on her. He relished his power and impending glory. Was he also, perhaps, tempted by her? Enticed by the Erlking's daughter?

Countless lives flashed through her mind. Of Isaac Berrow and Lydia Brewer. Of Landon Killeneth and Shanron Leia. Most had been brief because the Erlking had willed it so. A hungry poet and his lover. A blacksmith fixing a noblewoman's wagon spoke . . .

The memories were overwhelming. There'd been so much love and hate. So much sorrow. She'd learned how impulsive mortals could be. How emotional too.

The *strannik*'s eyes blazed with desire as he plunged the dagger down to end her life.

The Erlking's daughter yanked the henchman into the path of the blade.

Eirika

CHAPTER THIRTY-FOUR

Raging

The harrosheth blade sank to the hilt in the henchman's back. There was no blood. There never was, not with a harrosheth blade. She saw his mouth gape in shock and agony. He released her, arching his back as the immutable cold from the blade spread throughout him. The *strannik* yanked his weapon free, staring in horror at what he'd done. Yes, the *strannik* could read minds and should have been able to anticipate it. But he could not read hers.

She pivoted on the smooth wooden plinth and kicked the dying man in the chest, knocking him away from her. His legs were already useless, and he sank to the floor, trying to grab the plinth to hold himself up. He was suffering. She could see it in his eyes as the cold took over. She knew the pain of death caused by a harrosheth blade. She'd experienced it in previous lives. There was a feeling of satisfaction that this cruel man's life was ending that way.

Her gaze shifted back to the *strannik*, who was backing away from her, holding the blade protectively.

Memories that she'd buried beneath the surface of consciousness were rising like a tide. She was Eiríka, the Erlking's daughter and forsworn heir. She was a Semblance who had been reborn nine hundred and ninety-nine times. She'd lived in the mortal world for thousands of years. One more life was all that was needed to fulfill her oath to her father. The oath that would lead to his banishment and the irrevocable departure of the Aesir from this world. One more life.

Determination swarmed inside her. She needed more time. She knew that having fully awakened, she would die soon. It was always that way. It felt like she had only seconds left to make a difference. A mortal's lifespan was so fleeting. She comprehended that. She'd endured it over and over for centuries.

The *strannik* must have seen his own death mirrored in her eyes. He was no warrior compared with her—she was Disir and had trained in the arts of warfare with her sisters.

He threw the weapon as hard as he could, knowing instinctively that he was no match for her skills. Even in this weakened mortal shell, she had the memories of lifetimes. The harrosheth blade struck the marble floor, blade first, penetrating the stone as easily as if it were snow. All the lights extinguished, plunging the room into darkness.

Hoxta-namorem, she thought. The memory of the pitch was embedded in her mind. She'd tried to bury her memories of magic earlier, knowing that each spell she cast would awaken her further, reducing her grasp on mortality. Her magic was always more powerful when she was fully aware.

Instantly, the whorl of chaotic light came, sizzling with raw power and chasing away the shadows.

Eiríka ran and drew the weapon from the floor, which smoked from the cold of its touch.

She saw the *strannik* twisting the door handle, turning back to her in fear as he tried to wrestle it open. The panicked look on his face revealed the depth of his true cowardice. Pulling her arm back, she threw the dagger at him, intending to bury the blade in his skull.

He ducked just in time, and the blade embedded in the door instead. He managed to get it open and she sprinted after him as he hurriedly scampered outside into the hall.

Eiríka paused at the door just long enough to pull the blade free. Once in the corridor, she squinted, pained by the light particles striking her mortal eyes while they were fully dilated. An Aesir's eyes could dilate so much faster, with a degree of self-control totally impossible for mortals. Their eyes could see perfectly well, even in the sun blindness of snow.

As her eyes acclimatized to the brightness, she noticed several people had collapsed in the hall, hands on their ears, twitching as the riotous noise from the tubes rendered them helpless.

There he was! The *strannik* had reached the end of a windowless corridor, where he hurried to open another door. Two lamps sat midway down the passage, their bright glow revealing the presence of the Aesir. She ran down the corridor in pursuit and shattered both tubes. The pain in her inner ears lessened slightly, but the noise was still causing harm.

She reached the far door and opened it, and two men dressed in uniforms of the Marshalcy instantly rushed at her with truncheons. This second corridor had windows to the outside, and she saw snow coming down in heavy sheets. She launched herself at the two men, ducking a swing aimed at her skull while using her leg to trip the man and cause him to tumble onto the carpet. The second truncheon was met with the harrosheth blade, which severed the weapon mid-stem, causing the other piece to spin wildly and thump against one of the windows on the wall.

The officer—a *strannik* minion, no doubt—gaped in surprise as she kicked him in the stomach. Her aim was impeccable, and the blow sucked his breath away. She didn't linger to kill either of the men. Her target was the *strannik* himself.

No glamour could deceive her. It was part of the blessing—or curse—her father had given her. It wasn't McKenna Aurora Hawksley's deafness that had protected her from glamour. The terms of her agreement with her father had done so.

The next door opened before she could reach it, and another Marshalcy officer appeared, bringing an elfshot pistol into the fight. His mouth was twisted with rage and fear as he commanded her—as she interpreted it—to stop or he'd shoot her. Aesir were incredibly fast, but they were not faster than elfshot. And this present body lacked the reflexes of her kin.

Thankfully, mortals were notoriously bad at aiming. She ducked and wove and then feinted hard one way. He fired, but she'd already changed directions, and the shot went wide. After closing the distance between her and the soldier, she grabbed the man's wrist, spun around him, and slid the harrosheth blade through his middle to finish him off. His legs spasmed and he collapsed in a heap, gazing in astonishment at how quickly he'd been defeated. She removed the ear cuffs from his ears and put them on her own. The throbbing pain ceased, giving her an immediate feeling of relief.

Two more men were charging down the corridor toward her, both of them drawing pistols. The *strannik* was among them, pointing at her, although his mouth wasn't moving. He was directing them through the transmutation of thought. This next corridor had windows on one side, revealing the inner courtyard of the university. In the center was a fountain, covered by a cupola. Snow had already covered the top of the cupola, but there was a smudge of dark against the snow on the other side of the courtyard. Someone had collapsed outside. She saw Aesir coming from the sky, floating down like angelic beings coming to harvest the lives of the sorcerers down below.

The two men charged toward her, leaving the *strannik* behind, and fresh anger rippled through her. The *strannik* was sacrificing their lives so he could escape her.

Kalispel, she thought, and the brunt of the magic knocked both of the men over before either could aim their weapon at her. One hit the glass window so hard it cracked before he slumped to the ground.

The other had dropped his elfshot pistol during his tumble and was scrabbling on hands and knees to find it. Eiríka raced to him and kicked him in the head, knocking him down. They wouldn't die, but it would be some time before they were fit to fight.

The *strannik* had reached another set of doors. He gazed back at her, panting for breath.

Flee, you sniveling coward, she thought angrily. *I'll find you just as you found me.*

And then she heard a yip. It wasn't a sound from her ears. It was a warning from an intelligence. A dog's intelligence. She paused in her chase and looked out the window again, at the crumpled body in the snow. The sound had come from there, amplified by the Unseen Powers. But she didn't need the Unseen Powers to recognize this particular intelligence. It had helped them find each other in many lifetimes. In this life, they'd named the intelligence Loyal. But it had been with them since the beginning.

That was Rob in the snow. Another yip sounded, the intelligence trying to get her attention.

Her heart swelled with relief and pain.

The Aesir were nearly to the rooftops of the majestic university.

She uttered a command that caused the cracked window to shatter, spraying glass on the snowy scene. Instantly, a chill swept into the corridor. She vaulted over the edge of the broken pane and landed in the snow outside. She sprinted across it, making an arc around the frozen fountain to try to reach her husband. Fog came from her mouth as the frigid air reacted to the moisture in her lungs. More memories collided inside her. Grief, joy, ecstasy, compassion, tenderness, violence—a wonderful and confusing cacophony of mortal feelings that she'd come to treasure in all their complexity.

She reached her husband before the Aesir did. A grimace of pain was on his handsome face as he clamped his ears to protect them from the tumult of noise. She ran a hand down his shirt, looking for the pocket that usually held the device. There it was!

A shadowy figure emerged from the hail of snow about two dozen paces away. Tall, majestic, imperious.

It was her father, the Erlking. Come to slay her love again.

She found the device and pulled it out, hurriedly flipping the lid. The familiar rings and dials. The philosopher's stone that reversed the entropy of his mortal body. His eyelids opened, and the suffering in them made her desperate to comfort him. She hastily removed the ear cuffs from her ears and slid them on his instead. Pain exploded in her skull, even more terrible than before, but she endured it and quickly began to arrange the numbering of the ring. The secret code she'd shared with him all those years ago.

Four digits: 1-6-1-8. The code of creation. The alchemy of the universe. She took one of his hands away from his ears and pressed the device to his skin. The combination would not work for just anyone. It would only work for him.

He gazed at her worriedly, in misery still, and then she used her thumb to push the button on the top of the device. It would take a little time for the damage to his ears to be repaired by the device's healing powers, but it would happen eventually. The device could do so many clever things. For example, pressing the button with the right combination would trigger certain spells in reaction.

As she pushed it, she could feel the hairs on her arms tingling, and not just from the cold. The cold felt marvelous actually. The shiver caused exquisite delight.

She watched as the magic worked on him. Watched his confusion turn to comprehension. She grinned with relief, feeling like sobbing, because she'd made it in time. Recognition filled his eyes. Familiarity. *Adoration.*

"Hello, Isaac," she breathed, leaning down and kissing him again.

The inspiration for founding the Invisible College came on a bitterly cold winter day. There is a courtyard within the grounds of the University of Nirshoye that had a little decorative fountain in the center. Some miserable wretch had died there and lay frozen in the snow. No one knew the young woman's name or where she came from. No one understood the desperation that must have driven her to crawl to that spot in the snow or why the gate had been left unlocked that day.

My heart was moved by that pitiable creature's death. But my mind was fixated on it. How many, like her, die in the cold of winter, when a simple bespelled contraption can provide heat. How many starve for lack of food when much food is wasted? How many experience sorrow and feel they are of no worth because they simply have no one to talk to? These thoughts weighed heavily on me for many years, even after my graduation from and acceptance of a fellowship to teach at that very university. How many times did I cross the courtyard where the unknown woman died and think on her?

What if there was an organization that would dispense the knowledge of sorcery without prejudice toward wealth, sex, or geography? Where men and women could gather together and discuss the principles of arithmetic, chymistry, poetry, or Aesir lore. A quorum, if you will, like in the universities of olden times. Each quorum would be independent but subservient to a grander structure. I began to conceive of a system of ranks and degrees to safeguard such knowledge but also to ensure certain ideals were valued and rewarded. The pinnacle of this order would be responsible for perpetuating its reach and inspiring its influence. Food and warmth would be provided to those who participated. Comradery would ennoble it.

What would bind everyone together, though? Well, who does not enjoy a puzzle or riddle to be solved? The head of the order would be responsible for maintaining a secret. A royal secret. Speculating about the nature of such a secret would keep things interesting.

—Isaac Berrow, Master of the Royal Secret,
the Invisible College

Isaac Berrow

CHAPTER THIRTY-FIVE

FOUND

Fifteen years before the founding of the Invisible College

Isaac followed the footprints in the snow for as far as he could, until they literally vanished before his eyes, hidden by the heavy snowfall. He trembled with cold, but he felt a drive of persistence pushing him on despite his discomfort and the growing numbness in his feet. He reached the end of the narrow street and halted.

"Now, where did you go?" he murmured, stamping clumps of snow from his shoes. Looking back, he could see his own trail well enough. But there was no indication of which direction the poor creature had gone next. The university gates were on his left, fixed to square pillars with Aesir decorations atop them. The building beyond it had huge stained-glass windows and steepled spires. Looking the other way, he could find no trace of his quarry.

Reason suggested she would have gone away from the university. The gate was closed, after all. No students or professors were attending classes because of the break, and it was also late in the day. He glanced back and forth, trying to determine which way to go. Toward the university or away from it?

He wished he had the senses of a dog. They didn't rely on vision or reason—they could simply sniff the air and determine the right course. Mortal noses lacked that power, unless one was searching for a cesspit. Well, it wasn't possible to transform into a dog. But what about harnessing the intelligence of one?

Cats were much more abundant in Nirshoye than street dogs. And cats, although highly intelligent, were not all that interested in being of assistance. However, Nirshoye was known for its sorcerers, and many of them did prefer canine companionship. Perhaps an unfettered dog intelligence might be lingering about in the city.

He rubbed his arms, trying to invigorate warmth, and closed his eyes. He tried, unsuccessfully, to quell his agitation about the person he was searching for. Why it should be any of his business he didn't know, but the intense urge to follow after her hadn't lessened. On a night like this, the poor creature was doomed.

Hello, he thought, sending the impulse into the aether. *I'm in need of assistance to find someone in trouble. Someone sick and bleeding and in need of medical attention. I need help.*

He infused the thoughts with his worry for the person he was searching for. It was that combination—the mind and the heart—that appealed to intelligences.

Instantly, he sensed an intelligence at his side. A powerful presence with an eager and attentive manner. He could sense a friendly nature, one inclined to a great deal of tail-wagging, no doubt. The dog must have belonged to an impressive sorcerer during life to have responded so quickly to his summons.

Thank you, Isaac thought as he smiled. *I saw someone lying in the snow. Sick as can be. I followed her this far. Can you lead me to her?*

Again he sensed an energetic response from the intelligence. Instantly, it went in the direction of the university gate.

"Really?" Isaac said aloud with an equal degree of surprise and confusion. "Are you sure?"

He almost felt the dog's wagging and then a little inaudible yip came from the direction of the university.

Shrugging, Isaac marched the way it led. He was startled to discover that the university gate was unlocked *and* ajar. The grounds were always secured at night because the town was known for its unsavory miscreants. He'd have to report this lapse. After pulling open the gate enough for him to pass, he gently closed it behind him. The bars were so frigid they stung his flesh.

The doglike intelligence led him beneath a scalloped entry, which opened to a courtyard with a fountain. He gazed around at the area and saw no sign of the person he was chasing. But the doglike intelligence led him around to the other side of the fountain, and that's where he found her. He heard the coughs before he saw her, the wheezing breaths of a soul dying of some lung sickness. He summoned an orb of light to see better in the darkness, and it hovered over his shoulder.

As Isaac moved closer, he saw the shivering woman and her frostbitten nose. Blood was smeared against her chin. Her clothing was absolutely threadbare. Her fingertips were gray. The sight filled him with horror and worry.

He came and crouched near her. "We need to get you somewhere warm," he said. "Then I'll go seek a physician."

Her head lifted up. Her eyes were dull with suffering, but a little smile tugged at the corner of her lips. "You came."

That was an odd thing for her to say. Had she been expecting someone? He tugged off his coat and spread it across her. The exposed hair on his neck sent shivers all the way down to his feet.

"What's your name?" he asked her. He thought about how he could get her to stand, but she looked so weak and spent that walking might not be possible.

"L-Lydia Brewer," she said. That name sounded vaguely familiar.

"Well, Lydia, my apartment is not that far away. You need a doctor. Let me try to help you stand up."

She began to cough again and shook her head.

"I insist," he said soothingly, gently taking her bony arm with one hand. Maybe he could drape her over his shoulder? Would that make it easier to carry her? He wasn't as big a fellow as his roommate, but his roommate was gone.

"Isaac, I'm going to die here. I'd rather this body die in the cold than coughing up blood in a bed."

He stopped trying to help her rise and gazed at her in surprise. "How did you know my name? Have we met?"

"I know you because you're my husband," she said faintly.

That was even more surprising. "I'm a student here at the university."

"I know, Isaac. We were just married by the magistrate." Her head began to loll. "And we were married before that in a little village near Halt. And before that, we met at the ice trenches. You were a soldier that time. Before that, a poet."

Her words made absolutely no sense to him, but something stirred in his heart. It was a feeling that she was telling the absolute truth. His skull began to throb with pain.

Beneath the blanket of his coat, she produced a folded piece of paper and handed it to him. Isaac felt he should recognize it, but he didn't. After accepting the paper, he unfolded a marriage license and saw his name and Lydia Brewer's. Joined that day in matrimony by a magistrate judge. It was a trick. Surely. But his heart began to pound.

"A glamour spell," Lydia said. "That's what keeps you from remembering. Why I have to keep explaining this over and over again. But it's nearly over. Nine hundred and forty-seven times we've found each other. When we marry for the thousandth time, the Erlking and the Aesir will be banished. It will take another few centuries. But we'll do it." Her head began to sink.

"Lydia," he whispered, feeling several emotions knotting together in his chest. He couldn't even understand what the emotions were. He didn't understand what she was talking about. Was it the raving of a dying woman? Or was it possible she was truly the infamous Erlking's daughter from the legends?

He was about to stuff the paper in his pocket.

"I wrote on the back," she whispered. "The spell that will release the glamour. It is a spell that cannot be uttered. Only spoken with the mind."

"You? A sorcerer?" he asked in bewilderment.

"I am a Semblance," she said. "And so are you. When we die, our intelligences are sent to other bodies. And we must find each other all over again. But I know I'll find you." She began another uncontrollable cough. It sickened him to hear it. "We've always found each other," she wheezed after it stilled. "Goodbye, Husband. Until we meet again." She'd been reaching for his face when her hand dropped to the snow. A tear trickled from her closing eyes. And then she was gone.

Isaac watched as a plume of fog came out of her mouth after she'd taken her last breath and lay still. It was vaporous, and then instead of dissipating, it seemed to be yanked like a fish on a hook and taken away.

He sensed a mournful moan from the doglike intelligence.

Isaac turned over the paper and found she'd written on it with her own blood. One word.

Alítheia.

A spell not to be uttered but thought. He didn't know the language in which it was written, but it had an Iskandir feeling to it. There was more than one possible pronunciation based on the spelling. Alith-eeya? Ale-thay-uh? Isaac bowed his head and thought the word with the first pronunciation.

Alítheia.

Nothing happened. Had he thought it correctly? He tried it again with the second one. How many different ways could he—

The fog of glamour sloughed off his mind, and memories buzzed awake inside him. Eiríka! The marriage. All she had taught him about her people, the Aesir, over the past few days. Equations. Anatomy. The orbits of objects in the universe. How to make a philosopher's stone.

He gazed at her again, this time in full recognition, and his heart clenched with the agony of losing her. Tears stung his eyes, and he had to clamp his mouth to keep the sobs from bursting into the empty courtyard. She'd saved her final revelations for the last. She hadn't just been married hundreds of times, she had married *him* that many times!

He was a Semblance, just like she was, and both of them had been sent from body to body. Why had her father allowed her to keep her memories but taken his from him?

He gazed at Lydia's lifeless corpse and then wrapped his arms around her, burying his emotions in the fabric of his coat. With his memories back, he remembered the glamour spell she'd used. *Eshi omorfi matia.* She'd used it on the magistrate judge, and then she'd used it on him before eluding him in the streets. She'd written the counterspell on the paper. Had she intended for the authorities to find her body, the note, and then him? Or had she hoped against hope that he'd come after her himself even with his memories snatched away?

Lowering her body into the snow, he gazed at the face he'd grown to care for. To love, even.

What if he could find her again? If he made a philosopher's stone, it would prevent him from aging. Then, instead of her having to find him over and over, *he* could find *her*. He could search the world for her. But how?

He felt the doglike intelligence approach him, invisible tail wagging incessantly.

Isaac Berrow

CHAPTER THIRTY-SIX

The Erlking

Present day

As the memories came flooding back into his mind, he felt like he had so many times before—as if he'd awakened from the Skrýmir, gasping for breath.

Isaac Berrow knew himself again.

The Aesir ear cuffs that McKenna had put on him had drowned out the noise that had been ruining his ears. The philosopher's stone in the device he'd invented would heal him, but the situation was dire. He was surprised that one of the fail-safes in the device hadn't triggered before then to remove the glamour. Lifting his head, he saw the Erlking approaching them in the courtyard, his face both haughty and familiar.

McKenna was within the shield his device conjured around him, but her father's power was formidable. Even for an Aesir, he was tall, over seven feet in height, with a powerful build. The forked crown of Aesir gold was a symbol of his majesty and dominion. His white hair flowed like a lion's mane, and his entire being was incandescent with magic. The armor itself was vulnerable to elfshot, but Isaac lacked a pistol and the deadeye aim of a member of the Brotherhood of Shadows, the Semblance hunters.

He felt McKenna tugging on his arm to help him stand. His legs trembled, but he managed to rise with her help. His ears were ringing.

"Percutis malleo," he sang, trying to shatter the tubes in the courtyard, but the magic was countered by the noise permeating the air. He'd have to shatter them, one by one.

The Erlking reached them, standing imperious and confident of his victory. To him, it must appear to be a sure thing. His warriors were coming down from the stormbreaker overhead, arriving in a city vulnerable to their blades.

Isaac had the thumb ring on, so he reached out quickly with his thoughts. *General Ambrose, can you hear me? The bulbs must be destroyed. They've been tampered with. The Aesir are attacking Nirshoye. They are going to destroy the Invisible College. The Erlking is here in the Vernal Courtyard.*

KNEEL BEFORE ME!

The thought rolled like thunder in Isaac's skull. It rattled his bones with its ferocity and implacability. The compulsion to obey was strong after such a pointed command, but he did not. He felt McKenna squeeze his hand. He looked at her, feeling the pangs of love and devotion that had compelled him to defy the Erlking in a different lifetime.

Isaac faced the Erlking meekly. *We have one more life to fulfill the covenant. It is almost over.*

YOU WILL NOT SUCCEED.

Again, he felt the rattling in his mind. The wavering of his resolve. Against such powerful thoughts, who was Isaac Berrow? He was an insect in comparison to the intelligence of this being.

You may be right, of course. But we've succeeded thus far.

INSOLENT MORTAL.

Isaac shrugged his shoulders. *Our natures make us prone to insolence, I'm afraid. I have honored the terms of our covenant. You must abide by them as well.*

The Erlking took a menacing step forward, and Isaac felt his heart quail with fear. His shield wouldn't protect him for long if the Erlking attacked him. And with the shrieking taking away his ability to conjure magic of his own, he was helpless indeed.

YOU ACCUSE ME OF TREACHERY?

The Erlking was surprisingly sensitive. Isaac had learned, over the centuries, to be careful in provoking him. He could move as fast as a lightning strike. His magical abilities were without peer. Yet even he could only operate within the paradigms set by the Mind of the Sovereignty.

A figure emerged from the whorl of snow. It was the *strannik*, holding a magical device in his hand—a scepter containing an enormous jewel. Isaac recognized it as belonging to the Erlking.

Master! I have done as you bid me! the *strannik* thought with a groveling tone. He prostrated himself near the Erlking, giving Isaac and Eiríka a sidelong glance. He bowed his forehead until it touched the snow. *Master, I have done it! I have gathered them all here to be destroyed. Fulfill your promise to me. Grant me the kingdom in the other world!*

The Erlking's face twitched with disappointment and resentment.

YOU HAVE BROUGHT MY DAUGHTER AND THE ACCURSED COLLEGE FOR JUDGMENT. I WILL REWARD YOU AS PROMISED. RETURN MY SCEPTRE.

The *strannik* lifted his head, a gleeful smile on his lips. He bowed again, holding up the scepter while still on his knees. The magical scepter floated from the *strannik*'s hand and landed in the Erlking's outstretched one. He closed his fist around it.

I WILL STUDY THE INTELLIGENCES YOU HAVE CAPTURED FOR ME. YOUR PART IN THIS IS FINISHED. PASS THROUGH THE MIRROR GATE AND NEVER RETURN.

The *strannik* lifted his head, his expression showing relief. *What of these two? What will you do with them?*

YOU ARE IRKSOME TO ME.

The *strannik* bowed again and began to scuttle away. His eyes lingered on McKenna, and it made Isaac roil with impatience. Was he going to ask for more? To ask for the Erlking's daughter to be his instead? It was never wise to test the Erlking's limited patience. The *strannik* seemed on the verge of speaking, but he must have realized the foolishness of it and slunk away, bowing as he retreated.

You used him, Isaac thought to the Erlking pointedly.

HE GAVE HIS ALLEGIANCE TO ME COMPLETELY. DOES IT NOT BEHOOVE ME TO REWARD LOYALTY?

It is just for you to do so, Isaac agreed, inclining his head. *And wise. You send him to prepare the way for your coming. Is that the world you have chosen to conquer next?*

YOU BELIEVE I WILL LOSE.

Isaac bowed in submission without contesting the statement.

BID MY DAUGHTER RETURN TO ME, AND I WILL FORGIVE HER.

Bid her yourself, my lord. Let her choose.

SHE CANNOT HEAR MY THOUGHTS. THEY ARE SHROUDED FROM HER.

Isaac looked at him knowingly. *That is also your doing. But in this form, she can still understand you. She can read your lips. Say the words, and she will know them.*

A look of consternation came over the Erlking's impassive face. He was the sort of being who inspired an attitude of worship. But he had no mercy. Only a fixed sense of justice.

Isaac turned his head and looked at McKenna's defiant face. *"Your father wishes to speak to you,"* he mouthed to her.

She nodded and faced the Erlking.

His expression was mottled with disgust and despair. She had rebelled against him thousands of years ago, choosing to forsake her own people and enter into a covenant to become mortal. He'd been so certain she would come around eventually—that the rules he'd created would be impossible to fulfill, but she and Isaac had found each other almost a thousand times.

Isaac watched the Erlking speak. He could not discern his voice through the incessant noise, but the look on the father's face showed a plea for reconciliation. Was he asking her to end the conflict between mortals and Aesir? Was he pleading with her to return to the fortresses built beneath the glaciers?

In a previous life, Isaac had wandered into the ice caves with their whorls of prismatic colors, otherworldly in their beauty. He had visited their world while the inhabitants were under the Skrýmir, their most vulnerable state. He'd seen them sleeping with their eyes open.

He'd been looking for Eiríka's material body. He hadn't known where the Erlking kept it hidden. If he found her, he hoped to find a way to break the spell her father had put on her—to fully awaken her as herself.

SHE REJECTS ME STILL.

Isaac wasn't stunned by that information. Only someone with a will as implacable as his own stood the chance of defying him and surviving. McKenna gripped Isaac's hand, gazing at her father with conflict but determination.

All they needed was to find each other one more time, and then the Aesir would voluntarily leave. It would end the war permanently.

She has made her choice over and over, my lord. Accept it.

The Erlking's lips twisted into a sneer. He shifted his gaze from McKenna to the sorcerer. His fist clenched around the haft of the scepter, and the jewel began to glow with power.

HEAR ME, MORTAL. I CANNOT ABANDON WHAT I PROMISED. IF I DID, I WOULD NO LONGER BE THE ERLKING. ONLY SHE CAN ABANDON IT. SHE REFUSES. YOU WILL REGRET TAKING HER FROM ME. YOU WILL LOSE. I WILL SEE TO IT. PERSONALLY.

A flash of intuition came to Isaac's mind. In all their previous encounters, the Erlking had sent minions to thwart him and Eiríka from finding each other. Semblances had been sent to hunt them both. Isaac had protected himself from them by creating the device. Even still, their mortal marriages had never lasted very long before they'd felt the sting of the Erlking's wrath.

This last time, this final time, the Erlking would take on a body himself. That was the implication of his threat. He could not lie. If he became a Semblance himself for this final incarnation, then it would be that much more difficult for Isaac to find Eiríka next time.

Isaac felt his stubbornness flare to life. Well, if that's the way he wanted to play the game . . .

You will become one of us? How . . . uncomfortable that will be for you.

DO NOT MOCK ME, MORTAL. I WILL TRIUMPH. YOU WILL FAIL.

There was no use arguing with him. The Erlking could not be reasoned with. He'd been confused by the machinations of mortals, deeming them like dung beetles with an equal significance. But he was wrong. He could not change his view of his superiority, no matter what evidence prevailed on him to think otherwise.

Professor, this is Mr. Stoker. Retreat three steps. I have him in my sights.

With all the Aesir magic on display, the tubes had not altered in the slightest on the arrival of mortals wearing kappelin cloaks. He was relieved General Ambrose had hearkened to his message and sent soldiers into Nirshoye. Isaac had been stalling this whole time in anticipation of it.

Take out the tubes, Mr. Stoker, Isaac thought. *You can't win this fight.*

I have my orders, Professor.

Don't shoot the Erlking! Isaac thought in warning.

But he knew, from Mr. Stoker's previous examples of temperament, that it was exactly what he would attempt.

CHAPTER THIRTY-SEVEN

Orbit of Chaos

Isaac grabbed McKenna's hand and tugged her with him as he stepped forward so that the Erlking would be within the radius of protection from the device. Part of the covenant he and McKenna had agreed to was that they would not try to ambush and assassinate the Erlking—as mortals had done to the Erlqueen. If that happened, this second covenant, the redeeming one, would be irrevocably broken, and the Aesir would be under no obligation to depart the world voluntarily. But there was no memory of that promise made. Only Isaac knew of it and, of course, Eiríka. But the outcome would affect all of humanity if they succeeded. The Aesir would have to leave. Even if mortals wouldn't ultimately remember *how* they'd been saved as the centuries rolled past.

The noise of the elfshot rifle couldn't be heard over the shrieking of the tubes, but Isaac saw the flash of ignited saltpetr. The elfshot was deflected off the shield and then ricocheted once more off one of the columns of the fountain's cupola.

The Erlking's head jerked, his sense of hearing too acute to have missed the sound of the shot. His nostrils flared with outrage.

BETRAYAL!

No. I just saved you. My shields will protect you.

I DO NOT NEED YOUR PROTECTION, MORTAL.

Isaac knew there wasn't time to explain what he needed to do next. His memories as Isaac Berrow and all he'd mastered had been restored. He connected his mind with the intelligences powering his device. The shields were empowered by housefly intelligences. A typical fly had compound eyes and thus possessed a field of vision of nearly three hundred sixty degrees. Which meant the intelligences had indelible aim. He directed them to angle the shields so the elfshot would be redirected to strike the glass tubes in the courtyard.

Another shot came from a different rooftop, and the ricochet struck one of the tubes as predicted, shattering the glass and lessening the deafening noise coming from them.

The Erlking leaped away from Isaac and McKenna, his movements a blur of speed. Isaac's stomach twisted with dread as he saw plumes of gray smoke ignite from the rooftops surrounding the courtyard. The Brotherhood of Shadows all had Aesir-powered artifacts, giving them the ability to jump to great heights, turn invisible, and kill the immortal race. He'd seen them before. He'd *fought* them before, for they had strict orders to hunt Semblances, and he was often marked as one.

He looked to McKenna and took in the stern line of her mouth.

General—if your men kill the Erlking, we're done for! It violates an ancient treaty. Make them stand down!

One of the brotherhood came tumbling from the roof and landed on the cobblestone ground. Suddenly there were five Erlkings—all but one a refraction of the original. The shots continued to swarm like hail. Isaac felt some of the bullets rush by him, but his shields deflected them, knocking out another tube. Then another. The noise dissipated.

Professor, this is our chance to end the war! He could easily read Ambrose's tone. He was possessed by the single-mindedness of a military commander certain he had the upper hand. But it was quite the opposite. The covenant was the only thing keeping the Aesir from utterly exterminating everyone in their path.

No, General. They've been holding back. If he dies, they'll come in their might.

He could feel indecision in Ambrose's thoughts. The real Erlking, atop the wall, grabbed a soldier by the collar and hurled him off. Isaac could see the panic in the man's face as he tried to activate his magical artifacts, but the devices were subservient to the Erlking. They would obey his will. The man died on impact.

With the last of the interior tubes shattered, Isaac could hear again, and the device had healed him enough that the ringing in his ears was gone, though his hearing was still slightly muffled. The pipes beneath the courtyard were fed by underground cisterns, so he summoned the intelligences used to heat the water for the university and asked them to boil it. The pipes were all made of copper, which conducted heat well. If he could raise the temperature enough, it would be intolerable for the Aesir.

The Erlking had power over Aesir artifacts, but he could not so easily counter another sorcerer's powers. And all intelligences bound by sorcerers were compelled to obey the true Master of the Royal Secret. A hierarchy existed among magic users. The spells of lower orders could be countermanded by those of a higher rank all the way up to the highest rank of all.

Isaac Berrow.

Him.

Steam began to writhe from the fountain.

Isaac used his thoughts to extend the command beyond the university, to every intelligence that could hear his mind. Heat—expand the heat!

McKenna clutched his hand as another soldier was flung from the rooftop. The Erlking was a blur of action as his projections, each acting individually, pretended to fight the soldiers surrounding them. More shots rang out as the military tried to end this enemy who had destroyed so many mortals' lives. Some of them continued to use magical weapons forged by the Aesir against the ruler of the Aesir without realizing their own weapons would forsake them. As Isaac's mind raced to prevent the carnage, he judged he could not stop it. He was a mortal too, vulnerable to the speed and power of the Aesir. Soon, so very soon, the half-dozen or so men who had been sent after the Erlking were dead. Were more coming, though?

Isaac watched the Erlking's images rejoin into one as he lifted Mr. Stoker from the roof by the neck and plunged a triple-pronged sword into the soldier's middle. Isaac had never liked the man, but he'd been a relentless foe of the Aesir and had worked, with others, to try to protect mortalkind. Stoker's legs convulsed with the pain, his face a mask of hurt and fear. And then his head drooped down.

The Erlking drew his bloodied weapon and held it high with one hand and the body of the soldier with the other. The best warriors that Society could produce had been sent after him, and he'd taken them out effortlessly.

But Stoker had only been feigning death. Isaac saw him draw an elfshot pistol from his belt and bring it to the Erlking's head.

Isaac could not stop the trigger from being pulled. It was a mechanical device, one based on science, not sentience. He sucked in his breath.

The Erlking must have sensed the danger, for he turned his head just as the flash of saltpetr came, and the explosion rocked the courtyard.

"No!" McKenna gasped.

Stoker was dropped. He thumped to the roof, rolled to the edge, and then crashed onto the ground, the fuming pistol still in his now-lifeless hand.

The Erlking's shoulders were hunched. A hand came to his face, where the blast of heat from the saltpetr had scorched him.

A feeling of dread bloomed in Isaac's stomach. Was the Erlking dying? Had the elfshot struck his skull? Was it all over, after everything?

In that tremulous moment of uncertainty, the fountain suddenly exploded in a plume of scalding water, a geyser spraying its spume a hundred feet into the sky. Rubble rained down on them, sludge and mud splattering everywhere, but Isaac and McKenna were protected by the shield from his device. Isaac should have heated the pipes more gradually. He'd accidentally caused the explosion by introducing sudden heat to a compressed space. The snow was already melting, turning into rivers of soot.

The haze of steam reduced visibility. The Erlking was still standing on the rooftop, one hand pressed over his cheek and eye.

KILL THEM BOTH!

The Erlking grabbed the jeweled scepter in his left hand and invoked its power. He'd been drastically weakened. Only his immense strength and power had kept him alive. He would need to sleep in order to heal and recover. He needed the Skrýmir. That would preserve their lives for a time. Isaac knew the limits of an Aesir's immortality, and the gruesome wound must have brought him to the brink of death. Eiríka had revealed so much to him during their lives together.

Until the next cadence of Awakening came, which would be—according to Isaac's previous calculations—in another twenty-three years. A short cycle this time, unlike many of the previous ones.

The bodies of the fallen soldiers began to twitch. Isaac realized instantly what was about to happen. The Erlking had made them all into Semblances. It had to do with the scepter he held, the one he'd temporarily given to the *strannik*. No wonder the sorcerers of the Invisible College had struggled so much to capture him. The warriors rose, one by one, testing out their new bodies.

The Erlking was veiled in a sheet of the steam that was still gusting from the destroyed fountain. He straightened, still imposing, and lowered his hand. Isaac could see the devastated area of his face. His eye was gone, part of his nose with it. His rage seemed to feed off the agony he must have been enduring.

KILL THEM BOTH!

The battle wasn't over. It was just starting.

Eirika

CHAPTER THIRTY-EIGHT

Surrounded

She was losing her hold on McKenna's body. Ever since the drowning at the beach, her connection had been tenuous. Eiríka's intelligence had been connected to McKenna Aurora Foster since her host had died of the redoubtable fever in early childhood. She would have drowned in the ocean if Eiríka hadn't taken over and saved her, but that second breach had started an unraveling of the magic binding her to the host body. The unraveling was speeding up. Soon Eiríka's intelligence would be ejected from the tether of a mortal body and taken back to her lifeless body entombed in ice. Until the Erlking saw fit to send her into her final incarnation. The most important one.

Being trapped in a deaf girl's body, deprived of magic, had been a great challenge for the Erlking's daughter. She'd longed for it fiercely. But she'd found ways to compensate for the loss of hearing. In fact, she'd learned a great deal from the experience and had grown because of it. She'd retained her fascination with words and their meanings, much in keeping with her personality. And she was grateful, so very grateful, to the Fosters, who had raised her with loving kindness and sympathy, whereas another family might have rejected her. The Fosters hadn't been able to fully overcome the prejudices of Society, but they had made her feel important, respected, and loved. They were her parents, and even if they and she hadn't understood the complexity of that relationship, the connection they shared was still real and powerful. The Fosters were her family. And they would die on this island if she did not help Isaac save them.

A half-dozen Semblances were stalking toward them, reloading their weapons with fresh elfshot. She gripped the harrosheth blade tightly, trying to keep an eye on her surroundings. She glanced at her husband's face.

"We're surrounded," Isaac said, shaking his head. He summoned light to hover between them.

She'd seen the damage done to her father's face. And he was a man keenly aware of his perfect features. He took pride in them. His philosopher's stone would repair the damage, making his problem only a temporary one, but for now he was disfigured. She wondered how it must feel for him, being suddenly imperfect. Imperfection had become all too familiar to her. But each weakness she'd experienced during her many mortal lives had provided opportunities to gain new strengths.

"We have been in worse situations, you and I," Eiríka said to Isaac, flashing a smile.

"Really? I think this may be the worst."

"You wouldn't remember the previous times, before you were Isaac Berrow," she said.

"No. I sent Loyal to find the Fosters."

"Thank you. I don't want them to be harmed."

He turned to look another way. The Semblances were gathering around them, eyes filled with rage and disgust. Some of them were fluttering their eyelids compulsively. They must be getting used to the bodies and the need to blink. She remembered how strange it had felt at first.

The first soldier rushed at them and instantly was shoved back, meeting one of Isaac's invisible defensive spells. A second took his place while another attacked them from the rear with a harrosheth blade. Eiríka intercepted him, blocking the downward thrust with her forearm and kicking him hard on the knee. She spun around and landed another kick on a separate soldier, who'd lunged at her with his own blade. She disarmed him easily, his weapon careening through the air.

Isaac was casting a flurry of spells. He'd never been one to fight with his fists, but he did know an enormous number of spells, and she could see his lips moving as he conjured them in the midst of the fray.

Eiríka blocked a Semblance trying to strike Isaac from behind. She tried to stab him with the blade, but his reflexes were just as honed as hers, and he easily evaded the thrust. Their arms were tangled for a moment, but she kneed him hard in the ribs and somersaulted to engage another Semblance trying to get through.

This soldier aimed a pistol and fired at her, but the elfshot was deflected by the device's shield. She cut off the man's hand with the harrosheth blade, sending a grimace of pain across his face, before she reversed the knife thrust and stabbed him in the chest. As he slumped to the ground, a puff of mist came from his mouth. But that did not eliminate the threat entirely. His intelligence would wander to find another mortal body that had recently died, and there were plenty to choose from.

The steam, rising from the crater where the fountain had been, was sapping her strength. Through the mist, she saw a bog beast swoop down. The Erlking leaped atop it, heading away from the scene. There were no more Aesir within sight after he was gone, but that didn't mean others weren't attacking soldiers elsewhere.

Her gaze tracked her father, and a punch caught her on the chin in that moment of distraction, sending spots of light dancing in her eyes and making her drop the blade. Another blow landed on her ribs, but she blocked a third strike. Using the man's shoulders as leverage, she spun around and then caught him by the neck and flipped him over her back. As he impacted on the muddy cobblestones, she picked up the fallen blade and slammed it into his chest, causing another temporary death.

Then she blacked out for a moment, her intelligence slipping away from the body. In desperation, she tried to cling to it, feeling that if she fell, she wouldn't rise again. Her eyelids fluttered.

Isaac grabbed her beneath her arms, hoisting her up, and then cast a displacement spell, which caused them to appear in random locations throughout the courtyard. It was disorienting, but she managed to stay conscious. The random repositioning brought them near a university door. The door exploded inward, and Isaac helped her into the corridor. It was ghastly hot inside, and she felt herself growing drowsy.

"Out-side," she panted.

Isaac hurried her down the corridor, and the next door blasted apart before they got there. Her ribs were throbbing in pain, but her legs were still working and she was able to run with him. Spots were dancing constantly in her eyes.

Gulping down air that was too hot for her lungs made her fear she would suffocate. Memories of her ordeal in the ocean crowded her mind. She could feel it tugging on her dress, crowding her mind.

They reached yet another door, this one leading outside, and Isaac stopped at the handle, looking back the way they'd come. She saw him mouth another spell, and glass shattered within the corridor, sending razored shards into the confined space.

Then he twisted the door handle and pulled it open. A welcome breath of wintry air greeted her. There was still snow in the street outside. It was a blessed relief.

Isaac tugged her outside with him. She paused to look up, knowing the Semblances had magic that could defy gravity. A soldier in Mr. Stoker's body came down at them from above, his mouth twisted with determination. He had an iron dagger in his hand, which was making his skin smoke as the metal burned him.

She shrieked in warning, but Isaac was already prepared. The blade and Mr. Stoker went hurtling away—and crashed into the wall on the other side of the street.

Her legs buckled and she dropped into the snow. Disorientation gripped her as she swayed, her eyelids fluttering. Isaac knelt in the snow, holding her to him. When her vision cleared, she saw plumes of saltpetr coming from rifles down the street. Soldiers were shooting at them, but the bullets were whizzing by harmlessly.

Isaac tried to get her to stand, but her legs wouldn't work. He grimaced with despair as he stared at her, urging her to get back up.

She shook her head. The threads of connection were gone. There was nothing holding her inside McKenna's body except for sheer willpower. When she had been Lydia Brewer, the sickness and freezing temperatures had triggered the same unraveling. The vagaries of mortal hosts were quite challenging. She reached up and touched his face.

"Find me," she murmured. "Find me again."

She looked down the street and saw the gate to the university. Down that street was the little apartment where Isaac had lived as a student. Back when her father had put her into the body of a dying, diseased young woman. How strange. That brief connection of only a few days had altered the course of their lives. He'd thought up the idea of the Invisible College. He'd made a philosopher's stone so that he couldn't die. He'd used the glamour spell to disguise himself and had even figured out how to disguise himself *from* himself, locking away his memories as he took on another life. But he was still Isaac Berrow, and she still recognized him since glamour didn't work on her.

A face she'd fallen in love with over and over.

Her shoulders drooped. Bullets continued to rain all around them. He shook his head, grieving at losing her yet again. The toll it took on both of them was severe. But the hope of finding each other again next time made it endurable.

He sank to his knees, holding her close, pressing her against him as he sobbed.

She touched his face, her fingers moving over the slight stubble on his cheeks, and she slipped away, eyes closing.

Once she was separated from McKenna's body, she could hear the blast of gunfire, the cries of the soldiers shooting at them. It was strange being able to hear again. In that moment, she thought she understood all their thoughts and could discern that they believed Robinson had lured them all into a trap to be destroyed. They'd seen him kill Semblance soldiers with his magic. They didn't know the truth of the situation or the new infestation among their ranks. She knew mortals were prone to hasty judgments.

She pitied them for their blindness of mind. For their limited perception and prejudices, their pettiness and distorted beliefs. But although she pitied them, she also felt compassion for them. They knew not what they did because they were convinced that what they did was proper and right. Grief struck her deeply at another separation and the ending of this particular life, which she'd grown to love so much. Over the centuries she'd learned that each ended life had its own particular brand of grief, even those that had been filled with sadness. Most of their marriages had been pitifully short.

She left McKenna's body as a puff of smoke. Freed from the coil of mortality, she felt the inexorable tug of her true body yanking her back home to its icy embrace but still she resisted. She heard his precious voice utter one last spell.

"Eshi omorfi matia."

Then bullets struck him violently, causing rips and blooms of blood in his coat. He twitched, trembled, and then the two of them collapsed into the snow side by side.

Find me, she thought to him as the magic finally yanked her away.

I will, came his gentle reply.

Isaac Berrow

CHAPTER THIRTY-NINE

The Ending of Another Life

Steam gusted from the sewer vents as Isaac walked down the slushy street of the familiar university town. He had lowered the temperature of the heating objects feeding the copper pipes and the air had a humid tang to it. The Aesir were retreating back to the stormbreaker, the island too uncomfortable for their kind. His shoes crunched in some broken glass as he passed another broken tube that had been destroyed. His heart was heavy with grief, having left the bodies in the street. One was McKenna's. The other one had been glamoured to look like his. There had been enough corpses for him to easily create the ruse. He suspected the soldiers would take the bodies to the Foster family to identify. He felt for them, but that was no longer his chief concern. He needed to find Eiríka, and it had never been all that easy to find her, one person amidst a civilization. But he had Loyal's help, at least.

A company of soldiers with rifles appeared from a side alley at a light jog. They were still scouring the streets for signs of the Aesir attacking. They headed his way, but Isaac was not worried. The glamour he was wearing was that of a lieutenant, so he outranked all of these men. He'd adopted a forgettable face.

The band of troops slowed and stopped as they reached him. "Sir, we've been down Chrysostome Street. No sign of action. Where should we go next?"

"Head to the university and await orders there," Isaac replied. "The Aesir are retreating."

"Thank the Mind for all this steam," said one of the other men. "Surely it helped drive them off."

"Indeed," Isaac answered and offered a crisp salute. They saluted in return and started jogging the way he had come.

Dickemore, please answer me. It can't be true. It can't be!

It was another mental nudge from Wickins. He would ignore it. He had to. With all the sharpshooters firing at them, he'd made the decision to shed the life of Robinson Dickemore Hawksley. Hawksley was an invention anyway. It saddened him that his friends and newfound family would grieve, but he couldn't bring himself to stay long. He would enter the Skrýmir, something he had discovered how to mimic with his human—though immortal—body, and sleep until just before Eiríka awakened. Twenty-three years would pass during his sleep.

Once again, he would need to relearn the world of mortals.

This time he would not use a glamour spell to fool others—and himself—into thinking he was anyone other than Isaac Berrow. He would need all his faculties to best the Erlking.

Still, he *did* want to see them all first.

He felt the loyal intelligence padding his way from a distance. The dog's intelligence had been a faithful companion for so many lifetimes. He'd ordered his friend to protect the Fosters, and since the fighting had ended, it was returning to lead him to them. So he was doing what he'd done for so many years—waiting.

The streets were full of memories and ghosts from his past lives. His shoes splashed in the puddles as he walked back to the row of small student apartments near the university. Earlier, he had seen gawkers standing outside the one he had lived in as a student. He rubbed his forehead and shook his head, awash in memories.

There were no longer any bystanders outside his old quarters. He walked up and used a spell to unlock the door. That particular apartment was no longer rented out but had been purchased by an investor—himself—as a tourist venue. He opened the door and stepped inside, feeling his chest tighten as he looked at the display furniture he'd purchased to re-create his old room and alchemy. He shut the door behind him, plunging the room into shadows.

"Hoxta-namorem," he hummed mournfully, summoning light to the dwelling.

There was the bed where she'd spent her last days until they were married by the magistrate judge. He still had the marriage license, the counterspell she'd written on the back in her own blood faded and tattered and fragile as a spiderweb.

After that awful night, he'd spent fifteen years thinking about the terrible burden on Eiríka of having to find him over and over again. He'd graduated with distinction and become a paid fellow at the university. He'd even given the most boring lectures imaginable to prevent students from getting close to him, afraid that he might reveal the secrets with which she'd entrusted him. And so he had made the philosopher's stone to keep himself young so he could look for her. So she would not have to shoulder that weight alone.

But the pain of losing her over and over again had eventually worn him down. And so he'd invented the device that would help him keep track of where they were in their journey. It also safeguarded his philosopher's stone, which kept him perpetually young, and unlocked the glamour spell he'd cast on himself to veil his memories. To numb the pain. Learning to Skrýmir had helped him fall asleep during the interim times and awaken when Eiríka's next cycle as a Semblance was underway.

It was a solution he'd finally found to endure the constant loss and short-lived marriages. He would create a new identity for himself, a part he'd enjoy playing, and block his memories with a glamour spell. There were fail-safes, of course, in case he got swallowed up in the role and forgot to look for her. If the combination that would return his memories had not been discovered within a year of his awakening, the device would utter the counterspell to revoke the glamour. If too many threats against his life occurred in short order, triggering the devices' protective spells, that would also restore his memories.

But this time, this final time, he had no intention of submerging his memories.

He wasn't sure how long he stood at the door reminiscing before he sensed Loyal's silent approach. Time to leave this part of the past behind. He extinguished the light with a thought and then exited and resecured the door.

"Show me the way, old friend," he said and followed the trail. It led back to the university. Soldiers posted at the gate saluted him as he passed. Wagons were being filled with the bodies of the dead.

The Aesir had come to exterminate the Invisible College. They hadn't succeeded, but they had done considerable damage to it.

Soldiers lined the ridgeline of the university walls as well, their rifles ready for action. The stormbreaker was gone, however.

Isaac passed one wagon that held the remains of a single Aesir, the lifeless eyes open and vacant. Of course, the Aesir might not be dead at all. Its intelligence might be animating a mortal body. Who knew how many Semblances were walking among the mortals?

He entered the university through a sturdy door and followed the dog's intelligence down to one of the dean's chambers. He knew the university well and could have walked it blindfolded. There were two sentries posted at the door with stern expressions.

When he stopped in front of them, they didn't move. "Sorry, sir," one of them said gruffly. "Orders from the general that no one—"

"Eshi omorfi matia," Isaac sang softly, and the soldiers' countenances changed as the magic invaded their minds.

Isaac was still wearing a uniform, but instead of the form of the lieutenant, he looked like someone who had been granted permission to enter. Mortal eyes were so susceptible to suggestion.

They snapped to attention, and one opened the door for him. He wondered who he looked like to them.

The office had a big desk and several couches, and he found himself face to face with those he'd come to love and respect. Professor and Mrs. Hawksley sat on one of the couches with stunned looks on their faces, his arm around her in comfort. Mr. and Mrs. Foster were also present, along with Trudie, whose head was nestled on Clara's lap. Wickins sat next to Clara, his expression grief-stricken.

This was his temporary family, and it hurt to see them suffering. He'd enjoyed the many surrogate families he'd discovered since his birth at Flamsteed. That original family had not been very close and warm, but he'd since found such familiar bonds with other families, most recently the Fosters.

He shut the door behind him and gazed at them, trying not to lose his composure. Of course, the glamour would conceal it if he did.

Mr. Foster looked up at him. His hair was disheveled. Indeed, they all had stains on their clothes and looked like they'd been through a gristmill together.

"Has anyone found it yet?" Mr. Foster asked, his tone suppressing anger.

"Pardon?" Isaac asked in confusion.

"The device. It was usually in my son-in-law's right pocket. It wasn't on his corpse. Did someone from the military take it? You were supposed to check on it."

Ah, so the family had seen the bodies with the gunshot wounds. That accounted for the mournful looks on everyone's faces.

"There was much commotion, Mr. Foster," Isaac said. He swallowed. "We'll keep looking for it."

"It has been stolen by the military before," Mr. Foster said indignantly.

"I'm aware of that, sir," Isaac said. He gazed around at all the faces looking at him with hostility.

"It doesn't belong to any of you," Wickins said, rising from the bench. He looked so upset. Like he was ready to throw a punch.

"Let's try to be patient," Mrs. Foster said. "We don't even know what happened."

Alítheia, Isaac thought, dispelling the glamour. He didn't feel any different, but their faces went slack with shock before shifting to excitement.

"Rob!" Trudie squeaked, sitting upright.

"I couldn't leave you all like this," Isaac said. He was wearing his old clothes again, which were scuffed and stained like theirs. They came to him in a rush, hugging him and choking back tears. He felt his own tears coming as they embraced him. They were his family. He hadn't felt such acceptance in a very long time.

"What happened?" Mrs. Foster pleaded. "What happened to McKenna? Did they really kill her? They're saying you invented those tubes to help the Aesir king defeat us!"

He shook his head. "No, that's not true. The Aesir found a way to use them against us. But McKenna is . . . dead. She saved my life. She saved many lives today. The Erlking and his *strannik* set a trap for us. The *strannik* is the one who made all the tubes shriek with violent sound. McKenna . . . she broke free and helped rescue me. But it was too much for her. She was . . . compromised already. I held her as the intelligence of the Erlking's daughter slipped away."

Mr. and Mrs. Foster frowned with grief and nodded. They'd lost her forever this time. There was no blunting that kind of blow.

"It was pretty much a mess after that. The Erlking was shot in the face. He was incensed, as you can imagine, and he made Semblances of all the fallen soldiers from the Brotherhood of Shadows, like Mr. Stoker. Stoker died too. Those Semblances were trying to kill us, and McKenna protected me again. But when General Ambrose's soldiers came, they saw us attacking our own people, or so they thought. So they shot at us. I cast a glamour spell so they would think we'd perished."

"You canny genius!" Wickins said, grinning through his tears. He hugged Isaac tightly and pounded him on the back several times.

"The Erlking was grievously wounded, though," Isaac said after they broke apart. "He will descend into the Skrýmir to heal, which means this Awakening is over already. The Aesir will not attack us again until the next Awakening, which will be in twenty-three years."

"How do you know this?" Mr. Foster pressed.

He gazed at his erstwhile father-in-law. "I am the Master of the Royal Secret," he said. "And I know things now that I didn't know before. I also know that Sarah was allied to the *strannik* and they've left to go to another world."

As they murmured and exclaimed over this unhappy truth, he wondered if he should tell them another. Would it be more painful to them to know the truth of who he was? He gazed at the Hawksleys. Should he tell *them*, at least? That they'd only had two sons, both of whom had died? The identity of Robinson Dickemore Hawksley was an invention born in a hillside graveyard in Covesea. He'd seen these two parents lay their remaining son to rest. They had believed he was their son because of a glamour spell. And he'd used them to infiltrate the world and seek out Eiríka, who had been in another guise herself.

No. It was better if they believed in the version of himself he had created.

It made sense that the *strannik* had kept saying that Robinson was an imposter. The man had gone to Covesea and found the birth records. Records that would not have shown Robinson's birth at all since it had never happened. Isaac was a victim of his own glamour too, of course, and had believed himself to be an elocutionist versed in the Hawksley method. He'd learned about the famous professor during one of his visiting lectures at Nirshoye and had traveled to Covesea to be tutored by him. He'd always had a thirst for knowledge.

Isaac gazed at their faces. "The military can't know I'm still alive," he said. "It is better if I do my work from the shadows. Know this, though . . . There was an ancient treaty with the Aesir, and the terms are nearly fulfilled. If it goes through, the Erlking will voluntarily leave this world. That is my mission. That is my intention. It will end the war."

Both families stared at him in confusion.

"What kind of treaty is it?" Mr. Foster asked.

"Was McKenna part of it?" Mrs. Foster begged.

"I can't explain it to you now." He sighed. "I need to go away. It may be for a long time. I have to fulfill the terms of the treaty. If I do, there will be no more wars. No more attacks. Our people can live in peace."

"What about the *strannik*?" Wickins asked. "He should be brought to justice for what he did. They say he murdered Mr. Guiteau."

Robinson nodded. "The *strannik* had taken over the Marshalcy. And the Erlking now has several Semblances in the military. If I stay, they will try to kill me again. That is why everyone must believe I'm already dead." He grabbed Trudie and hugged her. "You must keep it a secret."

Trudie nodded vigorously. "I will, Rob. I promise."

He heard footsteps coming down the corridor. Several sets of steps. He couldn't trust that they wouldn't be interrupted.

"I want you to know how much I appreciate all of you," Isaac said. "How much you mean to me. If I don't see you again, just know that I'm trying to stop this war permanently. And that McKenna helped too. If not for her, we would both have died today. All of us would have died." His words quavered, but he let them out. "Farewell."

Wickins gave him a final hug, squeezing so hard it hurt. "I'll help you. Any way I can. Just call on me."

"I will if I can. You're a good friend."

Isaac heard the steps arrive at the door and stop. The sentries were speaking in muffled tones.

Aóratos, Isaac thought, backing away, conjuring the spell that would disguise him once again. This time, it made him invisible. A powerful spell that could confuse the brain into seeing nothing.

He stepped aside as the door opened and General Ambrose and his entourage entered. He looked perplexed to see the family standing, holding each other in solidarity, unable to fight the smiles of relief on their faces.

"Is everything well?" the general asked.

"General, we are just overjoyed to be alive," Mr. Foster said. "I think the evidence will exonerate my daughter and her husband. They were not part of this scheme."

The general frowned. "We'll see, I suppose. I don't have further information on the trinket. It was not with the professor's body when he was put on the cart. It's possible one of the Aesir may have taken it. I do have news about the *strannik*, however. Would you like to hear it?"

"Yes, General," Mrs. Foster said.

"He and his followers went down to the docks during the attack and took some boats. I'm confident we will find them and bring them to justice on the sea. They can't have gone far. We'll find them shortly. I promise you. And our vengeance will be swift."

Isaac shook his head, once again amazed at the propensity of mortal beings for the most bewildering self-deceptions. Rather than accept facts and evidence, they were only so willing to conjure stories that justified their own limited thinking.

The *strannik* had fled to another *world.*

And good riddance to him.

EPILOGUE

Till Death Us Depart

Fifteen years before the founding of the Invisible College

The unknown woman was buried in a pauper's lot at the edge of the University of Nirshoye. A fresh dusting of snow had fallen during the night, giving a layer of white to the rugged slate roofs nearby. A sad, leafless tree hunkered in the corner of the yard, the branches intertwining with the iron bars of the gate. Isaac hunched beneath his cloak, watching the groundskeeper lean on his shovel and the curate doff his wide-brimmed hat and shake some snow from it.

The curate noticed Isaac on the other side of the gate and gestured for him to come inside.

Isaac had tried to be inconspicuous, but as there were no others in attendance beyond the gravedigger and the curate, his presence couldn't be overlooked. He walked to the gate and tugged it open, shuddering from the discordant sound made by the iron. He'd always been sensitive to sound. As he approached, he saw the canvas-wrapped body in the dirt pit. Lydia Brewer. His wife.

"I'm Henry Krabtree Todmorden," the curate said, extending a hand, which Isaac shook. The man had a thick gray beard and receding hair. He looked a little put out at being in the graveyard in such cold weather.

"Nice to meet you," Isaac responded, without offering his own name.

"Did you know the lass? No one claimed her."

"I'm the one who found her near the fountain," Isaac said. "Poor thing."

"Aye. They're all poor. We bury five or six such wretches every week, don't we, Sowerby?"

The man with the shovel sniffed and shrugged. He had gloves with the fingertips removed, showing crusty fingernails.

"That many?" Isaac said.

"Many die of the cold, you see. Like this one. Just froze to death. Ah well, but what can we do about it? Suffering goes on whether we want it or not. But even a streetwalker deserves the dignity of a grave."

"Get on with it, Krabtree," Sowerby mumbled. "I'm cold."

"Don't be sulky, Sowerby. Don't be sulky." He clasped his hands before him and gazed down at the dirt-spattered shroud. He cocked his head to one side and then nodded to himself. "The Mind of the Sovereignty knows each poor soul. Some lifespans are long. Some are cut short. Although no one claims this poor waif, her end will cause the wildflowers to bloom come spring. Ashes to ashes. Dust to dust. Justice claimeth its own."

"Finally," Sowerby groaned with relief, then gripped the shovel and started to toss dirt down on the bundle.

"Justice claimeth its own." The words were bitter in Isaac's mouth as he murmured them. He scrubbed a tear from his eye, angry at himself for showing emotion in front of strangers.

"Not so fast, not so fast," Krabtree said, waving at his companion to halt.

"Now what?" Sowerby complained.

"Do you want to say any words, young master?" Krabtree asked.

There was a lot Isaac wanted to say, but not in front of these men. He had learned so much in the last days. His life had changed forever. Ideas and ambitions had begun churning within him. How could he go about finding the next Semblance she embodied? Would she recognize his face if he found her, or were her memories dulled? Had her next life already started, or would there be a gap between them? His mind was full of so many questions. How to go about answering them? How could he find out as much as he wished about the lore of the Erlking's daughter? About his own past life? Would there be clues that would help him answer these questions? It would take a lifetime. Maybe two. Or three.

He realized both men were staring at him after the curate coughed discreetly.

"I hope her next life is more pleasant than this one was," Isaac said.

"Next life?" Krabtree said with a perplexed furrow of his eyebrows. "We only get one life, lad. We're all going to end as dust."

"I don't believe in a wasteful universe," Isaac said. "Or an indifferent one."

What about that invisible hound who had assisted him? Was it an intelligence just trying to be helpful, or was there a deeper connection? Had it tried to help them find each other before?

An inaudible yip came through the frozen yard.

Krabtree rolled his eyes and then nodded for his companion to toss more earth. As clumps of dirt showered down on the shrouded body, Isaac felt a resolution growing inside him. He thanked the two men and then left the gate and started down the street, following the single set of footprints in the snow that he'd made on his way there. Eiríka had taught him how to make a philosopher's stone. It would take ten years. He could use that knowledge to prolong his life indefinitely. Of course, he'd need to pretend to grow old—even die. But with a glamour spell, he could easily achieve that end. He could make a gravedigger like Sowerby believe he'd laid a body to rest, even if he hadn't.

Finding the Erlking's daughter alone would be exceedingly difficult. Did she always find him first, and he just kept forgetting her? Or was it like finding a pin dropped in a field of grass? He would likely need more help than just the dog intelligence to find her. Perhaps people who were trained to find Semblances . . .

Ideas continued to agitate within his mind as he walked.

He passed the university gates. The next batch of classes would begin in a fortnight, but all that suddenly felt meaningless to him. He wanted to study the Aesir lore. He wanted to find clues that might help him predict when and where he could locate Eiríka again. He would not be ignorant next time. He would notice the people around him. He would look for those who were compassionate by nature, who wanted to help alleviate suffering. Those who did good deeds invisibly, not for recognition or praise.

What if he gathered other like-minded people, like his fellow student, Alvin Thuernagle, who had begged him to borrow some coins because of his desperate situation? Could he prevail on Thuernagle to join such a cause? A different kind of college. A different kind of curriculum. They could share knowledge and insights with each other. Rather than keeping inventions to themselves, they'd share their knowledge and learnings so true progress could happen. They could be of service to their fellow mortals.

Of course, there would have to be a way to distinguish those who were part of this . . . movement.

Although his heart was heavy, the thoughts tingling in his mind made him excited and eager to commence. There could be layers in the order, just like there were ranks in a university.

He was lost in thought, until he tried to unlock the door of his little apartment and discovered it was already unlocked. He *had* locked it before leaving for the graveyard.

Isaac twisted the handle and opened the door—and found Blake Sherburn sitting at the little table, eating a bowl of soup.

"So you *did* get out at least once while I was gone," Blake said with a chuff. "I brought you some. Have you eaten at all since I left? You're as thin as a rail."

Isaac shut the door behind him and locked it. "How was your trip?"

"He speaks! You noticed I was gone, Berrow? I'm shocked!"

"Of course I noticed you were gone," Isaac said. "It was very quiet."

"Sorry to be such a nuisance to you."

Isaac approached the table and saw a little tub of soup next to the mug Blake was using to eat his. "That was thoughtful of you to bring some to share."

"Honestly, I was afraid you'd starved to death unwittingly while I was gone. You do look pale. You probably haven't been sleeping."

"You could say that," Isaac said, chagrined. He'd spent time cleaning up the place so that Blake would not notice anything amiss when he returned. But his friend had noticed a change in him rather than their environment. "How was the wedding?"

"A noisy affair, I should say. It would have driven you to distraction. But I'm glad I went, despite the frigid journey. I wish there were a faster way to cross this empire except horse-drawn coaches. One of the team went lame. We had to put it down, and then the other three struggled to move us at a tolerable pace. But there was plenty of food and pleasant company."

"Oh? What's her name?" Isaac asked inquisitively.

Blake chuffed out a pleased laugh. "You cut straight to the marrow, don't you? Yes, I did meet an eligible young lady named Priscilla Horrocks. To be honest, I was tempted not to come back to the university. We talked for hours at a time. She has such a keen mind."

"Why did you leave her, then?" Isaac asked, feeling pangs of loneliness in his heart. He missed those hours staying up all night talking to Eiríka. In that room yonder with the blanket tucked in neatly.

"Ah, but will it last? How can I know unless I leave her? I could think of little else all the way back here. But what will happen when classes start up again? Will the memory dull? Will these feelings fade like a flower? I don't know. You think I should have stayed?"

Isaac shrugged, sitting down across from his roommate. They rarely talked like this. Their relationship had always been so . . . transactional. Being companionable felt . . . nice.

"I can't say. I haven't met Miss Horrox. Did you leave her with any promises?"

"Why should I do that? We may never see each other again."

"Do you want to see her again?"

"I do." He leaned back in his chair and sighed. "I wish she were here at Nirshoye. That she could learn and we could talk together. Why is fate always so vague?"

"You think it was fate that brought you together?"

"I don't know what it is. I know I'm rambling. I bet you didn't expect me to come back besotted like this. You've probably been hunkered down in here, working on your little experiments while the world goes on its merry way. I'm sometimes jealous of your detachment from people. I don't think you'll *ever* marry. No offense."

Isaac started to chuckle. And then he felt like weeping. "Ah well, we're not all as handsome and promising as Mr. Sherburn. Maybe you should send Miss Horrox a message. You could write letters to each other. I imagine she's eager to hear from you."

"But what would I say? Maybe I should just forget the whole thing. I can't change my circumstances."

"Change is part of nature. We either change, or we are changed by it. What's to stop you? Tell her you enjoyed her company. That you hope to see her again."

Blake gazed at the mug on the table and twisted it around in a complete circle. "I'm getting advice from you of all people? But what you say does make sense, despite your lack of experience in matters of the heart. Ironic."

"I admit I'm woefully inexperienced," Isaac said. "But then, that is my own fault, is it not?"

Blake slapped the table and nodded with confidence. "I'll write her today."

"I don't think you'll regret it."

"So what have you been up to while I've been gone? Everything looks just as it did when I left. You are so scrupulous. Not a thing out of place."

Isaac smiled. "I've been doing a lot of thinking," he said.

Author's Note

I'm often asked where my imagination comes from, why I can dream up so many ideas. Creativity and inspiration come from a variety of sources and often get woven together in new and interesting ways. Robinson's device, for example, was inspired by a trinket in a television show I watched in the 1980s called *Voyagers!* It was about a group of people who time traveled through history to put events back on the right course. These time-traveling historians each had a device called the Omni that showed them where they were and whether the timeline was wrong, and then they'd use it to teleport to the next broken part of history. It was a great show but didn't last many seasons.

I had planned from the very beginning that Robinson was Isaac and McKenna was Eiríka. It was always intended to be a love story, inspired by Alexander Graham Bell and Mabel Gardiner, as well as the history of Sir Isaac Newton. The whole idea of a secret society of sorcerers came from Newton actually. After reading about Bell, I wanted to use another famous inventor as Rob's earlier life and began to search about Newton. One biography, *Isaac Newton: The Last Sorcerer*, practically begs for a TV show adaptation. His personality and diverse interests were so fascinating that they helped inspire the characters (the name Isaac Barrow was discovered in that book as well). It is said that Newton never married. It was fun to imagine an alternate world where he did.

For those of you who have read the "Bonus Chapters" from the first book (which you can find on my website), it was the opening scene at the gravesite where Isaac decided to cast the glamour spell on himself and became Robinson Dickemore Hawskley. I'd been planning this from the start!

I also want to share a tidbit about the soundtrack that played a role. I was very moved at a Piano Guys concert by the performance of Christina Perri's song "A Thousand Years." Whatever you may think of the *Twilight* series, the lyrics of the song were evocative to me of this romance that had been going on over and over for a thousand years. As I was thinking of the setting for these star-crossed lovers, I chose a world I'd invented long before my publishing deal with Amazon and borrowed two characters and the map from that world. If it feels there is a rich backstory, it's because there is one that I may choose to write about someday. The tie-ins with the Semblances also fit very well in that context. But before I consider going way back in time to learn about the first covenant with the Erlking, I'm sure you are on pins and needles, wanting to know what is next.

There will be one more book in the *Invisible College* series, and as you can probably tell, this series ties into my other worlds, where the *strannik* will continue to be up to no good! I had always intended for book three to end with the big revelation of Rob's and McKenna's pasts. To me, it sets the stage for what is to come, their meeting and determining who wins the struggle of wills between the Erlking and his daughter and the mortal man who fell in love with her.

I'm pleased to announce another twist—that story is available *now*.

Uncover the thrilling conclusion to Jeff Wheeler's Invisible College series in *Master of the Royal Secret*!

Acknowledgments

My wife and I celebrated our thirtieth wedding anniversary with a trip to France and Switzerland, and less than a year later, we were back to England, taking a side trip to Paris to see Notre Dame. We've been involved in the production of the film *Seeking Persephone*, so you will not want to miss it (and might even catch a glimpse of us in the wedding scene!). It was in Paris that the idea came of publishing the last two books of the series concurrently. So I'd like to acknowledge my French publisher, Milena Schwarzburg, for the brilliant idea to do this as she did with the French editions of Harbinger. And speaking of which, join my newsletter to learn about the English hardcover editions of my Harbinger series! This is good timing because my next project with Amazon Publishing will be a continuation of the Harbinger series.

I would like to thank Elizabeth Agyemang, my new editor, for her input while jumping into a series at the third book. That could not have been easy, but she caught up and offered some great suggestions. I'm always grateful for my editorial team: Angela, Wanda, and Dan. Angela has become a bestselling author in her own right and will no longer be my dev editor after the *Invisible College* is done (though she did agree to help with the last book). Kudos and congratulations are in order to her, and I'm just so grateful to everyone who has been part of my journey so far. Especially you, dear readers.

About the Author

Photo © 2021 Kortnee Carlile

Jeff Wheeler is the *Wall Street Journal* bestselling author of more than forty epic novels, including the Invisible College series, the Kingfountain series, the Muirwood series, and many more. Jeff lives in the Rocky Mountains and is a husband, father of five, and devout member of his church. Learn about Jeff's publishing journey in *Your First Million Words*, visit his many worlds at www.jeff-wheeler.com, or participate in one of his many online writing classes through Writer's Block (www.writersblock.biz).